Photograph by Nadav Kander, courtesy of Yancey Richardson Gallery

About the Author

John Biguenet's fiction has appeared in such publications as *Esquire, Granta, Playboy, Story,* and *Zoetrope.* The winner of an O. Henry Award for short fiction, he lives in New Orleans. Ecco published his debut collection of stories, *The Torturer's Apprentice,* in 2001. *Oyster* is his first novel.

Also by John Biguenet

The Torturer's Apprentice: Stories

"An outstanding first novel . . . full of mollusks, menace, and murder."
—*Esquire*

"A rich gumbo of incest and longing that simmers with tension."
—*Playboy*

"Biguenet . . . catches the scents and sounds of the bayou, and his characters bristle with a dark intensity."   —*New York Times*

"Harrowing and often brutal. . . . John Biguenet is an accomplished craftsman who has produced an arresting and evocative story."
—*Chicago Tribune*

"Stunning vistas, a magical feel for life on the water, a freshly thrilling way with the thriller, and an utterly satisfying ending."   —*Baltimore Sun*

"*Oyster* is a smartly conceived, crisply written modern version of a Greek tragedy. Yet it moves so swiftly and persuasively you can barely detect its impeccable ancestry."   —*Newsday*

"Biguenet possesses a rare lyric gift."   —*San Francisco Chronicle*

"A finely wrought tragedy."   —*Minneapolis Star Tribune*

"A whiz bang of a murder story."   —*Orlando Sentinel*

"Biguenet's gripping debut novel . . . is unforgettable."   —*Booklist*

ecco

An imprint of HarperCollins*Publishers*

Oyster

a novel

JOHN BIGUENET

*No similarity is intended between the characters and situations
depicted in this novel and any persons, living or dead.*

FIRST ECCO PAPERBACK EDITION 2003

Designed by Claire Vaccaro

Library of Congress has catalogued the hardcover as follows:

Biguenet, John.
Oyster / John Biguenet.—1st ed.
p. cm.
ISBN 0-06-051447-7 (PBK.)
1. Louisiana—Fiction. I. Title.

PS3552.I424 O97 2002
813'.54—dc21   2001050170

02 03 04 05 06 07 bg/qbm 10 9 8 7 6 5 4 3 2 1

for Sha

Acknowledgments

The author wishes to express deep gratitude to Daniel Halpern and his talented colleagues at Ecco and HarperCollins Publishers and to Jim Rutman at Sterling Lord Literistic, Inc. Captain Tom generously provided detailed information on fishing practices of the period and place, as did Professor Robert Thomas on marsh ecology and related topics. Some of the material here included was suggested by reading, its sources long forgotten, and by tales recounted by fishermen, many now long dead.

The essential American soul is hard, isolate, stoic, and a killer.

D. H. LAWRENCE

Plaquemines Parish

Louisiana

1957

One

1.

The muffled slap of the paddle against the black water betrayed Horse's impatience as the pirogue nosed into Petitjean's bayou, clinging to the darkness of the overhanging trees along the bank. But half-submerged cypress knees rasping down the hull of the narrow boat and low-slung branches, perhaps sagging under the weight of fat cottonmouths, slowed the pirogue's progress. Thinking of the snakes, Horse unsheathed his knife and drove it into the seat beside him.

Though it was nearly midnight, the air was still thick with heat. Later, before dawn, a chill would settle. Sleepers, waking under the slow blades of ceiling fans, would reach down among their feet to drag sheets over cold bodies. Wives would sit up to put on the nightgowns their husbands had stripped from them hours earlier. Children would crawl into each other's beds. But until then, for another few hours, the heat would continue to ooze up through the floorboards of the houses, to drip from the needles of the pines. And a man's hand would cut through the humid air like a fin splaying the water.

A light flickered through the tangled darkness. It blinked again and again as the boat glided past the black tree trunks lining the bank and sometimes rising out of the bayou. Horse knew the beacon was Petitjean's yard light. It occurred to him that to get to the dock on the far side of the clearing, he would have to slip past his old rival's landing without trees to conceal him. The full moon, though low in the sky, worried him.

Even as he considered how to pass unseen, the trees began to thin. He could make out the house, set back twenty yards from the bayou. All the inside lights were out; the family would be asleep by now.

Horse bent over, dragging himself hand over hand along the bank where he could, paddling as well as he was able when he had to. Though, after a beer or two at R&J's, he would boast that he was the fittest fifty-two-year-old oysterman in Plaquemines Parish, he knew he shouldn't have made the run all the way from his camp on Bayou Dulac. His shoulders throbbed, and even his back was starting to ache. *Why the hell did it have to be by boat?* he asked himself.

As the pirogue sidled up to the splintery dock, he grabbed hold of a piling. He let the sluggish current pin his boat against the rubber tires nailed to the crossbeams. On the other side of the pier, the *Mathilde* slept lightly in its moorings.

Horse lifted himself up a bit and whispered into the darkness, "Therese?"

Among the pines beyond the dock, a figure slowly stepped out of the shadows. A barefoot girl in a thin dress approached. Horse started to tie up his boat.

"No, take me for a ride," she insisted, slipping his bow line off the piling.

"Sure, *ma chère,*" he said, "we'll go for a ride." He helped her down into the wobbly pirogue. "Is that why you had me come by boat?"

"You just get us out and away from my daddy's house," she answered with her back to him in the bow.

Horse pushed off from the dock toward the bayou's deep water. With the girl in his boat, he felt suddenly emboldened, even with the moon waxing in the sky. Despite the sharp pain in his shoulders, the paddle dug deep. His powerful strokes nearly lifted them out of the water.

As they reached the channel, a quarter mile from her house, the girl told the man to tie up the boat. Horse eased the pirogue into the reeds, grounding on the slushy mud of the marsh bank. The aft still stirred in the eddying current, so he dropped a bucket filled with concrete over the side as an anchor and tied off its cord around the thick handle of the knife he had driven into his bench.

"You think that'll hold?" Therese asked as she turned around in her seat.

"We ain't going nowhere," he assured her, wrapping one more turn of the line around the hilt of his knife.

Horse slapped a mosquito on his neck. "So why you wanted to see me so secret and all?"

"You set on marrying me, aren't you?"

"Therese, you're promised to me."

"You older than my mama, Horse," she protested, "and me, I just made eighteen last month."

"Girl, you more than old enough to be somebody's wife. Way more."

"Why you want me, anyway?"

The man shifted his weight, and the boat rocked ever so slightly. "You know why," he whispered.

"It ain't like the old days, Darryl. My daddy can't give me away."

Horse rubbed his face with his hands, then looked up at the girl. "If you'd just say yes, there wouldn't be no problem." He could see she remained unmoved. "Look, we neither of us can make a go of it without the other's oyster beds. There's red tide all over Barataria Bay, and you know ain't none of us is raking shit even way up in Bay Sansbois. How many sacks your daddy and your brother bring in last week, huh? But I got a plan." A frog bellowed somewhere nearby. "You know what I'm saying. We need each other."

"Yeah, I know your plan. You want to steal my daddy's oysters 'cause the state's gonna close your beds."

"Who says?"

"Everybody says. It don't take no genius to read the bacteria counts in the paper."

"That's a damn lie. My oysters are the cleanest in Plaquemines

Parish." Horse made a fist, crushing his anger in the palm of his hand. "Anyway," he said, taking a deep breath, "how could I ever steal your daddy's beds? They been Petitjean tracts for a hundred years."

"You already hold the papers to the *Mathilde*—and after last winter to our house, too."

"I did your family a favor, that's all. There wasn't no trick in it." The man raised his arm and squeezed a swollen mosquito battening there between his thumb and his finger. He dropped his hand into the water with a splash to wash off the blood. "When we get married, the boat and the house'll be yours. A wedding present. How's that?"

The girl looked out over the marsh. "You know what my daddy says? Says I ought to give you a chance."

"You ought to give me a chance. We need each other, your family and mine."

The tall reeds of the marsh trembled in the stillness. Therese, staring straight at Horse, began to unbutton her dress. In the moonlight, he could see she wasn't wearing anything underneath. "Well, Darryl, here's your chance."

"This ain't proper," the man wheezed.

"Take off your shirt," she said softly in answer.

Her dress was open as she felt her way to the back of the boat. She sat in his lap, facing him. The mosquitoes hovered around them like a halo.

Horse had never before been led by a woman. Her small hands worked down his damp shirt, undoing one button after another. She peeled the shirt off him, first over one aching shoulder and then the other. He pulled his arms free of the sleeves like gars slipping through holes in his nets. At first, he didn't know where to put his hands, until the girl rubbed her breasts against the thick, gray, wiry hair of his chest. He wrapped his arms around her, gently, as if she might break.

The breeze caught and lifted the skirt of her dress, pulling it away from her thigh on one side. He felt her trying to loosen his pants, but his belly was too tight against the belt. "You do it," she whispered, kneeling to unlace his boots.

He heard the heavy boots clunk on the floorboard, and he felt his feet wiggle free of the socks in her hands. Still crouching in the bottom of the boat, she snaked his khaki pants down each leg. Horse was breathing fast but trying to calm himself, to stay gentle with her.

She grasped his shorts with both hands and tugged them off. He sat naked in the pirogue, the gray hair of his body glowing in the moonlight. He felt powerful, mean. *All right,* he thought to himself, *if this is the way she wants it.*

"Close your eyes," she teased.

"Why?" Horse smiled, showing his bad tooth.

"I'm shy for you to see me all at once."

"Shy? You the least shy girl I ever met."

"Please?" she begged coyly.

Horse closed his eyes. "You see," he said, "we gonna be happy together."

He felt the boat rock and opened his eyes. Therese's dress lay draped over her bench, but she was gone.

For a moment he was confused, until he heard her surface behind him, five yards off in the channel. "What you doing?" he called in a hushed voice.

"What's it look like I'm doing? Taking a moonlight swim. Come on." Her long legs lifted above the water as she disappeared once more beneath the surface.

When she finally popped up, farther out in the channel, Horse was anxiously searching the water for her. "There's gators out at night, and sharks, too," he warned.

"Who you think you fooling, huh? Come get me. I'm giving you your chance."

The man sighed. He lifted himself over the side and eased into the black water. It had been a long time since his last swim. He sank up to his ankles in the soft mud and had to pull free with each step. But by the time he got a few feet from the pirogue, the dredged bottom of the channel had fallen away from him. He dogpaddled out toward Therese, who sculled against the strengthening current as the tide began to run.

"You some slow swimmer," she teased, spitting water at him.

"Come on, Therese, let's go back."

"OK, I'll race you." She darted forward in great splashes of water.

Horse shook the spray from his eyes and followed in her wake. "Girl, you stronger than you look," he shouted after her.

Swimming with his head up, Horse saw Therese emerge from the water, glistening in the pale light as she lifted herself into the boat. Her bright back rose above the cloven heart of her *cul*, as the old-timers still called it. Puffing in the dark water toward the pirogue, he smiled as he translated the word. *Some things just don't sound right in English*, he decided.

Therese sat in the back of the boat, dangling her feet in the water and playing with the anchor line. She kept teasing Horse. "I tell you, a girl could get lonesome waiting on a husband like you. Maybe I just ought to put my dress back on."

"I'm coming," he sputtered between slow strokes. He began to feel his age. The pirogue seemed to rise and fall, though the water was calm.

Finally, he reached the boat. Hanging on to its side with both hands, he tried to catch his breath. Therese had pulled her legs up as he approached, and now she put her face very close to his. "I got something for you, old man," she whispered.

"I know, but just give me a minute to rest, *chère*." He took another breath. "You wore me out."

"Come on," she said, grasping him by the arm, "let me help you up."

Horse bobbed once or twice, trying to get his footing in the muddy bottom, then lifted himself up, straightening his arms like an acrobat on a trapeze at the circus. As he gripped the gunnel, balancing half in and half out of the water, the boat shifted, its stern sliding off to the side. "Damn, the line's come loose," he said, surprised. Just as he turned his head to the bench where he had tied off the anchor, he felt his chest explode with pain.

My heart, he thought, fighting to stay conscious and flip himself into the boat. "Therese . . . Therese, help me." But Therese was pushing him back into the water. When he looked down to pull her hands from his chest, he saw the knife buried up to its hilt between his ribs. Something thicker than water was oozing over his lips and down his chin. "Jesus, girl," he coughed, "what you done to me?" His grip loosened on the little boat as he slipped back over the side.

Horse tried to say something else, but already his mouth was full of water. The mud grabbed his ankles, dragging him down into the muck, swallowing him. Suddenly, barely aware, he felt her naked body against his in the water, pushing him up. *A mermaid for a drowning sailor,* he thought, and almost smiled. He was rising with her, toward her. He felt himself sliding along her thigh, coming into her.

The water split open like a sheet torn in two. Coughing and wheezing, the man sucked hot air into his lungs. "Hang on, Horse," he heard her whispering, "I got you."

But she wasn't in the water with him. She was still in the boat. She had reached down into the water and pulled him up by the hair. "You hang on, you hear?" Dangling from the boat with one arm hooked over the side, Horse concentrated on holding fast.

As Therese backpaddled the pirogue out into the deep water of the channel, the mud let go his ankles, and his legs drifted up alongside the boat, thumping against its hull. The tide was running, and once in the current, the pirogue drifted toward the Gulf.

"Horse, can you hear me?" Her face was down close to his again. He opened his eyes. Her breasts were like two moons above him. "I don't get bought for the price of no damn boat, you understand?" The man couldn't force the words out of his mouth. He tried to nod.

He was still nodding when she wrapped the anchor cord around his neck three times and dropped the pail of concrete over the side.

2.

"Terry, where you been?"

Therese heard her brother's voice before she saw him. "What you doing up so late, Alton?"

"I heard the door open. Where you been?"

The girl stood on the dark stairs to her room, her hand held against the banister by her brother's strong grip. "Come on, let's go up before we wake Mama and Daddy," she whispered.

Alton, nearly six feet tall, stooped under the low ceiling. Nestled against the roof, Therese's bedroom was cluttered with stuffed animals and tattered dolls that glowered with moonlight from the open dormer window. She quietly closed the door and flicked on the lamp beside her bed.

"Look at you," Alton gasped. "Your hair's all wet, your dress is muddy, and where's your shoes?"

"I been swimming."

"Swimming? At one o'clock in the morning? You gone crazy or something?"

"I couldn't sleep."

The young man sat down on the bed next to her. "Terry, what's going on?"

"I couldn't sleep, that's all," she snapped.

Alton picked up from the floor a blue alligator with a red felt tongue. "You know," he said, looking out the window on the far side of the room, "you don't have to marry Horse if you don't want to. We gonna have a good crop this season. Everything'll be OK."

"Daddy don't think so," Therese responded softly.

"Well, he's old. He worries easy."

"You telling me he didn't have to sign the *Mathilde* over to Horse?"

"Daddy's sorry he done that. He just didn't think he had no choice at the time."

"Yeah, well sometimes," the girl bitterly mused, "people don't leave you no choice."

"Daddy panicked, that's all. But we won't lose the boat, you'll see." Alton got up, bending under the roof like a giant in one of the frayed storybooks in the pink bookcase at the foot of his sister's bed. "Look, all I'm saying, Terry, is you don't have to if you don't want to. We'll manage somehow."

Therese grinned at her brother. "You look out for me, don't you?"

"Just like you for me," he said without a smile, opening the door. "You better dry your hair."

The girl switched off her lamp and listened to her brother creaking down the stairs back to his room. Easing the straps of her dress over her shoulders and letting it slip to the floor around her ankles, she reached under her pillow for the nightgown she had stuffed there two hours earlier. The girl held it over her head for a moment, then let it fall, covering her shivering body. She kicked her soiled dress under the bed and ran her fingers through her dark, wet hair. Trembling even more, she turned off the rotating fan on her desk that she had left running and shut the dormer window. As she did, she saw a faint orange glow beyond the marsh grass off in the channel. She roughly pulled her curtains closed.

Lying in her narrow bed, Therese could not stop shaking. But she did not cry. Instead, hugging a rag doll she called Marie, the girl remembered the first time Horse had come to the house, perhaps a year ago or so.

Of course, she had known him all her life. Everyone still talked about the time at the tomato festival—she couldn't have been more than five or six—when she called out to the big man arguing with her mother beside the church, "Why they call you Horse, Mr. Bruneau?" And the man, drunk from an afternoon of Dixies, scooped up the little girl in one arm, turned to the crowd in front of the jambalaya pot, and roared, "This child wants to know why I'm called the Horse. Well, what you folks say? Think she's old enough to see?"

Therese's mother was hitting him, trying to pull her daughter loose. "In front of the church you act this way?" she shouted, furious and frightened. "You dreadful, Darryl, dreadful."

He ignored the woman. "What you say? You ladies want to explain how I come by my name?"

A voice silenced the clucking crowd. "You keep it up, people gonna think it's short for Horse's Ass."

Horse turned, flushed with anger, and saw Matthew Christovich step out of the crowd. "Oh, it's you, Sheriff," he said, his sneer twisting into a sly smile. "I didn't see you there."

"I believe Mrs. Petitjean wants her daughter back."

"No, not yet. I was about to show this child why they call me Horse." The man suddenly swung Therese onto his back, where she held him tight around the neck, and drunkenly lowering himself onto his hands and knees, gave her a ride around the churchyard. "See," he said, as even her mother smiled, "this is why they call me Horse."

There were other stories, of course, about the two families swerving in and out of conflict. Horse had always found the money, one way or another, to buy up the tracts of widowed and bankrupted leaseholders, and over the years he and his three boys had come to rival the Petitjeans in their holdings. No bay bottom under Horse's tongs, though, produced anything like Petitjean's beds. When there had been plenty of oysters for everybody, Horse seemed satisfied with his own fields. But as the oil companies cut their canals from the Mississippi River to the Gulf of Mexico, flushing the briny oyster beds of Plaquemines Parish with the heavy salt of open waters, his oysters shriveled and died. Then only the old family fields, like Petitjean's, in little bays without names, in tiny lagoons an hour's snaking bayou ride from the coast, kept producing like the old days.

But Horse's animosity toward Felix Petitjean ran deeper than a new-comer's envy of an old family. Though Therese had never learned the source of it, the bad blood between the Bruneaus and the Petitjeans had kept them out of each other's homes, until one Sunday afternoon the summer before, when Horse pulled into her father's driveway in his pale blue Cadillac.

Therese and her mother were sitting on the edge of their bayou, patching the nets Felix and Alton had used that morning trawling for brown shrimp. It had been a difficult summer, even for the Petitjeans. Only in the last few years had Felix even rigged the *Mathilde* for year-round shrimping, but now father and son scoured the coastal waters before dawn every morning with the other shrimpers. The big boats from Texas and Alabama and as far away as Florida didn't leave much for the local *petits bateaux*. But Hurricane Corinne had decimated the oyster beds in the fall, and shrimp were bringing fifteen cents a pound.

The two women had watched Horse struggle out of his car and lum-ber toward them with the rolling gait of a man who'd spent most of his life on the water.

"Mathilde," he called, doffing his baseball cap decorated with a Con-federate flag across the crown.

"Darryl," she answered, nodding back. The woman turned to Therese. "Go wake up your father."

Groggy from his nap, Felix, in an undershirt and baggy pants, had padded barefoot out onto the porch overlooking the bayou, where Horse joined him. Mathilde brewed a pot of coffee as the men spoke.

Unable to hear their conversation from the nets at water's edge, to which she had returned, Therese watched Horse gesture dramatically, even standing once as if to leave. She saw her father take him by the arm and lead him back to his seat again. Next to Horse, Felix looked puny. He was a little man and "skinny as a cigarette," according to the people in town. The girl felt ashamed: she didn't have to hear what he was saying to know her father was begging Horse for a favor. Then, just as Mathilde swung open the screen door with two shot glasses of black coffee on her old silver tray, the men spit in their palms and shook hands.

They sat silently, sipping their coffee and looking out over the marsh that stretched from the far bank of the bayou all the way to the horizon. Mathilde stood there for a few moments, staring at the two men, then disappeared into the house.

When the coffee had cooled, Horse downed what was left and, with a nod to Felix, heavily descended the porch stairs. But instead of heading for his car, he swaggered up to Therese.

"How you, little girl?"

"Mr. Bruneau."

"Been a while since I seen you," he said, studying her. "You ain't so little anymore, is you?"

"They feed me."

Horse snarled a laugh. "You still got a smart tongue, huh?"

"What were you and my daddy talking about?"

"Nothing," he said with a tight-lipped smile. "Just oysters." Horse was about to say something else, but he heard the girl's mother coming up behind him in the dry grass. "I'll see you, you hear?" He walked back to his car, mumbling, "*Au revoir*, Mathilde," as he passed her.

Half an hour later, Therese's father was still sitting on the porch, silently staring out toward the Gulf.

As she lay in her bed clutching her doll, that's what she remembered most vividly, her small father in his rocker staring at the horizon.

While the old man rocked on the porch that afternoon, her mother explained to Therese that the banks had refused to loan any more money. The Board of Health was threatening to halt the sale of contaminated oysters—too many cases of hepatitis in New Orleans, they said—and the state legislature was considering a bill to revoke everyone's leases and to auction off the beds to the highest bidders. It was all too uncertain for the bankers. "Daddy didn't have no choice," Mathilde sighed. Only Horse was willing to lend enough for another season's fuel and ice and lease fees, and only because she herself had gone to ask him.

"So what'd we put up?" Therese asked bitterly.

Her mother sighed again. "The boat."

Therese took a deep breath. "He's got us, Mama."

"I know," she admitted, "I know."

And it had all been for nothing. Though there was as yet no indication of it, the warm winter had brewed a new bacterium, which was floating into Barataria Bay with the summer tides. Felix may not have been good with money, but he knew more about oysters than the scientists at L.S.U. Returning early one September afternoon from his farthest fields, he staggered off the *Mathilde* and sat down on the dock, holding his head. His wife came running from the kitchen, shouting, "What's wrong?"

Felix sat there shaking his head. "They gonna die—all of 'em."

"Who's gonna die?" Mathilde asked, her arms around him.

In answer, he opened his hand, in which he held a stunted, blackening oyster.

By October, the state health office had closed nearly all the beds in western Plaquemines. By November, the whole year's crop was gone.

Two days before Christmas, the blue Cadillac slid up the drive once again. This time there was no haggling. The whole family stood around the kitchen table as Horse accepted their house as collateral on a second loan.

Listening to his car crush the gravel backing out of their drive, Alton said, "Next time, he'll get the beds."

Felix slammed his fist on the table. "There won't be no next time, damn it."

Mathilde, weeping, made the sign of the cross.

"No," Therese said angrily, "Daddy's right. There ain't gonna be no next time."

Crabbing and a disappointing brown shrimp season barely saw them through the spring and early summer. Horse waited until late August before he came again; laughing gently with her father as the two men whispered on the porch, he made Therese nervous. A second visit had sealed the bargain.

Finally, at breakfast after Mass the following Sunday, Felix told

Therese that now that she had graduated from high school, it was time for her to marry. Following custom, he and her mother had arranged a match. Of course, they couldn't force her. They only wanted her to give the man a chance.

Therese suddenly understood the visits of her father's old rival. "You want me to marry Horse?"

"His name is Darryl," her mother corrected.

"How can you even ask?" she gasped in disbelief.

"He's a wealthy man," her father said, looking away. "He's promised to take care of you."

"I don't need no taking care of." Felix refused to look at her. "Mama, help me."

"I can't help you, baby," her mother whispered in a voice chafed by tears.

Alton stood up slowly and confronted his father. "What the hell deal did you make with that bastard?"

"It wasn't no deal," Felix said feebly. "It's just an arrangement. And it's the right thing for Therese. She'll be the richest woman in Egret Pass."

Alton shook his head and slammed the door behind him as he stormed out of the house.

"It ain't right, and I ain't doing it," Therese said matter-of-factly.

"Just give the man a chance, that's all I'm asking," her father had insisted. "Just give him a chance."

It still angered Therese, the memory of last Sunday morning, but now, lying in the dark, she found comfort in that anger—and justification. Her trembling passed, and she rose from her bed to open the dormer again. Pulling back the curtains, the girl took a deep breath.

"Well," she said aloud, "he got his chance."

The moon was slung low over the marsh, and as far as sound would carry, nothing could be heard but the buzz of mosquitoes.

3.

Though a drunken shrimper told Sheriff Christovich he had seen a "basket of flames" off in the distance floating down the channel that night, nothing but a few charred pieces of trim from a pirogue floated into anybody's nets the next day.

"Don't prove nothing," Christovich told Ross, Horse's middle son. "Everybody down here has a pirogue."

"Yeah, you right, but my daddy's Cadillac is sitting over at our camp on Bayou Dulac and the big pirogue's gone."

Christovich started walking back to his car with Ross following. "I didn't say it ain't your daddy's boat been washing in. Just said there ain't no proof it is, that's all. Anyway, you ever hear of a pirogue catching fire out on the water? No motor, no gas—it don't make sense."

"That's just the point. You think Daddy pulled his lighter out of his pocket and set himself on fire?"

"Look," the sheriff said, swinging open the door of his squad car and getting back in, "you tell your two brothers I've checked with every captain putting in this morning. I even talked to old Boudreaux about what he saw last night. Nobody knows nothing. You boys got to give me some time to do my job."

Ross put his hands on the door, keeping Christovich from shutting it.

"I can tell you right now, Little Darryl ain't gonna be satisfied. When him and Rusty left this morning in our boat to go look for Daddy, he told me to make sure you don't forget what Alton Petitjean said at R&J's the other night."

Ross pulled his hands back just as Christovich slammed the car door shut. "Listen, son," Christovich warned, "you tell Little Horse he and the rest of you better leave the Petitjeans be. You mess with them, I'll lock you up. I swear to God."

"You don't never change, do you, Sheriff? You know what they say about you and Miss Mathilde."

Christovich was out of the car before the boy could jump back. The door knocked Ross into the ditch that bordered the road of crushed shells. "One more word," Christovich said calmly, straddling the boy down in the ditch, "and I'll take off this badge and whip your ass from one end of town to the other."

Ross stayed down, but as Christovich got back in the car, the boy shouted, "Shit, if you wasn't so old . . ." Before he could finish the sentence, the sheriff had roared off, choking him with a great cloud of white dust.

When the *Squall* backed into its slip two hours later, Ross was waiting for his brothers. "Any sign of Daddy?" he shouted from the dock.

"Nothing," Rusty answered, tossing him a line. The baby of the family, Rusty started handing up some baskets of shrimp to his older brother.

"Where'd you get these?"

"Little Darryl said we might as well do some trawling on the way in, so we dropped the nets when we come into Bay Batiste. The water's too hot, though. We just got these five hampers."

Darryl, Horse's firstborn, emerged from the bow hold. "The bastard's leaking again. I told Daddy we needed to recaulk the damn thing." Then he saw Ross taking a basket of shrimp from Rusty. "So what'd Christovich say?"

His brother hopped down into the boat. "Just like you thought," Ross said, sitting on a heap of wet nets. "Said stay away from Alton and his family."

"That son of a bitch," Darryl hissed, kicking over the last hamper of shrimp. Rusty bent down and started scooping them back into the basket. He pricked his hand on a ragged barb but said nothing.

"And what's he expect us to do? The sheriff tell you that?"

"Sure," Ross said with a sarcastic smile, "just leave it all to him."

Darryl reached up to the crossbar of the boom and, leaning forward, hung his weight from the pole. "I think we ought to have a talk with Alton."

Rusty looked up from the shrimp he was trying to reach under the winch. "But we don't even know what happened to Daddy yet. Maybe we ought to see what turns up first."

Darryl looked at Ross, and the two older brothers laughed. "Yeah, babe, maybe we ought to see what turns up, but in the meantime maybe we ought to hear what Mr. Petitjean has to say for himself."

"Yeah," Ross agreed, "we haven't talked with him since Monday night at R&J's. We ought to see how he's doing."

Darryl nodded to a few shrimp that Rusty had missed near one of the trawl boards. "There's some behind the tongs, too," he added. As Rusty tossed the last few shrimp into the hamper, Darryl said, "You go weigh in and tell the buyer we'll have a full run for him tomorrow. Me and Ross are going for a little drive. You get yourself a ride home, OK? Ask Glenn."

"And fix something decent tonight," Ross interrupted. "I'm tired of that shit you been cooking."

As the sun declined hours later over the open water of Bay Batiste, Rusty sat on the stone breakwater that jutted out from the levee behind the house. Protecting the inlet to the lagoon on which his father had built their home, the breakwater was a gift from a local politician and member of the parish council. A road gang brought down from the state penitentiary at Angola "inadvertently"—it was the explanation favored by politicians in those days for such projects—dumped their loads of broken rocks, which had been destined for an eroding state highway, at the end of Horse's levee. (The levee had inadvertently been built by a parish work crew a few months earlier.) The road gang made a good job of it; nearly twenty years later, the breakwater continued to rebuff the swells of the bay. On one side, choppy water nervously splashed against the gray stones that had been split under the sledgehammers of convicted murderers and other hard-timers at Angola. On the other side, though, the lagoon was as unperturbed as a kettle of cold gumbo.

It seemed to Rusty, watching the bay go pink and then purple, that there was a kinship between stone and water. The wall of stone restrained, it was true, the plunging waves of the sudden storms that lashed the bay all summer, and one need not spend much time on the beach to see the scars worn in stone by the steady running of the tides. But the slap of stone against water, water against stone, obscured the fainter music of their shared qualities. He tried to enumerate, like a schoolboy for his teacher, their points of intersection. Color, he thought; he'd often seen the sea go stone gray, blond as pebbles, black and green as St. Martin's marble altar. There was the face of it, too. In the jaws of a storm on Barataria Bay, how many times had he seen a sheer wall of water rise over the bow like a cliff; on the sandy spit around the bend, how often had he mistaken in the failing evening light a flat stone at water's edge for the gray mirror of a puddle stranded at low tide? And there was more that he sensed between the two—the way a stone fit in the hand, and the feel of water scooped up in the palm—things for which he could not find the words but that he understood, down in his bones he understood, knit stone and water together.

Like an oyster, Rusty realized. It seemed to him, the more he thought about it, a kind of marriage of stone and water, the oyster. Inside a stone, water thickens into an oyster, and then it pulses within its shell like the gray heart of a gray stone. He felt he was getting close to something he needed to understand, not about oysters, about something else, but then he heard the truck grinding up the road of crushed shells that crowned the levee. He sat a bit longer, staring out over the water, guilty that he had forgotten his father, even for a few minutes. He already knew in his heart that somewhere out in the bay, Horse was caught in the drift, five or ten feet down, and slowly tumbling toward open water. He closed his eyes and swam after his father, but the current was too strong; he watched the body sink, disappearing into murky depths.

"Hey, asshole, where's dinner?" Ross shouted from the truck.

Drunk, Rusty thought, opening his eyes.

Darryl started to walk out to his brother on the breakwater, but he was a little wobbly, too, and retreated to the levee after a few tentative steps. "Come on in, Rusty," he called. "Let's eat."

Ross was already inside by the time Rusty caught up with his big brother. "So what'd you find out, Darryl?"

"Not a damn thing." He sat down on the steps to the porch. "We went to find Alton, but their boat was gone when we pulled up—probably running crab traps. So we took a drive over to Happy Jack on the off chance Daddy might have made up with Cecile, but she says she hasn't seen him in months."

Rusty interrupted him. "You two've been driving all over the parish in this condition?"

"Hell, no. Cecile was in no mood to offer us a drink; she's still pretty pissed at Daddy over that little girl from Magnolia. So we come all the way back and wound up at R&J's. Figured we'd talk to some of the boys, find out if anybody seen anything last night."

Rusty could hear Ross inside clanging the lid on the cast-iron skillet. *Son of a bitch,* Rusty thought, *he's eating without us.*

"Nobody seen nothing," Darryl continued. "We bought Boudreaux a beer, but that old drunk's even crazier than your mother was."

Rusty had been trying all day not to think of their mother. He fought back the pounding memories of her last night and the numb days that followed. *Not now,* he repeated to himself, *not now.*

Darryl, perhaps realizing what was going through his little brother's mind, pulled up Rusty as he stood. "Come on, let's go eat before Ross cleans us out."

Ross was dabbing a sop of bread into the butter and garlic in the bottom of the skillet. Looking up guiltily from the stove, he mumbled with a full mouth, "Shit, I was too hungry to wait for you two." A heap of shrimp shells were mounded on his plate next to the sink.

"You better've left us something to eat, I'm warning you, Ross," Darryl said, standing in the door.

Rusty walked over to the stove, then turned and shook his head at Darryl.

"Goddamn you, Ross, what the hell are we supposed to eat now?" Darryl was suddenly sober.

"I'll fix something," Rusty said quietly, pushing his brother away from the stove.

"Well, shit, I didn't know," Ross mumbled by way of apology.

"You gonna do the dishes tonight, you hear me?" Darryl growled.

"Aw, Little Horse, why can't Rusty?" he whined.

"Don't give me any of that 'Little Horse' crap. I fuckin' can't believe you. And pick up the rest of the shit in here, too. I'm sick of living like this."

After a plate of beans and andouille, Darryl turned on the radio.

"Hey, it's Elvis," Ross said from the sink.

Rusty, about to go to the room he shared with his middle brother, asked Darryl if he had heard anything else at R&J's.

"Yeah, Eisenhower's threatening to send federal troops into Little Rock to integrate the schools."

Ross whistled. "How about that shit?"

"I mean about Daddy," Rusty said, turning back to Darryl.

"Just that Daddy had a couple beers before he took off last night. Everybody figured he was going home."

"And he wasn't with nobody?"

"Not when he left," Darryl answered.

Rusty shook his head as Ross turned up "Blue Suede Shoes" on the radio.

Lying in his bed, trying to concentrate on the *Reader's Digest,* Rusty felt again the aching loneliness that had shaken him the night his mother died. He had come home from school on a wintry afternoon to find her slumped over the table, unconscious. An empty bottle of bourbon lay at her feet, and sleeping pills were scattered like insects over the red checkered cloth. He tried to wake her, he remembered, propping up her head with his hand and shaking her, harder and harder, until he realized he was crying. He gently lowered her head and telephoned for help.

Rusty closed the *Reader's Digest* and tried to remember where everyone else had been. His father and Darryl were somewhere out in the oyster beds. Ross was at football practice.

By the time the ambulance arrived, darkness was falling. He scribbled a note and left it on the table among the pills. Squatting in the back next to her stretcher, the boy held her cold hand all the way to the hospital in Port Sulphur. She was still alive when a young doctor checked her pulse in the driveway of the hospital. As they carried her into the little emergency room, Rusty collapsed into a chair, full of elation. *We made it,* he told himself. But ten minutes later, the doctor returned and grimly sighed, "I'm sorry."

They let him see her while the room was being cleaned. A nurse patted him on the shoulder as he stood wiping the hair from his mother's eyes. "It wasn't her fault," he insisted to the nurse. "She did her best."

He stood inside the glass doors of the hospital for an hour, straining over every approaching pair of southbound headlights for his father's face. When the new blue Cadillac finally pulled into the parking lot, Rusty could tell his father was angry. Seeing his son on the hospital steps, Horse shouted, "Where the hell is she, that crazy woman?"

"Dead," the boy said in a growl, and he flung himself at his father. It took both older brothers to pull him off Horse. Twisting in their tight grip, crying hot tears, he snarled, "And you all know why."

Horse, shaken, got up from the asphalt and stood in front of Rusty. "Hold him still, boys," he said softly, the fury welling up in his eyes.

Rusty saw the fist falling toward his face. The next thing he knew, a doctor was kneeling over him, flicking a vial of smelling salts under his nose.

That night, lying in bed, the left side of his face swollen and throbbing, he had felt utterly alone, an orphan in a house of strangers. Tonight, as his brothers in the next room argued over the radio, he tasted again that bitter loneliness, and as he bobbed between sleep and wakefulness, he was stricken to find that he could not remember his mother's face.

4.

Two days later, a trawler out of Grand Isle, making one last swing through Bay Ronquille, winched in Horse's tattered body along with a light catch of white shrimp. Though a shark had taken away most of the belly and crabs had nibbled the bloated flesh, the anchor cord—broken free of its cement bucket—still dangled from his blackened throat.

The captain of the *St. Catherine* had the mates ice the body and radioed the coast guard with his position. An ensign, fresh from New London and recently assigned to the station, insisted the boat come in immediately. Laughing, the captain flipped off the radio and turned his boat west toward Cat Bay. He had heard the shrimp were running there in the late afternoons.

By the time the body had made its way to Grand Isle and from there to the coroner's slab in Golden Meadow, another day had passed, but news of the *St. Catherine*'s haul reached Egret Pass in just a few hours. An oyster lugger working the shoals of Cat Bay had picked up the conversation between the coast guard and the *St. Catherine*. Later, on its way in, the lugger radioed the sheriff's office back home. Signing off, Matthew Christovich pulled out the charts of the whole Barataria system and traced the currents backward from the point where the trawler had snagged the body. His finger came to rest just east of Egret Pass. He got in his car and headed for the Bruneau house.

Darryl was alone; his brothers were working on the boat down at their slip at the launch. Sitting on the porch, oiling a reel, he saw the sheriff's car coming slowly down the levee path. The air was full of mosquito hawks. *A storm must be on its way,* he thought. Then, almost offhandedly, he said to himself, *Daddy's dead.*

Darryl waited for Christovich to get out of the car and start up the steps before greeting him. "You got news?"

"Maybe," the sheriff said, sitting down next to the young man. "A trawler found a body out in Bay Ronquille today."

"Daddy?"

"Don't know. Don't know nothing yet, but it could be."

"Where's the body?"

"I imagine in Grand Isle by now. I told Mary Beth to call over there in a little while." Christovich brushed away a sand fly. It lit a second time on his leg, so he slapped it onto the floor and crushed it beneath his heel.

"Why'd you come out here then? If you don't know shit."

"I thought we oughta talk. If that does turn out to be your father down in Grand Isle, then I'm real sorry. But if it is, you boys need to take it easy." He turned and looked Darryl in the eye. "You know what I'm saying?"

"You saying we supposed to sit around with a thumb up our ass while you let the murderer go free."

"See," Christovich said, shaking his head, "that's just what I mean. Who said anything about murder? There must be a hundred ways a man can die in open water. You know that."

"I'm just telling you, Sheriff, Alton Petitjean ain't walking away from this—no matter what goes on between you and his mother."

"If Alton had anything to do with it, I'll put him away, don't you worry. Just like I'll put you and your brothers away, you mess with him." Christovich lifted himself out of his chair. "And one more thing, Darryl. I know you upset about your daddy, so I'm gonna forget what you just said about me and Mrs. Petitjean. But you ever again so much as hint there's anything improper between me and that lady, I'll break you into so many pieces they'll use you to bait crab nets."

He walked back to his car. As he swung open the door, the sheriff shouted, "I'll call you we find out anything from Grand Isle."

It was raining by the time Sheriff Christovich got back to his office. His dispatcher had reached the police station in Grand Isle, but the *St. Catherine* had not yet put in. "They say she's rigged with lights, so she may be doing a little night trawling," Mary Beth explained.

"Well," Christovich said, pouring a cup of coffee, "this storm'll drive them in soon enough."

Outside, peals of thunder rumbled in from the Gulf, and boats scurrying to safe harbor sloshed through whitecaps in the bay.

It was still raining the next morning when Christovich left for Golden Meadow.

"I didn't think you could get there from here," Tony Ruiz joked as the sheriff filled up his car at the Esso station in Happy Jack.

"Shit, you just about can't. Got to go all the way up to New Orleans to catch Highway 90, follow that to Raceland, then take 308 down to Golden Meadow."

"All that just to see a dead man." Tony laughed as he leaned on the hood to latch it.

"Yeah," Christovich agreed, shaking his head in disgust, "the dead are just as big a pain in the ass as the living."

The weather cleared as the squad car approached New Orleans, and the sheriff arrived in Golden Meadow around noon. By the time he had eaten and checked in with the local police, it was well after one. The autopsy, he was told, had been delayed until the afternoon; the ambulance the coroner had sent to Grand Isle for the body that morning broke down on the way back.

Christovich was napping in the hospital's parking lot when a tow truck pulled in, blasting its horn and dragging the ambulance behind it on a hook. The driver jumped down from his cab, clearly agitated. "Nobody told me I was gonna have to tow a corpse twenty miles," he complained to the nurse who had come out to see what all the noise was about.

Christovich followed the body into the hospital. Dr. Campo, the parish coroner, asked him to take a seat. "We get 'em all the time, Sheriff, after they've been in the water a few days." He shook his head and made a face. "Let me take a peek first."

When Dr. Campo finally led Christovich into the tiny morgue, huge fans were driving the air out through a wall of open windows. "Smell's the worst part," the coroner shouted over the fans.

Lying on a stone slab, the body was draped with a sheet. A small cloth covered the face. The doctor gently peeled back the cloth as if he were unveiling a treasure. Horse's puffy face, blackening in spots, stared up at the ceiling. "I can identify him," the sheriff said, taking a deep breath.

"Fine," Dr. Campo shouted. "Why don't you wait outside? I'll come get you when I'm finished."

Christovich lifted the unraveling anchor cord that hung off the edge of the table. "Strangled?"

The doctor pulled the sheet away from the bruised neck. "Looks like it."

The sheriff touched Horse's throat. "Could it be an accident?"

"Sure. The son of a bitch could've got his neck tangled in the rope if he was drunk enough, I suppose. You can't imagine all the damn fool ways people manage to wind up dead. Of course, it might be suicide."

A few minutes later, the doctor opened the door into the hall, where Christovich was waiting. "It's not a suicide."

Christovich went back in, and the doctor folded down the sheet, careful to conceal the gaping wound in the stomach.

"All these," the coroner said, pointing with a ruler to ragged, inch-long cuts, "some shark did. But this one wasn't from any fish."

"How do you know?" Sheriff Christovich shouted over the fans.

In answer, the doctor inserted his steel ruler into the clean, wide wound. It went in nine inches. Dr. Campo left the ruler in the wound and looked up. "You got yourself a homicide, Sheriff."

Christovich spent the long ride home putting together what he knew. Horse had been drinking at R&J's the night he was killed. Ronnie, the bartender, said he had a couple of beers. *Knowing Horse,* the sheriff thought, *that probably means four or five.*

Horse had left the bar around 10:30. *Figure twenty minutes or so to get to his camp on Bayou Dulac—if that's where he went first.* The sheriff backed up to 10:30. *That's all I know for sure,* he reminded himself, imagining the big blue Cadillac swerving out of the shell parking lot of the roadhouse. *Then what'd the son of a bitch do?*

He knew that at some point during the night, Horse had wound up at the camp on Bayou Dulac. The house was still locked when his sons went looking for him the next morning, but one of the pirogues was missing.

The sheriff concentrated on the pirogue. *It's a hunting boat,* he thought. *What was that big bastard hunting?* Christovich knew there were only two things he might be after in the middle of the night—money or "poontang," as the boys descending on the East Bank whorehouses after two weeks out on an oil rig called it.

There were all kind of ways that Horse made money, the sheriff knew, but he couldn't think of any that required a pirogue at midnight. On the other hand, whether it was Sidney Eustace's wife again or Beryl Zeringue or—he tried to remember whose name had come up a few weeks ago—Cindy Landry, Christovich could think of plenty of reasons for the drunken old fool to venture out at night. *Hell,* he thought, *if I have to check out every man who's got a wife or daughter Horse bragged about, I might just as well lock up the whole damn town.*

And then he added, *Or mother or sister.* He had heard the next morning about the trouble Monday night at R&J's between Alton and Little Horse. Alton wasn't much of a fighter, but he was just as big as Darryl. Like most of the boys who raked oysters, they both could crack a pecan in the crook of their arms. The mean streak in Darryl ought to have given him the edge, but as Ronnie explained when the sheriff stopped by the man's bar the next day, "you shouldn't push an easy man too hard." That night, with Big Horse off somewhere else, the usual taunts about Alton's father had given way to some sneering insinuations about his mother and sister. Little Darryl was drinking more than usual, Ronnie had told the sheriff. "Something had scratched him the wrong way. But when they went out back, if Ross hadn't jumped in, Alton would have knocked the shit out of him." According to Ronnie, when Alton went down the final time under a pair of kicks by the two brothers, he looked up at them through bloody eyes and whispered, "I'm gonna kill you and your daddy, too. Y'all ain't getting away with it, what you done us." Coming from Alton, that had surprised everyone. "Tell you, Sheriff, it sounded more like a curse than a threat," Ronnie said, making the sign of the cross. "The *gris-gris*, if you ask me." Christovich smiled, thinking of the anxious little bartender.

But the smile faded as he picked up Route 23 out of Belle Chasse for the last leg of his trip. He heard a ship on the river, just over the levee, bellowing for its tug. "Now the trouble really begins," he said out loud. "Goddamn that Horse."

5.

The pews of the suffocating parish church were filled by all the women in town, who flicked cardboard images of the Sacred Heart, supplied by the funeral home as fans, beneath their perspiring faces. Except for blood relatives, the men, by economic—and superstitious—tradition, did not attend Horse's funeral. The white shrimp season was too short, and the sea too dangerous, to mourn a drowned man.

Borne by Horse's three sons, two cousins from Buras, and the undertaker, the coffin entered the church. The priest, sprinkling the cloth-draped casket with holy water and perfuming it with little clouds of incense from the altar boy's censer, intoned the ominous prayers for the dead. "*Si iniquitates observaveris, Domine: Domine, quis sustinebit?*"

In a stiff black dress like all the other women, Mathilde Petitjean followed the Latin liturgy in her missal. "If you observe our iniquities, O Lord: Lord, who can survive?" She began to weep.

At the end of the *Miserere*, the congregation of women responded with a fluted "*Amen.*" But Therese, handing her mother a tissue, clung to the last words of the antiphon, "*ossa humiliata.*" "These humbled bones," the missal translated.

Shit, yeah, the girl thought, imagining the body, feet first, within the coffin, *I humbled those bones, all right.*

But as the service continued, Therese's bravado yielded to the gnawing insistence of what she had done. Against the image of Horse clinging to the edge of the boat, blood dripping from his mouth, the girl tightened her heart into a fist of anger. She would not let herself pity the old man to whom she had been promised in payment of her family's debt. Darryl Bruneau had taken advantage of them, she continued to maintain, struggling to suppress other memories of that night. *He got exactly what he deserved,* Therese answered the accusation welling up inside her, and she tried to fix upon the rage she had felt, the fury and disgust, as the fat old man, huffing and bobbing in the moonlit water, had dogpaddled back to the pirogue to seize his prize. *One way or another, he was gonna ruin us,* she defended herself. *He didn't leave me no other choice but to do what I done.*

Father Danziger, perspiring profusely beneath cassock and alb and chasuble, hurried the funeral to its conclusion. Though he had relented in finally allowing the body to be buried from the church, the priest knew Horse to be a "carnal sinner" and did not wish to waste more time than absolutely necessary on the interment.

Following the coffin, the women escorted the body to the small cemetery that adjoined the church. Though Cindy Landry and a few others wept openly—including, to her daughter's dismay, Mathilde Petitjean—most took snide satisfaction in Horse's demise. Some had better reasons than others to celebrate his death, but they showed no more emotion than Therese.

The cemetery, beside the town's main road, had only a few moss-draped oaks to shade the mourners as they lay Horse to rest beside his wife. The stubbly grass of the narrow plots obscured the names of those families whose descendants now prayed for the repose of Darryl Bruneau's soul. Two Negroes waited with shovels some distance away, trying to stay out of sight behind a tree at the edge of the cemetery until after the ceremony.

When the priest had concluded the service with a final blessing, the women lingered in little groups beneath the trees, greeting one another and shaking their heads over Horse's death. Then, in twos and threes, they crossed the yard to the Bruneau boys to offer their condolences. Darryl, his face hard as one of the low granite tombstones among which he stood, filled his father's old suit as if it had been made for him. Mathilde remembered Horse as a young man, waiting behind the church in his new suit, holding a rose; she felt faint in the heat and took her daughter's arm. Ross and his little brother simply wore short-sleeved white shirts and garish, old-fashioned ties. Some women returned from their cars and trucks with casseroles and cakes for the boys, which Rusty stacked behind them.

But when Mathilde and Therese approached with a small group of women, Darryl stepped out of the shade and into the sunlight to meet them. "You tell your son, Mrs. Petitjean, we know who done this. We know."

The other women began to chastise Darryl, but Therese hushed them, stepping in front of her mother. "Don't you boys go threatening my brother. Alton ain't never hurt nobody. He's got nothing to do with this, and everybody knows it."

Ross started forward as if he were going to grab Therese, but Rusty— to everyone's surprise—stopped him. "This ain't the time or the place," the youngest brother said. "These people are here to pay their respects."

Darryl put his hand on Ross's shoulder. "We'll settle this later." Then, looking past the girl to her mother, the man almost whispered, "You tell Alton, you hear?"

No one followed Horse's three sons back to their house. Though Ross had ripped off his tie as soon as they got into the car at the cemetery, the boys stayed dressed in their white shirts until after they had finished a dish of mirlitons stuffed with shrimp that one of the women had prepared for them. They ate in silence, taking long drafts of beer between bites. All three boys were lost among memories of their father.

Ross, though he would angrily deny he had done so if asked, had been the only son who wept for Horse. Little Darryl, offended by his father's murder and intent upon vengeance, continued to resist the tide of grief sweeping in upon them like a storm surge ahead of a hurricane. Rusty still blamed his father for the foundering of his mother's life upon the unhappiness of her marriage; in fact, he was ashamed he could not summon a sense of loss sufficient to numb his anger long enough to mourn his father. But Ross, the only one who felt orphaned by his father's death, had cried himself asleep the night he came home to the news that Horse's body had been found.

Emptying his beer, Darryl stood and said, in a tone Rusty had never heard before from his brother, "We got work to do." While the youngest cleaned the table, his two brothers changed into their blue jeans and T-shirts. "C'mon," Darryl shouted to Rusty, "we gotta go."

As he stood with a foot on the pier loosing the mooring lines of the *Squall,* a skim of fuel on the water swirled with color in the sunlight, reminding Rusty of the marbled end pages of his mother's old Bible. He hopped down into the boat as Darryl muscled the engine into gear. Clear of the slip, the stern swung sharply about, and the *Squall* eased into neutral. Ross, who had been floating just off the trailer ramp in a small wooden skiff, yanked the cord on the little outboard two or three times before the engine turned over, sputtering mud and gasoline and water behind as it lurched toward the trawler. Tossing a line to Rusty, he killed the motor. As he drifted alongside, Ross grabbed his brother's hand and lifted himself onto the bigger boat. Then Rusty let out a few yards of line and tied it off to a stern cleat. As the *Squall* nosed toward the channel, its gentle wash was lost in the thick reeds of the bayou's far shore and the creosoted pilings of the launch on the nearer side. Just as he passed the last pier, Darryl leaned on the throttle. The grumble of the engine rose like a church organ wheezing into its music. The steady, piercing hum reminded Rusty of the hymns they'd sung a few hours earlier as the priest laid his father to rest. He turned his face from the hot breeze, gritty with gnats, and hunkered down among the empty baskets in the stern. He watched the battered skiff chase after them, skimming over the green water as it kicked back and forth between their port and starboard wakes.

Darryl set his youngest brother adrift with a pair of eight-foot tongs just outside the shoals off St. Mary's Point. Anxious to catch the tide, he nearly forgot to leave Rusty a canteen.

Though it might look like open water to the sport boats that criss-crossed Barataria Bay on weekends, oystermen never had to check the charts to find their leases. Even after a storm had heaved the sandbars every which way and left nothing to navigate by but a scrubbed blue sky and muddy water, the oyster luggers homed back to their family fields like farmers on the way to their pastures, using faint landmarks like dead trees on a barely discernible shoreline to locate their beds.

Rusty dropped the arm of his outboard and followed the narrow channel between two bars into his own waters. Killing the engine, he poled himself along the bottom with his tongs. A slight scraping of shell against the iron teeth of his rake told him to drop anchor. For the next hour and a half, straddling the center bench as he stood, the boy dredged up encrusted shells, flipping open the dripping basket of his tongs in the bottom of the boat until the oysters around his feet reached the top of his white rubber boots. Exhausted, he sank down on the bench and took a long swig of water from his canteen. He was careful not to tip the boat, settling low in the water. It had been a good haul; he worried whether he had enough draft left to slip back through the channel now that the tide was out. He didn't want to throw overboard what he had broken his back to raise up.

As he sat motionless among the shells, waiting for his brothers to return from their trawling, small memories broke the shimmering water like a school of mullets chased by a shark. He recalled his eighth, maybe ninth, birthday, waking to his mother's kiss, cowboys twirling lariats on his tan and green flannel pajamas, his father standing at the foot of the bed he shared with his middle brother. He remembered the huge man tossing a box bound with bright ribbons next to him on the bed. He saw himself standing on the mattress, dressed in the yellow raincoat and hat he had seen in the Sears catalog, the slicker that he had pointed out to his father months before and forgotten. Now, ten years later, he could still smell the sour yellow rubber, see the small boy and girl sharing an umbrella as the rain puddled around them over and over again on the stiff canvas lining within the coat, hear the click of the black metal clasps snapping shut. And he remembered the man carrying him out of the house into the cold rain that pelted the tin roof above their heads, his mother's voice from the porch begging her husband to bring the boy in, and his own laughter as his father danced with him in the storm—the rain spinning off the brim of his hat, sluicing down the wrinkles of his yellow slicker.

A fin splayed the water forty yards off. Rusty looked for the tail, but nothing trailed the dorsal; it was dolphin, not shark.

His mother's voice, calling from the porch, lingered until it was lost in the drone of the *Squall*, which dropped anchor beyond the sandbars as he poled his way into deep water.

Little Horse was pleased with their haul. The wind had died as the tide began to run, and their nets had swept the milky green waters of a few hundred pounds of white shrimp. As Ross crouched in the hold of the boat chipping shards of ice from the blocks still whole among the afternoon's catch, he suddenly called out to his brothers, "Lookee what I found," and flipped a big redfish onto the deck. "We caught ourselves some dinner, boys." Rusty, his white boots still buried in the oysters filling the skiff tied up beside the *Squall*, shoveled the gnarled shells into the burlap sack Little Horse held open for him. Nodding to the redfish that flopped once or twice on the slippery deck, the eldest brother judged, "We done good."

When they had emptied the small boat and loosened its lines, retying its bow line to a stern cleat, they stacked the bulging burlap sacks and dragged an oily tarp over the oysters. Rusty, exhausted, hunched down on the damp shrimp nets. As the engine thrummed into gear, the bow of the *Squall* lifted, and the ice pick Ross had forgotten beside the lip of the hold clattered across the deck.

"Hey, asshole, we home." It was Ross, poking his little brother with an empty beer. Rusty pushed the bottle away and shook himself awake; he had slept the whole way in. They were already in the bayou, about to back into their slip.

It was nearly seven before they had come to terms with the buyer, off-loaded their catch, and hosed down the boat. Once home, Rusty baked the redfish in lemon butter. As they finished their meal, dipping hunks of

French bread into the drippings, Ross announced he was taking a run over to R&J's.

Rusty started to clean the table. "Leave the dishes, little brother," Darryl insisted. "Let's all go. We gonna drink to Daddy tonight."

The bar was crowded with shrimpers and oystermen. Their pickup trucks, pocked with rusted scabs from the salt air, filled the shelled strip beside the highway. When the blue Cadillac eased into the lot, one of the local men who had been sitting on the fender of his truck with a young woman hopped down and walked over to where Darryl had stopped, looking for a place to park.

"You boys pull in behind me," he said, leaning into Ross's window. "That little girl's got her knees glued together. We ain't going nowhere tonight." He started to get up, then leaned down again. "Sorry about your daddy. Damn shame."

Only the rotating fans nailed to the walls and the hum of the overheads offered any relief from the pulsing heat inside R&J's, but the bar was packed. Girlfriends in loose blouses and cascading skirts sat sulkily in pairs at tables around the room while their dates cocked their hips against the scarred cypress bar, laughing with the other men and keeping one eye on their women. As the Bruneau boys made their way toward the pool table near the fire exit, men thumped their shoulders in sympathy over their father's death.

"I hope they find the son of a bitch done it," Ronnie told them as he put a tray of Dixies on the table the boys had taken against the back wall. "Son of a bitch," he repeated.

"Everybody in this goddamn room knows the bastard that done it," Darryl answered, barely moving his lips. He pulled a roll of bills from his shirt pocket.

"No, forget it, Little Horse," Ronnie said, waving the money away. "The drinks are on the house for you three tonight—in honor of your daddy. He always done right by me."

Darryl nodded his appreciation to the short bartender.

The brothers drank silently, listening to the twang of a cowboy tune.

Suddenly, Ross turned to Rusty. "Gimme a dime. I hate that shit."

Taking the coin his brother had laid on the table, he started toward the jukebox.

"Hey, Ross." It was a girl he had gone to school with. She was wearing a sundress of pink and black camellias. "You OK?"

"Yeah, Yvonne, yeah." He tried to think of something to say. "You want to pick a song? It's three for a dime."

"Sure."

As they stood over the glass dome watching a stainless steel sleeve rotate the amber record onto the turntable, Yvonne slipped her hand into Ross's. "I feel real bad about your daddy." Ross turned to her and was about to speak when the first raw notes of "Maybellene" interrupted him. He smiled, tapping his boot to the nervous drumbeat.

Yvonne's blonde hair flounced above her bare shoulders as she bobbed her head to the music. "Wanna dance?"

"Not tonight," Ross said quietly, looking away.

"Oh, you poor baby. I'm so sorry. I wish there was something I could do."

They listened to Chuck Berry sing of faithless Maybellene's Coupe de Ville scorching through the night.

"You got that Cadillac of your daddy's here?"

Ross nodded as the guitar whined.

"Why don't you take me for a ride?"

As she stood behind him, shifting from foot to foot, Ross asked his big brother for the keys to the car.

Rusty hissed, "You going on a date the same night they buried your father?"

Ross ignored him, appealing to Darryl in a whisper. "She wants to fuck, Little Horse. I just know it."

Rusty started to stand, furious with his brother, but Darryl reached up and pulled the boy down by the collar. Then he tossed the keys on the table. "Don't you leave us here all goddamn night, you hear?"

"Don't worry, Little Horse, I'll be back in an hour, an hour and a half tops. Promise."

"Don't you forget us."

But Ross was already pulling Yvonne toward the door, grinning slyly to the men who nodded at him as he passed.

"You let him go screw that girl and Daddy's not in the ground twelve hours?"

Darryl put his hand on Rusty's forearm. "Listen, babe, Ross is more broke up than he shows about what happened. It's like when he was a kid and that damn dog of his died, that Catahoula with the bad leg. Don't say nothing about it all day, then Daddy finds him on the levee that night crying his eyes out. Ross needs a little ass tonight. It's the best thing for him. Fact is, wouldn't hurt you or me none, neither."

Rusty pulled loose of his brother's grip.

Taking a slow swig from the bottle in front of him, Darryl leaned back on just two legs of his chair. "What you think Daddy did the night Mama died?"

Rusty suddenly forgot about Ross. "What? What did he do?"

Darryl shrugged as if it were obvious. "You know what he always said: 'The living can't stop living just 'cause somebody else does.' "

"The son of a bitch," Rusty cursed under his breath. "The goddamn son of a bitch."

6.

Well, I'll be damned if you wasn't right."

"I told you, Little Horse," Ross boasted, pleased with himself, as the three Bruneau brothers sat in their pickup the next night, backed deep into a dark turnaround on the long gravel road that led, a hundred yards or so farther on, to the Petitjean house. Handing a pint of sloe gin back and forth, they watched a big Buick pass by their hiding place and creep down the road. "That's her daddy's car," he whispered excitedly. "It's just like Yvonne said. Sherilee don't want to get laid in the back of some truck that stinks of shrimp, so she does the driving. Hell, she probably even pays for his rubbers."

Ross laughed at his own joke.

"Shit, why don't we just invite her daddy down here?" Ross went on. "One look at Alton's hairy ass up against that back window, and Mr. Sonnier'll kill him for us."

Rusty stirred, half asleep after two hours waiting in the truck. "What do you mean 'kill him'? Darryl said we were just gonna talk to him."

"Yeah, that's right, babe," Darryl assured him. "We just gonna have a little talk, that's all. Find out what really happened."

The Buick turned off its headlights as it slowed to a stop not far beyond. Through the pine trees and bushes, the Bruneaus could see the parking lights of the car.

"That Yvonne knows what she's talking about, don't she?" Ross marveled. "And you didn't want me to hide the snake with her," he said, giving his little brother an elbow in the ribs.

"Shut up and leave him be," Darryl growled. "You want them to hear us?"

Another half hour passed, the silence broken only by night birds calling to their mates and the crackling of the brush as predators and prey scurried over the rusty pine needles strewn across the forest floor. Suddenly, they heard the Buick roar awake and a car door slam shut.

"That'll be Alton," Ross explained in a whisper. "Yvonne said Sherilee don't want his parents to see her car, so she makes him walk home. She told Yvonne she wants to keep it secret. Can you believe he puts up with that crap?"

"He's an asshole," Darryl said, his teeth clenched.

"Hell, we already knew that," Ross chuckled.

As the Buick backed down the road, something occurred to Rusty. "What if she tries to turn around right here?"

"She won't," Darryl assured him. "She's afraid she'll scratch her daddy's car—too many branches and shit to turn around in the dark. No, she'll just back all the way to the highway. It's not that far."

"And if you wrong?"

"Well, then, little brother, we just three drunk bastards lost in the woods. She won't give a piss what we're doing here, just so we don't tell her daddy what she's doing here."

"Look out, she's coming past," Ross interrupted. The brothers ducked down.

The gnashing of the gravel faded even before the dust lost the ashen glow of her headlights. The Bruneaus waited for the darkness to settle again before they climbed from their truck. They left the doors of the pickup open and silently followed single-file the soft shoulder of the road. They were nearly upon Alton when he abruptly turned and faced them.

"Darryl. Ross. Rusty." He greeted them, one by one, as if they had bumped into him at the grocery.

"Alton," Darryl responded, nodding.

"You boys coming to visit?" His voice was almost defiant, as if he were threatening the three men in front of him.

"Not exactly, Alton," Ross said, picking up a thick, gnarled branch beside the road and testing it against his other hand.

Rusty strained into the night, but the Petitjean house was still out of sight. "We got some questions for you," he said, trying to remind his brothers why they had come.

"That's right," Darryl agreed. Rusty felt relieved; Ross would not dare do anything to Alton unless their big brother let him.

"About your daddy?"

"What do you think, asshole?" Ross took a step forward, but Darryl put a hand on his brother's shoulder.

Alton didn't back up. "Don't know nothing about it." Ross was so close he could smell Alton's breath. It was sweet, like mint. "I'm sorry he's dead, but I don't know nothing about it."

Rusty realized the thick September woods would conceal any struggle, muffle any shouts. He spoke up from behind his brothers. "Well, that's what we were after—whether you knew anything about it." Something had frightened the animals; everything tensed in silence. "So we'll be going, right, Little Horse?"

"Yeah, babe, we'll be going." Darryl hadn't taken his eyes from Alton. "We'll be going right after we get an answer about one more thing."

"What's that?" Rusty could hear Alton's voice relax just the slightest bit.

"Well, Alton," Darryl said as he reached into the back pocket of his jeans, "I was just wondering . . ." Rusty saw the switchblade flick open, still behind his brother's back. Before he could take a step, the knife swung down past his brother's leg and then disappeared as it came up between Darryl and Alton. Rusty heard Alton suck in his breath, as if he had been punched in the stomach. "I was just wondering," Darryl suddenly continued, "how you like a knife between the ribs, you mother-fucker."

Alton teetered for a moment, staring at Rusty over Darryl's shoulder, as if he were confused, unsure of what had just happened. Then he fell to his knees. One hand held him up; the other dripped with the blood of the wound it covered. Ross circled around him.

Alton looked up at Darryl. "You wrong. I never—" But Ross caught him in the back of the skull with the heavy piece of wood before he could finish the sentence. He crumpled to the gravel.

Even in the dark, Rusty could see the blood gushing from the back of his head. "You told me," Rusty sputtered, "you told me—"

"Shut the fuck up," Ross said deep in his throat. He turned to Darryl, who still gripped the knife. "Think he's dead?"

"Better not take any chances. Let's drag him to the bayou. And get rid of that branch you used."

Rusty grabbed Darryl and spun him around. "You said nothing but questions. Just talk to him, you said."

Darryl bent down and wiped the blade on the back of Alton's shirt. As he folded the knife into its hilt and reset the spring lock, he looked up at his baby brother. "Now I'm only saying this to you once. This mother-fucker killed Daddy. He said he was gonna do it, and he done it. And we weren't gonna get no justice from Sheriff Christovich. I know that. You know that. So we done what had to be done. For Daddy."

"You two killed him. You killed Alton."

"You a part of it, too. Just as much as me and Ross. So you grab one of those legs and help your brother throw this son of a bitch in the bayou." Darryl stood up; he slipped the knife back into his pocket. Rusty felt as if he were staring at his father. "I mean it, goddamn you. Right now."

For a moment, Rusty hesitated. Alton had fallen with his head twisted, his mouth agape. Now a sliver of the moon sliced through the ragged clouds, casting its pale light over the contorted body. A hand jut-ting out impossibly from the shoulder, its fingers curled like the talons of a marsh owl, twitched. Rusty took a step back, then turned and ran, head-long down the dark road, the gravel shifting, slipping beneath his feet with every sliding stride. When he stumbled too close to the edge of the road, branches lashed his face, thorns of tangled vines stung him. Still he ran, till the uncertain road hardened into asphalt on the lip of the highway. As he gasped for breath, he realized he was crying.

Almost instinctively, he turned toward home but stopped himself and started walking in the opposite direction, toward town. He wanted to stop, to sink down in the culvert along the highway and rest, just for a little while. But he kept walking.

The highway, almost violet in the moonlight sifting down through the shredded gray clouds, seemed the only solid thing in the whole world as Rusty let one foot drop in front of the other. His head clotted with fear, which had already begun to congeal into guilt. The crickets paused in midrasp as he passed, a silence advancing through the darkness like a wave, still far out in the Gulf but swelling toward a distant shore.

In the heart of that silence, the boy walked. Having grown up among hunters and fishermen, he had seen many things die. He had never forgotten his first trip out with his father and brothers. They hooked into a school of croakers, pulling in thirty, maybe forty, of the bellowing little fish. "Why they make that noise?" the child had asked, concerned. Unthreading the barb of a treble hook from the eye of a small croaker where it had snagged as the boy reeled in, his father explained, "Why, they crying for their mama. But she can't hear them. Not anymore." Every time one of boys lifted the lid of the battered metal icebox to toss in another fish or to take a drink from the army surplus canteens chilling in the bottom of the cooler, Rusty heard the pathetic croaking. After a while, he secretly tore the shrimp meat from his hook and dropped his line in the water without bait.

But the nets of the *Squall* that dredged up thousands of shrimp, each curling around a tiny black heart that frantically pulsed beneath its transparent skin, hardened him soon enough. The baskets of still twitching shrimp, the sacks of oysters frothing from their corroded shells, the traps heavy with crabs desperately clambering over one another offered him the same lesson. Every living thing in the water that fell onto the deck of a boat cried out for its mother, the sea; and as he watched each wither in the harsh light of his world, he finally learned—almost by rote—how to let things die without flinching, without indulging in what he began to think a girlish sentimentality. Eventually, even his brothers relented in their taunts about his squeamishness.

But what he found as he wandered through the night toward Egret Pass was a kind of revulsion that had never before gripped him. He sickened not from the whimpered entreaties or the wretched throes of a violent death—Alton had fallen too quickly for that—but from . . . what? The ruthless ease with which his brothers had brought the man down? His own cowardice, or whatever it was, that had held him back, that had let him deceive himself into believing Darryl's lies? Or perhaps, merely the ripe, hollow thud of the club against a human skull? He was fleeing, he realized, not the body that already floated facedown in the murky waters of the Petitjeans' own bayou. No, he told himself, suddenly alert as a rabbit hunted by a hound, it was something else.

Rusty kept moving as if pursued. He tried to understand what Darryl had done. It was simple: Little Horse hated Alton. His brother had always hated Alton, though why such hatred had welled up so early and so intensely he had never been able to discover. As boys, they had wrestled daily in the school yard. Bad blood, everyone called it, though with a smile, as if amused to find such inexplicable antipathy in two small children. As teenagers, the boys avoided each other. Alton was slow to anger, diffident in the face of trouble. Little Horse was famous for his temper but seemed to grow wary of Alton. Some said, though they found it hard to believe, that he was afraid of the big Petitjean boy. But Rusty knew that their father had forbidden Darryl to fight with Alton. "Don't you touch him, you understand me? Don't you so much as look at him." Even a few days ago when Darryl and Ross had beaten up Alton at R&J's, the old man threw a fit, raging at his oldest son and whipping Ross from the house with a belt. "I warned you to leave that boy be," Horse had bellowed from the porch at the two of them. "I done warned you." Darryl insisted he had fought for Daddy, for the sake of his name—and tonight, crouching beside Alton's bleeding body, he had said the same thing, that he'd done it for their father, for justice—but Rusty sensed he had his own reasons.

Ross, on the other hand, was easier to understand; he had simply reveled in the murder. Rusty had seen the same blaze of excitement in the eyes of the butcher at a holiday *boucherie* when the long-bladed knife drawn across an exposed, pink throat silenced the squealing piglet, the little *cochon de lait*. And with a start, he realized he had seen the same barely contained exultation in Ross's eyes the night before as his brother led Yvonne by the hand outside into the darkness. Rusty knew this because, as Alton's fingers had quivered feebly beside the crushed head, he, too, had tasted blood, the exhilarating liquor of the heart's blood, if only for a moment, before he spit it out onto the white dust of that gravel road and ran away.

It wasn't revulsion that had dazed him—and the realization left him stricken—no, not revulsion, but elation. The pathetic twitch of Alton's contorted hand had engendered a shiver not of pity but of delight. Grimly, he remembered his father: he was one of Horse's sons after all.

A slash of lightning out over the marsh interrupted him. He waited for the thunder. It was five, maybe ten miles off—a storm sweeping in across the bay.

So this is what it's like to kill a man, he thought. And he hoped that if he kept walking long enough, eventually he would begin to feel ashamed.

7.

The rain, dashing itself against the dormer window, battering the corrugated tin roof above her head, startled Therese from her sleep. She had been dreaming, and she awoke groggy, troubled. Sitting up in bed, she opened her eyes wider. She couldn't remember what she had been dreaming—vague images flitted like fish darting just beneath the surface—but her nightgown was soaked with sweat. Something about Horse, the girl began to recall, something about Horse again. She threw off the chenille spread. Unsteadily, she stood up and felt her way through the dark room to the dormer. Her bare foot recoiled from the cold water on the floor; she shut the window.

Therese looked out and saw the plunging rain in the little yellow circle cast by the yard light. It took her a moment to realize she was shivering. Lifting the damp gown over her head, she dropped it to the floor and climbed back into bed. She curled beneath the covers, letting her breath warm the tent she had made. Muffled by the bedspread and the shut window, the rain sounded far off, like a memory, like the dream she had lost. She cupped a breast in one hand and sleepily played with her nipple.

Was it more thunder, she wondered as she woke again an hour or so later. The thick darkness of the room was untinged by any hint of day-break.

But her father's voice at the door, calling her name between his timid knocks, frightened her wide awake.

"Daddy, what is it?"

Felix opened her door. The light rose up the stairs and draped the old man like a cape. "It's your brother, baby. He ain't home yet."

"What time is it?" Therese started to sit up, then remembered she didn't have any clothes on. She gathered the covers to her throat.

"Five o'clock. We ought to be on the boat already. But Alton ain't here." Felix's hand floated up and brushed back his thin hair. He looked old to his daughter, and weak. "He didn't say nothing to you last night, did he? I mean about where he was going."

"No, Daddy, not a word. But he's been seeing that Sonnier girl from town. Maybe they still out somewhere."

"Five o'clock in the morning? Nah, her daddy'd never put up with that. I wouldn't be so worried if it wasn't for them boys—"

Therese interrupted her father; she had been thinking the same thing. "You sure he's not out by the boat or something?"

"I checked. This ain't like Alton." The old man looked over his shoulder, down the stairs. "Go sit with your mama. She's at the table, crying. I don't know what to tell her."

"You go on down and call the sheriff. See if he knows anything. I'll put on my robe." She waited while the old man slowly descended the stairs. Then the girl threw on a fresh nightgown and her robe. The air had chilled. She found a pair of socks and hurried after her father.

She kept pushing the Bruneau brothers out of her head. Maybe drunk, maybe arrested—she went through the possibilities, all unlikely for a boy like Alton. Maybe an accident, it occurred to her. She was about to tell her father to call the hospital in Port Sulphur after he had spoken to the sheriff when she saw her mother. The woman sat at the table, the bright light overhead turning her cheeks the color of ash. She was weeping quietly.

"Mama, don't cry. Alton's all right."

The woman looked up and simply shook her head. "You heard what Little Darryl said at the cemetery. They blame Alton."

"No, Mama, that was just talk. Everybody knows Alton didn't have nothing to do with what happened to Mr. Bruneau. Those boys, they talk big, but they just mouth."

Felix hung up the phone. "Sheriff's office hasn't heard nothing. Nobody's in jail, and there hasn't been any accidents far as they know." The two women were looking at him. "Maybe I'll take the truck and have a look around, drive to town and back." He was waiting for Mathilde or Therese to suggest something else, but neither spoke. He waited another moment, then said under his breath, "Yeah, maybe I'll do that."

By the time the pickup crunched back down the gravel road, the light was writhing in the treetops and already slithering down the long, scaly trunks of the pines. Therese followed her mother onto the porch. "Anything, Daddy?" she called as he stepped down from the running board of the old truck.

Her father shook his head. "Nothing, not a trace."

While Mathilde made coffee, Therese called Sherilee Sonnier. Sherilee, annoyed at being awakened early, allowed that she might have run into Alton the night before, but she couldn't remember for sure.

With her hand cupped over the mouthpiece to keep her parents from hearing, Therese hissed into the phone, "You can cut the crap, Sherilee. Everybody knows you've been screwing my brother. Now either you tell me where you left him last night, or I'm coming over there right now and we can have this talk in front of your father. You rather that?"

Sherilee, pouting, confessed that she had dropped Alton off halfway down the gravel road just before midnight.

Exasperated, Therese cut her off. "You couldn't drive him all the way home?"

"I got my reputation to think of." Then Therese heard a new tone in Sherilee's voice. "You don't think something's really wrong, do you? Alton didn't say he was going anywhere else."

Therese felt a twinge of sympathy for the girl. "We don't know. I'll call you when we find something out."

"No, let me call you."

The sympathy evaporated. "Afraid your daddy might pick up the phone?"

"There's no need to get him in the middle of this."

"You know, Sherilee, what people say is right: you one cold bitch." Therese hung up before she could answer.

Felix turned expectantly.

"They had a date last night, but that's it. She don't know where he is."

Only a few minutes had passed when Sheriff Christovich knocked at the door. "I heard you called the office last night."

"Just an hour or two ago, Sheriff," Felix explained.

"I guess Alton's still not home?"

"No, we don't know where he is."

Therese came up behind her father. "Why don't you come in, Sheriff," she said.

Christovich reached for the thread spool Felix had screwed to the screen door as a knob; it was so small in his hand that he had to use his fingertips to grasp it. As he swung open the door, he let himself think, for just a moment, about Mathilde's fingers, unwinding the thread from this bobbin.

He took off his broad-brimmed hat and nodded to the woman, who sat in a rocking chair, her hands clenched together. "Mrs. Petitjean," he nearly whispered. She turned to him, her face now blank as a stone.

Felix told Therese to get the sheriff a cup of coffee.

"Black," Christovich said before she could ask. He sat down next to her mother. Across the room, above the worn sofa, a framed picture of Jesus stared back at him; two delicate fingers pointed to the Sacred Heart, faded to pink and ringed round by a crown of thorns. Wedged between the frame and the wall, a tendril of a yellowed palmetto frond—blessed by Father Danziger, he knew, last Palm Sunday—curled. He thought of the palm from church his own wife had laid beneath their mattress last spring, a habit from the old days when she still had hoped to bear him a child. He looked away.

"When was the last time anyone saw Alton?" he asked to no one in particular.

Therese placed a cup of coffee beside him on a small table. "Sherilee dropped him off last night . . . just down the road."

"Sherilee Sonnier? What time?"

"Midnight." Even as she said it, she stopped lying to herself. *Alton's not coming home*, she admitted.

The sheriff took a sip of coffee. "That's some hot," he said, trying to smile. "But good." He stood up. "Maybe I'll take a look around while it cools."

Therese, still in a robe, followed him out of the house and pulled on a pair of white rubber boots on the porch. Everything still hung heavy with water though the rain had ended. Puddles gullied along the road. Sheriff Christovich walked slowly, nearly all the way back to the highway, pausing only to kneel beside two deep ruts full of water that swerved out of the turnaround. As they made their way back to the house, the sheriff suddenly stopped. "Wait here," he said.

She watched him slog through the wet underbrush. He seemed to know where he was going. Without thinking, she ran after him. Her robe snagged on bushes, its hem trailing through the mud. She caught up with him just as he stopped.

"Oh, shit," he whispered in a voice of the deepest disappointment.

"What is it, Sheriff?" Therese couldn't see over his shoulder.

"Go get your daddy," he told her softly.

"Why? What d'you see?"

"Please, Therese, go do like I say. Get your daddy."

The girl took hold of Christovich's shoulder and tried to pull him out of the way. He turned, facing her, and put his arm around her. But before he could block her view, she saw the body, facedown in the bayou. She recognized the shirt, the pants. "Jesus, no," she gasped, sagging for a moment in the sheriff's arms. But then she struggled free and ran to the edge of the water. The body was caught in a web of cypress roots that arched out of the bank and disappeared in the murky water.

She reached out to touch her brother and started to slide into the bayou as the soft bank gave way. The thick mud and roiling water sucked at the boots, loose on her small feet, as her legs churned, trying to find footing among the slick roots and crumbling clay. She reached behind her for a branch, a bush, something to hold her fast, but even as she threw herself backward, she slipped deeper, the cold water rising along her thighs. And suddenly, without thinking, to keep from going deeper yet, she caught hold of Alton's body. As she did, it shifted and rolled toward her, till her brother's face turned and settled just under the surface, the eyes imploring and the lips parted—as if, it seemed to her in that infinite moment, he was trying to say, "Oh, sister, look what they done to me."

A strong hand grabbed her arm and pulled her up.

She struggled to wrench herself free of the sheriff's grip, to help her brother from the water. And then, all at once, she understood she could not help him.

"I'm sorry," the sheriff said in a low voice as she wept against his chest.

"I got to go tell Mama," she sobbed. "I got to go."

"Come on," the sheriff said gently. He put his arm around her and led her back toward the house.

8.

Christovich was waiting for the *Squall* when it backed into its slip that afternoon.

As Ross half-hitched the stern line around a piling, Darryl watched the sheriff swat at something. *Gnats must be bad*, he thought. Then he turned to his brother. "Goddamn it, Ross, tie us off with a proper fuckin' knot." The younger man smirked. "Throw a clove hitch around the damn thing, asshole. You know what Daddy taught you. We get a storm tonight and she come loose, the pier'll knock the shit out of her."

Christovich walked down to where Darryl was securing the bow line. He nodded. "Boys."

"Hope you here to tell me you finally figured out who killed Daddy," Darryl said as he stood up.

"Alton's dead."

"Alton Petitjean?" Ross called out from the stern as he lifted a basket of shrimp up onto the pier.

Christovich ignored him. "I told you boys to stay away from him, Darryl."

"Us? What we got to do with it? We were over in Happy Jack last night."

The sheriff cut him off. "I didn't say it happened last night."

"And neither did I," Darryl said slowly, narrowing his eyes. "I just said we had a few drinks up in Happy Jack, that's all." He tried to change the subject. "Anyway, what happened to the son of a bitch—fall off his boat and drown?"

"Yeah," Ross echoed, "he fall off his boat?"

"I'm waiting for the autopsy. But it looks like a knife in the ribs." Christovich noticed a lone seagull circling overhead. "Just like your Daddy."

"Well, Sheriff," Darryl offered, "looks like you got yourself some mass murderer on the loose, huh?"

Ross, still off-loading their catch, brayed a laugh.

"It don't take no genius," Christovich said, looking Darryl hard in the face, "to see one's got to do with the other." His chin lifted ever so slightly. "You know what I mean, don't you, boy?" He drawled that last word, dragging it between them for a moment, before he snapped it taut.

"No sir." Darryl strangled the anger that rose in his throat. "Can't say I do."

The boat rocked, and in the corner of his eye, Christovich saw Ross already on the pier, moving toward him. The sheriff's hand, scratching a mosquito bite on his chest, slid down and came to rest on the butt of his revolver. He shifted his weight onto the other leg. "Smells like gasoline," he said.

Ross, taken by surprise, blurted out, "Oh, shit, it's the damn fuel line again." Forgetting why he had lifted himself onto the dock, he hopped back down into the boat. Bilgewater, glistening with iridescence, sloshed against the transom. "Little Horse, look at this shit."

"Take it easy," his brother cautioned him. "Tape up the line." Darryl hadn't taken his eyes off the sheriff. "And make sure you use the water-proof tape, not that black electrical crap."

"You boys ought to tend to that leak. You playing with trouble."

"Don't you worry about us, Sheriff. You just find yourself that mass murderer." He smiled. "Ain't none of us gonna feel safe till you put that madman behind bars."

"You better look to your engine, Darryl." But before the Bruneau boy could turn to help his brother, Christovich added, "Where's Rusty? I thought you three always went out together."

Ross stuck his head out from behind the plywood panels he had swung open to get to the engine. "Sick," he assured the sheriff. "Got the virus." He paused, losing confidence. "You know, the bad one going around."

"That so, Darryl?" Christovich knew Ross was lying.

"Well, you tell me, Sheriff, where else would he be?"

That's a good question, Christovich thought to himself as he followed the planks of the pier back to the crushed shells of the parking lot. *Where else would he be?*

Sitting in the patrol car, his door open, watching the two brothers work on their boat, Christovich checked in with Mary Beth on the radio. She told him that Terry Petitjean had called for him.

The sheriff walked across the lot, the shells scrabbling under his feet, to the pay phone on a lamp pole. He dropped a nickel into the slot and dialed the number he had kept memorized for years. Little Horse and his brother were trying to flush the fuel from the bilge. He watched Ross fumble with the hose. "Jackass," the sheriff muttered, keeping his eye on the boat.

He heard Mathilde's voice and stiffened. "Oh, Mathilde, it's me, Matthew. I think Terry called me a little while ago. She around?"

"No, she's with her father. At the funeral parlor." Mathilde's voice was scrubbed raw. She sounded to the sheriff like someone speaking in her sleep.

Christovich thought she was about to say more. He hesitated, straining to hear her, but there was nothing in the silence—just the vague, insistent crackle of the copper line. It sounded, he thought, like something in the distance shattering over and over again.

"Mathilde?" he whispered. "You still there?"

As he listened, his eyes followed the telephone wire up the creosoted pole. The black line sagged overhead on its way to a utility pole beside the highway. He imagined its path along the road, bellying and rising from pole to pole, all the way to the drawbridge. He saw the line plunge into the bayou beneath huge warnings forbidding trawling or dredging or even anchoring in the channel. He imagined its conduit settling into the mud of the water bottom and on the other side the pipe rising out of the bayou and halfway up a bare pole as solitary as a stripped cypress, dead in the water. And the wire, spewing out of the conduit with the others, carried his whisper, his sigh, on till it diverged at the Petitjean drive and followed the trees along the road of gravel and crushed shells all the way to the house. Then the small wire snaking through the wall to the baseboard, where the phone cord found it in the small square metal box. And then to her hand, to her ear, to the silence itself.

"Yes, Matthew," she said, surprised that he had had to ask. "I'm here."

"I just wanted to say, Mathilde, how sorry I am."

The pause was not so long this time. "He was gentle, even as a boy. Wouldn't you say so, Sheriff, even as a boy?"

It hurt Christovich to be called "Sheriff" by Mathilde. "Yes, Mrs. Petitjean, even as a boy he was gentle."

"Exactly," she said, "gentle as a lamb."

He could tell she was growing distracted. "I'll call back later."

"Yes," she said weakly. "Call back when they come home."

He waited for her to hang up before he put the phone back on the cradle.

The anger was pulsing in his chest, or constricting around his chest, really, making it harder and harder for him to breathe. He sunk into the seat of his squad car and watched the Bruneau brothers through his windshield. He knew they had murdered Alton. But they were laughing just now. He wanted to get out of his car and walk down the pier toward the *Squall*. Instead, he turned the key and slowly drove out of the parking lot so quietly, the boys never noticed him drive away.

9.

The screen door creaked open, then slammed shut.

"Well, look who's here. If it ain't the little pussy himself, sleeping like a baby." It was Ross's voice.

Rusty tried to shake himself awake. He didn't know what time it was, but he could tell it was late from the shadows in the folds of the curtains.

"What's the matter, babe, had a bad dream?" Rusty's brother was standing in the bedroom door.

"He here?" Darryl called from the porch.

"Oh, yeah, Little Horse," Ross shouted back, "he's here all right."

The screen slammed shut again.

Ross smiled. "I think our big brother wants to have a talk with you."

Darryl pushed past Ross, grabbed the neck of Rusty's T-shirt, and jerked him half off the bed. Their faces were inches apart. "Don't you ever fuckin' open your mouth about what happened last night. You understand me?"

Rusty tried to struggle free of his brother's grip. "You didn't say nothing about killing nobody."

"You miserable little asshole." Darryl shoved him back against the mattress. "That son of a bitch killed Daddy."

Rusty saw his brother's free hand tighten into a fist.

"I'm warning you, babe, you take up for that bastard Petitjean, and I'll knock the crap out of you."

Ross moved closer. "Hit him, Little Horse. Teach him a lesson. Just like Daddy done."

Darryl looked over his shoulder at his brother, who was leaning across the foot of the bed. "Why don't you shut the fuck up?"

"What did I do?" he whined.

Looking into Ross's face, Rusty forgot about Darryl. Suddenly, before his big brother could react, he ripped himself loose of the hand that pressed him against the mattress and lunged for Ross. The man stumbled back as his brother's shoulder caught him just below the throat. Catching himself against the wall, Ross smiled. "You gonna fight me?" he taunted, laughing. "Come on, baby. Come see me."

But Rusty was on top of him before he could throw a punch. Even Darryl was surprised by his little brother's ferocity; he stood back, alert, as if watching a dogfight. Rusty was pummeling Ross, but the blows glanced off the hunched shoulders and bowed head. Bent over under the rain of punches, Ross managed to push his brother back with a kick to the stomach.

Upright, still smiling, Ross bobbed his head. Rusty had seen it before. Ross always attacked the same way, the way he had learned in football. Arms wide, head down, he would charge and drive his opponent into the ground. Then it would all be over. Pinned beneath the squat, powerful body, the other man would be beaten into raw meat, would be beaten till Ross could not lift his arms even once more. Rusty let his hand fall upon the sheet crumpled on the edge of the bed.

As Ross rushed him, Rusty, in a single motion, stepped aside and cast the sheet, like a throw net, over his brother's head. Before Ross could even turn, Rusty had slammed his fist into the peak of the sheet. He heard a muffled groan. Dazed, Ross turned. Rusty could feel the ridge above the eyes, the soft cheeks, the sharp nose as he battered the head beneath the cloth. Like an enraged, blinded bull, Ross staggered, almost bellowing, in the direction of the punches. But already the blows were falling on him from another direction and with such fury that he could not lower his hands long enough to pull off the sheet.

Only the stains of blood, smeared along the folds of the cloth, finally slowed Rusty's anger. As he hesitated for a moment, he felt Darryl's grip tighten on the back of his shirt and pull him off his brother. Darryl jerked the sheet free.

"Shit," he sighed. Ross, his hands still up in front of his face, squinted through eyelids nearly swollen shut. Blood oozed from his nose, drooled from the corner of his mouth. He coughed on the blood when he tried to talk. "I'll kill him," he choked.

Darryl nodded to Rusty to get out of the room, but the boy didn't move.

"Get the hell out of here," Darryl said in a low voice as he dabbed with the sheet at one of the cuts on his brother's face.

Through his narrowed eyes, Ross saw Rusty moving toward the door. "You a dead man, you hear me?" But he started to gag again on the blood and spit it onto the sheet sprawled at his feet.

Rusty, suddenly paling from the fight, leaned against the back of the sofa as his legs sagged beneath him. Steadying himself with a deep breath, he walked uncertainly onto the porch, sinking down on the steps. But even there he could hear Ross cursing him through swollen lips. He climbed the levee and then let himself fall back against its slope near the edge of the water. The light had soured; a yellow skim sheathed the calm surface of the lagoon.

He was still trembling with rage and adrenaline and, most of all, guilt for what they had done the night before. He was tired of being used by his brothers, tired especially of Ross. He couldn't stay here, not with them.

One of their skiffs had been hauled up on the muddy batture, its motor tilted. They had meant to paint it, but there had been no time in the last week to tend to it.

Rusty slid the boat into the water and stepped into the bow. He threaded the fuel line from the red gasoline can onto the prongs of the outboard. Then he pumped up the pressure with the hand cock and pulled the cord. It caught on the second try. Snapping the engine into reverse, he puttered out into the lagoon backward, his eyes on the house just over the crest of the levee. His brothers hadn't heard the motor, he guessed. He eased off the gas and shifted into gear, cutting a hard circle toward the edge of the breakwater. Just as he crossed into open water, he twisted the throttle open. The bow of the weathered boat lifted as the prop screwed deeper. It was too fast this close in, Rusty knew, but he didn't care. The stern skittered over the light chop, and the whine of the outboard, like a siren on the water, pulled Darryl and Ross out of the house. He saw them on the levee, though he could not hear what his brother was screaming at him. Ross hurled a chunk of concrete in his direction; it splashed just a few yards from the shore.

The house disappeared behind a stand of cypresses as Rusty followed the shoreline toward the channel. He saw an old black lady with a straw hat and cane pole fishing from the remains of a pier that had been shattered in a hurricane. Neither of them waved to the other.

At first, he didn't know where he was going. But slowing in the middle of the channel, he saw the piece of plywood nailed to a tree that once had read, *Bayou Petitjean*. All that remained now was patches of white paint, streaked here and there with black. No one bothered, though, to repair the sign. Everyone knew who lived a quarter mile up the still water.

He shouldn't do it, he understood. He shouldn't go anywhere near their house. Out of respect, if nothing else. But he dropped the speed as low as he could make it without killing and slipped up the bayou, the engine no louder than a swarm of mosquitoes.

As he came upon their property, he could see the *Mathilde* in her mooring on the far side of the clearing. Shifting into neutral, he drifted up into the roots of the big trees descending into the water.

It was still terribly hot even though the falling sun was at his back. Through the trees, he caught sight of the sheriff's car in the driveway behind Mr. Petitjean's truck. It wouldn't do to run into the sheriff here.

He kicked his skiff out from the tree roots and swung the boat hard back to the channel, keeping the throttle low. As he turned into the face of the sun, settling over the saw grass of the marsh, Rusty did not see

Therese in the cabin of the *Mathilde* looking for her brother's knife among the charts. She crouched on the deck and watched the Bruneau boy drift back toward town in his little boat. *What does he want, the son of a bitch?* she wondered.

Making her way to the house, she handed the knife in its leather scabbard to Sheriff Christovich but did not tell him what she had just seen. *Not for now,* she told herself.

The man slid the blade from its case and held it up to the light above the table. Satisfied, he sheathed the knife and gave it back to the girl's father, who walked the sheriff to his car, where the two men lit cigarettes and continued their talk away from the women.

Therese and her mother still sat at the kitchen table. The woman started to cry, and Therese covered her mother's hand with her own.

"It's punishment for what I done," Mathilde said.

"You?" Therese shook her head. "It's not your fault."

"It is," Mathilde insisted, weeping. "You don't know."

The girl had her mother go lie down and, not knowing what else to do, started dinner, though no one was hungry.

There was a little andouille in the refrigerator and a half bowl of shrimp, enough for a jambalaya. Therese picked up her mother's heavy kitchen knife and leaned on its handle over the pepper she had plucked from the bush beside the porch steps. Dicing the green flesh on the scarred cutting board Alton had made in his woodworking class at school, she remembered the gawky fourteen-year-old, beaming as his mother unwrapped his Christmas present to her.

The girl let the kettle heat till the black cast iron was almost smoking. Adding oil, and a few moments later the garlic and onion and green pepper, she sautéed the sausage and then the shrimp in cayenne and black pepper and thyme. It was the onion, she told herself, that made her weep. When the gray shrimp had sizzled into pastel curls of white and pink stripes, she dumped in rice and stock and brought the pot to a boil.

As the jambalaya simmered, Therese sat at the kitchen table, shelling peas and thinking about what remained to be done. The arrangements for the funeral were complete, but there was the boat to deal with. Her father would not be able to handle the shrimping by himself, let alone the oystering. She would sail with him, but she didn't know what they would do about the reefs of oysters in the back bayous of their leases.

Though she tried to distract herself with worries about the future, the fin of a terrible truth had circled her all day, the shadow just beneath the surface thickening each time it approached and was driven away. Therese, alone of everyone in Egret Pass, knew Alton to be innocent of Horse's murder. And it was her fault, she knew, Alton's death.

Unable to resist any longer, the girl yielded and let herself remember her brother snagged in the cypress roots, the cold rain lashing his back all night. She saw the face, its eyes sprung open, staring into the murky green water.

As she sat there, stripping hulls from the meat of the peas, guilt hardened into resolve: she would kill them, she would kill all those bastard Bruneaus.

Two

10.

A rain that began before dawn strengthened through the morning. At eight o'clock, everyone's lights were still on, and the streets were dark with the weather. Therese tried to hurry her parents, but Felix sat on his bed in an undershirt and brown pants, his small, bare feet leaning against each other. Her mother was out on the porch, watching the rain over the bayou.

Therese called without opening the screen door, "We got to go, Mama."

She helped her father with his tie and into his brown coat. Looking at the old man, she smoothed his thin hair. "It'll be all right," she whispered.

The three squeezed into the truck. The rain picked up as they followed the winding road of crushed shells and gravel from their house to the highway. Therese looked out through the pines and cypresses toward the crook in the bayou where the sheriff had found Alton's body.

The windshield wipers, clicking like locusts caught in a jar, flicked back and forth, skimming a veil of water from the window. But the storm, billowing out of the marsh in blinding gusts of rain, buffeted the pickup. In the curves, they could feel the wheels slip on the black asphalt.

Therese could not guess what they were thinking, her parents. They drove on in silence, the rain muffling the noise of the truck, the rattle of its fan, the slow breaths of its occupants. The girl drew a face on the fogged window of the door.

The weather relented, a bit, as the family approached the Gautier Funeral Home, a former bank that had failed in the thirties. The old-fashioned vault, anchored into the foundation, still interrupted the back wall of the building, and each window was barred with sturdy iron arabesques cast in a New Orleans foundry at the turn of the century.

Henry Gautier Jr. hurried down the three stone steps with an opened umbrella for the two women. Ushering them into the lobby decorated with biblical scenes in ornate frames, Henry asked them to wait while he got his father in the back office. Mathilde weakened as she turned toward the coffin, sequestered in an alcove beneath a simple crucifix; her daughter caught her by the elbow and steadied her. The lid was propped open, and a garland of flowers was draped along the side of the casket. The undertaker returned with the old man.

"Our sympathies, Mr. and Mrs. Petitjean. A terrible loss."

Felix shook hands with old Gautier.

"I do hope you'll like what we've done with Alton."

Therese felt a fury welling up within her. She backed away from the others and stood by a window, watching the rain slither down the glass.

Henry, who had assisted his father in the mortuary since childhood, sidled up to the girl. "I'm sorry, Miss Petitjean. Your brother was always kind to me. He was the only one."

"That's all right. He was good to everybody."

"Yes, ma'am, that's the truth." The young man, so skinny his neck bobbed freely in his buttoned collar, stood there a moment. "I did my best on Alton. I really did."

Therese had never before noticed Henry. Younger than he was, she couldn't remember ever speaking to her brother's classmate. "We appreciate it, Henry. Very much."

"I just wanted you to know." His father was calling him. "Maybe you'll tell your parents for me."

The girl took his hand and nodded.

Henry blushed and gently withdrew the hand from her grip.

It was Therese who had decided to forgo an evening wake. Her mother was too distraught to endure a long night of visitors. Instead, the girl had instructed Mr. Gautier to arrange a viewing of the body for two hours before the priest's arrival to escort the funeral cortege to St. Martin's for the requiem Mass.

As she stood at the window, she watched a car, as if looking for an unfamiliar address, slow and then pull into the rutted parking lot. The headlights, casting their beams over the broken oyster shells, illuminated shafts of rain as the automobile swung to a stop before a tarred log.

It was family. Extricating herself from the steering wheel that pinned her heavy thighs to the seat, Aunt Eunice, from Pointe a la Hache, followed by Patrice, Therese's cousin, tottered on high heels through the worsening shower toward the porte cochere on the side of the building, where a black hearse was parked. Neither hurried; both were big women and used to being wet.

Henry, having heard the car crunching across the shells, hovered next to them, uselessly trying to keep the rain from their faces with his umbrella. *He's a good boy,* Therese thought, still watching, then shook her head. *I sound like my mother,* it occurred to her.

Therese looked over her shoulder. Supported by Mr. Gautier, Mathilde sobbed beside the open coffin. On the other side of his wife, Felix, like a man already dead but still on his feet, swayed. As the girl crossed the room, the undertaker ushered her parents to a settee beneath a rendering of Christ's entry into Jerusalem. She took her place beside them.

Eunice, her whole body seeming to swell even larger with each labored breath, slowly crossed the lobby to her brother and sister-in-law. Therese offered her seat to the woman and let Patrice kiss her.

"We're sorry, Terry," her cousin whispered and then, as if an explanation might be needed, added, "about Alton."

"Thank you, Tricia. It was kind of you to come."

"Oh, we wouldn't miss it." She paused again. "The funeral, we wouldn't miss it."

Though Patrice was four years older, Therese had always felt sorry for her. Fat even as a child, the girl had endured endless taunts growing up and, protected by a ferocious mother, early adopted the habit of referring to herself as if she and her mother were indivisible. That was how she came to be called "the we-we girl." Though a term of affection among her doting family, the nickname was immediately corrupted into "the wee-wee girl" by merciless schoolmates. In junior high, the joke found new life. Spending the night with her older cousin, Therese read what one vicious boy had written in Patrice's autograph book: "If there was that much of me, I'd call myself we." And in high school, the nickname served to smear her reputation when snide rumors Frenchified her into "the *oui-oui* girl." But years of torment had not broken her of the habit.

"We just felt awful when we heard the news . . ."

Therese finished the sentence for her. "About Alton."

Patrice nodded, her pink cheeks shimmering with tears.

As the two cousins embraced, Therese fought back her own emotions, concentrating on the framed picture above her parents. It was a simple scene: a crowd, cheering and waving palm branches, jostled the donkey on which the Messiah entered the gates of the city. The same mob, she remembered, that nailed him to a cross five days later.

For the next two hours, family members and women from town arrived and whispered in small groups, taking turns to kneel at the prie-dieu before the coffin and offer their prayers for the salvation of the boy's soul.

Therese had not yet looked upon her brother when Father Danziger arrived. Knowing Henry and his father would soon lower the lid of the casket and latch the bolts in place, she excused herself from the old friends who hovered around her parents. Everyone had withdrawn from the alcove in which the body rested, gossiping in little knots of neighbors and family scattered around the lobby of the defunct bank. Therese, alone with Alton, faltered as she raised her eyes to his ashen face.

Powdered and rouged by the undertakers, her brother looked like one of the figures they had seen as children in the wax museum in New

Orleans. They had thrilled to the exhibit of Jean Lafitte and his band of pirates fighting shoulder to shoulder with Andrew Jackson against the advancing line of British redcoats. They had puzzled over the forbidden scene of a Storyville brothel glimpsed behind a curtain not fully drawn and vainly restricted by a worn sign to *Gentlemen Only*. And they had been haunted for weeks after by the tableau of the beheading of a famous queen, whose little face—still crowned by a glittering tiara—stared back at them with pursed lips from a basket beneath the executioner's block.

She hadn't thought of it in years, but she remembered asking her big brother why none of the wax figures were smiling.

"Well, how'd you like it if you was in the middle of winning the battle of New Orleans or getting your head chopped off or something, and here come all these people gawking and pointing at you?"

"I wouldn't like it," she admitted.

"Neither do they," Alton explained. "They's pissed, that's what they is. They want to get on with whatever they doing, but we won't let them. We froze 'em in their tracks. That's how come they kill you and turn you into one of them if you get locked in here at night."

"Why would they do that?" the little girl asked, terrified.

"They don't like us," her brother had assured her. "They don't like us one little bit."

Looking at Alton's waxen face, she realized how right he had been.

Therese wanted to soothe him, to comfort him, to ease his anger. But when she stroked her brother's massive hands clenched above his heart and bound with a black rosary wrapped around his wrists and threaded through his fingers, she recoiled from the cold flesh.

One thumb, crossed over the other, slipped loose as she brushed the hand, and it fell slack against Alton's chest. The girl lifted the thumb gingerly, like a piece of shattered porcelain, and felt the bone unhinged in its skin. She leaned it back in place and raised the next finger on his hand; it swiveled beneath her grip. The undertakers had broken them, she realized as the nausea rose in her throat, broken all her brother's fingers to clasp them together in prayer.

What other insults and indignities had Alton suffered on the mortuary slab?

"Oh, my poor baby," she sighed and, overcome with pity, pressed her lips against her brother's. They were chill and unresisting.

Therese felt as if she were about to faint, and dropping her head onto the chest of the corpse, she caught the tang of alcohol or bleach, maybe, issuing from the parted lips as her weight slumped against its lungs.

Then Henry had her by the shoulders and was pulling her away from Alton. She tried to struggle against his grip but felt her legs buckle.

"It's OK, *ma petite*." Her mother was patting her hand when she jerked upright on the settee where Henry had laid her. "You're OK, baby."

The scent of bleach still filled her nostrils as she stared back, unfocused, at the faces floating above her. She batted away a hand that grazed her chin, then realized Mr. Gautier had been passing a little bottle of smelling salts under her nose. "I'm all right," she insisted weakly. "Just let me sit."

"Yes," Father Danziger agreed, "let Mrs. Petitjean and Terry sit there while the rest of us recite a rosary for the deceased."

Dropping to their knees, the gathered women grasped their beads of faceted crystal or worn wood and kissed the feet of the crucified Christ dangling at the end of a single strand. Some men knelt, too, though few had rosaries in their pockets.

"Let us not forget," the priest reminded the mourners, "that the rosary is sacred to Our Lady. Like Mathilde, she lost her only-begotten Son. So we mustn't doubt the Blessed Mother's pity for our suffering. We are her children and have only to ask for her help. Let us ask her this morning, on this dark day when the sky itself weeps with sorrow, to comfort our friends the Petitjeans, and to give succor to all those who have lost loved ones."

The rain continued to pelt the roof of the funeral home.

"Our Father, who art in heaven," Father Danziger began.

"Hallowed be thy name," the huddled group continued. Together, they and the priest repeated the prayers of the rosary for the next fifteen minutes. Mindful of Mathilde, Father Danziger announced, one by one, as the Our Fathers yielded to Hail Marys and back again, the five joyful mysteries, then the five sorrowful mysteries, and finally the five glorious mysteries of Mary's life. And as he proclaimed the annunciation of the Messiah's birth by the angel Gabriel, the finding in the temple of the lost twelve-year-old Jesus, the scourging of her son at the pillar and his crucifixion on the rude cross at Calvary, the glorious resurrection three days later and Christ's ascension into paradise, the descent of the Holy Spirit, and the assumption of the Blessed Virgin into heaven and her crowning there, Mathilde suffered beneath the lash of memory after memory of her own son's life and of his martyrdom, she did not doubt, for her sins.

The unbidden images tormented her with long-unremembered moments: nuzzling her plump baby into giggles and battening on the milk-sweet scent of his flesh, cupping water with her hand over the five-year-old's fevered body as he trembled in the tub, enticing the boy on her hands and knees out from under the house where he had hidden from his father after breaking a favorite pipe, waving on the pier as the nine-year-old came home on the bow of his daddy's boat from his first fishing run, turning from a pot of crawfish étouffée simmering on the stove to discover her high school son had grown taller than she.

Mathilde took deep breaths to calm herself, but her very fingertips felt as if they had just pressed the stone-hard muscle the proud boy had flexed for her in the kitchen that afternoon six years ago, the golden stew bubbling behind her, the damp air fragrant with garlic and onions, peppers and roux. Ravaged by the relentless litany of vivid memories, inexorable as dreams, she numbly repeated the formula of the Hail Mary over and over and over.

When Father Danziger had concluded the rosary with a blessing of the faithful, he motioned for the altar boy in cassock and surplice who had accompanied him. Sprinkling the coffin with holy water from the silver bucket the boy carried, the priest intoned the despairing opening of the *De Profundis*. But when he chanted in Latin the fiftieth psalm and Mathilde read the English translation from the prayer card the funeral home had provided, she could not contain her grief and guilt. "For, behold, I was conceived in iniquities," the priest recited in the dead language, "and in sin did my mother conceive me."

The woman began to sob into the shoulder of her daughter, still beside her on the little sofa.

"Mama," the girl comforted her. "Mama, nothing can touch him now."

But Mathilde turned a bitter face on Therese. "He didn't deserve this, what they done him."

"No ma'am," she whispered, "not Alton. But they can't touch him no more."

"Yes," the woman nodded, stanching her tears with an embroidered handkerchief, "he's safe now."

At the end of the psalm, Father Danziger announced that the assembled mourners would travel in procession behind the hearse to St. Martin's for Mass. Then, as people filed out of the funeral home to their cars and trucks, the priest turned to Alton's parents, taking Mathilde's hands in his and assuring the couple that, though it might be hard to accept in this moment of grief, providence had ordained their son's fate. They should remember, their pastor instructed, that not a sparrow drops from a branch without its Creator allowing that small death.

Therese, standing behind her mother and father, stiffened with anger as the priest exhorted the family to resign themselves to what no one could hope to comprehend, God's inscrutable plan: "Our only comfort is to give ourselves up to the mystery of his wisdom."

Over Father Danziger's shoulder, the undertaker and his son tightened the brass bolts that fastened shut the lid of the coffin.

11.

Though the liturgy was the same requiem Mass that only days before had laid Horse to rest, a more somber mood fell on Alton's funeral at the church.

The mothers attending the service, most of whom had tasted the salt of satisfaction on their lips at the death of the old man, lamented the loss of the boy. They saw in him their own sons, and each of their daughters had, at one time or another, mooned over the good-looking boy. Many wept quietly as they prayed along with the priest.

The family members, too, who had joined Eunice and Patrice in comforting Alton's parents and sister regretted the death, though not only in grief over the loss they had suffered. The family had looked to Alton to preserve the Petitjean oyster fields and sustain the tradition of their holdings in Plaquemines Parish. One by one, the others had lost their own beds over the years and were forced to crew other men's boats or, when the catch dwindled, to endure the humiliation of working the slime line of a shucking house. Some had even moved upriver to New Orleans for city work. Their sons had signed on with the oil companies, hoisting fifty-pound drill bits as roughnecks on the big rigs scattered off the coast. So now they had only to look at the boy's father, withered beside his weeping wife, to know the fields, the boat, the last of everything was in jeopardy, the last of everything that had made Petitjean—for more than a century—a name to be spoken with respect.

A scrim of sorrow diffused the candlelight that flickered on the altar as if against the dark day. Even Father Danziger, usually crusty with his parishioners, seemed moved by Alton's death, recalling the boy's service as an altar boy in a brief homily on the Mass's scripture. But Therese paid no attention to the anecdote the priest recounted. Instead, she disputed the words of the gospel he had just read about the raising of the dead: "Thy brother shall rise again," Jesus assured Martha, the sister of the buried Lazarus. Alton's sister, her fury growing as the service proceeded, scorned Martha's submissive faith.

Therese studied the casket, draped with a black cloth and garlanded with flowers, resting before the communion rail. She had followed the pallbearers down the aisle of the church and watched them ease their load onto a bier between six candles as tall as the girl. She had grown dizzy in the front pew as the priest circled the coffin, aspersing it with holy water and incensing it from a silver thurible that clattered against a long chain. Then nearly swooning in the close and humid air, heavy with the sickly sweet perfume of the censer, she had averted her eyes from the dark and airless casket in which her brother lay. Now, though, she fixed her gaze upon the wooden box and saw, inside, the limp body—no doubt jostled in its journey to the church—with its broken fingers awry and its head lolling askew on the satin pillow. She inhaled, again, the tang of Alton's sour breath. She shuddered as she tasted his waxen lips against her own.

And the girl understood, despite all the claims of affection protesting the admission, that her brother was dead and would not be met again in this world.

When the Mass had ended, the other mourners allowed the family to follow the coffin down the aisle before they filed out into the drizzling rain. Taking her mother's arm as they passed the rows of friends and neighbors, Therese glimpsed, hunched in the last pew, Rusty Bruneau. Mathilde, too, saw the boy, and as she felt the girl tense, the woman clenched her daughter more tightly to her side. "Don't you start anything," she whispered. "Don't you dare."

"He got no business here," Therese hissed.

"You leave him be, you hear me?" Softening, the woman added, "He come to pay his respects is all. He's a good boy." Then they were outside, covering their eyes from the rain that continued to fall.

At the cemetery, crowding under an umbrella with her cousin Patrice, Therese watched rivulets of water sluice down the heaped earth beside the empty grave and splash into the pool at the bottom of the hole. When the pallbearers, their shined shoes clumped with mud, lowered the coffin onto the wooden planks across the mouth of the grave, the flowered garlands lost their petals under the pelting downpour.

"The whole world's turning to water," a man's voice sighed behind the two girls.

"Yeah," Patrice whispered to her cousin, "that's what we always say, too, when it rains like this."

But Therese did not answer. She was thinking of the water rising in her brother's grave.

After the brief burial service, as the mourners dispersed to their cars, the girl wanted to wait until the lowered coffin was covered with earth, but her parents urged her back to the truck. "The people will be coming," her mother explained.

As her father pulled away from the cemetery, Therese kept watching the forlorn and abandoned grave until it wavered and disappeared in the glaze of rain on her window.

By the time they parked beside their house on the bayou, friends were already waiting on the porch for the Petitjeans. The women held baskets of food, pies, casseroles. The few men who had attended the funeral carried liquor by the necks of the bottles. Children, restless after hours of silence, continued to be shushed by stern adults.

"Come in, come in," Felix invited the visitors as more headlights approached, following the gravel road toward the house.

Inside, Mathilde put out glasses and plates, knives and forks. Therese served the guests from the dishes they themselves had prepared for the grieving family: bell peppers stuffed with eggplant and shrimp, links of homemade boudin, dirty rice speckled with flecks of gizzards and livers, a daube glacé, baked yams sweetened with cinnamon and vanilla, butter-milk pies, pecan pralines, molasses bread, fig preserves.

Polite reminiscences about Alton and expressions of sympathy for his parents quickly gave way to gossip about the murder. The town took for granted that the Bruneaus had killed the boy. The same women who crowded together on the sofa or stood in a little group in the kitchen, commenting on the tastiness of the oyster dressing on their plates, had heard Darryl's warning to Mathilde at the cemetery a few days earlier. No one thought it an empty threat. But people had also heard the rumors linking Alton to Horse's death, the story of the fight at R&J's. And who didn't know at least something of the bad blood between the two fami-lies? So the uneasiness that had troubled the town since the first murder dissipated with the second. Everyone, of course, regretted Alton's loss— he was well liked everywhere he went—but the small community was unprepared for the uncertainty, the anxiety of an unresolved mystery. They were used to knowing where things stood. And now it felt as if things had found their balance again, death for death. Even the children sensed the muted relief of the adults, whose restrained voices soon gave way to subdued but unresisted laughter.

Matthew Christovich stopped by only long enough to apologize for missing the funeral; a New Orleans civil sheriff and his assistant had tried to repossess a Pontiac from a trapper in Nairn, who took the men for car thieves and chased them off with a pistol. Sheriff Christovich had spent the morning trying to calm down the two New Orleanians and straighten it all out. Now he had to follow them back down the river to Nairn to pick up the car. "I'll stop by tomorrow," he promised. "Candy sends her regrets, too. She hasn't been well lately. You know how she is; she didn't want to come by herself."

Mathilde let Matthew kiss her on the cheek. "You tell Mrs. Chris-tovich we understand completely. This is no weather for her to be out in. Not if she's been ill again."

Felix put his arm around his wife. "And we know you got a job to do, Sheriff. No need for apologies."

"I just wanted you to know how sorry . . ."

"It's all right, Matthew," Mathilde nodded. "We'll talk tomorrow."

As the visitors waited out the rain and the hours wore on, husbands, returning from fishing runs cut short by the unrelenting storm, joined their wives at the Petitjeans' house with six-packs of beer chilling in metal ice chests in the back of their pickups. Brown bottles—emptied of local brews like Dixie or Jax—began to fill grocery bags on the porch next to other garbage from the gathering.

In fact, Therese was taking out another bag of trash when she encountered Sherilee alone on the porch. The girl wiped tears from her cheeks with a tight fist.

"If I'd have known, Terry, I never would've left Alton to walk the rest of the way home."

Therese was not ready to take pity on the girl. "I bet your daddy still don't know about you two."

"What difference does it make now what he knows?"

Therese shook her head, keeping her eyes fixed on her brother's girlfriend.

Sherilee sighed. "No, he don't know nothing." Then she turned toward the bayou and asked, "You want me to go tell him? I don't give a damn. I'll go in there right now and tell everybody. I loved your brother."

Therese put her hand on the girl's shoulder.

"We had plans, Alton and me," she whispered, starting to cry again.

"It wasn't your fault, Sherilee. It didn't have nothing to do with you, what happened."

"It was them Bruneau boys, wasn't it? That's what people are saying."

"That's what people say."

Sherilee turned back to Therese. "They say Alton killed Mr. Bruneau, too. But it ain't so. Alton told me he didn't have nothing to do with that."

"Alton wouldn't hurt nobody."

"No," Sherilee agreed, "that boy wouldn't hurt nobody. He was the sweetest thing."

Therese lifted the lid of one of the coolers the men had carried from the trucks. Pulling two Dixies from the ice chest, she popped off the caps with the bottle opener her father had screwed to a post of the porch railing. *Drink RC Cola*, it encouraged. She handed Sherilee a beer.

The two girls sat on the bench against the wall, drinking without talking and watching the rain fall.

Inside, Felix was persuaded to get the guitar from his son's room and handed it to Luke Lukijovich. Atwood Thibodeaux, already an old man when he had moved from 'Tit Mamou to Egret Pass twenty years earlier to live with his widowed daughter, had brought along the fiddle he took with him everywhere he went. Atwood bowed a melancholy complaint on his violin while Luke tuned the guitar, a Christmas present to Alton at the end of the big year everyone had had in 1946, the last big year for the oystermen before the oil company canals had indifferently begun to flush the brackish marsh lagoons with a flood of salt water and shrivel the crops of oysters seeded in the shallow-water leases of the coast.

Luke waited for the old man to finish the melody, then joined in on a second tune, "Aux Natchitoches." Emelda Abadie, Atwood's daughter, picked up the song, recalling in French two young lovers separated by their parents. Even as she began to sing, the two instruments stopped, letting the words lilt across the room without accompaniment, in the Cajun style, all the way to the last stanza. *"Et si que vous avez une habille-z-à prendre,"* the old woman sang, drawling the Acadian French, *"prenez-la donc couleur des cendres, parce que c'est la plus triste couleur pour deux amours qui vit qu'en langueur."*

A gloom hung over the gathering as the instruments repeated the final measures of the song.

"But what did Mrs. Abadie say?" one of the little girls asked her mother. Most of the inhabitants of Egret Pass were not Cajun, and few children of the other families heard French in the house anymore.

"She was singing about two people who miss each other. She said if you have a dress, it should be the color of ashes."

"Why?" her daughter demanded, indignant at the idea.

Mrs. Abadie had heard the girl. "Because, *ma chère*," the singer explained, "it's the saddest color."

The child climbed down from her mother's lap. "Well, I won't wear a sad dress," she declared.

Atwood laughed. "How 'bout a pair of red shoes, *mignonne*, you wear them?"

"Oh, yes sir," the girl decided. "I'd wear red shoes."

"Then I got a song for you." The old fiddler nodded as he launched into "Mes souliers sont rouges."

The little girl began to dance across the wooden floor to the lively tune. Her mother tried to stop her, but the child slipped away.

Mathilde motioned the woman not to worry. "Let her play."

Outside on the porch bench, Therese listened to the music rising. She slowly sipped her beer until she had drained the very last drop, then tossed the bottle with the other empties and stood up.

"Your brother," Sherilee said, still staring off across the bayou, "I would've married him if he'd asked."

Therese nodded slowly. "He would've asked. Sooner or later, he would've asked you."

"You think?"

"I know my brother. He wouldn't have touched you otherwise."

"That's right," the girl realized, turning to Therese, "not Alton."

Inside, the music had softened to a slow waltz.

"You stay out here long as you want. I'm gonna go check on Mama and Daddy. It's been a hard day on them."

"On you, too," Sherilee said.

"I'll manage."

The girl smiled. "I don't doubt that."

Therese returned the smile and swung open the screen door. Inside, restless children were playing on the stairs. The adults, having eaten and drunk all afternoon, dozed in chairs, listening to Atwood Thibodeaux's fiddle whine old songs like a sharp saw drawn across wet wood. Luke Lukijovich had put down the guitar to get another plate of the mirliton casserole, so the old man played on by himself, his eyes closed and his polished shoes keeping time against the worn planks of the floor.

12.

B y the time the last car had followed the road from the Petitjeans' house back to the highway, it was already growing dark.

Alone at last, the family sat together around the kitchen table, but no one spoke. After the long afternoon of voices and clatter, the silence settled upon the room like a sheet cast over a bed, draping them in its folds.

Therese had been staring at her two hands folded on the green plaid tablecloth, the fingers knit together, she suddenly realized, like her brother's in the coffin. Startled, she looked up at her parents; exhaustion lined their faces. "Why don't you two go lie down for a while?" she suggested. "I'll put the food away."

"It's been a long day," Felix agreed.

But Mathilde wanted to help clean up.

"No, you go with Daddy," Therese insisted. "There ain't much of anything needs to be done here."

Felix pushed his chair back and stood up. "*Allons*, Mathilde. The girl's right."

"You sure, baby?"

"Yeah, you go on." Then she whispered as she leaned over to give her mother a kiss, "Don't leave him be alone. He needs you tonight."

"And what about you, 'heart?"

"Don't worry about me, Mama. You just go on and look to Daddy. He don't say much, but . . ."

Mathilde nodded and returned her daughter's kiss. "You get some rest, too. Everything fell to you. You go to bed."

"As soon as I'm done. It won't be a minute."

When her mother had followed Felix to their bedroom, Therese ladled the last of Mrs. Balfour's gumbo into a large jar and screwed on its lid. She wrapped a basket of corn bread muffins in a dishcloth and put a bowl of strawberries in the refrigerator next to two casseroles neighbors had left.

Before leaving, a few women had washed and dried the dishes stacked in the sink, but Therese found dirty plates under chairs, half-finished glasses of milk beside the rockers on the porch where the children had been playing, coffee cups along the mantel of the fireplace. Ashtrays, full of nubs of cigarettes and still wet stubs of cigars, rested on windowsills, the arm of a chair, the stove, the top of the radio.

Even in her brother's room, a bowl of cold gumbo, the spoon still resting on its lip, waited on the boy's desk as if Alton might yet come home, hungry from a day on the water. The guitar lay on his bed; Luke must not have known where else to put it when the music had finally ended.

Therese sat down beside the instrument and cradled it in her lap. She let her palm trace its varnished curves—*The shoulder, the waist, and the hip*, she repeated to herself, *and the biggest damn belly button you ever seen*, remembering from childhood one of her father's jokes. She sighed and let her fingers fall across the steel strings. Taut as leaders at the end of lines weighted for bottom feeders, the six strings hummed, refusing to hush until she damped them with her hand. Gently, she leaned the silenced guitar against the wall beside the headboard.

The girl slipped off her shoes and lay back on her brother's bedspread, a quilt stitched of scraps of fabric going back generations. Therese, who had grown up to the family stories of her great-grandmother Mémère and had heard them retold by her own mother as she learned to sew, knew the history of each bit of cloth pieced into the compass-rose design. Mémère had begun the blanket for Mathilde's trousseau when Therese's mother was still a little girl.

Her hand, lolling on the edge of the bed, brushed a button snug in its buttonhole. She did not have to look down to know four others, all aligned with it along a strip of calico near the hem of the quilt, buttoned close a long pocket, the bride's purse, as they called it in English. It was a tradition, its origins long since lost, for wedding guests to slip money into the pocket of the quilt on the couple's new bed. *"Une bourse bien garnie,"* Mémère would joke, "a well-lined purse." An old superstition equated the number of buttons on the pocket to the number of children the bride would bear her husband. It was a running joke, grandmothers adding buttons to wedding quilts and brides-to-be snipping them off with shears. And no wedding ever passed without coarse jokes about the bridegroom unbuttoning his bride's purse that night and what he would find inside it.

But it was the buttons themselves over which Therese paused, letting the tip of her finger spiral down the worn disks to the cross-stitched threads affixing them to the thin fabric. The buttons were carved whalebone, she knew, yellowed, aged almost blond with use. She wondered how many shirts and dresses they had clasped until Mémère chose them for the bride's purse on Mathilde's wedding quilt. As Therese slipped her thumb over another button, she thought back even further and imagined a whale breaching in the middle of an ocean, tearing open the skin of still water at the surface, like a human being bursting through a crystal dome. Each of the five buttons had been to the bottom of the sea, she understood, like Jonah, inside the whale. And now, a hundred years later, they were stitched to a blanket, five small circles in a straight line, here on Alton's bed. It was a miracle, really, that such things could happen in this world, like Jonah spit up after three days onto the beach, or Jesus rising from the dead.

The girl wished she could believe it, any of it. But only the buttons, carved from the bones of a whale, gave her hope.

Lying in the bed, Therese could see on the low shelf of a bookcase toy soldiers, some missing heads or legs, crowded into the backseat of a plastic model of a convertible, a Chevrolet, she guessed. The car was carefully glued together, but the paint job was crude and garish, a silver hood inset between two red fenders. Beside the car on the shelf, a jar of marbles caught the hall light, glistening like so many eyes. *Arab genies trapped in a bottle waiting for a chance to escape their glass prison,* Therese told herself with a smile. It was a game they had played at night, she and Alton, trying to find a story to scare each other. She had used the cat's-eyes to her advantage more than once, she remembered, though it was usually Alton who frightened his little sister, on the verge of tears, into their parents' bed.

Higher up on the shelves, a few books were piled. She couldn't recall ever seeing Alton read, except for the hours they shared at the kitchen table doing homework after school.

Mémère had told them—Therese couldn't remember how many times—the tale of the man who read too much, a windmill maker from Bretagne. Young and out for his fortune, he had come to Louisiana to show the farmers how to pump water into their rice fields. Succeeding, he married the daughter of the richest farmer in Terrebonne Parish. But a few years later, by then a satisfied husband and father, with three children and his own house, he thought of the parcel of books he had left in New Orleans with a friend of his French family, an old man with whom he lodged when he had first landed. The windmill maker sent for the books but, embarrassed, hid them in his barn when they arrived. By candlelight that night, he read in the hayloft. When his wife came to the door of the barn to call him to bed, he told her to go to sleep; he would be in later. But the man read all night, afire with the magic of the stories in the books. The next night, the same thing happened. And the next. The following day, exhausted and preoccupied with what he had read, he left to repair a windmill at a nearby farm. As he returned home, though, the man saw smoke billowing from the yard. Racing the rest of the way, he came upon his wife poking with her rake at a bonfire of his books. His children, their eyes glowing with the flames, danced around the fire, shouting, "Burn the devil, Mama, burn him good." At first angry, the man looked upon his family as the gilded pages of French rose in singed flakes with the smoke. But then the windmill maker realized, Mémère assured

Alton and his sister, that he had never before been truly happy until that moment.

Therese, shaking her head as she thought of the old woman's tale, glimpsed on top of the stack of school texts a notebook, its taped binding at an angle to the others.

Expecting a journal or maybe even a diary, Therese was surprised when she pulled the black notebook from the shelf to find on page after page not musings or poems or old class assignments, but lease numbers of their oyster fields, dates, and the hauls taken. Sometimes the lease number and the haul were circled, and a comment beneath noted the salinity of the water that day, a cold snap the week before, a steady wind that had roiled and muddied the water. Frequently, Alton had sketched a shifting sandbar at the mouth of a lagoon or a landmark, usually a solitary cypress, to fix the position of a bed. He gave names to most of the trees. "Brokeback," he described one on St. Mary's Point. Another, with a ridged trunk, he called "Three-fingered Joe." "Hardon," a short, thick branch bending out halfway up the tree, guarded the inlet from Bay Long into Billet Bay.

The log had other notes, drawings of clouds banking up over the horizon with arrows pointing at the features that revealed in what direction the storm was headed, more arrows to show the currents in a rendering of Quatre Bayoux Pass, and another arrow to pinpoint the wreck sunk off Coup Abel. Therese recognized her father's handwriting. He had added the arrows to his son's sketches. The trembling of the hand, of both hands, suggested these were lessons learned at sea, probably drawn at the helm of the *Mathilde* as man and boy lumbered home with a hold full of shrimp or gunnysacks of oysters after a day's run.

The girl, desolate, let the notebook slip to the floor as she lay back again on her brother's blanket. She fingered one of the quilt's coarse wool triangles cut from her great-great-grandfather's Confederate tunic, the moth-eaten jacket the old man had worn as a fifteen-year-old at Vicksburg, then later at the battle of the Wilderness, and finally at Cold Harbor. Those were Alton's favorite scraps, Therese knew. Pointing out the gray tips of the compass rose that covered his bed, her brother had more than once told her the story of the women of Vicksburg promenading with their parasols every afternoon at two o'clock to show their disdain for the muzzles of Grant's artillery on the bluffs above the besieged city. "Great-great-grandpa wasn't much older than me," Alton had nodded, conveying to his younger sister the glory of the uniform, "when he defended those ladies against the Yankees on the hill."

Like the other boys, he had played the war over and over again in the school yard, one day as Stonewall Jackson, the next as Nathan Bedford Forrest, the next as some other hero of the Confederacy. The unpopular boys—like Henry Gautier, she recalled—were impressed into the enemy ranks as their foes, the drunken and honorless General Grant, the thieving Spoons Butler, the detested Sherman. Therese had burned to join the boys' battles as they rewrote Northern victories into routs by fearless Rebels. She still remembered the recess she had followed her brother up Cemetery Ridge as the twelve-year-old General Pickett succeeded, at least that once, in breaking through the Union lines at Gettysburg. And she heard his laugh as he clambered to the top of the jungle gym and hooted at the cowardly Yankees scattering toward the strawberry patch that abutted the playground.

The darkness, thickening, chilled the room. Therese wrapped herself in Alton's quilt and did not try to resist the sleep sweeping in upon her like a heavy tide.

13.

Whether an hour had passed or a whole night, she could not tell when her mother patted her awake. "What time is it?" she whispered.

"Well after two. It's late." Mathilde brushed the hair from the girl's brow. "You should go up to your own bed, get a good night's rest."

Therese nodded. "Yes ma'am." Then rubbing the sand from her eyes, she asked, "Why you awake? Everything all right?"

"I woke up and couldn't fall back asleep. I was gonna warm some milk."

The girl tried to see her mother's face in the dark. "I'll sit up with you."

As Mathilde filled a saucepan with milk in the kitchen, Therese straightened her brother's bed and remembered the abandoned bowl of gumbo on the desk. She felt vaguely nauseous.

The house still savored of caramelized onions and baked eggplants, of sweet mayonnaise and *sauce piquante*, of cigarettes and souring beer. The odors crowded the kitchen like shadows. But under everything else, Therese could smell the mold after a day of rain.

"Why don't you get down the cocoa from the cupboard," her mother suggested as the girl placed the bowl from Alton's room in the sink. "I'll make us some hot chocolate."

"Yeah, that's a good idea. My stomach's not right." She swung open the cypress door of the cabinet above the counter and lifted herself on her toes to reach the canister on the top shelf.

"You sit down, baby. I'll fix it."

The woman spooned a heaping mound of cocoa into the pot and a little sugar, stirring the swirls of chocolate into the scalded milk. When she brought the drinks to the table, the two women sat there, hands cupped around the steaming mugs.

"The other evening, Mama, what did you mean it's punishment for what you done? You got nothing to do with what happened to Alton."

"You don't know, girl. Nobody knows but me."

"Knows what?"

Mathilde seemed to slump in her chair.

"You all right, Mama?"

The woman sighed. "I tell you, you can't never tell your daddy a word of this, you understand? And I mean never."

Therese waited for her mother to go on.

"Promise me. No matter what, not a word to him. He's a good man, your father. And it's not his fault, what I done. It's on me, all of it."

"I won't say nothing," the girl assured her mother.

Mathilde held her breath for a moment. "I never told nobody this before, nobody but the priest. Guess you have the right to know, though, if anybody does. He was your brother, Alton." The woman closed her eyes and rubbed them with the heels of her hands. "And I think I'll never sleep again if I don't tell somebody."

Therese put her hand on her mother's bare arm. "Nothing you say tonight ever leaves this table. I swear."

Moths clicked against the kitchen window, drawn by the light over the sink.

"You know Mémère raised me."

"Yeah, after your own mama died."

"I know that's what Mémère told you, but it wasn't quite like that. Not exactly."

"Complications from childbirth, that's what she said."

"That's what she told me, too, complications. And that's sort of what it was, but not the way you think. It was Mama's sister, my aunt Jolene, I got the real story from her after I'd been married a few years. Mémère would never have said nothing, but my aunt thought the reason your daddy and I hadn't had any babies was on account of my mama. That I was afraid to get pregnant 'cause of what had happened to her. So Aunt Jolene told me the truth. Therese—her name was Therese, too, she's the one I named you for—Therese, my mama, didn't die from childbed complications. That's just what Mémère gave out as the story later on when somebody would ask. Like I said, she wasn't exactly lying, neither, not really. Happened all the time back then, too, women dying of childbirth. Nobody thought nothing of it. And the ones who knew the real story, well, you don't speak ill of the dead."

"How come nobody ever told me that's what they called her? I didn't know I was named for your mama."

"There's good reasons the family never said nothing about it."

The girl tried the chocolate, but it was still too hot. "What reasons?"

"She ran off, my mama."

"Ran off? Why?"

"Didn't have no husband. Aunt Jolene said Mama never let on to nobody who the man was, the one got her pregnant. Anyway, as soon as I was born she lit out for California. I can understand it, too. You know what it would be like around here for a girl with a baby and no man."

"And we never heard from her again?"

Mathilde shook her head. "No, darling, we know what happened to her. She died in a car crash three years later. In the desert."

"California?"

"Things always come to grief out there."

"What was she like, your mama?"

"Pretty. That's the first thing people always said when they talked about her. And full of fun. 'Ya mama, she was a pistol,' that's the way old man Gaspard used to put it. But a baby would've meant the end of her fun, I guess."

"So Mémère just told you she died giving birth."

"Like I said, I was full-grown before I found out any different. Made it easier all around, I guess that's what Mémère was thinking. And I suppose you could say she died of complications from pregnancy."

"You never found out who the daddy was?"

"Nobody ever knew. But that part of the story, the part where I was nobody's child, everybody in Egret Pass knew that."

"How did Mémère explain that to you?"

"Never did. First time I asked, she said, 'Some children have daddies, some don't. You don't.' That's as much as she ever had to say on the subject."

"You never wondered?"

"When I was old enough, yeah, sure. Cherie Daigle, that was her name before she married Jules Robin, I remember at school one day we was fighting at recess. The teacher, Mrs. Heine, she pulls us apart, holding us off like two dogs by the collars. Well, Cherie—she was some mad, I'd gotten her good—she goes and calls me a bastard."

"You mean the Mrs. Robin died of cancer a few years back?"

"Yeah, poor Cherie. We couldn't have been more than nine, ten years old. Well, Mrs. Heine just about had a stroke, to hear language like that coming from one of her little girls. So she tells Cherie cussin' like that ain't ladylike. Cherie wasn't one to be cowed, though, even by a teacher. She looks up into that old lady's face and says, 'It ain't cussin'. It's fact. I heard my daddy tell my grandpa.' Of course, I didn't know what she was talking about. But then Mrs. Heine says it don't make a difference whether I got a daddy or no, Cherie's not going around using vulgar words, not if she wants to be able to sit down again anytime soon."

"That's a hard thing for a child to learn in front of her friends."

Mathilde nodded. "But when I got older, in junior high, maybe, I was thinking one time about that day in elementary school and Mrs. Heine saying what she did, and I realized, wait a minute, I did have a daddy. The problem was that Mama didn't have a husband. That's when I started my search."

"Search?"

"For my father. I figured he still had to be around here somewhere. It wasn't like there were strangers ever passing through town my mama might have met. And nobody had been killed in the Great War, not the two or three that had gone off and come back, and they were too young anyway. Considering my age, I guessed he had to be at least thirty years old, my daddy. So I'd study my features in the mirror, then keep an eye out for some man with my nose or chin or hair my color. I remember for a couple of weeks I was sure it was Mr. Donaldson."

Therese smiled. "The bait man?"

Embarrassed, Mathilde laughed. "Yeah, it was his cheeks, high up like mine. And the way he walked, too."

"The way he walked?" The girl cocked her head. "Now that should've told you something, Mama. You know what people say about Mr. Donaldson. When it comes to women, I mean."

"I was thirteen years old. What did I know about that sort of thing?"

"Still, Mama, Mr. Donaldson . . ."

"Yeah, well, I never did find him, my daddy. Or at least I never knew, if I did." Mathilde sipped her chocolate. "I still wonder sometimes, though, even at my age, who my father might have been."

"Married man, probably. A man who couldn't say nothing about it."

"I suppose. Particularly with everybody knowing everybody else's business down here."

"People keep their secrets, even down here," Therese said, suddenly serious.

"Not forever," her mother assured her, "not forever."

Therese tried to change the subject. "So you forgot about your father?"

"If I did, I was the only one. When I got in high school and the dances started sophomore year, none of the boys asked me. I guess it wasn't their fault, really. The parents, they wouldn't allow it. That went on for a year, nearly two years. Then one afternoon, I'm sitting at the table with Mémère, just like this, when there's this knock at the door. It was a boy. He'd come to ask me to the junior spring dance, the one they held the Saturday after Easter, the first one since Lent began."

"Who was it? Who asked you out?"

"Matthew Christovich."

"Sheriff Christovich?"

"He was a sweet boy, and his parents, well, he just didn't tell them. Not only was I not a Yugoslav girl, but I was the girl with no father. In fact, when they found out, they threw such a fit, he had to sneak out through his bedroom window to take me. But that was Matthew. Nobody could make him go back on his word. If he'd asked me to a dance, then he was gonna take me to that dance."

"What happened when you walked in the gym?"

"Everyone sort of held their breath when they saw me. I hadn't told nobody I was coming. I guess I was afraid it wouldn't work out or something. So the music kept playing, but not a single person was speaking. Everybody was looking at us. Then one of the teachers, I don't remember her name, she taught algebra, she came up to me and said, 'Miss Follain, that's a lovely dress you wearing. And Mr. Christovich, you look very smart, too.' That's all it took. Just like that, the spell was broken. People started talking again. Matthew got me a glass of punch. And I was at a dance with a boy. I thought I'd died and gone to heaven."

"I didn't know, Mama, they treated you like that."

"You not just one person, baby, you part of a family—for good or bad. Maybe my mama was the one that done it, but I was what she'd done."

"It ain't fair, blaming the child for the parents."

"Yeah, but it works the other way, too, praising the child for the parents. You think Darryl, God rest his soul, would've wanted you for a wife if you hadn't been a Petitjean? You may be pretty, girl, but pretty don't trump blood."

The mention of Horse caught Therese by surprise. "All I'm saying is they should have treated you better, that's all."

"Well, once I was a Petitjean, they treated me just fine."

Therese softened her voice. "So how come you not Mrs. Christovich?"

"If it had been up to Matthew, I would have been. We saw each other for the next year, despite his parents. But they never gave up, they never let it rest. Matthew, he just ignored them, but it was hard for him, I know. He loved the old man, Mr. Christovich. It was always 'Daddy says this' or 'Daddy says that.' I liked that in Matthew, the way he loved his father. But graduation was coming. Half the girls in my class were already wearing engagement rings; the other half were holding their breath waiting."

"You, too?"

"I didn't know what to wish for. To be Matthew's wife, that would've suited me. To be daughter-in-law to the Christoviches, though, that I wasn't so sure about. But before I could make up my mind, before Matthew could make up his mind, I guess, your father came calling."

"Daddy?"

Mathilde nodded.

"What was Daddy like when you met him?"

"Met him? I always knew him, knew of him, at least, a Petitjean and all. But he was eight years older than me. And the Petitjeans never had anything to do with the family, not after the scandal with Mama. I never saw him take the slightest notice of me, not until the day I walked in after school and found him sitting in the parlor with Mémère."

"How come he hadn't married someone sooner?"

"He was proud. He wanted his own boat. And that took time. He crewed for his daddy, put his share away, year after year. Mr. Petitjean, Paw-Paw, he thought Felix was crazy. I can still hear him telling the story. 'We go partners, what you say to that, boy?' But that wasn't good enough for your father. He wanted a boat of his own."

"The *Mathilde?*"

"Paw-Paw used to tease me his son got married just to have someone to name the boat after."

"So how'd you come to marry him instead of the sheriff?"

"Well, Matthew wasn't the sheriff then. He was just a sweet boy. His daddy was an oysterman, but they weren't making a go of it. Barren leases, hard luck, nothing to fall back on, neither."

"But Daddy, he had plenty to fall back on, huh?"

"Mémère, she saw right away what it could mean, a Petitjean come calling on her granddaughter. By the time your father got up from the table with her that first time, the deal was done. They hadn't spoken of it, of course, neither one. No talk of marriage or anything like that. I doubt my name even came up till I walked through the door. But it was settled, just that quick."

"You told me that's how they done it in those days."

"Sometimes. If the match made sense."

Therese looked skeptical. "But how did it make sense? You didn't have nothing, did you, not even a father?"

"Well, whatever it was I had, it's what your daddy had set his heart on. By the time we graduated, I was one of the girls wearing a ring."

"He didn't waste no time, did he?"

"Well, there really wasn't no question about it. As far as Mémère was concerned, if he wanted her grandbaby, that's all there was to it. And you got to remember I was Therese Follain's daughter. Only a Petitjean could overlook that."

"Or a Christovich."

"That's right, the only men would have me were too rich or too poor for it to matter."

"But you loved him, didn't you?" Therese asked plaintively.

"I came to. The boat, me—your father didn't give a damn what anybody else thought. His sister once told me about the fights in the house when he told his daddy who he was gonna marry. The old man cursed him up and down the bayou, Eunice told me. And Maw-Maw, she was weeping like he'd struck her a blow. But none of it changed your father's mind, not for a moment. It means something when a man stands up to his family for you."

"And you had two men doing that."

"Yeah, but only one of them asked me to marry him."

"What did you think of him then, of Daddy?"

"Your father was a good man, and gentle. Easy about everything. Like Alton, just like Alton." Mathilde smiled to herself. "Of course, he wasn't so big as the other boys. A little fellow—but strong. He always surprised you, Felix. One day I remember his father and his uncle Avery were wrestling a sack of oysters onto the back of a flatbed. Felix comes along and takes the sack in either hand and—easy as you please, like it's nothing but a great big pillow—sets it on the back of that truck. The two men, they give each other a look, but Felix he just keeps on his way, not thinking twice about what he just done."

"Yeah, that's Daddy all right. And Alton, too."

"There was something about him. Maybe his age, being older than me. I just felt safe, I guess. It was like he knew things, saw them coming before they got here."

"How'd he propose to you?"

"Took me out to see his new boat. The shipwrights had just finished with it that morning. He brings me down to his slip, and there's a tarp over the stern. He has me yank it off, and I see the name he's christened his boat. My name. Then he tells me it's woeful bad luck to change a boat's name."

"He didn't make that up. Mr. Boudreaux, he's always saying that, every time he sees a paint can."

"Yeah, I knew that was true. So your father says I shouldn't wish bad luck on him and would he have to change it. No, I say, leave it be. I was proud. No one had ever named nothing after me. Leave it be, I told him."

14.

Mathilde brought the pot to the table and refilled her cup and Therese's with the warm milk, dark with cocoa.

The marriage, she continued, had been happy enough at first. Felix, having lived with his parents until he wedded in his late twenties, was awkward with his young bride, unsure when to bend and when to stand firm. Mathilde, on the other hand, sometimes brooded over her husband's silence; he was not a man to waste words. She chafed under his authority; he wondered, exasperated, at her moods. Neither found what had been expected, but habits of affection fashioned their marriage into something that grew sturdier with each year.

Just as the seasons determined the meals they sat down to each night—crawfish in the spring, shrimp in the summer, strawberries in May, figs in July—their life together followed its own calendar of seed and harvest, rain and heat.

Everything, of course, depended upon the oysters, but their first years together were buoyed by large crops and stable prices. With two boats between them, Felix and his father had expanded the Petitjean holdings as he worked new fields off Grand Island Point and beyond Manila Village all the way into Hackberry Bay. "The oil rigs in those days were few and far between," Mathilde explained to her daughter. The big canals had not yet been cut, and the beds still produced as they had for a century. From one end of Barataria to the other, she remembered, oysters were as thick as "roses on an April bush." Nobody called the Gulf an oil patch; Mathilde said she hadn't even heard that term until just a few years ago.

But all those days of easy pickings and good fortune ended for the Petitjeans one summer afternoon on Lake Grande Écaille when the old man, still half drunk from a lunch of Dixies and salted crackers, took a screwdriver from his tool kit to dislodge cable twisted in his winch.

Paw-Paw's mate, a new man related to the Gallaudets in Socola and just out of parish prison in New Orleans after serving three months for assaulting a bartender on Bourbon Street, had thrown the shift into reverse when the winch jammed. The steel cable, attached to an iron-toothed basket dredging the muddy bottom for clumps of oysters, had looped back on itself when he switched gears, catching in the chain sprocket that turned the winch. Realizing his mistake, the mate forced the shift into neutral, but he was unable to disentangle the cable from the sprocket. Paw-Paw, cursing the man, idled the engine and let the dredge hold his position as an anchor. Leaving the wheelhouse, he bent over the winch and used a screwdriver to lift the drive chain, link by link, free.

When he reached the cable, though, locked between the chain and the sprocket, the old man couldn't ease the tension. Cursing his mate again, who sulked on the engine housing out of the sun, Paw-Paw ordered the man to pry the cable loose with the screwdriver while he lifted the chain with a crowbar. Later, the man would insist that he had objected but Mr. Petitjean had threatened to hit him "upside the head" with the crowbar if he didn't do as he was told.

The boat had a following sea that afternoon, the swells rolling in against the stern. The mate was sure a rogue, shearing the steady waves out of the southwest, had hit them square along the port beam just as the cable came loose. The two seamen, riding the deck as it rose and fell stern to bow with the gentle swells, would not have been ready to shift their weight sideways for the unexpected wave as they muscled the cable free. And with the dredge skittering across the lake bottom, nothing held the boat fast against a sudden surge. That, at least, was the explanation the mate chose to offer at the inquest of why one of them had lurched against the shift lever and knocked the winch back into gear just as the cable came free.

It was over before either was aware what was happening. As the winch suddenly churned back into action, the dislodged loop of steel cable closed and tightened around the left hand that had held the crowbar in position, drawing the wrist between the drive chain and the spinning teeth of the gearwheel.

The hand flopped to the deck like a pulsing squid tumbling from a shrimp net, its thick tentacles twitching in the sunlight.

The old man calmly reached out with his right hand and shifted the winch back into neutral. The mate, the Gallaudet cousin, tied a tourniquet he cut from the bow spring line around the bloody forearm, but by then Paw-Paw was already clammy with shock.

Panicked, the crewman forgot about the heavy dredge still in the water; it slowed the vessel as he made for port. Old-timers scorned the radios new boats had installed, so it was more than an hour before the mate sighted another boat and signaled he was in distress. By the time it maneuvered alongside, the old man had been dead thirty minutes.

Everything, Mathilde told Therese, changed after that. Felix, grief stricken and guilty that a stranger had been crewing his father's boat the day of the accident, blamed himself for the old man's death. "It was nothing but damn fool pride," he told his young wife, "getting my own boat. I should have been out with Daddy on his rig, not halfway across Barataria on my own. He offered to go partners with me, too. What kind of son says no to that?" But though she tried to comfort him, telling her husband of his father's pride in the independence of a son who had gone out on his own when he didn't have to, Felix never fully recovered.

"Call it bad luck," Mathilde explained. Felix, a cautious man who had tried to sail out into his own waters, was driven back in to his home port by an unlucky wind that fixed his character for life. From then on, he husbanded the Petitjean resources, letting risky leases in western Barataria lapse and focusing his work on the old beds his family had held for the last hundred years. Selling his father's boat out of superstition more than the need of his widowed mother, Felix never again considered operating a fleet of vessels. And in a single day, he changed from an ambitious young man, full of plans, to the patriarch of a family, hanging on to what he already had.

"It was as if," Therese's mother continued, "Felix was the one who had died and I found myself the wife of his father."

The girl shifted in her chair, uncomfortable at the revelation.

Mathilde sensed her daughter's unease and added that, if anything, she felt safer, more protected. "I guess, in some ways, it was what I had always wanted."

But one question, more than any other, troubled their marriage. Felix, who had delayed marrying and then, having finally taken that step, told his bride they would have to wait a few years—until the boat was paid for—before they could have children, now postponed the decision about a family over and over again. "I'm twenty-eight years old," Mathilde had finally protested.

Catholics, the couple were constrained in their intimacy by the church's prohibition against birth control. Though Felix seemed relieved that fewer and fewer occasions arose to test his decision to postpone a family, Mathilde felt more and more abandoned by her husband. The grim resolve with which he began to attend to business, the anxiety about the changes he noticed in the oyster crops wherever the oil companies set up their operations, the sense of a family inheritance beginning to drip away like water cupped in a hand—everything that weighed on him increasingly tainted his relations with his wife.

Mathilde, of course, did not tell her daughter everything. She remembered but said nothing, for example, about an evening in late summer a few months or so after Paw-Paw's death. The rain that night clattered against the tin roof of the rented cottage in which the young couple had lived since their marriage.

It was a small, dark place, with mildew speckling the old wallpaper along the seams and near the ceiling. Felix had insisted they pay off the boat before buying a house, and his bride had agreed. She had tried to make a home of it, the battered cottage just off the highway, hanging fresh curtains on its few windows and scrubbing the grit from the grooved floorboards and the cockeyed corners left unsquared by the amateur carpenter who had built it fifty years before. Mathilde could do nothing, though, about the water stains that bruised the walls above the kick molding. Tottering on brick piers three feet higher than the canal that dead-ended behind it, the house had flooded at least twice, the landlord admitted, and probably more than that. Felix, never in his life having been far from a boat, kept a pirogue in the crawl space under the house, but raccoons and cats often took shelter there as well. In fact, the cats crowding under the overturned pirogue often woke Mathilde in the middle of cold nights with wails that sounded like babies, human babies, crying out in pain. Though her husband ignored the keening beneath them, the young woman had wept herself back to sleep more than once in the mahogany bed that was much too big for the room it filled.

Even in a rainstorm at seven o'clock at night, the house was suffocating with the humid heat of the long day, Mathilde still recalled. Felix had gone off to see his mother; worried about her loneliness, he had visited her, at least briefly, every day since the old man had died. Alone in the darkening house as the rain dashed itself against the metal roof, Mathilde unbuttoned her smock and stepped into the bath she had drawn for herself. The huge tub, beside the squat hot water heater in the kitchen, was the one luxury the house offered. Poised on menacing talons curled playfully around iron balls, it ran the length of one wall and dwarfed the stove and icebox across the room.

The woman was still standing in the water when a stroke of lightning filled the house with blue light. It seemed to persist, the illumination, until a peal of thunder, a deep roar she felt even more than she heard, tore open the fabric of the sky overhead. The rain gushed down the kitchen window, a curtain of water. The lamp above the little kitchen table, the table she had painted yellow with its two chairs, flared, then died. The storm had knocked out the power, she realized. Suddenly chilled, Mathilde lowered her body into the tub of warm water and lay back, listening to the rain gust and fade.

When Felix returned, stumbling through the dark house, calling out for his wife, she did not answer. She let her husband find her on his own.

"Mathilde?" he whispered.

She heard him breathing across the room.

"Mathilde?"

In answer, she rippled the water with her hand.

But Felix did not come to her. Instead, he said, more loudly, "I'll be in my chair when you done."

The woman had never forgotten that night and had never forgiven her husband. Even now, all these years later, she was still stung by it and angered.

Though Mathilde did not mention that evening to Therese, she did tell the girl about the next morning, a bright Saturday when Darryl Bruneau married Arlene Metzger.

"Mrs. Bruneau, who killed herself?"

"We don't know that for a fact."

"Mama, the priest wouldn't even bury her from the church, not until Horse made a big stink and the diocese declared her insane."

"What do you know about all that? You were in eighth grade at the time."

"Everybody knew about it—and Horse's donation, too, the one they bought the holy water font with."

"That was a memorial to his poor wife."

"Where'd she come from, anyway, Mrs. Bruneau? She didn't have any family here, did she?"

"No, Arlene was born in Des Allemands. But her father died when she was a baby, and her mother moved to Algiers for a job at a chocolate factory."

"A chocolate factory?"

"They made Easter candy there, and for Halloween. Doughnuts, too, in boxes."

"What did they come down here for?"

"Just Arlene by herself, after she graduated. To teach grammar school in Magnolia."

"That's where Horse met her?"

"At a store. You know how Darryl was, a big tease, even with strangers. They got to be friends standing right there in a little notions store. What in the world Darryl was doing in a shop like that, I don't know."

"Probably followed her in. She was pretty, huh?"

"Red hair—just like the baby of the family, Rusty—green eyes. And young. Darryl must have been thirty, at least. With a boat and money, and so good looking. She didn't stand a chance, that girl."

"But crazy?"

"No," Mathilde sighed, "that came later. And it wasn't her fault, neither. Others done it to her. Others drove her to what she done."

"Others? You mean Horse."

"His name was Darryl. But no, not just him. He didn't do it all by himself."

"You and Mrs. Bruneau were friends?"

"When your brother was small. We both had babies."

Therese shook her head. "And look what they growed up to be, those Bruneau boys."

"It was Darryl's influence, not Arlene's."

"I mean," Therese continued, "take Little Darryl and Alton. Same age, but different as night and day. Some babies, we'd all be better off if they just tied 'em in a sack and flung 'em in the bayou."

"Don't you say such things, even in jest. They were sweet little babies, every one of them. What happened afterward, well, that's just something else. Little Darryl and Alton, they played together on the same blanket, like twins."

"What are you talking about, Mama? Little Horse would cross the street to pick a fight with Alton. They couldn't stand each other. People used to make jokes about it, how they hated each other."

"That's when they were bigger, when they went to school."

"How come I don't remember Mrs. Bruneau? You two had a falling-out?"

"Yeah, 'heart, that's exactly what happened. We never spoke again."

"What'd she do to you, to make you stop talking to her?"

"It's what I did to her."

"With good reason, I'm sure, whatever it was."

Mathilde took a sip from her mug. "Arlene was a fine woman. She just wasn't as strong as Darryl."

"I guess they didn't call him Horse for nothing."

"There wasn't many could stand up to him. Arlene least of all."

Therese yawned. "It's a sad story, Mama, Mrs. Bruneau killing herself and all, but what's this got to do with my brother? And what's it got to do with you?"

15.

W hat's it got to do with me and Alton?" Mathilde repeated, shaking her head as she looked down into her cup. "I'm gonna tell you."

She began by describing the Bruneau wedding to Therese and the big party Horse threw in front of the church after the ceremony. The bride, in a dress of ivory satin her mother had stitched by hand and trimmed with heirloom lace her father's own grandmother had brought from Germany, seemed more bewildered than entertained by the festivities. She was basically a city girl, having grown up in Algiers, and new to country ways. As the afternoon pressed on toward dark, the music growing more raucous and the men drunker, the uncouth local wedding traditions and leering jokes unsettled her into tears. Horse, to no one's surprise but his own wife's, was the most callous to her feelings, mocking her blushes and taunting her modesty. When, angry and hurt by the rough treatment at the hands of her groom, she fled the party and wept behind the church doors her mother shut on the guests, the women berated their husbands and sons into silence. Horse, apparently shamed, forced open the doors and, in front of the whole town, apologized on his knees to his wife. She stanched her tears with a linen handkerchief embroidered by her mother with the girl's new initials, *AB*, and Horse had a friend drive the woman and her mother home to his house.

"I'll just finish up things here, and then I'll be along," he promised. But as soon as she had been taken away, Horse invited the guests to make a supper of the still-warm jambalaya and gumbo and bread pudding. "I don't know about you folks," he boasted, "but I'm not ready to call it a night yet." He had the band start in on another tune. "Now, who hasn't had a dance with me yet?" he shouted over the din of violin and accordion, guitar and harmonica, drum and bass fiddle.

That was how he came, eventually, to waltz around the churchyard with Mathilde. Felix was displeased, she knew, when she let Horse take her hand and lead her to the center of the dancers, still catching their breaths after a two-step. But hurt by the night before, her husband's turning away from her in the dark kitchen as the storm raged, she did not decline to dance with his chief rival in the oyster business. The waltz, whining and insinuating, drew all the couples on the dance floor into each other's arms. Mathilde felt Horse's hand in the small of her back, a powerful hand that lifted her onto her toes as they glided across the ragged lawn, little puffs of dust kicking up about their ankles with each step.

The woman tried to keep her eyes down, but she knew her hand, lifted up beside their faces, had been swallowed in the man's huge grip. His breath, sighing above her, was sweet with the whiskey sauce of the pudding he had finished off between dances. He had rolled up the sleeves of his white shirt, unbuttoned the collar against the heat of the evening; the sweetness of his breath mingled with the salt of his body. Strong as he was, Mathilde was moved by the gentleness, almost tenderness, with which he held her, as though he feared she might shatter if he closed his arms too tightly around her. A kind of pity came over her for this man always constrained by the weakness of those around him. She allowed herself to look up into his eyes as their bodies surged and fell back together waltzing before the church.

Horse, too, allowed himself to look into the woman's eyes, and the longer he looked, the less he smiled. When the band wheezed to a stop, he released his rival's wife as if he were returning a fish to water, his hands loosening enough to let the creature swim free, back to its own world.

Mathilde, without a word, took a step, two steps toward her husband, who waited beyond the dancers now spinning in pairs to a jig the band had taken up. But then she looked over her shoulder. Horse stood unmoving in the midst of the dance, his eyes fixed on her, his arms limp at his sides. The dancers swirled around him as, abashed, he watched Mathilde take Felix's arm and walk away.

The look on his face when she glanced behind her after the dance—that, she explained to her daughter, was the moment she fell in love with Darryl Bruneau.

"Love?" Therese repeated, shocked.

"There ain't no other word for it. No other word I know," her mother continued. "I thought he was afraid he'd crush me if he squeezed too tight when all the time I was holding him in my hand."

"On his wedding night you fell in love with him?" Therese was stunned by Mathilde's confession.

"You think I was the only wife in the world in love with another man? Don't fool yourself, girl."

"But you didn't do nothing about it, did you?"

"No, neither one of us. Knowing Darryl's reputation, I was surprised, too. I thought he would have found an excuse to see me somehow. At church the next day, he was there with his new bride and his mother-in-law, but he didn't even look at me, not as far as I could tell."

"And what about you?"

"We was in church. I prayed."

"But what were you praying for, Mama?"

Mathilde eyed her daughter. "I prayed for strength." Then, tasting her warm chocolate, she described her visit to the Bruneau house the following Friday, a day she knew Horse would be out trawling.

Arlene, lonely after her mother's return to Algiers, was delighted to have the company. The young woman had no friends yet in Egret Pass, and Mathilde was only a few years older than she was. The plate of pecan pralines her guest had brought reminded Arlene of her mother's house. "The one thing we always had," she smiled, "was candy."

Mathilde admired the house, but Arlene was embarrassed by the stains on the sofa and the broken light fixtures, the hole in the window screen and the closet door that would not shut. "Darryl hasn't taken the place too seriously, I'm afraid."

Her visitor laughed. "I don't know any man around here does take his house seriously. That's what they got us for, I guess. You should've seen what our place looked like when Felix showed it to me the first time. And he didn't think there was a thing wrong with it."

They liked each other, the two women, and commiserated over the life of a fisherman's wife, though one had known it for only a few days. "They're used to being out on the water with no one to talk to. That's why it's so hard to get them to say something. You got to ask them questions," Mathilde advised.

By the time she rose to leave, the two were friends. "You come see me next week," the older woman insisted. "We'll bake some pies. How's that?"

But if she had hoped to ward off the husband through friendship with the wife, she learned when she got home her strategy would do little good. Horse was waiting for her, sitting on the edge of her canal.

"Darryl, what you doing here?" The woman realized how happy she was to see him. "How come you not out on your boat?"

"Done early today," he said, looking out across the marsh grass, "engine trouble." Then he turned back toward her.

She was leaning against the corner of the house. "Why you come by, Darryl? You ain't never been to our house before."

"Ain't never been asked," he explained. "On the way in, I seen your husband heading into Bay Ronquille. He'll be late tonight. Wind's against him."

"Don't make no matter. I never fix dinner till he walks through the door."

Horse turned back toward the marsh. "You got 'coons, you know."

"At night I hear 'em. Under the house."

"Want to see where they live?"

The woman smiled. "Where they live, those raccoons?"

He looked over his shoulder with a grin. "I'll show you."

Mathilde let go of the house. "OK, Mr. Bruneau, show me."

Horse stood up and hauled the pirogue out from under the house.

"Where you think you going with Felix's boat?"

"Won't hurt it none." He flipped it over onto its keel and slid it into the water. "Getting wet's good for it." Mathilde started to object, but he flicked the water from his hand into her face. "Good for a woman, too."

The boyish impudence made her laugh. "You a bad one, aren't you?"

In answer, Horse held out his hand. She hesitated, then put hers in his, and took her seat in the bow while he steadied the pirogue with his boot. The boat rocked when he settled himself onto the back bench, and Mathilde grasped the sides with both hands. She wanted to object, to get out and go inside and lock the door. But Horse had already pushed the boat out into the torpid canal, and she felt the pirogue lift as the man's paddle dug into the still water.

With two in the little boat, the water skimmed just inches from her fingers, curling over the gunnels. She felt the hint of a breeze as the pirogue glided around the curves of the canal. Obscured by the tall *roseau* canes and three-cornered grass of the marsh, the roof of her house was all she could make out, sitting so low in the water. And soon she had lost sight of her roof, too, even before the boat slipped into the marsh that opened at the mouth of the canal.

Therese woke her from the reverie. "What were you thinking, going off that way? What if Daddy had come home early?" She did not tell her mother, of course, but the girl could not forget the pirogue in which Horse had taken her for a ride.

"Thinking?" Mathilde shook her head. "If only I had been thinking."

Horse followed the bank a few hundred yards, then let the boat drift. It sidled against a pair of cypress knees rising out of the swamp.

"So where's all the 'coons?" the woman demanded.

"You just hush a minute," he whispered.

She could hear frogs burping among the roots of trees. An owl burst from an overhead branch, the flutter of its wings like a man huffing just behind her. Then she heard something roar.

"Gator," the man explained calmly.

Finally, a scrabble of claws caught her ear. She turned around. Horse was nodding, pointing with the heel of the paddle toward a clump of palmetto. She looked carefully, saw a masked face of fur among the sprawl of green fronds.

"How'd you know where to look?" she whispered. But the raccoon had heard her. She lost it in the underbrush.

"I lived out here my whole life, woman. You think I can't find you a 'coon—or any other damned thing you want?" He laughed, and the chirp and bellow all around them died away. Now she could hear nothing but the water barely eddying around the boat.

The silence frightened her. "Take me home, Darryl."

On the way back in, Mathilde told him she had been to visit Arlene.

"She's a sweet girl, that one," Horse agreed. "But she's got a lot to learn about life down here. It ain't like the city."

"Maybe you's the one got something to learn."

Horse seemed to turn serious. "You right about that." A small alligator roiled the water near the bank in a thatch of roots. "It's just she ain't the woman to teach it to me."

Mathilde didn't let herself ask who that woman might be.

"And that was the end of it?" Therese wanted to know, interrupting her mother.

"Well, yeah, Darryl took me home, shoved the boat under the house, went off. I made your daddy a dinner of all his favorites, baked cushaw, corn fritters, a buttermilk pie for dessert. I figured it being a Friday he'd bring home a speckled trout or something I could panfry. But he didn't come home for dinner that night, your daddy. Got in late because of the wind, he said, and stopped by his mother's. Then he had to see a man about a new net. I was asleep by the time he come home; I didn't even bother opening my eyes when he climbed into bed. So if you mean was that the end of Darryl and me, then, no, baby, that wasn't the end of it, not by a long shot."

"You blame Daddy, don't you?"

"For what? He wasn't doing nothing different from any other husband down here. I don't blame nobody but me. It falls square on me, all of it."

"But what does, Mama? I still don't see—"

"You ain't heard the whole story yet."

Arlene came by the next week, just as she had been invited. Mathilde taught her to make a yam pie of sweet potatoes laced with cinnamon, ginger, and brown sugar. They made a simple pecan pie together, shelling the nuts on the porch and then adding the meat, dusted with flour, to corn syrup and sugar, eggs, and butter flavored with vanilla. But Arlene could cook, too. She showed Mathilde a recipe for fudge her mother had learned at the chocolate factory in Algiers. Mathilde wanted her new friend to stay to meet Felix, but Arlene was afraid to be late for Horse.

The next morning, Mathilde was startled by a knock on her door. She didn't have many visitors so early in the day.

It was Horse. "I hear you serve pecan pie, ma'am. Got a piece for a hungry fisherman?"

"What you doing here, Darryl?" Standing at the front door, they could be seen by anyone passing on the highway. Mathilde looked in both directions, but no one was coming. "Come inside for a moment." She closed the door behind him.

"I could use some coffee, too," the man said. Then, surveying the place, he added, "This the best Felix can do for you, a house like this? A man with as much money as a Petitjean?"

"There ain't so much money with Paw-Paw gone. And we got the boat to pay for."

Horse laughed. "Darlin', that boat was paid for a year ago. Your husband never told you?"

"How would you know that? You just tellin' tales, you."

"I know the banker. We play *bourré* together, so I know him real good. You ask your husband how much you got left to pay on that loan of his." He wet his thumb with his tongue and glued a loose seam of wallpaper back in place. "I tell you, you were my wife, I wouldn't keep you in a shack like this."

Now Mathilde laughed, though she was still upset about what he had told her about Felix's boat. "I seen the house you put a wife in. It ain't no great shakes, Darryl. That poor girl, she got her work cut out for her, fixing your place up."

Horse frowned. "What's wrong with my house?"

"Holes in the windows, furniture a muskrat wouldn't sleep on, doors that don't close—"

"Sure," Horse interrupted, "maybe it needs a little work here and there. I'll get around to it. Arlene been complaining?"

Mathilde caught the edge in his voice. "No, 'course not. She hasn't got a bad word to say about anything. I'm the one seen it with my own eyes." She started to tease him. "It's a shambles, that's what it is."

Horse smiled. "All right, I'll fix it. But it'll cost you a piece of that pecan pie I been hearing about."

"One piece and then you go, you understand?"

He followed her into the kitchen. "And a cup of coffee."

She put the food before him and watched him eat. She liked it, the way he ate her food, like a man who hadn't eaten in a long time.

Felix had told her that morning he was heading out for Lake Grande Écaille. He would be home late. While Horse finished his pie, the woman looked out her kitchen window to the sky over the Gulf. It was blue, without the trace of a cloud. No storms would drive the boats in early today.

She poured Horse more coffee.

16.

Y'understand?"

"Yes ma'am," her daughter answered softly. "You and Horse . . ."

"That's right."

The two women sat in silence for what seemed like a long time. Then Therese, gathering anger as she spoke, lashed out at her mother. "What Daddy ever did you to deserve that? You tell me."

"It's what a man don't do."

"You talkin' like a crazy woman. He give you a house, put food on your table, a dress on your back, and you, you take a son of a bitch like Horse Bruneau into your husband's bed."

Now Mathilde was angry. "His name was Darryl."

"I don't give a damn what you call him. You put that bastard where Daddy ought to have been."

"You don't know, girl. You think a house, food, a dress, even a goddamn gold ring buys a woman? It was my bed I took Darryl into that morning. Not your daddy's. If he had made it his bed, then maybe none of this would have ever happened. But it was my bed that day. Mine."

Horse could read a shifting wind like any man who lived his life on the sea. He didn't make Mathilde say the words. Instead, ignoring the fresh coffee steaming on the table, he took her hand and led the woman from the kitchen.

"This way?" he asked, pointing to the bedroom door. Peeking out her curtains, flowered with a print of twined roses, Mathilde had shut the door when she had seen Horse on her front porch, knocking.

All she could do was nod in answer to his question.

It was like a raft, he thought, swinging open the door, the big bed wedged into the small room like a boat in its slip. "Tight fit, huh?" he joked.

Mathilde couldn't find her voice. Nodding, she leaned against the four-poster mahogany bedstead, its corner posts carved into tall corn-stalks, tufts of corn silk budding from the tip of each ripe ear.

Horse bent to one knee to slip her feet from their sandals, taking the calf of her leg in his palm and lifting her foot from the shoe he held in his other palm. When he had lowered the second bare foot to the floor, she felt his huge hands beneath the skirt of her dress sliding up her thighs until he cupped her slim waist in his fingers. Then she felt him ease her panties over her hips and let them fall to her ankles. She felt her feet lifted free of the soft cloth. And then he was standing in front of her.

"You all right?" he whispered.

She nodded again, reaching behind her back to grasp the bedpost in both hands.

He kissed her while his hands fumbled somewhere below. Suddenly, she felt herself lifted up, split open. She squeezed her eyes shut, tightening her grip on the wooden stalk behind her, until the pain rippled back inside her as a kind of numbness thickening into something that loosened her fingers, one by one, from the wooden post along which she rose and fell.

Her face was buried in his shirt of black and white checks. She forced her gaze down, but there was nothing to see except the flounce of her skirt against his pants.

And then, a few moments later, she felt herself being lowered, one hand cushioning her head against the bedpost, another hand—in which she was surprised to discover she had been sitting—easing her back to the floor.

When she looked down again, weak in the knees, breathless, Horse had already buttoned his pants.

She took a step toward the door but staggered, catching herself against the edge of the bed with an outstretched hand.

"Where you going?" Horse asked, watching her from the straight-backed chair into which he had slumped.

She was too shy to look at him. "I thought we was done."

"Done? Darlin', we just gettin' goin'. You'll know when we done, I guarantee. There won't be no question. Now you come here."

Mathilde was in new waters, but she trusted the breeze.

Loosening her smock, Horse slipped it over her shoulders and her long arms but caught it up at her hips, rolling it over on itself like a belt. Then, with his huge hands, he unclasped her brassiere and tossed it on the floor. Bare breasted, she stood before the only man other than her husband who had ever had her. He seemed to be waiting for something.

Mathilde eased her hands along her sides until the dress slid to the floor. The naked woman stood there for a moment, the dress frothing around her feet.

"*Chère*, you look like Venus on the half shell," Horse teased.

It was an old joke, but it made her blush, and she lost her nerve, hopping into the bed and pulling the covers up to her throat like a schoolgirl.

Horse laughed. He liked sex with married women. In fact, as far as he was concerned, there wasn't anything sweeter than another man's wife. But it wasn't just the men, screwing their wives, pissing in their faces. Married women knew something, something you didn't find in younger girls, a kind of sudden shamelessness. And they weren't such a pain in the ass when you were done with them, either. They always had more to lose than you did if the story got out. So they kept quiet about it, when you'd had enough.

He kept telling himself all this as he smiled at the little face poking out among the pillows on the bed. But he knew he was lying to himself about this time. This was something else, what was happening in this bedroom. *Get up and walk away,* he told himself. Instead, he undressed and joined the woman under the covers.

He was curious, that's how he explained it to himself, like a shark worrying a turtle, trying to figure out what in the hell this creature was. He smiled to think of it that way, but that was what he was doing. She confused him, shying, then suddenly growing bold. He didn't know what to make of her, so he spent the morning worrying her, again and again.

For her part, Mathilde had never before realized how different it might be with a different man. Felix wasn't much bigger than she was—strong, maybe, but a small man. Everything about Horse, though, was big. When he was on her, she quickly discovered, if she lifted her chin, she could just nuzzle the cleft beneath his shoulder between his arm and his chest; that's how much bigger he was than she. When he rested above her, she felt like a mouse pinned beneath the paws of a lazy cat. She liked that, and played at lying still, barely breathing beneath him. His weight pressed her, for a moment, like a heavy stone. But then he joked he was a Southern gentleman. "You know what a gentleman is, don't you?" he explained. "A man who holds himself up on his elbows." She was surprised by that, too, how much he made her laugh.

Ignoring her daughter, Mathilde rested her face against a palm. The chocolate had grown cold as the night wore on. She thought she heard Felix cough in the bedroom.

"What you thinking about, Mama?" Therese asked, softening. Her mother had had nothing else to say after their angry words a few moments earlier.

"Confession. I went to confession about it."

"You tell the priest?"

"What else could I do? It was a sin. I told him it had been a month since my last confession and I had committed adultery."

"Did he know you?"

"Yeah, sure. It was old Monsignor Aubert. He knew us all since we was babies—he'd baptized every one of us. The monsignor was half deaf by then, to boot, so he had them take down the privacy screens in the confessional. That way, he could see our lips move. But he was staring straight at us. Knew exactly who it was telling him all these terrible sins. The worst part, he was so hard of hearing, he used to shout, and he'd call you by your name the whole time you were in there with him. Anybody in line for confession or saying their penance on the kneelers in front of the confessional, they could hear every word. The nuns from school, they made us scratch our collars when we was standing in line so we couldn't hear nothing. And they told us the seal of the confessional extended to little gossips like us. Straight to hell, we divulge one word of what we hear coming out of there."

"That keep people quiet about what they heard?"

"What you think? Confessing on a Saturday to the monsignor, you might just as well have gone up into the pulpit at Sunday Mass the next morning and announced what you done to the whole town."

"So what did you do?"

"I got him in the rectory on Friday. Told him I had a mortal sin on my soul and couldn't wait till confession the next day—in case I died in the meantime."

"So he heard your confession right there in the rectory?"

"He wasn't none too happy about it. The housekeeper had gotten him up from his nap. While he was putting on his stole and getting ready, he kept grumbling, 'What kind of mortal sin could a girl like you commit, anyway?' He shut up with that in a hurry, though, when I told him what I'd done."

Therese allowed herself a smile. "I guess that woke him up, huh?"

"It wasn't funny. This priest had known me all my life, like a grandpa or something. I was ashamed. And he knew my mother's story, too, the one Aunt Jolene had told me. The whole time, I'm worrying he's gonna think I'm just like my mama."

"What did he say?"

"He had me make my act of contrition. Then he said he couldn't forgive me—he couldn't grant absolution, was the way he put it—unless I was heartily sorry, like it says in the prayer I'd just recited. And also, from then on, I had to avoid the near occasions of sin."

"He got that right out of the catechism, didn't he?"

"Maybe they got the robe, but we all read the same book."

Now Therese laughed. "You sound like one of those Baptist Bible thumpers on the radio, Mama."

"I listen to them sometimes. It makes sense what they say, some of it."

"Better not let Father Danziger hear you talk like that. He find out the Protestants are worming their way in down here on the radio, probably go pull down that radio tower on the river, if I know him." Therese laughed again.

But Mathilde was smiling about something else. The next time she saw Horse, she told him he was a near occasion of sin.

"Well," he sighed, "that's one thing the priest is right about, I'll give him that."

She had believed, she had wanted to believe as she recited her act of contrition, that she regretted her infidelity to her husband, that such a lapse would never, could never happen again. She had begged forgiveness with a sincere heart, and on Sunday at Mass she had avoided Horse's eyes.

But a few days later, lying beside him in the big bed, she had given up all hope and all desire of avoiding the occasion of sin. She yielded to it, to its unforeseen consequences, to all the catastrophes she risked, to everything she endangered, in the same way she had yielded to the man's insistence that morning—with a single sigh. From that moment on, she was his to do with as he wished. That was how she comforted herself when she grew frightened by what she had embarked upon. She was adrift without rudder or compass or star to steer by, a ghost ship under tattered sail, driven by gusts no mariner could forecast on a course no navigator could plot. She took refuge in her resignation to a fate, she persuaded herself, that could not be forestalled.

Horse did with her as he wished, and she did not protest. Forcing her head down with a heavy hand or pinning her body against the mattress with a thick forearm, the man introduced her to intimacies she had never imagined. In fact, she hungered for them, what others might describe as degradations, for they confirmed that she was at the mercy of a passion beyond her control.

Enslaved by desire, as she was willing to describe her infatuation with Horse, Mathilde found herself freed of the constraints that had curbed her curiosity and had checked her inventiveness in bed. But she was surprised to find Horse cool to her when she encouraged his indecencies. As soon as her confusion reawakened a modesty that resisted his advances, though, he again fell upon her with an eagerness and an indifference to her protests that left her aching and purring.

It was as if the man were devouring her, gnawing upon her very bones. *Is it a sin,* she defended herself with images drawn from scripture, *for the lamb to lie down with the lion?*

A month passed of this life, then a season. It was winter already. She baited traps of hardware cloth with chicken necks to crab the canal behind their house. Felix brought home oysters she stewed in milk with cayenne and shallots. She knit a vest of red wool for him to wear on the water. One afternoon, he crawled under the house to wrap the pipes in scraps of cloth to protect them against an early freeze that was bearing down on Plaquemines from the north. The next morning, they woke to find the elephant ears and other exposed plants had swooned to the ground before the cold wind; already, the long fronds were yellow with death.

As the year progressed, Arlene came to depend more and more upon her friendship with Mrs. Petitjean. Mathilde taught Horse's wife to mend nets, to gut and fillet a redfish, to coon oysters at low tide in the shallows. The new bride even learned to skin a muskrat, then run the hide through a ringer and stretch it in a rat mold. And after the freeze had passed, the two of them shared a winter garden of cauliflower, squash, radishes, onions, and cabbages.

Two or three times one December afternoon, weeding the garden and laying down a thicker mulch of cypress chips, Arlene started to ask her friend something, then stopped, embarrassed. Finally, Mathilde shook her head. "If you don't tell me right now, we gonna be out here all night."

Arlene sat back on her heels between two rows of onion bulbs she was weeding. "It's just silliness, I guess, but I've heard things about Darryl."

Mathilde stiffened. "About Darryl?"

"You know how people are, always talking about what they don't know the first thing about. It's just . . ."

Again the woman hesitated to continue.

"Is that the moon up there in the sky already?" Mathilde teased.

Arlene laughed. "All right. I know I'm silly. It's just they say Darryl is something of a lady's man, if you know what I mean."

"They jealous of you, is all that means. A pretty little thing like you comes along and steals Darryl's heart, what you think they all gonna say?"

"You're right, Mathilde. I'm just new to . . . well, you know. I want to be a good wife to my husband. But other women know more than I do."

"All you got to remind yourself is you the one Darryl chose to marry. Ain't nobody gonna take that away from you."

"Yeah, I know. He just leaves me alone, you know, at night. I can't help wondering—"

"At night?" Mathilde interrupted. "Darryl goes out at night?"

"I tell him to take me with him, but he says the places he's going to aren't fit for a person like me."

"Bars?"

"I guess. He doesn't like me to ask too many questions."

"They all do it, the men. Just something a wife gets used to."

"Felix goes out drinking at night?"

"Sure," Mathilde lied. "They all do."

"If it was just drinking, that would be one thing. But people say he has girlfriends."

"Girlfriends? More than one?"

Arlene laughed. "You mean it would be OK if there was only one?"

"No." Mathilde smiled back, recovering her poise. "It's just how would Darryl have time for all these women, the ones everybody talks about?"

"You're right. I just—when he leaves me alone so much, I guess I just think up things to worry about. I never did like being alone. And being married, I thought that would be the end of it, loneliness."

"You need children. Fill up the house that way."

Arlene blushed. "I hope it won't be too long till we have a family."

Mathilde looked at her friend. "You keeping a secret from me?"

17.

I hear you got more than one girlfriend. That true?"

Horse was half asleep. He opened one eye on Mathilde, whose head against his chest rose and fell with each breath he took. "Nah, that's just talk by all those women wish they were my girlfriends."

"I mean, maybe I ain't got no claim on you, but you hold me up to ridicule, so help me, I'll—"

"What you talking about, ridicule?" Now he was wide awake. "Who puts these ideas in your head, anyway?"

"Never you mind. You just better not go round—"

"Woman, I don't know what the hell you talking about." Horse took a deep breath. He began again in a softer voice. "You think you just another girlfriend? You know how much money I been losing lying here in your bed half the week? You way too expensive to be just another girlfriend."

She was almost convinced. "I don't know. It was summer and the shrimp were running, bet I wouldn't see you nearly as much."

Her ear still to his chest, she heard a chuckle rumble deep inside.

"You know, you don't fool me, Darryl, not one little bit."

"Hush," he said, stroking her hair. "Can't we just lie here in peace for a minute?"

She started to say something else, but then she thought better of it and closed her eyes, lulled by the steady echo of his heart.

"Mama?" The voice was far away. "Mama? You asleep, Mama?"

Therese was shaking her mother's arm.

"No, I ain't asleep. What makes you say that?"

"Your eyes were shut. I thought you were falling asleep, the way you were nodding there with your eyes closed."

"No, I was just thinking, is all."

"About Horse?"

"And about Mrs. Bruneau."

"So what happened to her?"

"We got to be friends, best friends. Then that winter, Arlene got pregnant, but she was afraid to tell her husband. They hadn't been doing so well lately. Darryl wasn't bringing in what he usually did. He kept telling her they had to tighten their belts. So she worried about how he'd take the cost of a baby. And she said he'd gotten moody. Never knew what to expect out of him."

"I guess she didn't. And she had no idea what was going on between you two?"

"Oh, Arlene sensed she wasn't the only woman in her husband's life. She just didn't know who the other woman was."

"You'd talk to her about it? About this other woman?"

"She'd talk about it. I'd nod, tell her every wife is jealous—particularly wives expecting a baby. Tease her who would want Darryl anyway."

"How you do that, talk to your friend that way when you the one she's worried about?"

Mathilde's voice thickened, as if she were forcing back anger. "It didn't have nothing to do with her, what was going on between Darryl and me. It was something else entirely."

"It didn't have nothing to do with her? Her best friend screwin' her husband?"

"Don't you use language like that with me, girl. And don't talk about what you don't know."

"All I'm saying," Therese began again, backing down a bit, "is here's this young bride confiding in you, her friend, and you—"

Mathilde cut her off. "I was pregnant, too, by then."

"What?"

"I was carrying Darryl's child, too, just like her."

Therese blanched. "You sure it was his? I mean, you and Daddy must have . . ." The girl stopped. Mathilde was shaking her head no.

"There wasn't no doubt. Your daddy, well, he was a man, so it wasn't like he never touched me. But there wasn't no question about who had fathered this child on me."

"You tell anybody?"

"Darryl, even before I was sure. With Arlene expecting a baby and maybe me, too—I took this all for a sign we have to break it off, what we doing. I sit him down next time he come over, and I take the chair across from him, and I tell him I'm carrying his child. We got to stop, I tell him."

"How'd he take that?"

"Not like I expect. Instead he's quiet, thinking on it, I guess. And tender, sort of, like he feels sorry for me. He don't put his hand on me, don't stroke my hair, nothing, just comes and sits next to me, not saying a word. I don't know what to make of him, Darryl. And when he goes, he gives me a kiss on both cheeks. He never done that before."

"And you didn't tell nobody else, not Mémère, not nobody?"

"Nobody. I need time to think, everything coming to a head like this all at once."

Outside, something chirruped, a toad, maybe, in the garden. They had been sitting at the table for a long time.

"But Darryl don't give me time to think," Mathilde continued. "The very next day after I tell him we got to break it off, he's at my door at six o'clock in the morning. Felix hadn't been gone an hour yet, and already here's Darryl knocking on my porch. I'd gone back to bed after breakfast. I hadn't slept well. Darryl, it turns out he hasn't been to sleep at all. Drinking, wandering all over the parish the whole night, he looks like a wild man, like he's been chased through the woods by some mad dog or something at his heels. He come in, and he sits me down on the sofa.

Then he says am I sure about the baby? Sure as a woman can be, I tell him, not wanting to give him any excuses to keep things going. Well, he says, he's made up his mind to it. Wants me to come away with him. Leave Felix, he tells me, right this minute, and marry him."

"No, Darryl wants you to run off?"

"Says we can make a go of it up and down the coast, don't make no difference to him where. What about Arlene, I say, what about your wife? She can go back to her mama in Algiers, he says. She never was happy in his house anyway, he tells me, not since day one."

Therese waited for the rest of the story.

"I tell him he's talkin' crazy. Just 'cause he got me pregnant don't mean he got to marry me. But he says it don't have nothing to do with the baby. The baby just sealed it, that's all. No, he can't live without me, he keeps insisting. He don't know what it is, why he wants me so bad. But it's me, it ain't the baby. Though he's glad about it, he says at the end, proud to have me the mother of his child."

"How's that happen to a man, go crazy over a woman, throw away everything he's got just like that?"

Mathilde smiled. "Darryl, he once was telling me how you hunt big alligators in the swamp. Said you take your flatboat out in the middle of the night and bait a one-pound hook with a dead chicken or, you don't have a chicken, just some oily rag. Then you hang the bait from a pole maybe a foot or eighteen inches above the water and wait till some monster gator comes bursting out of the bayou and swallows it whole. So you got this ten-footer hooked in the gut with a pound of steel, and you drag it over to the boat—the whole time with the gator snapping those jaws to take somebody's arm off and smashing everything in sight with its tail—and you lay the barrel of a .22 between its eyes and pull the trigger. That's how you go fishing for alligator, he told me. But then he says it's just like love."

"Love?" Therese laughed. "That was Horse's idea of falling in love."

"Yeah." Her mother nodded. "Only thing is, according to Darryl, you just can't tell whether love is the bait dangling over your head, the hook in your gut, or the slug buried right between your eyes."

"Maybe that's what it feels like, all right, but how does it happen, a man risk everything he's got over a woman?"

"Just as well ask how that happens to us. Only difference is, a woman don't know any other way to love somebody. The surprise is when a man loves us the way we love him. Why'd Darryl feel that way toward me? I don't know. I don't think he ever knew. Maybe he's just looking to love somebody like that and I come along at the right time."

"No, you done swept him off his feet, Mama."

"Well, I put the broom away soon enough. He don't know yet Arlene is expecting. I'm the one got to tell him he's gonna be a father on two women. So there can't be no question about us running off together or whatever he has in mind. I won't let him abandon my friend."

Therese was exasperated with her mother. "Your friend? You been sleeping with her husband. You gonna bear his child. How can you call her your friend?"

"It's one thing," Mathilde explained to her daughter in a voice the girl had never heard before, "to sleep with another woman's husband. But to steal away the father of her child, that's a sin won't be forgiven."

Therese nodded. She could see the truth of that.

"And Darryl, he didn't put up no argument. He looked, he had this look on his face, it was like a boy just found out his mama died. Halfway between tears and curses."

"So you sent him home?"

"I told him go home and see to his wife. See to the mother of his child. But he looked at me like he never done before and whispered, almost under his breath, he whispered, 'You the mother of my child. Always will be.' And that's how he left it."

"He never came again?"

"That was the last time Horse come by, the last time he visits me on the sneak. Except for church, I didn't see him after that till Little Darryl's christening party."

"And what you done, Mama, about your pregnancy?"

"Done? Why, I didn't do nothing. What could I do?"

Therese began to understand what she had resisted. "You don't mean . . ."

"That's what I'm telling you. I had your brother, Alton, eight months later."

"Alton was Horse's son? A Bruneau?"

"No, he wasn't no Bruneau. He was one of us. None of this we talking about changes who Alton was."

Therese didn't know what to say. "And Daddy . . ."

"Your daddy never guessed nothin'."

"How? How'd you keep him in the dark all these years?"

"How'd I keep you in the dark? People don't see what they not looking for."

"Still . . ."

Therese's unasked question embarrassed Mathilde. "That night, that same day I saw Darryl, I made sure Felix would think Alton was his, that's all. And a few weeks later when I told him I was pregnant, I didn't put up with no excuses. I said what with a baby on the way, it was time we had a decent house. When he said there was the boat to pay for and all, I was ready for him. Said it seemed to me we ought to be damn close to having that boat paid for. I was tired of that story. But I didn't want no new house anyway. I told him we should move into his father's house. That suited your daddy just fine. Keep an eye on Maw-Maw that way. Easier, too, with the *Mathilde* right there in Paw-Paw's slip on the bayou. Maw-Maw, she was tickled pink we was finally having a grandbaby for her. She moved upstairs into what's your room now. So that's how we come to live here."

"I can't believe Alton was Horse's son," Therese whispered, as if her sleeping father might overhear. Then something occurred to her. "What about me?"

Mathilde was offended. "You think there was any question, I would've let you almost marry Darryl?"

She had not thought of that. "No, 'course not."

"You your father's daughter. You doubt me, go look in the mirror. A little thing like you, who else would your daddy be?"

Therese relented. "And Alton never knew what was what."

"You think I was wrong not to say? Who wins, I tell the truth, huh?"

"How you live a lie like that all these years, Mama?" There was sympathy in the girl's voice.

Mathilde laughed. "Just look around, 'heart. Half the people in this town living some kind of lie. Ain't nothing out of the ordinary in that."

Therese was aware of the secret she herself carried. She wouldn't argue the point with her mother.

"You know the hardest part? Living in the same place as Darryl all these years. He never touched me again, not even to shake hands. You imagine what that's like? But he looked out for Alton and me, both. I think he was proud of the way Alton turned out."

"Then how come he was always at Daddy's throat?"

"Jealous, I guess. And he couldn't forgive Felix for being a Petitjean. It got worse over the years, too."

"I'm sorry, but he was a son of a bitch, Mama, the way he treated Daddy."

"Darryl had to scrap for everything he got. That makes a man mean, after a while," Mathilde explained, defending him. "He didn't have to help us, you know, giving us those two loans when nobody else would."

"Help us? Are you crazy, Mama? He just wanted our beds."

"Could've waited and picked them oysters up for a song when we lost them to the bank. That's why I went to see him about it all. After he told your father no deal."

"Some favor he does you. The crop don't come in this year, he winds up with everything—boat, house, and the Petitjean tracts, too, by the time he's done with us."

"Don't speak ill of the dead."

"Seems to me, Mama, you got on them rose-colored glasses when you talk about Horse."

"I'm not saying Darryl was a saint. He had his faults just like any man. He wasn't a good husband to Arlene."

Therese smirked. "That was plain enough."

"I mean afterward. Darryl seemed to blame Arlene for the way things had worked out, as if she was the one responsible somehow. He got worse with her. She would tell me about it. Especially when she got pregnant the next year with Ross. He got worse with her then. He got worse with everybody. But if you had seen him as a young man. He looked just like Little Darryl does now. Big, strong, handsome. And could he make you laugh. You wouldn't think a man like that could make you laugh so hard."

Therese remained unconvinced. "Nobody else knows about all this except for me?"

"With Darryl and Arlene gone, nobody else but you."

"Mrs. Bruneau found out?"

"Like I said, Arlene's second pregnancy seemed to set him off, Darryl. It was tough going then. Things were just starting to change, to go bad in the oyster fields. And Darryl was mixed up in something with two men here in the parish, too. There was this prosecutor sniffing around, though nothing ever came of it. But for a while, it looked like maybe there'd be a problem. So one night after Ross was born, Horse got drunk. Things weren't going well for their marriage, either. I think Arlene had already started drinking by then."

"I thought you two were like sisters."

"All right, Arlene was drinking pretty good by then. When I first knew her, it was candy. That girl loved candy more than anybody else I ever knew. Always had a piece of fudge or a candy cane on her some-where. But then—you know, Darryl left her alone at night too much, just her and a crying baby—so next thing you know, instead of candy it's gin she's always got nearby or whatever else Darryl keeps in the house."

Therese was shaking her head. "He drove her to it."

"I did my part, too."

"I didn't mean it that way, Mama. I meant like you said, leaving her alone all night."

"Well, this particular night Darryl had been out drinking more than usual, I guess. He come home and Arlene says something about me, about why can't he be like me, a friend to her—not even a husband, just a friend—and he laughs and tells her the whole story about him and this friend of hers. When it started, how it kept going, he tells her the whole story. And then he tells her the truth about Alton."

"He was a cruel man, Mama."

"She carried her babies over here the next morning, dragging Little Darryl by the hand and with Ross bundled up in a blanket of blue wool I knitted him myself when he was born. Arlene, she repeated every word between them from the night before. And then she asked me was it true. She didn't believe it, not for a minute, she said. Darryl would say anything to hurt her, she knew. But she had to ask me, to put her mind at rest. She was standing on the porch, wouldn't come in. She just had to know, she said."

"And you told her?"

"That girl, looking into those green eyes of hers, I don't know, I just couldn't lie to her."

"God, Mama."

"She never spoke to me again. Not to the day she killed herself all those years later."

"And that's what you meant, it's all your fault what happened?"

"I ought never have told her the truth, Arlene. That was the last thing she needed to hear. Who's the truth good for anyway but the guilty?"

"So why you told me the truth tonight, Mama?"

"You blame the Bruneau boys for what happened to Alton, don't you? But even if the Bruneaus had something to do with what happened, it didn't start with them. It started with me and their daddy. And what's it led to but Arlene a suicide, Darryl murdered, Alton in a damp grave, and me without my firstborn? If those boys done it, they struck down their own brother. And if you try to even the score—"

"How's a girl like me gonna even the score against them boys?" Therese interrupted.

"You think you fool me? I know what you got in mind. But you find some way to even the score, you ain't doing nothing but hurting your brother's brothers. You think on that for a while."

"Mama—"

"This is all on my head. You want to get even with somebody, you get even with me."

"It's not your fault, Mama. How can you say that? You just weary with all that's gone on."

Mathilde would not be comforted. "It's punishment for what I done. All of it. Arlene, Darryl, Alton—everything. Don't you go making it worse, baby. Let it rest, you hear?"

The two women looked up as Felix padded into the kitchen in his underwear. "What you girls doing up so early?"

Mathilde answered for them. "What you up for already, honey?"

"It's 4:30. Time to go to work."

Therese looked at the clock above the sink. "You can't take the boat out by yourself, Daddy. How you gonna manage the wheel and the dredge at the same time all by your lonesome?"

"I done it before."

"Maybe when you was thirty years old," Mathilde chided.

"We ain't got no choice. There's bills to be paid. We lost a lot of days this week already."

"You insist on taking the boat out, I'm going with you, then," the woman told her husband.

"No, Mama, you exhausted. You need your rest. I'm going with Daddy."

Her father laughed. "You? What you gonna do?"

"Learn to crew a boat, that's what."

Felix shook his head. "Don't be crazy, girl."

But her mother agreed. "She's right, Felix. Till you can hire a man, we got no choice. She can steer while you handle the baskets."

"I don't know." The old man hesitated.

"She's a strong girl. She'll do just fine out there."

Felix was still scowling at the idea.

"It's her or me," Mathilde continued. "Make up your mind. You ain't going out on that boat alone."

"He'll take me, Mama," Therese said firmly, getting up from the table. "I'll go get dressed. You make us some breakfast."

Felix, mumbling and shaking his head, retreated to his bedroom to get ready. Therese turned to her mother, who was taking eggs from the refrigerator, and whispered, "Don't you worry, Mama, not a word of what we talked about tonight will ever leave that table."

"I know that, 'heart. Just don't you forget what I said, neither."

Already the night birds had grown still in the trees along the bayou, and the first light of dawn smudged the eastern sky over the marsh.

Three

18.

There was enough light to see the slight wake of the *Mathilde* as Therese checked the trawl boards and other gear in the stern after they had fueled the tank and picked up a load of ice for the hold. The boat was settled deep in the water, its engine barely turning, slowly making its way back out to the channel. To keep from eroding the banks of the canal with his wash, Felix did not rush to catch the tide.

Therese could hear the mosquitoes still humming above the mudflats in trembling brown clouds. The whine of locusts, like a motor ratcheting against its casing, revved from a low octave into a higher pitch, then plunged down the scale suddenly, as if a switch had been tripped. Already two squawking gulls were trailing the boat, eager for chum.

The girl smiled to see a muskrat at water's edge nervously back into the tall wire grass when the ripples of the wake surged over its paws. Among all the voices of the marsh, Therese had always found that the sweetest sound was the water itself, churned by the prop, splayed by the bow, shredded by the grille of reeds rising in the shallows. She even liked the sound of it at home, of water sloshing in a bottle, of dew dripping from the eaves after a humid night, of rain splattering against a window, of the tap plinking drop after drop into the still bath she had drawn.

Felix, too, was glad to be making a run on the boat. It was like taking a breath—that's how it always felt to the old man at the wheel, like a body lifting to its full height as it inhaled all the air it could squeeze into its lungs—when he throttled up as the Mathilde entered the channel and headed for open water. Now the boat rose on its stern, skimming across the flat water. The spin of its engine drowned out even the gulls complaining overhead.

Nobody else was on the water yet, so Felix let the boat run. He had to strain to see over the bow from the wheelhouse. It was like getting carried around on your daddy's back when the boat stood up on its tail, stretching to look around the old man's head at what was coming. He still remembered that, his daddy hauling him around that way, his arms locked around the man's throat, his cheek against a shoulder hard as a knob of cypress. How many years ago must that have been, he tried to figure.

It made him think of carrying Alton on his own back, the time the bayou rose when a hurricane came through one year. You had to step carefully in the murky water, a child on your back, your wife with the baby in her arms hanging on to your belt not to fall in the storm, and the rain lashing you across the face like a nine-tailed whip.

But they had survived the hurricane and everything else, his little family, had come through the scarlet fever, the dog bite in August, the rusty nail in the leg. "You outswum the sharks this time, boy," that was how his daddy had always put it after a close call. Only this morning, the wet breeze running down the windows of the wheelhouse like rain, the sun half risen on the horizon like a bloody egg in a nest, did Felix understand the "this time" for what his father had meant by it.

The old man looked over his shoulder at his daughter. Therese was sorting the nets in case her father decided to drop them for shrimp on the way in that afternoon. He sensed the sharks were still in the water, but he knew that's where the oysters were, too.

The girl turned over a wire measuring basket as a seat. "How much this hold, Daddy?" she shouted over the engine, but the wind carried her voice aft across the transom and into the spindrift of the wake. She went forward to where her father stood at the wheel, tapping his shoulder to get his attention.

Inside the three walls of the cabin, it was easier to talk. "What you need, babe?" Felix asked.

"How much one of them hold, that shrimp basket back there?" She pointed to where she had been sitting.

"Ain't no basket. It's a champagne, holds a third of a barrel. Seventy pounds of shrimp," he shouted back. He kept going with the lesson. "See that stack back there by the floats?"

"Yes sir."

"Those are baskets. Four baskets, that's the same as three champagnes."

"So four baskets to a barrel?" Therese calculated.

"That's right. Each basket's fifty-two and a half pounds of shrimp." Felix checked the stern, looking for boats overtaking him. They were still alone. "You ought to write this down," he suggested. "There's a lot to know."

"No, I got it," she assured him. "You got 210 pounds to the barrel, and that's three champagnes or four baskets."

"You quick, girl. Alton, he used to write it all down, things worth knowing."

Therese nodded. "I seen his notebook." It was the first time on the boat that morning either one of them had mentioned Alton. "I can't believe he's gone," Therese said softly, but her father did not seem to hear her over the engine.

A half hour later, Felix eased the throttle down and shifted into neutral. "Maybe we make a short day of it, huh? I don't want to leave your mama alone too long."

"She'll be asleep for a while, Daddy."

"Let's just see we can't find some oysters right here in Bay Batiste. You know how it all works?"

"Some," Therese shrugged.

"You seen our lease sign over there when we come round the point, didn't you?"

"The white sign with the numbers stuck out on that pole in the shallows."

"That's right. We got three hundred acres here."

"With a lease this big," Therese wondered, "how you know where you planted your oyster beds? From up here, it ain't nothing but water all the way to the shoreline."

Felix chuckled. "We sitting on top of one of our reefs this very minute."

"How you know? You mark it somehow?"

"Not unless you want some other fella come along in his lugger one night and steal you blind." Felix opened a locker in the cabin and pulled out a chart. He slipped off the rubber band and smoothed the map with his leathery hands on top of the plywood engine housing. "See the point behind us, that's right here." He laid a straightedge on top of the little peninsula noted on the chart. "Now here's where we are." He indicated the spot with his finger and pivoted the ruler until it stretched across the two points.

Therese interrupted him. "But how you know that's where we are? It all looks the same out here."

"No, it don't." Felix laughed.

The girl shook her head.

"See that cove?" He lifted his arm and pointed to the shoreline.

"Where? That little break in the marsh grass?"

"Right off our beam. Now look near the bow. At one o'clock."

Therese saw nothing.

"The tree," her father hinted.

"What tree?"

"There. Look."

The girl stopped fighting the rocking of the boat, letting it lift her. Waiting to focus her eyes until the boat paused at the top of the swell, she suddenly saw something different from the long swords of grass that edged the bay. "That's a tree?"

"A dead one."

Therese looked down at the chart again. She found the fingernail curve of the shoreline due east of their position. "But where's the tree?"

"Over there," her father smiled, pointing off the bow.

"No, I mean on the chart."

"Ain't on the chart. But when you here, it's at one o'clock. See? There it is, and here we are."

"How come you need the tree to know where you are? You got the cove and the point."

He took a mechanical pencil from his shirt pocket and laid it down on the chart between the cove and the *Mathilde*'s position. "You see the problem?"

In answer, Therese fixed her thumb above the peninsula outlined on the chart and slid the ruler back and forth along the pencil like a wind-shield wiper. "It tells you how far off the cove you need to be, right? If the tree ain't at one o'clock, you too close to shore or too far away."

"You some smart, girl." Felix stowed the chart. "Now let's go catch some oysters."

The man, as surefooted on water as on dry land, hopped up onto the port deck. Kicking the block in front of the winch to make sure its cable wasn't kinked, he wrestled the dredge to the side of the boat. The teeth on the five-foot metal frame scraped the steel protection plate bolted to the deck as he maneuvered the device into position. Felix checked the four lengths of chain that joined the frame's corners to the cable and shook the heavy netting attached to the back of the dredge that would catch the oysters scooped from the bottom.

"Give me some slack, baby."

Therese was standing at the wheel, watching her father. She reached over to the handle on the winch, unlatched the brake, and let out a few feet of cable before popping it back into neutral.

"That'll do." Felix eased the dredge over the side. "Give me another six feet."

The girl leaned on the shift lever, and the frame and its netting slipped into the water.

"Hold on for a minute," Felix called out. She stopped the winch while he muscled the dredge's cable over the roller on the edge of the deck. "OK, let her go."

Therese let the cable unspool, the drive chain running from the engine to the winch clicking as it engaged.

Felix was at the wheel again, shifting back into gear and urging the throttle just a bit above idle. "Here, Terry, you take over," he called. "Swing her in a lazy circle. Use that far inlet to keep your bearings."

The girl took the wheel. "Like that?" she asked after a minute.

"You got it. Now let's pick up the speed just a touch." The boat lifted slightly. "Yeah, that's good."

While Felix readied the dredge on the starboard side, Therese followed a long arc with the boat. She liked it at the helm of the *Mathilde*, the hot breeze—sharp with the tang of salt—washing through the cabin with its windows swung down on their hinges. She liked all of it, the rocking of the deck as the boat sidled between gentle swells out of the southwest, the swish of the bilge as she rode the troughs, the thump of water against wood, all of it lulling her, soothing the pricks of memory.

She could hear her father working in the hold, shoveling chunks of ice into one of the compartments. She looked over her shoulder and saw him spread a canvas tarp over the bed of ice he had made.

"Let's see we got anything," he shouted to the girl.

She throttled back and shifted into neutral. Her father engaged the winch. The steady whine of the cable wrapping around its bobbin deepened with strain as the dredge, heavy with oysters, came free of the bottom beneath the boat and was lifted straight up the twenty feet to the surface. When the links of chain, joining the cable to the metal frame of the dredge, clanked against the roller on the deck, Felix flipped the handle of the winch into neutral. The whole rig was slimy with black seaweed and dripping muddy gobs of water as it dangled just above the surface of the chop. "Put her into gear, and we'll let the wake from the bow wash these off," he told the girl.

When she shifted back into neutral after rinsing the catch, Therese was distressed to watch the old man try to muscle the oyster dredge aboard, sliding it over the roller. *He must be used to Alton pulling it up*, she thought.

"Let me give you a hand, Daddy," she offered.

It troubled her even more that he did not attempt to refuse her help. The load of frothing shells chafed against one another with each tug of the netting. Finally, twisting the frame onto its side, the two of them managed to drag the dredge over the roller and onto the protection plate.

"Shall we empty it?" Therese asked.

"First we drop the other dredge over the side and get under way again. Then we see what we got in this one."

So the morning was spent, alternating from port to starboard, emptying one oyster dredge while dragging the heat-forged teeth of the other through the thick muck of the bay bottom.

Each haul brought up clumps of shells that Felix split into singles with a culling hammer for the sacks of "selects" the buyer preferred. Spats, baby oysters that had anchored themselves to mature shells, had to be scraped free and washed overboard back to the bed. Crabs scrabbled across the deck, menacing every obstruction with barbed claws. Broken shells, too, the aggregate Felix had dropped year after year to stabilize the muddy bottom into a firm reef, were littered about his feet.

With nothing before her but gray water bounded by wetlands as she piloted the *Mathilde* along the slow circles her father ordered, Therese sorted through the stories her mother had spent the night telling her. She had never imagined that one of her parents might have lived a life of such passion, might have risked so much on . . . what? She couldn't dignify Horse's feelings for her mother as love. Maybe the woman, in confessing to Therese, had used the word in talking about the father of her son, but there were simpler ways to understand what had happened between them.

Yes, maybe Mathilde and Darryl weren't teenagers when it had happened, but Therese would not accept the notion—it pained her even to think it—that Horse had been the great love of her mother's life, that her mother had been the object of Horse's devotion. It was ridiculous. And yet, the more she derided the idea, the more it cast a light over her mother and even over Horse that explained things in them both she had never thought to question. Her mother's restraint around her father, the way the woman ladled out caresses to Felix like half helpings of gumbo from a nearly empty kettle—Therese had always thought it mere modesty in front of others. The mean streak in Horse, having it in for her father all the time, that made sense, too, if he was a man living in the same town as the woman he loved and could never have again. Even worse, she realized, he had to watch another man raise the son he had fathered on that woman, and not just another man but his rival in love and in work.

Therese remembered asking Horse, that night in the pirogue, "Why you want me?" She began to understand how many answers there were to that question.

19.

When Matthew Christovich stopped by to see Mathilde just before lunch, Felix and Therese were still dredging oysters on Bay Batiste.

Matthew's knock had wakened the woman, asleep on the sofa. Rinsing the breakfast dishes after her husband and her daughter had gone out to the boat, she had taken her coffee into the parlor to finish. The next thing she knew, a pounding on the front door had startled her awake. The bright sunlight confused her. *What time is it?* she wondered, sitting up. She heard her name called from the porch.

Matthew greeted her through the screen door.

"I'm sorry, Sheriff. I fell asleep." She held open the door for him. "Terry and I were up all night talking."

"She upstairs?" he inquired, looking toward her room.

"No, Felix took her with him on the boat. He needed to make a run, but there's no way he can handle the leases by himself, Matthew, no way."

"I can't tell you how sorry I am, Mathilde, about Alton." Then he remembered to add, "Me and Candy both."

"I know, Matthew. Thank you. Yesterday, everybody, they all said the same thing. He was such a sweet boy. You could tell just to look at him, couldn't you, that he was a sweet boy?"

"He was a good boy." Matthew nodded grimly. "Never heard anybody say different, not once."

Mathilde sighed, and the man could see her eyes, her gray eyes, welling with tears.

He tried to distract her. "Candy wanted to be here yesterday. She was afraid to come, though, by herself. Particularly in the rain."

The woman took a deep breath and turned her face to his. "How's she doing, Matthew? Things going any better with her?"

He looked away. "I don't know, Mathilde. Ever since the operation, she seems to be going downhill."

"What do the doctors say?"

"I took her to the Touro Infirmary in New Orleans last month, but they don't know nothing. One says one thing; the other, something else. You don't know who to believe."

"But I thought they said the operation was a success."

"Yeah, that's what they said then. But now it's a different story. The operation, now they say it was only meant to slow things down. Now they say there's only so much they can do in cases like this."

"I didn't know, Matthew."

"Neither did we. We just finding out little by little ourselves. They a pack of liars, every one of them. They don't know what the hell is going on with her. I tell you, might just as well go see Marie Deux-Chiens up on the Hermitage and buy one of her potions for all the good these doctors do."

Mathilde laughed. "Mary Two-Dogs? She still alive? I haven't heard that name in twenty years."

"Oh, yeah, she's still got her place over on the river. I thought she was about as old as a human being could get back when we were in high school. But I seen her a year ago. A fisherman found a man's body over that way, been in the water for a while. Nobody knew who it was. So me and Huey Hebert, the sheriff up in Magnolia, we take a flatboat from the Hermitage launch and follow the river to Lake Laurier to check it all out, see what we can find. The sun had just come up, and everything was still wet, you know, with the chill of the night. There was this little blanket of fog, maybe a foot or eighteen inches of it, lying right on the water, caught between the two banks. It was just the way a river would look if it was made of nothing but clouds. And everything muffled by it, quiet. You could barely hear the outboard, we were going so slow, since we couldn't see the water ten feet ahead of us under the fog. Then we come around a bend, and there's her place."

"The old cabin?"

"Just like you remember it—old barge boards nailed like planks to oak trees for the walls, rusted sheets of corrugated tin overhanging everything for a roof, muskrat and nutria pelts stitched together for a door."

"She still got the dogs?"

"Yeah, must have been a pack of ten or twelve of them, mean-looking curs, too. Everywhere you turn, there's one rooting around the bank or rushing out of the woods, barking and growling."

"That time we went, I was so scared of the dogs."

"I don't mind telling you now, so was I. Vicious animals, she kept."

"So did you see her, old Mary?"

"We saw her all right. The dogs must have woke her up, 'cause just as we passing in the boat, floating down this river of clouds, a gnarled black hand pushes aside the pelts over the door and out she comes."

Mathilde was like a girl listening to a ghost story. "What did she look like?"

"Same as you remember, only worse."

"She still wearing the bones?"

"All around her throat like some kind of necklace. And she's got this shawl of furs around her shoulders that's decorated with chicken claws and feathers from crows and I don't know what else."

"She say anything?"

"No, she come down to the water's edge—the fog's edge, really—and she hikes up her skirt and, well, she pees right there in front of us."

"Oh, don't tell me."

"Right there in front of me and Huey, and both of us sheriffs. 'Course that don't stop her."

Mathilde smiled. "Probably why she done it."

"Or maybe she's just too old to care anymore. That's what she does when she wakes up, and it don't make no matter to her whether there's somebody passing by in a boat or no."

"I'm starting to feel like that myself."

Matthew gave her a sidelong look. "You ain't no old woman, Mathilde. Not by a long shot."

She ignored his compliment. "I can't believe Mary Two-Dogs is still alive. After all these years."

"She's alive all right. But so old. Her hair's white now, not even gray. God knows what she's got living up there in it, too. It ain't never felt a comb or a brush, I promise you. Not in the last hundred years or so, at least."

"I can't believe we went to see her, you and me."

"We were young, Mathilde."

"And who else could we turn to for help like that, huh? Especially around here back in those days."

Matthew laughed. "Yeah, we couldn't exactly ask your grandmother."

"Mémère, she probably was the one person knew what to do."

"She was something, all right, your grandmother."

Mathilde's smile faded. "You ever sorry, Matthew, old Mary didn't have what we was looking for?"

"Maybe we were lucky, you and me."

"Lucky? How's that?"

"I always thought Marie, she liked it, these two kids crazy in love with each other showing up in a boat on her riverbank one morning when they supposed to be in school. I think maybe she did give us what we were looking for. We just didn't know what it was we wanted."

Mathilde was nodding. "It was kind of a relief, I guess. I was glad we tried—it made me proud of us. But, yeah, maybe old Mary, maybe she wasn't so crazy as she wanted you to think."

"It just seemed to me afterward, when we started back up the river to where I'd left the truck, I don't know about you, but I was happy. Not that I would have admitted it at the time, but I don't think I've ever been any happier than I was that morning, after she shook that gray head of hers *no, no, no* at us. I still remember you in the bow of that little boat smiling back at me—you were happy, too."

"She did talk sense to us, didn't she? If you don't count that poultice for a jealous heart she made you buy."

Matthew sighed. "I got my money's worth. Before we were done, I had plenty use out of it."

"I'm sorry," the woman whispered. She put her hand on his. "I wish it could have been different."

"I don't know. I wonder if the whole thing wasn't like our visit to Mary Two-Dogs. Maybe it's just better, sometimes, for things not to work out the way you want them to."

Mathilde lifted her hand and returned it to her lap. "You mean you have no regrets, Matthew?"

"Regrets? Oh, yeah, *chère,* more than you know. But I couldn't have taken care of you back then. And what would have happened to us? No job, no money, no house. We wouldn't be sitting here right now, I'll tell you that."

"You probably right, Matthew. I wouldn't have thought so back then, I know. But you probably right. Maybe Mémère, she knew what she was doing, eh?"

Matthew laughed. "Oh, she knew what she was doing all right. But I don't think what she was after is what we talking about."

Mathilde laughed, too. "I'm glad you come by today. It done me good to see you, think about something else for a while."

"The past, it's like quicksand. Swallow you up you don't watch where you step."

"Everybody says that, Matthew, says I got to be brave and get on with my life. But you, you never been a parent. Lot's wife, the one God turned to a pillar of salt in the Bible, she must've been someone's mama. That's why she looked back when they fled Sodom. Once you a mother, you spend the rest of your life looking over your shoulder."

"Nobody expects you to forget Alton."

"That's what it feels like, they say you got to be strong and get over this. What kind of woman gets over her son?"

"People just trying to help, Mathilde."

"I know. They think they being kind, saying that."

Matthew tried to change the subject. "Y'all gonna manage?"

"We was just getting by. Now I don't know. You heard, I guess, about the loans we took from Darryl, God rest his soul."

"Heard he held the papers on your boat."

"House, too, after last season."

"Jesus, Mathilde."

"We got a big payout comin' end of the year—everything we still owe. Maybe Little Darryl will give us some grace on the loans, with what's happened and all."

"I wouldn't count on it. He's a lot like his daddy, especially when it comes to money."

"Well, we'll see how Therese does out there today. Won't be easy, but then, we ain't got no choice."

"Let me see I can't find you someone to give Felix a hand, at least for a while."

"Matthew, you got problems of your own to deal with."

"Me and Candy, we'll be OK. But let me see what I can do for you. Everybody in town feels for y'all. Somebody'll want to help."

Mathilde got up and walked the sheriff to the door. "Just don't let Felix know it's a favor, if that's what you got in mind. Alton hit him real hard. He don't show nothing, but he been hurt bad."

"I know. If I find someone, I'll make sure it gets done right."

He hesitated just inside the screen door. Mathilde lifted herself on her toes and kissed his cheek. "I'm glad," she whispered, "even after all these years we still understand each other."

As Matthew slowly followed the gravel road in his car back to the highway from the Petitjeans' house, he looked over to where he had found the boy dead in the bayou. He knew the body had been dragged there and dumped in the water. He looked out his own window as he passed the turnaround in which he was fairly certain some kind of vehicle, probably a pickup truck, had waited for Alton to come home the night of the murder.

The sheriff stopped and backed into the graveled recess cut into the line of cypresses and pines that edged the road. He kept backing up until he heard the branches of scrub bushes scratching the trunk of his police cruiser. Then he got out of the car and walked a few yards toward the highway. Even in full daylight, he could make out nothing of the parked vehicle. At night, with its lights off, a pickup would have been invisible hunkered back in the turnaround. Alton could've driven right past it and never seen the truck waiting there for him to get home.

The sheriff knew from Therese that Sherilee hadn't driven the boy all the way to the house. So walking home down the dark road after midnight, he would have been all alone. Matthew reached up and ran his fingers through the thick foliage of the overhanging trees. From where he was standing, the house was not visible through the heavy vegetation, already rusting with the coming autumn. Any sounds of a struggle would have been muffled, dying in the buffer of dense leaves and pine needles. He looked in the other direction. The highway, too, was out of sight behind the bends of the road. And who would have been out on this stretch of highway at one o'clock in the morning?

Water from all the rain they'd been having the last week still gullied in the ruts worn into the road. Whatever traces of the murder—a magnolia leaf splattered with blood, hair snagged in the bark of a branch used to club a man to the ground, tire tracks in mud—whatever remained afterward had been washed away under the steady downpour that night or in the slow currents of the bayou.

The sheriff got back in his car and pulled out of the turnaround. He noticed the wide arc he had to follow to avoid the low branches of the cypress on his left. He remembered the swerve of tracks, filled with rainwater, he had seen at that same spot the morning he found Alton's body.

Next to him on the seat of his car was the autopsy report he had picked up at the office with the morning's mail. There were a few details the coroner had omitted in a phone call two days ago with the basic findings, all confirming what the sheriff had already guessed. But the new details didn't change anything important. The victim had died of a fractured skull, though he would have eventually died of a stab wound anyway. He was dead before the body was dumped in the bayou. Whoever did it was lucky they had thrown the corpse in the water: the coroner couldn't fix the time of death with any accuracy, and if there was any evidence under the fingernails or elsewhere on the body, the bayou and the rain had scrubbed it all away.

As Matthew paused at the lip of the highway, waiting for a tanker to rumble past, he added up what he knew.

Alton had been stabbed and clubbed. The club killed the boy, so he must have been stabbed first. Why would someone with a knife then use a second weapon? The sheriff remembered the most important lesson he had learned as a deputy: the simplest explanation, that's what happened. The one with the knife wouldn't use a club. He must have had an accomplice.

Alton was big, strong, and smart. He wouldn't be easy to bring down, especially not so close to home. The murderers needed a plan.

Whoever killed Alton, they were lying in wait. And they knew about Sherilee, it occurred to the sheriff, so they weren't strangers. They had a plan, and it worked.

These murderers, they must have been big and strong, too, to drag the body to the bayou.

They had a car or a truck, whoever it was.

They had a motive.

Anyway you cut it, Matthew concluded, suddenly realizing the truck had passed and he was still sitting at the intersection of the road and the highway, *it comes up Bruneau*.

But as he pulled onto the asphalt and headed toward town, the sheriff also recognized he didn't have the first piece of physical evidence or the slightest hope of turning any up. He could ask around about who might have known that Sherilee didn't drive Alton all the way home, but a story like that—only a boy as gentle as Alton would have let a girl get away with it—a story like that was too good not to have made its way all over town.

What I need is a witness, he thought, then added, *a witness willing to talk*.

As he followed the highway past Mathilde's first house, still nestled beside the canal, it occurred to the sheriff who that witness might be.

Now he was the one with a plan.

Kill two birds with one stone. He smiled to himself, thinking about it. And suddenly he was laughing out loud.

20.

Matthew wasn't wearing his uniform when he caught up with Little Horse that night at R&J's.

"You gone undercover, Sheriff?"

"Off duty, Darryl."

"Wouldn't hardly recognize you. Look almost like a human being dressed this way."

"Well, you wouldn't want to mistake me for one of them, now would you?"

"No sir. You a wolf in sheep's clothing tonight."

"Where's your brothers?"

"Ross, he's off with Yvonne LeBlanc."

Matthew raised an eyebrow in surprise. "Ross got himself a girlfriend?"

"Hell, somebody married you."

"And your baby brother?"

"Don't know where the fuck he is, little asshole. Had to cook my own damn dinner tonight."

The man laughed. "You the one need a wife, Darryl."

"Shit, find me a girl with some money, I'll let you know."

The sheriff shifted his weight to the other leg. "You mind if I sit a minute?"

"No law against it far as I know." Little Horse took a long swig of his beer. " 'Course, I guess you'd be the one to tell me if there was a law against it, wouldn't you?"

"Suppose so." Matthew took a seat at the table. "You go for another Dixie?"

Little Horse eyed the sheriff suspiciously. "Long as you paying."

"Hey, Ronnie," the man called, turning in his chair toward the bar, "let me have two beers over here."

The two men sat in silence, waiting until the bartender had brought their drinks.

"So what you doing here, Mr. Christovich?" The boy carefully measured an insult. "Looking for a little female companionship maybe?"

Matthew would not be pushed. "Like you said, Darryl, I'm a married man."

Little Horse sipped his fresh beer. He decided to push harder. "To hear people talk, that never stopped you before, having a wife at home. How she doing, anyway? Hear she been sick. Guess it wears a man down."

"You just keep talking, boy. I ain't wearing a badge tonight."

"Got nothing to protect you, huh?"

"And I always thought that badge was the only thing kept me from beating the crap out of you."

"So you get all dressed up just to pick a fight with me? Could've done that in your underwear if that's all you want."

"Fight? I'm here to do you a favor, son."

"You do a Bruneau a favor? That'll be the fuckin' day."

"First time for everything, Little Horse."

The boy cocked his head. "What kind of favor?"

"People know you and your brothers hold the papers on the Petitjean place."

Darryl smiled. "Yeah, and on their boat, too."

"Well, people got ideas you boys mixed up somehow in Alton's murder. You know how they talk, people."

Darryl started to object, but the sheriff interrupted him. "Ain't saying I agree with them. I mean, you didn't do it, did you?"

"I thought we decided it was some mass murderer on the loose."

"Yeah, that's my theory, too. But the way you threatened Alton at your daddy's funeral—you know, what you told Mrs. Petitjean about her son—all those ladies heard that, Darryl, heard what you had to say. Then the boy turns up dead in his own bayou. Makes people think."

"Where you going with this?"

Matthew took a slow sip of beer, put the bottle down on the table, leaned toward the boy, and continued nearly in a whisper. "Thing is, when people put two and two together, the threat and the murder and you boys holding the papers on the Petitjeans' house and boat and poor old Felix trying to work his beds without a son to help him, well, it all adds up, don't it?"

"Adds up? How's that?"

"I mean, all of a sudden, we got ourselves a motive stands up in court."

"The fuck you talkin' about?"

"Money, Little Horse. Why you think people kill one another?"

"You saying I killed that son of a bitch to get his house and boat?"

"I ain't saying nothing, not me. It's people, they the ones pointing the finger."

"My family helps out another family in hard times with a couple of loans, and that makes us a bunch of murderers?"

"That ain't quite how people see it, Little Horse. They know an old man like Felix Petitjean can't make a go of his oyster fields by himself. And they also know if he don't, you and your brothers get everything he owns. A sweet deal, that's what people are calling it."

"Alton gets himself murdered, and it's all because of a couple god-damn loans."

"Like I say, me, I'd go with the mass murderer theory. But the rest of the people down here—hell, a lot of folks in this barroom right this very minute—they take a look at you Bruneau boys, it sort of makes sense to them."

"I can't fuckin' believe—"

"But I got an idea, Little Horse. That's the favor I was talking about."

The sheriff took another swig of beer. "Something that'll prove you ain't trying to ruin the Petitjeans."

"I ain't trying to ruin the Petitjeans. I don't give a fuck about those people."

"I know you don't, Darryl. That's what I been telling everybody. But you know how people around here felt about Alton."

"Felt about Alton? That motherfucker killed my daddy."

"We'll never know, now he's gone. But it won't matter. Not if you do like I say."

Little Horse was shaking his head. "So what's this idea you got?"

"I was thinking, it don't take three of you to work your beds. You and Ross could handle them easy enough by yourselves. So wouldn't cost you nothing you lend the Petitjeans Rusty to crew their boat till they get on their feet again and figure what they gonna do with Alton gone."

"Lend them Rusty?"

"Think about it, Little Horse, how it would look. Everybody sure you boys killed Alton so the Petitjeans can't make their notes and you wind up with the house and boat. But then you turn around and one of you volunteers to take Alton's place on the water, help out this family in need. You and your brothers would be saints to the people around here. Shit, they might put up a stained-glass window in St. Martin's to the Bruneaus."

Darryl smiled at the idea of a window in the church. "That'd shut them up, all right."

"All you got to do is send Rusty around to the Petitjean place tomorrow, let him offer to lend a hand. I talked to Alton's mama this morning. They desperate, those folks. And you can tell people y'all just want to make peace between the two families, say it's time for the Bruneaus and the Petitjeans to forgive and forget."

Little Horse was smiling slyly. "That's right. It's the Christian thing to do."

Matthew emptied his beer and stood up. "Told you I was here to do you a favor."

Darryl grabbed his arm and looked him in the face. "How come, Sheriff? How come you do us a favor?"

"Like I said, Little Horse, I think people are wrong. I don't think you killed that boy for the loans. I think the reason he died has nothing to do with money. And my job, it's to make sure justice gets done, that's all. For the Bruneaus and the Petitjeans both."

"You a real hero, Sheriff."

"You send your baby brother over to see Felix tomorrow, you the one gonna be the hero."

Darryl watched Christovich walk out the bar. He could not tell the sheriff was smiling.

"Let me have another one, Ronnie," the boy shouted at the little man pouring drinks.

When Ross swaggered in an hour later, pushing through the gauntlet of young men teasing him about where he had been all night, Darryl talked over the sheriff's idea with him.

"It makes sense, what he said. Except for tonging oysters in the shallows, what do we need Rusty for anyway?"

"I already told you, Little Horse, you and me, we don't need that asshole for nothing."

"Well, 'less you want to rake oysters from a skiff yourself, we can take him with us once a week out to Wilkinson Bay. The rest of the time, let him crew for old man Petitjean."

"Fine by me."

The two brothers drank for a while, listening to the songs on the jukebox complaining of fickle love.

Darryl was still thinking about the sheriff's suggestion. "Daddy knew what he was doing, taking those loans. Ain't no way the Petitjeans gonna make good on those notes."

"I don't know, Little Horse. Mr. Petitjean, he knows a shitload about oysters. And those beds of his in Bay Sansbois . . ." Ross whistled. "They fuckin' gold mines, them beds."

Darryl nodded. "Yeah, you right. And all those old fields he got hidden away up in the middle of nowhere—shit, I'd like to get my hands on them, too."

"Yes, indeed."

"Maybe we ought to do more than just stick Rusty on the *Mathilde*."

"What you mean, Little Horse?"

"Maybe we ought to protect our investment."

Ross was having a hard time following his brother. "How we do that?"

"Maybe Rusty don't just crew. Maybe we give him instructions of our own."

Ross still didn't get it. "Instructions?"

"We put Rusty on their boat, we got a spy in their midst, don't we? Rusty can keep an eye on them."

"You mean the sheriff tells them something about his investigation, we hear it from Rusty."

"That's right. But more than that. They start to turn the corner with money, Rusty slows them down."

"Yeah," Ross agreed, excited. "Mr. Petitjean's an old man. What's he gonna say Rusty drops a load of oysters overboard or forgets to tie off the shark net when they go shrimping?"

"There's a million ways to screw them out on the water. We could be absolutely sure they don't make their notes. And the whole time, everybody thinks we trying to save 'em."

"Yeah, I like it," Ross smiled. "I like it a lot."

"Shit, Rusty ain't no use to us anyway. This way, we can't lose."

"I tell you what, though. After what he done me, I get that son of a bitch alone . . ." Ross didn't have to finish the sentence.

"Yeah, well, that's another reason to put him on the *Mathilde*. Keep you two apart." Darryl took a swallow of his beer. "Just don't touch him till we get that boat and house. They ain't got a boat, they can't dredge their leases."

Ross grasped his brother's scheme. "We sell their house and we buy up those leases cheap."

"Maybe we sell our house and move in theirs."

"Daddy would have liked that, us living in the Petitjean house."

Darryl smiled. "And Daddy would have liked Sheriff Christovich being the one who shows us how to do it. Never did care for that bastard."

The two brothers got in the Cadillac and drove back to their house. They could see the lights were on inside when they pulled up. As Darryl had hoped, Rusty had come home.

"Listen, Ross, you let me do the talking. I don't want no shit out of you about what happened the other night. You let me deal with this little asshole."

"All right, I'll do like you say. But he starts anything—"

"He's not starting anything. He's come home 'cause he ain't got no place else to go. He won't be looking for trouble."

When they walked in, Rusty was asleep on the sofa. Darryl shook him awake. He jerked upright, ready for a fight.

"Hold on, little brother, it's just us."

Rusty was on his guard.

"You take it easy," Darryl said, calming him. "Ross and me talked after you took off. That threw you, what happened to Alton. I can understand how you felt. Ross, too."

"I didn't know you was gonna kill him," Rusty protested.

"Nothing none of us can do about that now. All we can do is stick together. We all equal guilty. They get one of us, we all go down. We a family. We got to act like one."

Darryl had his hand on Rusty's shoulder. He could feel the muscles start to relax.

"I just didn't know—"

Ross cut him off. "What's done is done."

Darryl gave Ross a frown. Rusty didn't see Ross shrug an apology to his older brother.

"We been thinking," the eldest Bruneau continued, "maybe we owe it to the Petitjeans to give them a hand—"

"Since it's our responsibility and all, what happened," Ross interrupted.

Again Darryl signaled Ross to be quiet.

"What Ross means is, Mr. Petitjean's gonna have a hard time dredging his oysters without Alton. We thought, me and Ross handle the *Squall* by ourselves for a few weeks, you could help out on the *Mathilde*. Give those folks a chance to get back on their feet. What you say to that?"

Rusty had been nodding as Darryl sketched out the plan. "Yeah, I think it's only right we give them a hand."

"Why don't you go by there tomorrow afternoon, tell 'em me and Ross gonna work the *Squall* alone so you can crew for Mr. Petitjean. Call it a gesture of goodwill."

"And that's not all you can do when you with them," Ross broke in. "Tell him, Little Horse, tell him the rest."

Darryl looked like he was ready to hit Ross.

"What rest?" Rusty wanted to know.

"Ross, he don't know what he's talking about. He means you can help out with the shrimping, rake their shallow beds with tongs—you know, everything you do with us."

"I'll go tomorrow," Rusty promised.

"Good, now you go get some sleep. I need to work out with Ross how we gonna handle our leases with just the two of us. We may need you once a week or so to go out to Wilkinson Bay, but I'm sure the Petitjeans will spare you."

After Rusty had gone to bed, Darryl explained to Ross why they hadn't told Rusty the rest of their plan. "Let's get him on the boat first. He hear the whole story, he'll never do it. But don't you worry. Once he's there, he'll do what we want."

"And if he says no?"

"We won't give him the choice. He'll do what we want, all right."

Ross started to laugh, but Darryl silenced him with a finger to the lips.

21.

Therese was on the bow of the *Mathilde* as Felix swung the boat into its slip the next evening. They had gone out at dawn, dredged some of their beds in Bay Ronquille, then dropped their shrimp nets on the way in but had little luck. It was only the second day of the girl crewing the boat, but already Felix was learning how much he had depended upon Alton.

Therese, too, had not known how much raw muscle fishing required. Strong as she was, she was exhausted after two days on the water. And she was shocked when they off-loaded at the buyer's dock by just how small a catch they had taken compared to the hauls of other boats. She was a girl not much given to crying, but the anger and frustration brought her to the point of tears as the buyer paid out a tiny sum to her father for ten hours of backbreaking work.

Her pride kept her eyes dry. The other oystermen and shrimpers were having beers on the dock, waiting their turn to sell what they had dredged up or netted. They offered their sympathy about Alton, every one of them, but Therese could see in their eyes the jokes they would tell as soon as she was gone about a little girl like her trying to do a man's work.

Neither she nor her father had brought up the problem of the shallow-water reefs. It was already clear to Therese after just two days of watching her father on the boat that he could not handle a pair of eight-foot tongs standing in a flatboat. Maybe he knew enough tricks to manage the *Mathilde*, but tonging would kill the old man.

Felix, of course, was even more aware of how much trouble they were in. He had taken Therese out to the easiest leases to dredge. But even those fields had presented problems the two of them had barely managed. And hard as the work had been for father and daughter, he knew they couldn't make a living on those beds alone.

Mathilde saw them from the porch as the boat glided down the bayou. She watched her husband swing the stern toward the far bank and nose into the slip. He had a gentle hand with a boat. It was something she had always admired.

Putting down the potatoes she was peeling, the woman walked to the dock.

"How y'all do?"

Felix was latching the windows in the wheelhouse. He pulled one back open and leaned his head through. "We did OK. No great shakes, but Therese, she's learning."

When Mathilde turned to her daughter, though, the look on the girl's face made clear Felix was exaggerating their success. Still, Therese called out from the stern where she was hosing down the walls of the hold, "Yeah, a pretty good run. We done fine, Daddy and me."

Felix was still leaning out the window. "You take the girl in," he told his wife. "Let her wash up. It was hot out there today."

"No," Therese protested from the stern, "I'll finish up down here. You go in with Mama."

Mathilde turned to her daughter. "No use arguing, baby. He won't be in for another half hour. You know how he is. Come on, now. You can help me with dinner."

Therese sighed. She let the hose keep running into the hold while she hopped onto the pier and turned off the faucet.

Her mother complained as she approached, "Girl, you are some sun-

burned. You got to wear long-sleeves out there—and keep a hat on, too."
Felix, still in the wheelhouse, peeked out to see what his wife was fussing
about. "And you," Mathilde snapped at her husband, "you gotta take better care of your child when you keep her out on the water all day. Look
at this girl!"

Felix shrugged. "She look all right to me."

Mathilde shook her head. "You useless, Felix. She's gonna take a bath
right now, and then she's putting lotion all over those arms. If she don't
come down with fever, it'll be a miracle."

Felix shrugged again, and Mathilde walked Therese back to the
house.

The girl, annoyed to be treated as a child, tried to change the subject.
"So how was your day, Mama?"

"Well, Rusty Bruneau come by a little while ago."

"Bruneau? What's he want?"

"Needs to see your daddy. Said he'd stop back later."

"Little Horse probably sent him for the note or something. How much
we owe this month, anyway?"

"I'd have to look in the book. More than we got, though."

"Sons of bitches, the three of 'em."

"Don't use that kind of language, girl. It's not ladylike." Mathilde
watched a jay tormenting one of the family's cats. "Anyway, we don't
know what he wants. Maybe he's just looking to offer his sympathy."

"Sympathy? Mama, those boys killed your son. They ain't got no sympathy for us. They the ones put us in this fix, and now they want their
money. I don't know about you, but I don't call that sympathy."

"We don't know they done it. Sheriff Christovich, he'll let us know
who done what once he finds out. But till we know for sure, I'd hold off
accusing people if I were you."

"Mama, there ain't no doubt—"

Mathilde stopped her in anger. "The people think the Bruneaus killed
Alton, they say it was just vengeance for Darryl's murder. But you know
damn well Alton never killed Darryl. Alton couldn't kill nobody."

" 'Course not."

"So if those boys did murder your brother, they went after the wrong person, didn't they? And now you want to go blame them whether you got the whole story or no."

Therese tried to object, but her mother cut her off again.

"Anyway, Rusty was always different from those other two. He favored his mother, looked just like her with that red hair of his. You could see it in church, even, the two of them together. Arlene doted on that boy. And he's the one found her the day she died, poor thing. He ain't like the other two."

"I don't know. They all the same, them Bruneaus."

"He's the only one of them come to your brother's funeral. You say people all the same, you just not looking very close."

When they went inside, Mathilde had Therese take a bath. Stretching out in the long tub, the girl felt her muscles unknot. As they relaxed, the scrape where the dredge had caught the back of her calf, the bruise where the handle of the shovel in the hold had struck her thigh, and all the batterings her body had sustained since morning began to throb, croaking their dull aches like frogs chirping hoarsely in the dark.

Her mother knocked at the door to check on her. "Don't you fall asleep in there."

Therese stood in the tub, the water almost up to her knees. She studied herself in the mirror over the sink across the room. The sunburn had seared a rash along her arms and across her face and throat. Wherever she probed the burn with a finger, her body flinched. Gingerly patting herself dry, the girl rubbed cocoa butter into tender skin. Chafed by gusting wind, baked by glare flashing off the water, burned by the salt always in the air, a body weathered quickly on a boat. Already she could see flesh was no match for water.

Throwing on a loose cotton shift, Therese waited for dinner on the porch, catching an evening breeze off the bayou. The sky, too, was bruised purple in the east, though to the west lazy clouds still floated like white ducks on a blue pond.

She heard a car rumbling over the gravel, then crunching to a stop on the other side of the house. A few moments later, Rusty walked around the corner of the porch.

"Evening, Miss Petitjean."

"Rusty."

"Your daddy in there?"

"Imagine he is."

"I come to see him."

"You got nerve, I'll give you that. You do what you done to my brother—right over there, you flung him in the bayou—and then you come round here to see his daddy."

"I didn't have nothing to do with what happened to Alton. I'm just sorry for it, and I come here to offer my condolences, that's all."

Therese was thrown off balance. "Yeah, well, your brother was singing a different tune at the cemetery the other day."

"Darryl was just upset. We were burying our daddy. He didn't mean nothing by it."

" 'Cause Alton didn't kill Horse. Alton never hurt nothing in his life."

"I know, Miss Petitjean. I always liked Alton."

The girl turned on him. "Liked my brother? You?"

"Yeah, I always did. I remember Ross was teasing me one day at school, had me crying and all—we were little, I must not've been in third grade yet—and Alton comes up and tells him to leave off picking on me. My brother Darryl never stuck up for me like that."

Therese was smiling. "And what did that asshole Ross say to Alton?"

"Ross stand up to Alton? Shit, your brother was already bigger than Little Horse, and you know that Ross ain't never stood up to Darryl. No, Ross gives me one more kick and takes off. That's what Ross does. And when he gets far enough away that Alton can't catch him, he shouts, 'You ain't nothing but a damn bully, Alton Petitjean.' You imagine that, Ross calling Alton a bully?"

They were both smiling.

"Listen, Miss Petitjean, the other reason I come over here was to offer your father a hand on his boat till things straighten out, till y'all figure out what you gonna do. I know Mr. Petitjean can't manage all by himself. And my brothers can handle our beds without me."

Therese looked hard at him. "We'll get by."

"Yeah, I'm sure you will, but one man can't do the job."

"My daddy won't be out there by his lonesome. He's got me."

Rusty laughed. "A girl? On an oyster lugger? You probably ain't a hundred pounds soaking wet. What can you do?"

"You think I can't handle the wheel of a boat or shovel shrimp into a hamper. It don't take no genius. Hell, you do it."

He realized he had insulted her. "I didn't mean no disrespect. It's just I ain't never heard of no girl raking oysters or seining for shrimp."

"Well, you heard of it now."

"Yeah, I guess now I have." Rusty seemed to turn thoughtful. "But listen, there's no way you nor your daddy can take a skiff back into your beds off Bay Sansbois, rake oysters all day, then pole a laden boat back into deep water. Mr. Petitjean's too old, and strong as you are, you just don't have the muscle. And you need those oysters."

Therese was angry. She knew the boy was right.

"Well, I don't care. Go talk to my daddy if you want. He'll never take you on, but you go ahead. Go knock on the door."

Rusty started up the porch steps, then stopped when he was next to the girl. "You look real nice tonight, Miss Petitjean. That's a pretty dress you got on."

Therese sniffed. "Pretty for a crawfish, maybe."

Rusty smiled. "Well, you a little red in the face, yeah. It'll cook you out there, you not careful. But you don't look so bad. Least your red's gonna fade. Me, I'm red for life."

"Guess they don't call you Rusty for nothing."

"No ma'am. My mama used to tell me, she and Daddy took one look when I was born, threw all the names they had out the window. I was the only baby ever named himself, she said."

"Not me," Therese explained. "I was named after my grandmother." She realized this was the first time she was telling somebody where her name came from.

"Like the Little Flower, huh, the one the nuns were always talking about?"

"Guess so. Guess there's always some saint mixed up in a name."

"St. Rusty?"

They both laughed.

"But they didn't baptize you that, did they?"

"No, the priest threw a fit when they told him how to christen me. Said he couldn't baptize no baby Rusty. So my daddy says, 'Well, you baptize that child whatever the hell you want, but I'm calling him what I damn well please.' Then the priest—I guess he was pissed at language like that in church—just to spite Daddy he names me Athanasius. That's what they got written down on my baptism certificate, Athanasius Bruneau."

Therese was still smiling. "So God must think that's your name, Athanasius."

"You ever want to look me up in heaven," Rusty joked, "you got to check under the As in the phone book up there."

They both laughed.

"Go knock on the door," Therese said, more softly than the first time. "Maybe he'll take you on, my daddy."

22.

The next day, watching Rusty pivot a dredge heavy with a load of oysters onto the starboard protection plate, Therese felt envy. With just one hand tipping the basket and the other guiding the cable from which it was slung, the boy had brought the dredge aboard the *Mathilde* almost effortlessly. And before the water from the dripping basket had drained down the deck and back into the sea through the scuppers, Rusty had already crossed to the other dredge and was lowering it away over the port roller.

It stung the girl to see her father nod at the boy's skill. She had not expected Rusty to last the day. *How could a damn Bruneau be of any help to us?* she had sniffed smugly when Felix decided to give him a try. Instead, she had spent the morning sorting the mounds of oysters he dumped on the deck with easy efficiency.

In fact, they had already doubled the haul they'd sold the buyer yesterday after a full day's work. There was more of the lease yet to dredge, but about noon Felix decided to give Rusty a break.

The sky and sea converged at the horizon without the ragged border of thunderheads that often began to thicken out of the west about lunchtime. "We may get in a long day, the weather holds up," Felix observed. "How we doing?"

Therese was standing nearly up to her hips in the cork-insulated hold, laying a tarp over the sacks of oysters. "We fine," she reported. "Got two compartments packed full. This one's about a third done."

"It stays fair, we'll have time to shrimp on the way in." Her father nodded as he thought about it. "Keep me a compartment or two free. We get lucky, maybe we'll pull in three or four champagnes going home."

Rusty was lying atop the engine's plywood housing, his cap over his eyes. His shirt was soaked with sweat.

Felix smiled at him. "We ain't working you too hard, are we, son?"

Smiling back, the boy lifted the brim of his cap and raised his head to answer. "No sir, not with Miss Petitjean here to do all the heavy lifting."

"I'm pulling my weight," Therese hissed, climbing out of the hold.

Rusty stopped teasing her. "Truth is, I ain't never seen a girl could keep up the way you do. You a lot stronger than you look." He lowered the cap back over his eyes. "I mean, for somebody as puny as you are."

"What you just call me, boy?" Therese was furious and tore the hat off his head. She saw he was smiling under his brim and threw the hat back in his face. "Very funny. You just a load of laughs, ain't you?"

"Guess I better watch my step around you. You got some temper, girl."

Therese was still annoyed. "Yeah, you better watch your step. You wind up shark bait you mess with me."

Therese could see Rusty was chuckling under his cap.

Boys are so stupid, she complained to herself.

"Let's eat something," her father called from the wheelhouse. "Rusty, go drop the anchor so we don't lose our position in the bed. We in the wind. This is a good spot."

As Rusty went forward, he asked Felix the depth of the water.

"Thirty feet or so." The old man understood the question. "Pay out about a hundred feet of line, then snub it around a cleat."

When the boy had done as ordered, Felix backed the boat off until the anchor set. He shouted to the boy to pay out another hundred feet.

Meanwhile, Therese took from the ice chest the sandwiches of hog head cheese and Creole mustard her mother had made. Out of habit,

Mathilde had prepared only two meals. Therese whispered to her father there wasn't enough food.

"You didn't bring no lunch, boy?" Felix asked when Rusty had snubbed the anchor rode a second time.

"Oh, no sir. We usually—since Mama died, at least—we just open up some of our oysters. And we keep a couple boxes of crackers aboard. There's always a lot of beer, too. That'll fill you up in a hurry." Rusty noticed the two sandwiches in Therese's hands. "Don't y'all worry about me. If it's OK, a dozen raw ones or so are all I need."

"You shuck all you want. And we got some Barq's root beer in the ice chest there."

Rusty slid a heavy screwdriver from one of the loops of a leather strip Felix had tacked to the wall of the wheelhouse for the ice pick, fillet knife, hatchet, and other tools he kept handy. Cupping an oyster in his palm, the boy slipped the flat tip of the screwdriver into the seam of the shell and popped open its hinge with a practiced flick of the wrist. Following the interior of the shell, he severed the stubborn muscle that tethered the oyster in place, first above and then below. The top shell snapped off with a little twist, and he flipped it overboard. The oyster was unmoored in its own juices.

He lifted the half shell to his lips. As the oyster liquor ran down his chin, his tongue riffled the damp and salty frills. Then the oyster slipped into his mouth. On the tongue, it felt like a ripe fig running to syrup, and its flavor reminded him of something sautéed in olive oil and shallots.

He had thought it was an egg, when he was a very little boy, the corroded shell cracked open and the gray yolk floating in its own slime. He had even asked his daddy what kind of chicken laid eggs like that. "Chicken sharks," his father had answered grimly. It became a family joke, his older brothers terrorizing him with tales of the monstrous bird. Though it could fly, the chicken shark nested in the sea, Little Horse and Ross had assured him, its beak lined with rows of teeth and its talons, of course, always locked around the crushed skulls of little children plucked from their beds in the middle of the night. The mere sight of an oyster, waggled in his face by one of his brothers, would terrify him into tears as he imagined the horrible and pitiless mother of such a malformed egg.

"How are they?" Therese wondered, waking him from his daydream.

"Want some?"

Rusty quickly lined up on top of the gunnel a half dozen in their shells. The girl and her father each tried one.

"The water's too hot," Felix noted.

"But they good, Daddy." Therese preferred the oysters to the sandwich her mother had made.

"You finish these up, then, Miss Petitjean."

"Call me Terry," the girl allowed without a smile. "And here, you take half this sandwich."

"I'm fine with just the oysters."

"No, go ahead and take it." She shoved it into his hand.

"Thank you, Terry. It's kind of you."

"No, it ain't. I don't like the stuff my mama made this sandwich out of, anyway."

His slight smile in response irritated the girl.

After lunch, the *Mathilde* finished dredging the bed. About 3:30, Felix brought the boat around and headed for home.

"Shall we drop the net, Mr. Petitjean?" Rusty asked after he had secured the dredges.

"Yeah, let's do a little shrimping," the old man shouted over the engine. He pointed to the sky. "With these clouds rolling in, maybe it'll cool off a little."

"Want to run a test trawl?" the boy called from the stern.

"Nah," Felix answered, "we'll just take our chances. See if we don't run into some on the way in."

Therese stood aside and watched Rusty run the winch cable through a block and over the boom. Then he threaded the lazy line through a pair of blocks and checked the rest of the rig.

The trawl boards, sheathed in metal frames, rattled their chains when he attached the big slabs of wood to the winch. The cork floats slung between the trawl boards lifted freely from the deck, and beneath them the heavy chain of the tickler line was free of kinks.

Therese had already examined the fine mesh that billowed behind the tickler chain in the water and the sturdy shark net dragging after it. The canvas that protected the webbing of the heavy net from snagging the bottom needed mending. The girl would repair it when they got home. She might not know how to dredge oysters or seine shrimp, but she had learned as a little girl how to mend net and patch canvas. She had been proud when her hand was finally big enough to use her mother's leather palm to push triangular sail needles through torn canvas, and now she was even quicker than Mathilde when it came to reknitting a net shredded by a school of barracuda or by one of the hammerhead sharks that fished the same tides the shrimp rode.

Rusty tugged the line at the back of the seine to make sure it was tied properly. The knot was trim as everything else on the *Mathilde*. He admired the old man's seamanship. On the *Squall*, things were jury-rigged, held together with tape and wrapped with rusting wire, or just abandoned to the vicissitudes of wind and water. Making do, that was all the Bruneaus knew. But aboard the Petitjean boat, things got done right.

The first trawl didn't bring in half a basket, but when they tried again a few minutes later, they hit a cloud of shrimp drifting across the bay. Rusty hauled in a swelling net that spilled its glistening catch across the deck. By the time they winched in their final run, Therese had layered two compartments of the hold with alternating sheets of shoveled ice and twitching shrimp.

When they weighed in at the buyer's that evening, the girl was not tempted to cry, as she had been the night before. Instead, she felt the exultation of bringing in a boat with a full load. She was filthy, exhausted, and jubilant.

"We done good, didn't we, Daddy?"

"Yeah, baby." Felix nodded. "We done real good."

They left Rusty on the dock to find a ride home, but before they cast off, Felix took the boy aside. "We didn't talk money last night."

"No sir. I ain't worried about getting paid. I'm just helping y'all out till you get on your feet again."

Felix stiffened. "We don't need no charity."

"Didn't mean to suggest you did, Mr. Petitjean. But neighbors ought to give each other a hand when they can."

Felix counted out a crewman's share of the day's take and handed it to the boy.

"Fair enough," Rusty said.

"We see you in the morning, yeah?"

"Yes sir, if you'll have me."

Over the next few days, even Therese began to acknowledge that the boy was indispensable. Any doubt she had preserved about his value evaporated at the end of the week when Rusty's brothers claimed him on Saturday to tong one of their shallow reefs. Without the boy, on the way in after a few hours of futile test trawls with a try net, Felix remarked, gesturing toward the small catch he and Therese had managed to bring in on their own, that they might just as well have stayed home that day and saved the money wasted on fuel and ice.

Therese, though, maintained her skepticism of Rusty's intentions. "A snake's a snake," she insisted, cutting off her mother's defense of the boy. "Don't make no difference how good he handles a dredge. I don't trust him." As Rusty spent more time with the family over the following week, she was dismayed to watch her parents' affection for him seem to blossom and thought it a betrayal of her brother's memory.

She was even more dismayed by her own emotions, though, for she, too, found a great deal to like in the boy. His courtesy to her father pleased her. And he seemed to worry as much over the old man's health as she did. Wrestling a net sagging with shrimp into position on the deck, for example, the boy had managed to keep Felix at the wheel of the boat and out of the fierce noon sun. It worried Therese that her father had yielded without any more complaint than a mumbled curse to Rusty's transparent excuse for getting the old man into the shade; Felix, she knew, would have been immovable if he had not felt his own weakness.

The girl was touched, too, by the trouble Rusty took to avoid bruising the old man's pride. Just as he never protected her father from the hard labor of the boat without finding some reason that required the old man to see to some less strenuous task, the boy never missed an opportunity to ask Felix's advice about the currents or the contours of the bottom. Though she said nothing, Therese had even overheard Rusty patiently accepting instruction from Felix on how to set a rig she had seen the boy handle without hesitation just the day before.

But it was at the buyer's dock each evening she felt the most gratitude toward him. Drinking beers as they waited for their hauls to be weighed in, sons of other fishermen, it seemed to the girl, went out of their way to boast of how they had surpassed their fathers, mocking the old men for seeking refuge at midday in the wheelhouses of the trawlers or taking naps under tarps lashed to booms as makeshift shelters. Therese understood without even bothering to acknowledge the recognition of it, knew in her bones that the sea itself had taught the young men to be pitiless to weakness—even in their own fathers. It was simply too dangerous on open water to coddle the infirm. Yet Rusty, alone of the boys flexing their fresh muscles in front of the girl on the dock, deferred to the greater expertise and physical prowess of his captain. "You ought to see Mr. Petitjean handle a dredge," he insisted between sips of a beer. "Maybe he don't look like much, but we get out there, that old son of a bitch puts me to shame. And in front of his daughter, too." Therese watched the other boys hoot their derision and Rusty shrug under their school yard taunts. She found herself almost tempted to tell them the truth.

Some of the boy's reticence about his own strength and Felix's weakness was merely the respect for age ingrained in every child raised to adulthood in Plaquemines Parish. An adult, regardless of the inadequacy of other marks of status, could expect the deference of any child encountered in the shops or on the roads of the parish. Even a Negro, if an adult, would be greeted with respect by a local white child. Such courtesy yielded to considerations of race and wealth and strength and beauty only when one reached adulthood. The boys on the dock, for example, were strutting their newly achieved manhood in denigrating their fathers. Rusty, however, persisted in the habits of his youth.

But in another sense, the boy did not exaggerate his admiration of the old man. Rusty was surprised at how much Felix knew and how little his own father had taught him and his brothers about oystering. Horse had no interest in and little patience for the biology of the oyster and the other sea life they harvested. The fishing seasons and catch limits enforced at the bidding of state marine biologists meant nothing more than the inconvenience of avoiding wildlife and fisheries agents and, when caught, the added expense of fines or—if the particular agents were amenable—bribes. So Rusty was shocked to learn, for instance, that oysters could change their sex up to twice during their lives. He discovered, as well, how little he understood about salinity levels.

Felix could tell the salinity of water just by looking at the plants growing in it. Already Rusty had learned to distinguish the border where swamp yielded to freshwater marsh by the sudden sprouting of cattails along the shoreline and the carpet of water lilies clogging the still surface. He could now recognize, too, the wire grass of the great brackish marshes, where the Petitjeans' oldest beds still flourished on shallow-water reefs. Soon enough, the boy could smell a saltwater marsh as well, its effluvium of rotting plants and dead bodies stirred into the air by the surging of daily tides. Like his teacher, Rusty shook his head over the misnamed oyster grass that distinguished a saltwater marsh from its rich brackish neighbor; it was not a good place to cultivate oysters.

Felix had also pointed out among one of the hauls emptied onto the deck from their dredges the little shell of an oyster drill, one of the deadliest enemies oysters faced in the wild. Unlike oyster grass, the small snail was aptly named, boring into the shell of an oyster to feed on its soft flesh. Fortunately for oystermen, the drill could not tolerate low-salt water, where oysters thrived.

Cajuns who farmed beds in Lafourche Parish and Terrebonne, Felix had chuckled to Rusty, had their own way of dealing with the snails. Each spring when oyster drills gathered to lay eggs, the Cajuns caught the drills and—never given to wastefulness—boiled them for an hour with plenty of salt, then ate them for dinner.

"But for pure destruction," the old man had gone on, "ain't nothing like a black drumfish. Damn things run fifty, sixty pounds, and the bastards, they got a mouthful of teeth, crush an oyster with one good chomp. Suck up the meat, spit out the shell. A school of drum hit a bed at night, by morning you got nothing left but empty shells broken in a hundred pieces."

Rusty asked whether there was any defense against the fish.

"Freshwater. But drum just like drills, they follow the salt. Some boys hang rotting drum carcasses from bamboo poles around their reefs. Maybe the scent scares the others off, I don't know. But figure you got three years invested building a bed somewhere on your lease, then another eighteen months, two years, maybe three, waiting for your seed oysters to mature. You talking five, six years before you get the first penny back for all that work. And in just one night, you lose it all to a school of drum never would have made it this far back into the marsh even ten years ago."

Rusty cursed with Felix the oil companies that had cut their canals through the marsh, flushing brackish lagoons with heavy salt tides that scorched fertile beds and carried oyster drills and black drum deep into waters once safe for oysters. He had heard the expression before, "saltwater intrusion," but he had never before understood into how much of his world that intrusion had advanced. He had heard his father cursing the oil companies and the state officials that had battened off the deals made in Baton Rouge and New Orleans. And he had heard oystermen talk about the old days. He knew there were fewer luggers now than when he was a child, and he could name the families that had given up oystering and moved "up front," as the locals called it, to the city. But for the first time, shifting his weight from foot to foot on the deck as the sea picked up into swells, the young man began to grasp how delicate a balance held everything together and how a single act of destruction could precipitate a catastrophe, rippling like a red tide into the farthest backwaters.

As the gathering storm loomed in the west, Therese saw the melancholy in Rusty's eyes as they all hurried to secure the boat's equipment before trying to outrun the weather. The look on his face reminded the girl of Alton. She could not guess that Rusty, too, was thinking about her brother.

23.

So how you making out with the Petitjeans?" Darryl asked as he reached across the table for a chunk of French bread on the edge of Rusty's plate.

"Real good. I'll tell you, some of their beds, like off Bay Batiste, you ain't never seen nothing like it, the oysters back there."

"We get lucky," Ross mumbled, his mouth full of jambalaya, "those'll be our leases before long."

Rusty looked up from his dinner. "How's that?"

"The Petitjeans decide they can't make a go of it," Darryl explained, "we might step in and take those leases off their hands. At least, the ones worth the trouble."

"Shit, Little Horse"—Ross laughed, a fork in one fist, a knife in the other—"what they got but an old man can't lift an empty crab trap by himself and a goddamn girl supposed to rake oysters? It's like Daddy always used to say, just a matter of time."

Rusty's voice tightened. "They wouldn't be in this fix, somebody hadn't thrown Alton in the bayou."

"Somebody wouldn't have thrown that motherfucker in the bayou," Darryl explained to Rusty, "he hadn't fed your daddy to the sharks."

"Yeah, asshole," Ross added.

"And don't you go forgetting," Darryl reminded his little brother, "you was one of them somebodies."

The three boys ate in silence for a few moments.

"Well, it don't make no difference," Rusty insisted. "Them beds they got, we been selling full hauls every night. They won't have no trouble keeping their heads above water."

"Yeah, you know, babe, you don't have to kill yourself out there when you're with them. We doing them a favor, is all. You just there for the ride, they gonna be grateful. You don't have to set no records. Ain't nobody gonna be impressed you do."

"Mr. Petitjean, he's been paying me. It ain't just a favor no more."

"Paying you?" Ross interrupted. "Well, where the hell's our share of that? Me and Little Horse, we working twice as hard on the boat without you there to do your part. We the ones making the sacrifice, not you. Tell him give us our money, Little Horse."

Darryl rubbed his eyes. "Will you shut the fuck up, Ross? That ain't what we talking about."

"Yeah, but it's our money he got."

"You hear me? I said that ain't what we talking about. Eat your dinner, goddamn you, and keep your trap shut."

"Make up your mind," Ross mocked. "Can't eat I don't open my trap."

Darryl started to get up. "I'm warning you."

Ross hunched over his food. "I ain't sayin' nothin'," he mumbled without looking at his older brother.

Darryl turned back to Rusty. "All I'm suggesting is you setting these people up for a fall. They get used to these big runs, what they gonna do when you come home and start working for us again? Tell me that."

Rusty shrugged. "I hadn't thought about that."

"It don't do them no favors you postpone the inevitable."

"Then why you send me out there in the first place?"

"It was the Christian thing to do. I told Sheriff Christovich I was thinking of sending you over, and that's just how he put it. 'You boys would be doing the Christian thing.' That's just what he said. And maybe, with Alton and all—despite what the son of a bitch did to Daddy—maybe we got ourselves a responsibility here."

"Yeah, you right about that."

"But on the other hand, if it don't work out for the Petitjeans, it don't hurt us none to know which of their beds are worth leasing and which ain't."

"You mean you got me out there as a spy?"

"Hell, no. It's just the reward comes of doing a good deed."

" 'Cause I ain't spying on those people."

"Nobody's asking you to. But let's say they decide to cash in their hand. It's a hard life for an old couple like them. And that girl of theirs, she's gonna marry somebody and he'll take care of her."

"Therese? She don't allow much taking care of, that girl." Rusty smiled. "Reminds me of a horse won't be broken."

"That's 'cause she ain't found a man yet knows how to handle her. Mr. Right come along, though, she'll take a saddle, you'll see."

"I don't know. Some horses won't be ridden."

"That's the kind of horse they invented whips for, little brother."

"Yeah," Ross agreed, "and I got a horse needs riding tonight."

Rusty looked to Darryl for an explanation.

"He's got a date with Yvonne."

"That's right, babe, so I gotta go change." Ross started toward the bedroom, then stopped. "Look, Little Horse, why don't you let Rusty take the pickup tomorrow morning, and we'll take the Caddy down to the slip? Then I don't have to get up so fuckin' early to run him over to the Petitjeans."

"No way. You know Daddy never allowed no one in the Cadillac after they been fishing. It ain't no work car."

"Aw, Little Horse—"

"I said no. And I hear one more word out of you about using the Cadillac for work, I swear to God I'll make you take the truck tonight. Then just see if you do any bareback riding with Yvonne."

Ross, cursing under his breath, slammed the bedroom door behind him.

"Anyway," Rusty sighed, "Mr. Petitjean, he won't give up. His family's been oystering their beds for a hundred years."

"You probably right, but just say one day he's had enough of it—the storms, the mosquitoes, the oil companies, the goddamn bacteria, the getting up an hour before dawn every day. Tell you the truth, I don't know why any of us keep at it. We'd be doing them a favor, we're ready to take over some of their leases. You know the other families around here, they'd rob the Petitjeans blind."

"No, they wouldn't."

"They wouldn't have no choice. Who could afford to pay a fair price for Petitjean tracts? Nobody's got any money. And what they got's already sunk in their own leases. But us, we know which tracts produce and which don't, we can offer some real money for the good beds 'cause we betting on a sure thing. Everybody come out ahead that way."

"So what you want me to do?"

"You just need to keep an eye on what's what over there with the Petitjeans."

"You mean, which leases are worth bothering with."

"Yeah, that. But also how they're doing when it comes to money. We don't want them to get themselves so stuck in the mud we can't pull them out when the time comes."

"You talking about the notes on the boat and the house coming due?"

"For starters. If they can't make the payments, we need to know now—before everything gets out of hand. Like, for example, they need a little more time to pay off the loans Daddy gave them, we come up with a new schedule. Losing Alton, that's a real blow to their business. We just do them another favor. We fold everything into a new loan—the boat, the house, maybe a few of their beds, too, the ones you were talking about off Bay Batiste—we fold everything together and start the Petitjeans off fresh. Let them take an extra few months to get back on their feet."

"Why would they throw in those beds? It's money in the bank, those leases."

"The Petitjeans, they a proud family. No way they'll take charity from us. They gonna want to put something up as collateral to extend the loans. You know, make it look like a business deal. But there's nothing else left. That truck of theirs, it ain't worth shit. 'Course, you find out they got things we don't know about, well, we talking something else entirely. Wouldn't be any need, then, to use those beds as collateral."

"So I see can I find some way to help them out."

"Exactly. You just sort of keep an eye on things, let me know how they doing."

"I ain't seen everything yet."

"How about the beds squirreled back up there in Bay Sansbois?"

"The ones Daddy was always talking about?"

"Yeah, the really old ones, up in the shallows."

"Ain't seen them yet. In fact, I haven't done no tonging at all for Mr. Petitjean. We've had our hands full just dredging the big leases."

"I want to know about them. Daddy used to say there weren't any richer beds between here and Texas than those old tracts."

"Mr. Petitjean, he'd probably be glad for me to go rake them. Him and Terry, they can do some dredging while I fill up a skiff for them."

"Yeah, you tell him you'll do that. He may just be leery of asking somebody doing him a favor, after all, to rake oysters in shallow water. He knows it's hard work, handling a pair of tongs."

"You probably right. Especially in weather like we been having. The damn sun don't never go in."

"Tell him."

"I will," Rusty promised.

"And don't just play the hired man with them. Let them know they want you to do anything else, you happy to do it."

"Mrs. Petitjean, she says I ought to spend the night with them when we going out early the next morning."

A smile yawned across Darryl's face. "Yeah, I like that. That's a first-class idea that woman's got. Wouldn't hurt to sleep there, get to know the family a little better."

"She says I wouldn't have to get up so early that way. Mrs. Petitjean, she wants me to have breakfast with them, too. She's worried I don't get enough to eat."

"Yeah, old Mathilde, she's onto something. Makes a whole lot of sense, you moving in over there."

"I don't think she meant for me to move in," Rusty objected. "Just spend the night is all when we're getting an early start."

"When does Felix Petitjean not get an early start? You think Daddy ever once got to the icehouse in his entire life and that old asshole hadn't already been and gone?"

"Yeah, he likes his early start, all right."

"Don't you remember Daddy used to say the one sure thing he could count on was the sun come up, the *Mathilde* was on the water?"

"But where would I stay?"

Darryl looked at him as if he were an idiot. "Think they got a spare room, now."

Panic filled Rusty's face. "I ain't sleeping in no dead man's bed."

"Why the fuck not? Poor Alton, he's sleeping over by the church from now on. He won't be needing his bed back anytime soon."

"I don't like it."

"You rather keep sharing a room with Ross? Listen to your brother snore and fart all night long? Shit, I'd think you'd be damn glad to get away from him."

"Well, we'll have to see does Mrs. Petitjean ask me to stay."

"Don't you worry, she'll be tickled pink to have you in Alton's room. You watch, she'll have you wearing his clothes next."

"Over my dead body," Rusty objected.

Darryl laughed at his choice of words.

Rusty smiled, too. "All right, maybe I'll sleep in his bed—I guess there won't be no way to refuse that—but I'll be goddamned I wear a dead man's clothes."

"This is Daddy's shirt I'm wearing," Darryl said, pulling the fabric up at the chest.

"Yeah, but you didn't kill Daddy," his brother sighed.

"Just you don't forget you did kill Alton."

"I know," Rusty whispered. He sat there at the table for a moment, aware of his brother's eyes on him, then started to get up to clear the dishes.

Darryl looked at Rusty. "And about that other thing."

"What other thing?"

"What Ross was talking about. You see your way clear to let me have some of what Petitjean's paying you?"

"Why? I'm the one doing the work."

"I know, babe. I wouldn't be asking for myself. But Ross, he's still pretty fuckin' pissed about you knocking the shit out of him the other evening. You can see what his face looks like. I mean, some of those cuts, I should've taken him to the hospital and had them stitched up. You beat the crap out of him. So he's gonna go on about this money till he drives me crazy. It don't have to be much."

"That was his doing, what happened."

"I know. I was there. It was his fault, all right. Got what he deserved. But we brothers. We gotta live together. A little money, it'll shut him up. Make him feel like he got even with you. And when you get right down to it, it's a small price to pay for peace in the house."

"Yeah, I see what you saying."

"Look, it don't have to be much. You just give me half of everything you make, I'll straighten it all out with your brother."

"Half?"

"Well, shit, Ross is right about we the ones carrying the extra load. You'd be working this hard for nothing, you was on the *Squall*. By rights, we ought to be getting equal shares. You should be passing on two-thirds of that money to us. I mean, you get right down to it, all that money is rightfully ours. Hell, you still getting free room and board here. Ain't paying no rent far as I know."

"It's my house, too. And a third of the *Squall*."

"That's just my point. You get a third of all our work. But us, we don't get nothing of what you do. You think that's a fair arrangement?"

Rusty could see where the argument was headed. "I'll go get half the money."

"Yeah," Darryl agreed, "that'd make a good start."

24.

Darryl was right about Mathilde. A parcel of Alton's clothes was waiting for Rusty a few days later when he arrived for breakfast before casting off with Felix and Therese for another day of oystering and shrimping.

Spooked by the long walk in the dark down the gravel road from the highway to the Petitjean house, the boy blanched when the dead man's clothes were thrust into his arms by the mother of the son he had helped murder. Rusty had wanted his brother to drive him all the way to the house, but Ross refused from the first morning to take him any farther than the break in the trees where the Petitjean road met the highway. Though Ross took every opportunity, especially after their fight, to make things difficult for his little brother, Rusty guessed it had more to do with Alton's death. Three weeks had passed since that night they had brought the boy down in the thick woods, yet Ross still marveled to his brothers over dinner at the sound the skull had made against his club, the sound of a ripe watermelon smashed against a rock. But Rusty discerned in his brother's relish of the details of the slaying a queasy fear. The boastful recounting of the murder, night after night at their dinner table, sometimes even embellished with a reenactment of the crime, began to sound to Rusty like a ritual practiced to hold a ghost at bay. Ross's swaggering and callous cruelty masked, his younger brother sensed, a festering terror. So every morning well before dawn, Rusty walked the moonlit path of gravel and crushed shells between the highway and the Petitjean house.

The boy saw immediately that he could not turn down the woman's gift. She had taken the trouble to wrap the clothes in brown paper and twine, and she hugged him as he held the parcel in his arms, hugged him until he worked a hand free and patted her on the back.

Rusty had not resisted Mathilde's mothering. Having nearly forgotten the tenderness of a woman's concern over whether he was well fed and clothed, rested and content, he savored the little smiles she offered him like pieces of candy to a child. He was a dog to her hand when she brushed the red locks from his sleepy eyes in the morning, clucking in jest at how he had left the house with his hair uncombed and his shoes untied. His own mother had been dead almost five years. He had not fully realized until he began working for the Petitjeans how much he missed her.

When Rusty wore one of Alton's shirts the next day, he saw in Mathilde's face how much she missed her son, and he was ashamed that he was responsible—no matter how many excuses he made to himself about his own role in what had happened—for depriving her of the boy she loved. Walking every morning down the same road where Alton had died, and then on the boat passing the bank of the bayou from which his brothers had dumped the bleeding, battered body into a tangle of roots rising out of the murky water, Rusty had had a great deal of time to contemplate the murder.

He did not think he was lying to himself when he insisted upon his surprise, his shock, at the sudden flash of Darryl's switchblade burying itself between Alton's ribs. But when he probed that surprise, asking whether he should have guessed what they were doing in their truck in the middle of the night backed off the road and waiting for the Petitjean boy to come home, he could offer only his innocence, his willingness to believe his big brother's lies, as a defense. Who would not have known, he asked himself, what was about to happen in those dark woods? There was only one answer that didn't sound like a lie: someone who didn't want to know.

Even more than his complicity in the crime, the elation Rusty felt as he watched the body crumple to the forest floor tormented him like an accusation he could not refute. When he argued that his emotions had betrayed him, he realized there was as much confession as defense in that admission. His emotions, he understood with an inexorable clarity, had no more betrayed him than had his brothers.

It did not ease his conscience to argue, as Little Horse vehemently continued to maintain whenever Rusty brought up the question, that Alton had killed his father and deserved to die. He had never been convinced, not from the very beginning, that Alton was the murderer. It made no sense. What motive did the boy have? How did it profit the Petitjeans? And weighing even more strongly, Alton's gentleness, it seemed to Rusty, would not have curdled into violence without some provocation. But what had Horse Bruneau ever done to provoke Alton? If anything, his father had gone out of his way to protect Mathilde's son, often arguing with Little Horse about the animosity between the two boys. No, Darryl had had his own reasons, Rusty came more and more to believe, for what happened in the Petitjeans' woods that night.

So in guilt and in restitution, Rusty threw himself into his work on the *Mathilde* to restore to the Petitjeans, in some measure, what he had allowed to be taken from them. And if the murdered boy's mother asked him to wear old shirts, to sleep in an empty bed, then that was penance he would not shirk for what he had done.

Rusty, though, was not the only one troubled by Mathilde's gift to him of the parcel of clothes. He did not know that the family had quarreled furiously over the few shirts and two pairs of pants. Therese insisted the gift was a betrayal of her brother. Her father defended his wife against the girl's angry charge that dispersing Alton's things was just another way to eradicate the memory of the boy. They were already forgetting their son, she accused them with hot tears.

When her mother tried to calm Therese by suggesting that getting on with one's life didn't have to mean forgetting, she turned on the older woman, venting the contempt suppressed over the last weeks as she had watched her brother slowly replaced—first on the boat and now in their own house—by the Bruneau boy.

They were no better, her parents seemed to her, than a pair of animals abandoning a dead cub after a few hours of prodding the lifeless body. She imagined them troubled, as they wandered away through the trees, but soon unable to remember, exactly, the source of their unease.

Therese used language, in quarreling with her father, that she had never dared use before. He struck her across the face and would have hit her a second time, but Mathilde grabbed his arm, begging him to stop.

The girl was unrepentant, though. She lifted her chin and defiantly goaded the old man to strike her again.

She didn't want the wound of her brother's death to close and so, ever since the funeral, had worried it at the edges to keep it from scabbing over. Now learning for the first time the way things reknit themselves more quickly than one might ever imagine, the way roiled water stills over a drowned body or grass sprouts over a buried corpse, she picked at that wound where it had started to heal, scratching a channel for the blood to flow.

Therese pitied neither her mother nor her father in their grief, and if the pain of losing an only son was so great as to drive them to coddling one of his murderers in his place, she would no more allow them that forgetfulness of their suffering than she would let herself be charmed by the sweet nature of the boy she worked beside on the boat every day.

Throughout the South, emblazoned on the bumpers of cars, embroidered on caps, stamped on T-shirts, a single slogan articulated common feelings about the war lost to the North nearly a century ago: *Forget, hell!* Therese well understood the bloodied but impenitent defiance of the sentiment. She imagined herself the last mourner standing vigil over the grave of her brother, of whose death she knew herself to be the cause. Out of loyalty to Alton, the girl would not forget Rusty was a Bruneau.

Nor could she forget. Though the stabbing of Horse might continue to disturb her sleep, Therese evaded responsibility, insisting he had brought it upon himself. Guilt over Alton's death, however, pricked her day and night, and she embraced the preservation of her brother's memory as atonement for her complicity in his murder.

Though Felix had sided with his wife against his daughter, he felt the same qualms Therese had voiced about Mathilde's gift. He, too, had caught himself thinking of Rusty as a kind of son, often in the turmoil of deck work nearly calling the boy by Alton's name. Unlike his daughter, however, he could not blame Rusty for his son's death. He sensed the Bruneau boy was no more capable of killing Alton than Alton was capable of killing Horse. Felix was an old man for someone who had lived the life he lived. Well more than half the boys with whom he had graduated from eighth grade were already dead. The only thing a long life had taught him, he often thought with no little bitterness, was a great deal about death. Felix knew grief was a current against which a swimmer would exhaust himself and be carried out into dangerous waters. It was like a riptide: just follow the shoreline, he counseled himself when the memory of his lost son was too great to bear, until the current weakens and you can make for the beach.

Rusty was confused by the reaction of both Felix and Therese the day he wore Alton's shirt. Therese increasingly had seemed to him a moody girl, swinging between the playfulness into which the two of them easily fell and an offended pique at some offhanded remark he had made. He never knew what to expect from her, laughter souring into scorn from minute to minute. But today her mood was steady and dark. And she wasn't the only one who seemed different this morning. Felix had warmed to him over the last few weeks; in fact, whenever they weren't busy dredging or trawling, Rusty was at the old man's shoulder, asking about oysters or navigation or weather. But today Felix, too, was irritable, answering the boy's questions with grunts. So Rusty was glad when they put him adrift in a flatboat to tong a reef in a shallow bay made treacherous to the *Mathilde* by shifting sandbars.

It was a burden to him, the shirt, and hot. He hadn't paddled a hundred yards before he stripped it off and continued in just his T-shirt. Settling his boat over the reef, he poled with his tongs until he felt the shiver of crusted shells against the metal frame of his basket. The boy worked with the slow rhythm of heavy tools, sinking the tongs to the bottom, scraping the clumps of oysters into the basket with the teeth of the opposing tong, and scooping the load into the boat against the weight of the water. When he had filled the boat two hours later, he covered his haul with wet canvas and laid his tongs across the tarp to hold it fast against the wind picking up out of the south.

The boat, low in the water with its stony cargo, began to ship waves breaking over its side, so Rusty turned the vessel into the wind and let its bow drift off a few degrees to take the seas at an angle. He knew if a storm was whipping up, he was in the worst possible spot to ride it out. Gentle swells in deep water would turn to whitecaps over a shallow seabed, the swells agitated into waves as they followed the shifting contours of the near bottom. Nothing was more dangerous than a squall in a shallow lake, with the chop doubling back on itself from the circling rim of the shore, like water sloshing in a bowl. Beach crabs, he knew, fattened on drowned men.

Rusty scanned the horizon for the *Mathilde*. Felix hadn't told him how long they would leave him as they headed off to trawl for shrimp in a pass some distance away. Having never tonged for the Petitjeans before, Rusty realized they might not know he could fill a boat in two hours. Maybe Alton had taken three hours, or four. Some men were slow with a pair of tongs. He didn't know whether he could keep afloat in heavy seas for another hour or two; with the draft of a full load, he had only a few inches of wood above his waterline.

Though the waves were beginning to run under the gusting wind, it was still hot. Rusty grabbed the plaid shirt he had crumpled under his bench and dipped it in the water, then wiped his face with it and left the sopping cloth on his neck for a moment to cool off. As he dipped it again, bringing it up in his hand to wring over his head, it occurred to him that he was holding the shirt of a dead man, a man he had helped kill.

In the south, out over the Gulf, a line of darkening clouds was advancing on him. The bay danced all around his little boat, burdened with oysters. He was too far out to make for shore with such a load in the heavy chop. The *Mathilde* was still nowhere in sight.

The boy remembered his brothers had dumped Alton's body in the water. He stood among the oysters, balled up the wet shirt in his hands, and hurled it leeward as far as he could manage. A gust caught the shirt and puffed it open before it fell into the water, only a few yards from the boat. Rusty watched it float, spread out like a flag, for a few moments, then sink beneath the waves.

His offering to the drowned lords of the underworld—crowned with coral and draped in seaweed, as a fearsome childhood tale once had described them—must not have satisfied their vengeance, for the storm now broke upon him with a wild and sudden fury. Rain lashed his face, and he felt his boat grow sodden with the downpour and the frothy waves that lapped over its sides. He struggled to keep himself into the wind, but the weight of his cargo made it difficult to maneuver in the rough seas.

He strained to hear a ship's engine, higher pitched than the shrieking squall, but the only sound in the bay was the slap of water against water and the whine of the wind. Rusty realized he would have to save himself.

Driving the fork of his tongs into the muddy bottom, he let the waves pin his boat against its sturdy arms while he dumped his oysters back into the sea with both hands. He could feel the water loosen its grip as the boat lifted a little higher in the chop. He kept throwing back oysters, nearly all he had raked from the reef, until he had room to bail the bilge sloshing around his feet with the tin scoop used to fill burlap sacks with the catch.

The tongs continued to hold his position until Rusty had lightened the boat sufficiently to come about in a trough between waves and make for a cove nestled into an outcropping of the shoreline. After a harrowing fifteen minutes of scudding before the sea, paddling desperately when he found lulls in the seething water, angling across the surges of ragged swells at his back, the boy let the unwieldy flatboat be driven into the reeds that bordered the mudflats, then worked his way around to the safe harbor of the little cove. Hunkered down under the tarp as the rain continued to pelt him, Rusty understood how close he had come to disaster.

Like most Gulf storms, the downpour suddenly slackened, then dripped to a stop in just a few minutes. The vast, black clouds racing inland were chased by a scrubbed blue sky and an unblinking sun. Except for the raindrops quivering at the tips of battered palmetto fronds and the skim of rainwater glazing the flat surfaces of the boat, there was no evidence of the squall that had just wracked the bay for half an hour. The sea had grown still, and only the slightest breeze followed the storm north.

Edging from the cove like a timid animal from its burrow, Rusty slowly paddled his boat back to the reef, where after circling for a little while, he found the handle of his tongs jutting just barely from the water. The boy was surprised at the effort required to dislodge them from the bottom until he remembered how forcefully, panic-stricken, he had driven their teeth into the seabed.

He had stowed the tongs and bailed the last of the bilge among the few oysters he had kept as ballast when he saw, still far out, the *Mathilde*. It was running wide open, he could see as it approached, and he knew it had taken a light haul by how high it rode in the water. He paddled his small boat out past the sandbars.

As they came alongside, Therese tossed Rusty a line. She was looking down into his flatboat and shaking her head. "We give you three hours and that's all the oysters you can rake. What you been doing, boy? Taking a snooze?"

"Where the hell you been?" he shouted at her. "I liked to drown out here."

"Drown? How? You go to sleep and fall overboard?"

"The storm that swept through here. It nearly flooded me."

"What storm? We were over trawling in Bay Ronquille. We didn't see no storm."

"Where's your daddy? I want to talk to him."

"Hell, if that's all the oysters I raked in three hours, I wouldn't want him to see me."

Rusty's anger was fueled with adrenaline left over from the squall. "Goddamn it, girl, I had oysters up to the gunnels an hour ago. If y'all hadn't left me to drown, we'd have three or four sacks to sell."

"Yeah, well, where are they now, all these oysters you got?"

"Where the hell you think they are? I pitched them overboard to save my ass."

"You threw my daddy's oysters back? 'Cause of a little rain? Shit, Rusty, I thought we were paying a man to rake oysters for us, not some scaredy-cat afraid of a little water."

"I almost fuckin' drowned out here."

"Yeah, I bet." Therese sighed with scorn. "Come on. Take your things, and let's tie up the boat and get on home."

Felix leaned out of the wheelhouse. "Everything OK?"

Therese smirked. "This little boy was afraid he'd get wet, so he dumped all your oysters overboard."

"It was a squall," Rusty explained. "It blew up out of the Gulf."

"That hit you?" Felix asked, surprised. "I thought it was heading west."

"Came right over my head," the boy explained. "And I already had a boat full of oysters. Three-foot seas—I didn't have no choice. I had to dump them before I got swamped."

Felix nodded. "You done the right thing. There's always more oysters where they came from."

"That's what I tried to explain to your daughter, but Miss Smarty Pants thinks she knows everything there is to know about the water."

"Where's my brother's shirt?" Therese interrupted, looking over the flatboat a second time.

She had caught Rusty by surprise. "I, I lost it in the storm. It got washed away."

Therese was skeptical. "You telling me a wave ripped it off your back and carried it away? What kind of idiot you take me for?"

"I don't know what happened to it. I was trying to keep this boat afloat, and I lost the goddamn shirt. What difference does it make? I got more shirts."

"What difference does it make? That was Alton's shirt you threw away."

"I didn't throw it away," the boy insisted. "It got lost, that's all."

"We send you out to rake our bed, and what do you do? You dump our oysters over the side and toss Alton's shirt away. That was a gift to you, that shirt."

"What are you talking about, girl? I almost died out here. You ought to be apologizing to me."

"The hell I will."

Felix was shaking his head. "That ain't no kind of talk for a lady to be using in mixed company."

The girl was on the verge of tears, though she didn't know why. "Daddy, he lost Alton's shirt."

"I know, baby. But there's nothing none of us can do about that now." The old man looked out toward the horizon. "Tie up the flatboat to the stern, and let's get in. That's another storm coming behind the first one."

When Rusty came aboard and started to help Therese stow the shrimp nets, she whispered to him as her father shifted the engine into gear, "I ain't forgetting what you done, Rusty Bruneau. I don't care how much you fool my mama and my daddy. I know you ain't nothing but a coward and a cheat."

25.

When Felix and Therese nosed their boat into its slip that evening, Sheriff Christovich was sitting on the porch of the Petitjean house talking with Mathilde.

Therese, securing bow and stern lines around the pilings with clove hitches, watched the man and woman approach. Mathilde kissed the girl and lamented to the sheriff the raw cheeks of her daughter after just a few weeks of daily scrubbing by the salt air of the open water.

Therese was proud of her rough looks, boasting of her ability to pilot the boat. She might not have the muscle to run a dredge, she admitted, but put her at the wheel and she could hold true to a course or cut a clean circle over a lease. "Daddy says I'm a natural," she bragged, insisting she could ride the peaks and troughs of waves better than a captain with twenty years' experience.

"Well, I'll say one thing for you, little girl," the sheriff teased, "you sure can blow your own horn as loud as most of them boys down at the launch."

"There ain't no crowing in what I'm saying. Just plain facts is all."

"Wouldn't doubt it," Christovich conceded. "That's Petitjean blood running in your veins, Terry." He smiled at Mathilde. "Probably half salt water, your blood."

Therese took that as a compliment. "At least half," she agreed, "maybe more."

Mathilde excused herself and joined her husband in the wheelhouse, where he was studying a chart he had pulled from a locker under a bench along one of the walls.

"I hear Rusty Bruneau is crewing for your daddy," Sheriff Christovich said offhandedly to Therese as she began to hose down the deck of the boat.

"Yeah, he gives us a hand. We just dropped him off at the launch. Don't know how much longer we'll need him, though."

"Really? People say he's moving in with y'all."

"Not if I have anything to do with it, he won't. That's my mama's foolishness, trying to get him to spend the night. Says it's too far for him to come to our house every morning so early. And Daddy, well, since Alton died, he don't have much to say about anything."

"I couldn't be any sorrier about that, Terry. He was a fine boy."

"Goddamn Bruneaus. Everybody knows they done it. I don't see how come you don't throw them all in jail."

"Rusty, too? What you gonna do without him?"

"Hell, yeah, throw him in jail. We'll find ourselves somebody else to crew the *Mathilde*. Don't take no genius to rake oysters." Therese splashed water in the compartments of the hold, letting it drain out into the bilge.

"No ma'am, it don't. But ain't that many young men hanging around with nothing better to do. Anyway, no proof they did it, the Bruneaus."

"My mama says the same thing. Says we don't know for sure them boys killed my brother, says before we go blaming anybody we got to wait for you to find the evidence to prove it."

"Your mother, she's right about that."

"Well, what's your evidence tell you, Sheriff? They done it, or not?"

"What you got to remember, Terry, not everything that tells you whether or no someone done something counts as evidence."

Therese was watching the sheriff's eyes as the water continued to flush the hold and its compartments. "So you might know who done something, might not have the slightest doubt who done it, but that don't mean you have the evidence to prove it, that what you saying?"

Christovich returned her gaze. "Yeah, that's exactly what I'm saying."

"So let's just say, for instance, you might know perfectly well them Bruneau boys murdered my brother, but there wouldn't be one damn thing you could do about it."

"Without evidence, yeah, you could say that."

"So they just get clean away with it?"

"Well, not necessarily. Let's say, for instance, the sister of this murder victim was in regular conversation with someone who might have seen everything that happened the night in question. And let's just say he let something slip. Then that would be a different story. We'd have a kind of witness, wouldn't we?"

"I get your drift, Sheriff."

"So, hypothetically, if somebody like you were to hear something that might, let's just say, strongly suggest what happened to your brother, then you could testify to what you heard and who told you. Now that might lead to some real evidence."

Therese twirled shut the faucet handle and looped the hose around it. "Yeah, well, I didn't mean we'd be getting rid of Rusty anytime soon. He's half useless far as I'm concerned, but neither me nor my daddy can rake oysters from a flatboat or handle a dredge the way he can. So I imagine we'll be keeping him on."

"Not that I'm talking about anyone in particular, mind you. Just saying if something should come up on the boat or somewhere, it'd be a help you let me know." Then he added offhandedly, "No chance, I guess, you already heard anything worth repeating, huh?"

"The subject ain't come up yet. But don't you worry, Sheriff. I guarantee it will."

"That's a good girl, Terry. Your brother was lucky to have a sister like you." They heard Mathilde and Felix laughing over something in the wheelhouse. "So how's your mama doing? She puts on a brave face, but there ain't nothing harder than this for a mother to bear."

"She doing good. Real good, as a matter of fact." Therese did not tell Christovich about the clothing her mother had given to the Bruneau boy. "But you never know with her. Her heart was broken in a million little pieces, she wouldn't let on. She knows how to keep a secret, that woman."

"Yes ma'am." The sheriff nodded thoughtfully. "That she does."

At dinner, after Christovich had driven off in his squad car, Felix insisted Therese apologize to Rusty. "I heard you today. You had no call to chew that boy out the way you did. We was in the wrong, not him. I never should've left him out there all alone for so long. We was begging for trouble, doing that."

"Aw, Daddy, how bad could it be, a little rain?"

"Girl, you better learn to show some respect for the water. You don't, it'll slap you down so hard, you won't never stand up. It can get bad in a hurry out there. And it can stay bad if it wants to."

"Anyway, he don't need no apologizing to."

"Oh, yeah, he does. We need that boy, we gonna get through all this. You run him off, we got a problem."

Mathilde rose from the table. "Look here, I made two sweet potato pies today. Why don't Terry bring one of them over to Rusty for his dessert tonight? That'd be a nice apology, don't you think?"

Felix put down his fork of speckled trout. "Yeah, that's just right. You take the truck after dinner, girl, go bring him one of your mama's pies. And you apologize, you hear me?"

"Yes sir." Therese pouted, playing with her food. "I don't know why you making me do it, though. He's nothing but a big baby."

"Have him heat it up," her mother suggested, wrapping the pie. "You get the full flavor that way."

"I can't believe you sending me over to the Bruneaus."

"They doing us a favor, those boys, sending Rusty over here. It's the least we can do," Mathilde insisted.

"Those boys killed your son," Therese reminded her mother.

"We got no proof of that. Sheriff Christovich was telling me just this evening before y'all come home he ain't got no evidence of what happened. Not a scrap."

Therese thought of her own conversation with the sheriff and relented. "Maybe y'all are right. Maybe we ought to be making peace with the Bruneaus. I'll run the pie by their house. Make sure Rusty's feelings ain't hurt, the little baby."

"Tell him to come early tomorrow," Mathilde instructed the girl. "I'll fix flapjacks."

"And take off those pants and put on a dress like a proper lady before you go over there," her father demanded. "I tell you," he complained to his wife, "she acts more and more like a boy every day."

"And whose fault is that," Mathilde snapped at him, "keeping her on the boat all the time?"

"What you expect me to do?" The old man sighed in exasperation. "The girl won't get off even now we got Rusty."

When Therese pulled her truck up to the Bruneau house, the pickup was gone but the Cadillac was parked beside the porch. She took the dessert her mother had wrapped and knocked on the cypress siding beside the front door. It was a hot night, and the house was wide open. Only a latched screen door kept out the mosquitoes.

When there was no answer to her knocking, she called out a hello.

She heard a gruff voice somewhere inside shouting back. "Hang on. I'm coming."

Through the screening, she watched a figure emerge from another room, probably the bathroom, and shuffle toward her. She recognized him. "Hey, Ross, it's me, Terry."

"Hey, yourself," he greeted her from the other side of the door.

"I'm looking for your brother. He here?"

"Which one? Little Horse? 'Cause he ain't here."

"No, I'm looking for Rusty."

"Well, he ain't here either. Neither one of them is here. They gone off together."

"I get it, Ross, they're not here."

"You got something there?" he asked, nodding toward the red dish towel covering the pan in her hands.

"Yeah, it's a pie my mother sent y'all."

Ross unlatched the door between them. "What kind?"

Therese smiled at his question. "Sweet potato." Thinking again of her conversation with Sheriff Christovich, she asked, "You like to try a piece? It's some good."

The porch door swung open, and Therese followed the man into the kitchen. Ross took a plate and a fork from the drainer beside the sink while the girl unwrapped the pie.

"What about me?" she wondered.

"Oh." Ross got a second plate and fork as well as a big knife that was resting on the drain board.

Ross sat at the table as Therese served him a slice of the pie. He did not wait for her to cut herself a piece before he tried the dessert.

"Good, huh?"

"Yeah," he mumbled, his mouth full, "good."

She watched him wolf down his food. "Want another?"

"Yeah, I'll have more."

As she served him again, the girl said he reminded her of Alton. "He did like his pie, my brother," she explained.

Ross grunted.

"That night he died, we had sweet potato pie that night," she lied. "You remember what you ate that night, Ross, the night my brother died?"

The man shrugged as he kept chewing.

"That's the strangest part when something happens, remembering all the little details had nothing to do with it. They just happened the same night, too, so you remember them. Know what I mean?"

Ross seemed to the girl to be making an effort not to look up from his plate.

"You remember anything about that night, Ross, anything at all?"

"Yeah," Ross answered, putting down his fork and defiantly meeting her eyes. "I remember plenty that night. But I ain't tellin' you shit about it."

"You don't have to be nasty. I was just trying to make conversation. You know, be friendly."

"Friendly?" the man smirked. "I'll show you friendly, girl."

He pinned her wrist against the table and got up slowly. She struggled to free her hand, but he had no trouble holding her fast.

"You hurting me," she whispered, too proud to show her fear by crying out.

"You don't know hurt," he threatened, tugging her by the wrist out of the kitchen and forcing her down onto the sofa in the front room.

"Maybe," he whispered as he lay on top of her, "this'll be one of those nights somethin' happens and you remember everythin', huh?"

Therese had shut her eyes under the rasp of his unshaved chin against her face. She could smell the sweet potatoes on his breath—and liquor. She continued to fight, cursing him furiously, but he was so strong, she could not loosen his grip or struggle free of his body pressing her against the lumpy cushions of the sofa. His hand grasped her breast and squeezed; she thought she was about to faint from the pain. Then his hand was sliding inside her skirt. "Let's see can I find that little oyster you got down there," he whispered into her ear.

Suddenly, the girl felt his body lifting from hers. She opened her eyes and saw Rusty standing over her, hurling his brother to the floor.

"Don't you touch her, motherfucker." Rusty leaned over Ross, both hands knotted into fists. "Don't you lay a finger on that girl."

Now Therese, a bit wobbly, was on her feet, standing next to Rusty. She picked up an empty whiskey bottle lying next to the sofa, gripping it by the neck. "Come get a kiss, asshole," she offered.

Ross looked ready to charge the two of them, but he sank back to the floor when the screen door swung open and he heard Darryl's voice, deep with anger, shout, "What the fuck's going on in here?"

Ross tried to laugh. "Nothin', Little Horse. I was teasin' her, is all. She just can't take a joke, that's her problem."

Rusty didn't take his eyes off his brother on the floor. "I come in here, Darryl, and this motherfucker's on top of Terry. She's cursing and scratching him, but he's got her by the throat."

Therese hadn't even realized Ross had had his hand around her throat.

Darryl stepped between Rusty and his brother. "What you doing here, girl?"

"My mama sent me over here with dessert for y'all. But Ross, he decides to help himself to more than a piece of pie."

Ross tried to make a joke. "That's all I wanted, a little piece."

Darryl looked over his shoulder. "You shut the fuck up." Then he turned back to Rusty and Therese. "You two get out of here. Rusty can spend the night at your place. I'll deal with this asshole myself."

The girl was still holding the empty bottle by its neck. "It's OK, Terry," Rusty promised, taking the bottle from her. "I'll bring you home."

As they got into the truck parked out front, they could hear Darryl shouting at his brother.

"I'm sorry about all that," Rusty apologized as he started the motor with Therese's keys. "Ross can be a real moron."

"I was asking him," the girl said softly, suddenly weak with exhaustion, "what he remembered about the night my brother died."

"Well," Rusty stuttered, "we don't know nothing about that."

Therese sighed, looking out at the dark trees flitting past her window. "Maybe so, but it sure set him off when I brought it up. That's when he got nasty with me."

"You just lucky me and Little Horse come home when we did. That Ross don't never know when enough's enough."

"Lucky for him, maybe. I would have killed the son of a bitch."

Rusty laughed softly. "Yeah, you might have. I thought you were ready to kill me this afternoon—and that wasn't an hour after I'd just come this close to drowning." He held up his hand, the thumb an inch from his finger.

"That's why Mama sent the pie. She and Daddy said I had to apologize to you. Daddy said we were the ones in the wrong."

"Well, no harm done. I'll go rake that bed again. There's plenty of oysters down there."

No one else was on the highway. The steady thump of asphalt lulled the girl; she realized tears were running down her cheeks. She kept her face turned to the window so Rusty wouldn't see she was crying.

The couple drove on in silence until they turned onto the gravel road to Therese's house. "You sleep in Alton's room tonight," she insisted, her voice hoarse. "There's more of his clothes in the dresser in there. You wear what you want in the morning." Then she added, "Mama's making flapjacks for breakfast."

"I ain't had them in a long time," Rusty admitted.

"Since your mama died?" Therese asked, almost tenderly.

"Yeah, since then."

As they slowed to a stop, the gravel under the truck's wheels sounded like the pock of boiling water, cooling to a simmer. The two of them sat in the cab for a moment before getting out.

"I appreciate what you done back there," Therese said without looking at Rusty.

"I'm just sorry," he sighed, "that something needed to be done." Then he smiled. "But I sure would have liked a piece of that pie."

Therese smiled, too. "I wouldn't be surprised we find you some inside."

26.

Therese was surprised when Little Horse came calling the next night. He began by thanking Mathilde for the pie she had sent. He agreed it was time for the two families to put aside their differences. They both had suffered terrible losses. They ought to help each other in these difficult times. He was glad that Rusty was seeing them through this rough patch until they could get on their feet again.

Felix was mostly silent, but Mathilde brewed coffee. "We real sorry about your daddy, Darryl," she said as she served their guest a pecan praline on one of her best plates. "And I don't know what we'd have done without your little brother. He's a lifesaver."

"I appreciate you saying that, Mrs. Petitjean. And you folks need any more time with those notes coming due from that money Daddy lent when you were in trouble last year, you just got to ask. I know we can work something out."

Now Felix spoke up. "We got ourselves a real good crop this season. Don't think we gonna need any extensions."

Darryl took a bite of the praline and smiled. "This real good, Mrs. Petitjean. Just like my mama used to make us."

Mathilde nodded. "That was my recipe Arlene had. When you and Alton were babies, we used to make pralines together, your mama and me."

Darryl ignored what she had just said. "I'm real glad to hear that, Mr. Petitjean. I'm thrilled to death you don't need no more time. I guess your little girl's turned into quite an oysterman, huh?" He nodded to Therese, sulking in an armchair across the room.

The girl smirked. "I do my share."

"I know you do, Miss Petitjean. All the boys down at the buyer's dock, they can't get over you. Nobody thought you'd last a week out on the water."

"Guess they were wrong."

"Yes ma'am, they all looking at you in a whole new light. Me, too, I don't mind saying."

"That's real nice of you, Darryl," Therese's mother offered when her daughter refused to respond to the compliment.

"Well," the man sighed as he rose from his chair, "I just wanted to come by and tell you thanks for the pie. I'm real glad to hear everything's working out so good for y'all." He smiled. "I got to admit, I don't know how we ever gonna entice Rusty back to his own house when he's got a place nice as this to stay. Your home shows a woman's touch, Mrs. Petitjean."

"Thank you, Darryl. And I hope you convince your brother to stay whenever he wants. We enjoyed him being here last night. Whole lot more convenient than having to come all the way over from your place at 4:30 in the morning."

"You right. I think he's just afraid he'd be imposing on you folks."

"You tell that Rusty Bruneau it ain't no imposition at all," Mathilde insisted. "We delighted to have him."

"I'll tell him he's got an invitation as soon as I get home, Mrs. Petitjean."

"You see you can't convince him."

"Yes ma'am." He nodded to Felix, then to Mathilde. "Evening, Mr. Petitjean, ma'am." He turned to Therese. "Maybe Miss Petitjean'll show me to my car. What you say, Terry?"

"Think you might get lost between here and our porch?" Therese snapped.

Mathilde scowled. "You show our guest to his car, girl."

Therese uncurled from her chair. "Come on," she told their visitor.

Once they were on the porch, Darryl smiled. "You have some mouth on you, little girl. You know that? I just wanted to get you out here to apologize for what happened at our house. You won't have no more trouble from Ross. He says he was drunk, but he learned his lesson good last night, don't you worry. I saw to that myself."

By the porch light, Therese noticed the scratches across Little Horse's knuckles and thought of Ross's unshaven jaw. She tried to change the subject. "Your two brothers, they don't get along so well, do they?"

The man smiled. "Yeah, those boys are sort of on the outs right now. I told them I come home tonight, they been fighting, I'll whup their asses all the way back to town, the two of them. They no better than little children, you leave them alone. That Rusty, he liked to kill Ross a couple weeks ago in a fight they had. And Ross, well, I told him the other day on the boat he ought to make peace with his brother. You know what he says to that?"

"No, what?"

"Says, 'I wouldn't piss down that bastard's throat if his heart was on fire.' He hates Rusty with a passion, I tell you. That's why I think it's a pretty good idea your mama's got. You know, my brother starts staying over here regular. The less them two together, the better for everybody concerned." Darryl stopped smiling. "Ross, he can get out of hand real easy. Like last night, for example. There wasn't no excuse for what happened. I don't know what gets into him, that boy. And he's always been like that. Since he was a little child, he's been like that. He done things back then—well, I just don't know why he does what he does sometimes."

"I don't want to talk about last night no more," the girl whispered. "Not out here in front of my parents."

"Yeah, you right. Less said, the better. But that wasn't right what he done you."

"He didn't do me nothing," Therese protested. "He had, he wouldn't be breathing right now, I promise you that."

Darryl laughed. "You are a demon, aren't you, girl? You gonna go and kill Ross? Hell, I barely can keep that boy in line, and look at you, tiny as you are. Ross is a bull. He's like a goddamn bear in a fight. How you ever kill somebody like that, a little girl like you?"

"Yeah, you make fun all you want, Darryl. But you just see what I do somebody hurts me."

Staring at her burning eyes, Darryl seemed as if he suddenly understood something that hadn't occurred to him before, and his smile faded into a kind of gape. "Jesus, girl," he sighed.

Therese turned away from him. "All I'm saying is lucky for him you walked in when you did."

"I can see that," Darryl said with a new seriousness in his voice. "You somebody to be reckoned with, ain't you?"

"You don't hurt me, you got nothing to worry about."

Darryl seemed to be mulling something over. He sat down on the porch steps. "Ever think where we going, your family and mine? Things won't keep on forever the way they been."

"We doing OK."

"Sure, this season, with Rusty running the dredge for you and tonging your reefs. But where's that put you two years from now, or three? Your daddy, he's running out of steam."

"Is not," Therese objected. "He's just had a bad spell, is all. The last two years, they been hard."

"On us all. I ain't saying it's just you. But you fooling yourself you think that old man and you gonna make a go of it by yourselves."

"We'll manage."

"Manage just won't cut it no more. You think them oil companies done with chopping up the marsh? Shit, you know how much money they talking about out there in the oil patch? You think they give a fuck how many coonass fishermen they run out of business?"

"So you gonna do something about it, Darryl?" Therese asked scornfully.

"It's a question of what *we* gonna do about it. The little man, they gonna grind him under. But we don't fit under their heel, they twist their ankle. Then they got to deal with us."

Therese saw his point. She sat down next to him on the steps. "How we do that? You tell me how we hold them off, those oilmen."

"The Petitjeans and the Bruneaus, you put together all our leases, it's a force to contend with. Shit, between us we control half of Bay Sansbois, a good chunk of Bay Batiste, and God knows how many little reefs and shallow-water beds all over Barataria."

"So?"

"So like I said, Terry, y'all can't make a go of it. Yeah, maybe you hang on another year or two. But then what? You get out now, you walk away with some money in your pocket. You wait, you lose everything."

"You just like your daddy. You want our beds."

"They ain't gonna do you no good, girl. I don't care how thick with oysters those old reefs are. You can't rake them. Neither can your daddy. But we work something out, you keep your house, maybe a little money. I'm talking about doing y'all a favor."

"Yeah, just like your daddy done us with those loans of his."

"Wasn't his idea. Your mama, she come round and beg him to lend y'all the money. Hell, the bank gets their hands on your boat, we pick it up for a song. And no boat, no beds. So then we scoop up those leases of yours, too. We home free. Don't have to risk a penny of our money, neither. I told Daddy he was crazy, giving your mama the loan. I don't know what he was thinking, the old man. Going soft, probably, just like your daddy."

"My daddy ain't soft. He's out there before you are every morning, and he's the last one in at night."

"I ain't here to quarrel with you, girl. Just saying you ought to think about where all this is headed. Maybe jump off before you run aground."

"You real smart, Darryl, for somebody as stupid as you are."

The man bristled. "Stupid?"

"You think I scare easy? Is that what you think?"

Darryl whistled. "Shit, no. I don't know what it'd take to scare a girl like you."

"More than you, I'll tell you that."

The man started laughing. "You a pistol, girl. Tell you a secret, too. I was looking forward to having you as my stepmama. That would've been something."

Therese was taken aback. That part of marrying Horse—being a mother to his sons—had never even occurred to her. "Well, I wasn't looking forward to it."

Again Darryl's smile faded. "No," he said thoughtfully, "I guess you wasn't looking forward to that, was you? I guess you wasn't looking forward to none of it."

"Don't make no difference now what I was looking forward to."

"Come to think of it, my daddy's funeral, I don't remember you shedding no tears at all."

"I was crying on the inside," the girl said flippantly.

"Bet you were. Must've been a terrible shock, my daddy dying on you out of the blue."

"No bigger shock than my brother dying must have been to you." Angry, the girl stood up. "I gotta get inside. My mama'll be worried."

Darryl rose, too. He looked the girl in the face. "You know, some people might say you and me, we got something in common. Something terrible."

Therese nearly spit the words at him. "What could we have in common? What could I possibly have in common with you?"

"We both lost someone, someone closer to us than anyone else. That's a terrible thing, isn't it?"

"So?"

"Maybe we give it a chance, we find we got other things in common."

Therese laughed in disbelief. "You ain't serious?"

The man shrugged. "Anybody else asking you out?"

"You some crazy, Darryl Bruneau. You think there's the slightest chance in the world I'd say yes?"

"Makes sense, you think about it. We got a lot in common, us two."

"Only thing in common is we got to get up before dawn tomorrow morning. I think it's time you get along home."

Darryl stepped down from the porch and started toward the Cadillac. "I'll drop by again, Miss Petitjean," he said without looking back.

When Therese went in, she climbed the stairs straight to her room and shut the door. Darryl had unsettled her.

He was right, she knew, about the future. She and her daddy, there was no way they could harvest their leases by themselves or bring in enough shrimp to pay the bills. And he was right about things changing for the worse. You saw it everywhere you looked—boats for sale, people moving out, oil rigs sprouting up all over the Gulf. Everything he said was true, the son of a bitch, and it all made her nervous.

But beyond that, something darker and more worrisome kept echoing as Therese thought about their conversation. "We got something in common. Something terrible," he had said. Yes, he had explained it was a terrible thing losing the person you loved most of all. But there was something else in his tone of voice when he said it, something woven through the words, that troubled her.

Had he put it all together? she wondered. Had he suddenly begun to doubt that Alton was the one who had murdered his father? Could he let himself believe a tiny little thing like Terry Petitjean could actually bring down Horse Bruneau?

And was he confessing to her brother's murder—or bragging about it—when he said they shared something terrible? He had twined them together, the two murders, so that in confessing to one he was accusing her of the other. That's what it felt like, at least, the way he put it.

It frightened her, too, that Darryl had suggested they were two of a kind. What was he hinting at, saying they might have other things in common? Everything about the man made her nervous. She didn't like being around him. How could he even think she might be interested in him? It's true, she admitted, he was a good-looking man, tall and muscular. And his eyes, those blue eyes of his, knifed right through you.

It was the eyes, thinking about Darryl's eyes, that made Therese remember her brother and his eyes sprung open under water. How many times had she dreamed that pale face staring up at her from the bayou?

She felt her own face harden. Darryl had as good as confessed to her, she decided. Lying in her small bed, surrounded by the worn toys of her childhood, Therese smiled. Maybe it wasn't evidence; maybe it wouldn't satisfy Sheriff Christovich. But it satisfied her.

She had been right, she told herself as she fell asleep: Darryl was real smart for somebody so stupid.

Four

27.

W hat's wrong with your arm, Daddy?"

"Don't know," the old man answered, unconcerned. Backing out of their slip, he turned the wheel of the *Mathilde* with just his right hand. His left arm hung limp at his side. "When I woke up this morning, couldn't move the damned thing. Thought maybe I slept on it funny."

"And you still can't move it, Mr. Petitjean?" Rusty asked.

"No, it's better. I'm getting my feeling back."

Therese and Rusty looked at him with worried faces.

Felix laughed. "This is what it means to get old." He chuckled, jerking his left shoulder so that his arm swung like a pendulum. "Every day, it's something else."

"You ought to have that looked at," Rusty suggested.

"Yeah, it don't get better, maybe I will. Ain't so bad, though. Nobody even noticed it at breakfast."

"Well, now the sun's coming up, it's pretty damn obvious," Therese said, shaking her head.

"Instead of worrying about my arm, you better worry we got enough fuel to get ourselves over to the icehouse. I smell gasoline."

"Yeah, me too," Rusty agreed, lifting open a deck panel next to the engine housing. The sharp odor of gasoline gusted into his face. He reached under the floorboards and let his hand feel its way back along the fuel line to the fitting where it joined the fuel pump.

"Be careful you don't burn yourself, boy. That gets hot in a hurry down there."

"No, I know where I am. And it ain't that hot yet."

As he drew out his hand, he rubbed his thumb against the two fingers that had brushed the fitting. Then he lifted them to his nose and winced. "You got a leak, Mr. Petitjean."

"Bad?"

"Will be, we don't do something about it."

"Damn it to hell."

"I think the fitting's just worked itself loose, is all. I didn't feel no gas till I got to the nipple at the fuel pump."

Felix tried to grab a screwdriver from the tools he kept handy on the wall of the wheelhouse, but his arm still would not respond. "Terry, reach Rusty that screwdriver," the old man told his daughter, nodding toward the leather strip holstering tools and weapons he might need in a hurry.

The girl surveyed the row of instruments on the wall. There were knives, an ice pick, a battered belaying pin to subdue any shark dumped onto the deck from one of their nets, a pair of long-handled pliers to clamp a catfish by the lip and yank it overboard without getting stung by one of its poisonous spines, a flashlight corroded by salt water, and other implements of the fisherman's trade.

"Which screwdriver, Daddy?"

"The one with the black handle. Next to the hammer."

Therese handed it to Rusty, who had exposed the fuel pump by removing the deck panels above it. "It's too dark to see."

The girl went back for the flashlight, but when she tried to flick it on, nothing happened.

"Batteries in the locker down there," Felix instructed, nodding to the other side of the open wheelhouse.

When Therese finally brought the light to Rusty, he had her shine the beam on the fitting. Three or four turns of the screwdriver fixed the problem.

"That's all there is to it?" she wondered, unimpressed. "You turn the boat upside down for that?"

Rusty and Felix laughed.

"Yeah, girl," her father explained, still laughing, "that's all the difference there is between a tight fitting and blowing yourself to kingdom come."

"What, we could've blown up?" she asked skeptically.

"Nah," Felix assured her. "Not unless those two vents there fore and aft got stopped up somehow. But that happened, then the fumes would build up under the deck, and we'd be riding a goddamn wooden bomb out into the bay."

"But the engine wouldn't start, would it? I mean with the vents clogged."

Rusty broke in as he replaced the deck panels. "That's one of the reasons the new boats, none of them have partial bulkheads like these old luggers. Not to mention they all got blowers, too, the new ones, for safety's sake. Plus the good ones, they use diesel now. But these old boats, there's plenty enough oxygen down there to keep the engine running for a while, particularly if it's a slow leak."

"Even apart from all that, there's the air intakes in the hull," Felix added. "Won't make no difference on a boat like this to the engine, those vents don't work."

"And gasoline's heavier than air," Rusty went on, "so the fumes, they just sit on the bottom. It's OK at first, but then you get out in the channel and open up the engine, that slow leak, now she's pouring into the compartment like water from a faucet. Next thing you know there's a whole lot more gas fume than oxygen down there underneath you. And without those vents, there ain't no place for it to go but all under your deck."

"So then you get out a ways and you turn on your propane burner to heat up some coffee," Felix continued with the lesson, ominously, "or maybe you light a cigarette near the fumes coming up through the deck—

and once you under way, you don't smell them 'cause of the wind—well, that's all she wrote for you."

"There ain't nothing more explosive than gasoline in a container," Rusty explained. "And a big boat like this makes one hell of a container."

Felix was nodding in agreement. "A teaspoon of gas, same as a stick of dynamite."

Therese smirked at the men. "You two think you can scare a girl with your stories. And you," she said, pointing a finger at her father, "you just trying to change the subject. I ain't forgetting that arm of yours. We get home tonight, it still don't move, you going to the doctor. I don't care you throw a fit."

"You see," Felix joked to Rusty, "that's why they say it's bad luck to take a woman on a boat. She drive you crazy, and you ain't got nowhere to go to get away from her."

"Except overboard," Rusty suggested, giving Therese a look.

"Don't you worry, you two," the girl responded. "I need to, I can get this boat home all by my lonesome."

Their easy banter sped the day along, though the three of them, used to one another after nearly a month on the water, had learned to work together almost silently. The shuffling of dredges over the side, the slow circling of the boat, the culling of the catch, and shoveling it into gunnysacks—every job on board meshed with every other. Felix, at the wheel of the *Mathilde*, anticipated the winching of a net by slackening off on the throttle; Rusty, ready to drop a dredge over its roller, waited for Therese to seal the near compartment she had been packing.

Rusty, especially, took care to keep an eye on the other two. Handling the chains and metal-toothed frames and heavy trawl boards of the *Squall* with his brothers, he had seen things go wrong so quickly one of them might easily have died. As it was, he still carried the scar of a gash across his thigh from a rusted cable that broke under the weight of a net it was winching aboard. The jagged wire threads where the line had snapped, like the fangs of a striking snake or the razor claws of a raking paw, had sheared his khaki pants so cleanly, he first thought the cable had miraculously caught a fold of cloth and missed his flesh. Only in the next moment as the leg of his pants began to stain red, and then something darker than red, did he realize his thigh had been shredded. On the way in for medical assistance, the hasty tourniquet of a knotted belt slowing his bleeding, his brothers had teased him mercilessly about how close they had just come to finally having a sister, but the tense set of his father's jaw as the man slammed the boat through the rough chop, racing home while radioing for help, left no doubt in the boy's mind about the seriousness of the injury he had sustained.

So Rusty not only did his own job, but he made sure the old man, whose frailty he had sometimes glimpsed, and the girl, always full of bluff and bravado, were never in harm's way.

But the boy was unable to protect Felix from the red tide that had burst from the canal of a weakened artery in his brain. Though the old man could twitch his left arm by the time the *Mathilde* headed in that afternoon, it was obvious that something serious was wrong

After they had off-loaded their catch and, as he did every night, Felix had signed the receipt for the total paid, the buyer asked with a laugh, "What's this? Some kind of joke?"

Therese looked at the sheet of paper. The signature wandered all over the page. "Daddy?" she asked, holding up the clipboard.

"I know," he said, grinning as if embarrassed. "Damnedest thing. I couldn't remember how to make my hand sign my name."

"You did this with your good hand?"

"Yeah," Felix assured her, "my right."

"Try it again," she encouraged.

He had trouble picking up the pencil Therese held out to him on the clipboard, so the girl, to spare him further embarrassment, threaded it through his fingers. Watching an erratic line scrawl across the page as Felix tried to scratch the three stripes of the letter *F*, Therese covered his hand with her own and guided his signature across the bottom of the receipt. She handed the clipboard back to the buyer, who had stopped smiling.

"Maybe," the man suggested, "your daddy ought to have somebody look at that hand."

"Yeah," Rusty answered for her, "they gonna run by the doctor tomorrow."

Therese nodded as she clasped her father's arm and started back to the boat with him.

"Terry," Rusty called after her, "why don't you let me come along home with you tonight? Maybe you can run me back to my house later on."

The girl started to refuse, then felt her father's arm limp in her grasp. "Probably wouldn't be such a bad idea," she yielded. "I might could use some help tonight."

Once on board, Felix seemed to manage the wheel without too much difficulty, even using a hand that would no longer sign his name. But getting on and off the boat was not so easy with only one good arm. Rusty stayed close to him in case he slipped as he mounted the gunnel.

With the boat tied up in their slip at home, Therese walked her father to the house while Rusty started to hose off the deck. She came back out after a few minutes to help clean the boat.

"How's your daddy doing?"

"I think he's starting to get a little worried about it all. Still can't move his arm, and Mama, well, she's pretty upset. She's in there putting him to bed right now."

Rusty tightened the nozzle to spray some dried mud from a corner of the transom. "She notice this morning?"

"Yeah, she been sitting in the house all day worrying about him."

"There's a lot on her mind, Mrs. Petitjean. I guess she don't need something else to think about."

Therese took a deep breath and slowly exhaled. "It's been harder on her than you know. Alton, I mean."

"Yeah . . ."

The girl thought Rusty was about to say something else, but then he seemed to change his mind. Turning to her work, she stowed the loose gear in the wheelhouse and made sure the drains in the hold were open.

"You done with that hose?"

"Yeah, all done." He twisted the nozzle shut.

"You didn't get these yet, did you?" she asked, standing over the open hold and its divided compartments.

"Not yet. You want for me to do them?"

"No, they're my job."

Rusty leaned on the transom and watched the girl rinse down the compartments.

"Mama says you gonna stay for dinner," the girl told him without looking over her shoulder. "Thinks you probably ought to spend the night in Alton's room, too."

"Let's see after dinner."

The girl had taken off the white rubber boots they used when they were on the water and walked barefoot on the deck. Her feet were long for somebody her size, but sculpted, it seemed to Rusty. At least, that's how he thought of them.

He found himself often thinking about her body. The hands were long, too, and her face. Compared to the round girls with whom he had grown up and gone to school, everything about Therese seemed angular, as if cut from rock. The other girls, they seemed made of water, pulsing, rippling under a boy's touch. But this one, she was all chiseled granite. Sometimes, at dawn, at twilight, he thought he could almost see the small facets, the slight chips pocking the stone, the tiny—almost impercepti- ble—shadows darkening her cheeks. He remembered once comparing water to stone, but looking at Therese, the boy knew it was stone he pre- ferred. Water, it took its form from the lashing wind, from the currents driving it across the worn contours of the seabed, from the tide drawn back and forth by the moon. But stone, stone resisted manipulation. Water accepted the shape of its container. Not stone. It insisted upon its own form.

Watching her work, Rusty admired the muscles of her bare back that he imagined under her shirt. He had seen her legs, crossed beneath a dress. The hard line of her calves had hinted at the tense curve of her thighs; the blue jeans, as she bent to get a better angle on the upper walls of the hold, offered a dark image of those long muscles.

His thoughts thickened, and he wrestled with images of the girl that, he knew, he had no right to savor. The lurid scenes to which he succumbed, unable to resist, were the impossible concoctions of an inexperienced imagination. The boy, despite opportunities he sometimes later regretted having declined, had never been with a woman.

Though still a virgin, mostly thanks to a shyness that a few girls in his class had found irresistible, Rusty had offered in defense against their desire for him a now fading religious fervor. He had somehow linked his resisting of the temptations of the flesh, as Father Danziger described such sins, with the salvation of his mother's soul; knowing her a suicide, the boy bargained his virginity against her place in heaven. He knew the priest had, at first, refused to bury his mother in consecrated ground. Lately, he had begun to doubt a church that would condemn a woman whose suffering had driven her to suicide: if such a sufferer did not deserve mercy, then perhaps such a church did not deserve his faith.

His eyes fell upon Therese's bare ankle just as she looked back at him. Embarrassed, he turned and put his hands on the transom, surveying the marsh on the far side of the bayou.

Now that it was October, the sunsets came earlier. Tonight the sky in the east was already purpling with evening. To the west, the blue was staining pink as the sun sank across the bay. It was still warm; mosquitoes, rising out of the marsh, buzzed in the breeze. The water, too, was still warm; at the buyer's dock, somebody had mentioned a hurricane was churning in the Atlantic, maybe heading their way. The season might be coming to an end, he thought, but it wasn't over yet.

28.

The next morning, Felix was no worse than he had been the night before. However, though he maintained that his left arm showed definite improvement and though he managed to wiggle it by thrusting his shoulder forward and back, no one else at breakfast could detect any change in his condition. When Mathilde demanded he write his name across an envelope on the table, he refused even to pick up the pen she had laid beside his right hand. He huffed, as if offended that the woman would put him to the test rather than take his own word for the inconsequence of his malady and the progress of his recuperation. But she was neither mollified by his attempt to downplay the disabling he had suffered nor intimidated by his bluster.

Despite Mathilde's objections, he insisted on taking the boat out. His wife did manage to extract from him the promise he would come in early so they could see the doctor in Magnolia that afternoon.

Rusty, mostly silent at the breakfast table, had spent the night. It was only the second time he had slept in Alton's bed, and just as during the first night there, his restless sleep in the Petitjean house was discomforted by troubling dreams. Though he strained to suppress any memories of Alton's murder by his brothers each time he nodded off in the fresh sheets, Rusty would start from his pillow minutes later, vague images of a twitching hand or an unblinking eye refusing to recede with the dream from which he had awakened.

Even more disconcerting, however, were the dreams about Therese— or women very like Therese—from which he awoke slick with sweat and embarrassed by their residue. The tangle of limbs, the sheen of bare flesh, the huffing breaths still echoing down the corridors of his ears as he awoke in confusion, unsure where he lay, teased him as he shook free of the clinging dream.

The desolation of that bed, to which he could hope neither to restore Alton nor to entice the sister of the boy he had helped murder, enwrapped him in its brambles. No matter how exhausted, whichever way he turned, he found himself pricked awake.

Worse, the long, sleepless night in a room stored with mementoes of Alton's life confronted Rusty with the tracks of a ghost. Like a mattress sagging under the weight of an unseen body and a fluffed pillow impressed with the indentation of its head, the room seemed to mold itself around Alton's absence. The shirts that hung over creased pants in the small armoire remembered the boy's shoulders. Toy soldiers, headless and one-legged after a childhood of tabletop battles, did not desert the formation Alton had last ordered. A half-finished model airplane on his desk did not complete itself. As Rusty pitched from side to side in the narrow bed, his eyes fell upon object after object, which each in its own voice seemed to utter Alton's name as a kind of question—a question, he well knew, that would never be answered.

This chorus of Alton's things, silently protesting their perplexed abandonment, disturbed Rusty's sleep like crickets chirping in the dark. It felt to him as if everything in the room was hardening around Alton's absence. And what was a ghost, anyway, he began to understand while lying in a dead man's bed, but a felt absence, a keen unpresence?

It calmed him, thinking of the melancholy of the room in that way.

As he lay there, recalling his other dreams, those woozy scenes of remorseless passion, he realized they, too, invoked their own ghosts of rapt longing. The ghost whom he had kissed in his dream and who had done more, much more, than kiss him in return was an absence felt along the whole length of his body as he remembered her imagined writhing and entwining, moaning and whispering.

Rusty tried to distract himself with a framed photo on the windowsill, a picture of Alton and Therese in a child's pirogue. But it was of no use. He had never liked photographs; now he understood why. *Reminding you what's gone*, he argued to himself, *all they good for.* That was the reason he kept no photo of his mother, he began to see, though he had never thought of it quite like that before. *Nothing but a ghost stuck to a piece of paper, that's all it is, a photograph*, he decided, a little unnerved, turning the frame facedown on the windowsill.

"You believe in ghosts?" Rusty asked Therese as they prepared their gear on the way out into Bay Batiste for their abbreviated day of dredging. As usual, Felix was at the wheel while they worked in the stern.

"You thinking about Halloween, boy? Wear a sheet and go trick-or-treating?"

"Not exactly." He tried to be cautious in his explanation. "I just was thinking about them and wondering what you thought."

"Thinking about ghosts? What kind? Some hobgoblins or devils or what?"

"Just plain old ghosts. You know, dead people who won't stay put where you bury them."

"Well, yeah, that would be a ghost, all right. Or come to think of it, isn't that really a zombie you talking about? The walking dead. One of those voodoo monsters."

"Like they do up on the Hermitage? Mary Two-Dogs and her people?"

"Yeah, if that's voodoo, what she's up to. I don't know, though. Mama, she won't have no talk of any of that around the house. Too superstitious, I guess."

"I never seen her, Mary, but I heard stories when I was a boy."

"Me, too. About the chickens, I heard all about that. And the thing with the snake."

Rusty blushed. "Yeah, I heard that story, too."

Therese smiled at his embarrassment. "You didn't believe all that, did you?"

"No," the boy insisted. " 'Course not. Who could believe anything like that? You'd have to be a fool."

"Those morons we went to school with, they didn't have no trouble believing all that foolishness."

Now Rusty smiled. "Yeah, well, Gaspar Hebert and Gus Bilich, yeah, they probably did think so. They weren't exactly the sharpest knives in the drawer."

"And that idiot Frank Kotor and his friend Eddie Allemand."

"No, not those two. They wouldn't have fallen for a story like that, not those boys."

"Who you think told me the story?" Therese assured him. "And their eyes as big as silver dollars while they telling me. Eddie, he even swears it's a water moccasin, the snake."

"You making this up."

"No, I'm not. I say, 'Hell, Eddie, a cottonmouth is poisonous. Kill you graveyard dead, it sinks those fangs in you.' Know what Frank says to that?"

"What?"

"Says she's got the immunity against it, Mary Two-Dogs. Says snakes, they can't hurt her. Then Eddie, he throws in, 'No matter where they bite her.' Those two, lucky to cross a street without getting themselves killed, they so stupid."

Rusty shook his head. "Vernon, too, I guess. That poor thing probably believed the whole story."

"Vernon Gremillion? Goes without saying."

The two of them laughed.

"No wonder you and me done so good in school," Therese joked.

"You mean, considering the competition?"

She gave him a smile and went to check on her father. A few moments later, Rusty heard her panicked call for help.

Hurrying around the dredging equipment positioned across the deck, the boy found Therese trying to talk to Felix. The old man couldn't pronounce whatever it was he was attempting to say. His eyes were clouded with confusion and, it seemed to Rusty, sadness.

Yet the boat was on course, the throttle open. Felix had held the *Mathilde* steady as it crossed Bay Batiste.

Therese, obviously frightened by her father's sudden inability to speak, begged him to turn them around and head home. "We got to get you to a doctor," she pleaded.

Felix ignored her.

When Rusty tried to take the wheel, the old man resisted and shook his gray head, growling incomprehensible curses. He was still the captain, even if he had only one good arm and even if his tongue had thickened in his mouth. There was enough of him left in working order to steer an oyster lugger, he seemed to be insisting.

"Mr. Petitjean," Rusty said softly, laying his hand on the old man's bony shoulder. "Mr. Petitjean, we got to get you home. You understand what I'm saying?"

When Felix turned his face toward Rusty, the boy saw that the sadness in the old man's eyes had driven out the confusion. The captain nodded slowly and swung the boat in a broad arc back toward home.

"Why don't you let me take the wheel, Mr. Petitjean, and Terry can see to you? You lie down on the cushions over the lockers. Rest a little till we get in."

The old man hesitated, then stepped back from the wheel, though still holding it steady until Rusty took over.

Therese sat beside her father and had him rest his head in her lap. Brushing the hair from his eyes, she put her arm around him. Rusty, glancing in their direction, saw Felix fumbling to take his daughter's free hand in his own. He was worried, the old man. He was beginning to admit to himself that he hadn't slept funny on his arm, that his hand hadn't simply forgotten how to sign his name, that his tongue hadn't really swollen in his mouth. Something was happening, the kind of thing that didn't get cured. Rusty knew what Mr. Petitjean would say if he could still speak: "Damn shame," he would sigh, cursing the inevitable, "goddamn shame, that's what it is."

Rusty had a following sea, the wind blowing in and urging the boat along toward home, so he made good time. He sensed Therese's relief when he dropped the throttle to just above idle as they neared their slip on the Petitjeans' bayou.

Even as they helped the old man from the boat onto the dock, his wife was running from the house toward them. She knew they were back much too early. "What's wrong?" she shouted as she approached.

Therese shook her head. "Daddy can't talk right, Mama. Something's the matter."

"You stubborn old man," his wife berated him. "I told you not to go out there this morning."

Felix responded with a dismissive garble of grunts, sputtering out of him like a dry cough.

"You going to the doctor right now, you hear me?" she resolved. "No ifs, ands, or buts about it. We getting in the truck and going to Magnolia right this minute."

Felix sighed, no longer able to put up an argument.

"All right," Mathilde went on, "let's get going."

All four of them walked together toward the truck. The old man tried to pull his good arm free of his wife's grasp, but she held fast to it. "You just lean on me for once," she said with a newfound determination.

When Therese ran ahead to the house for her mother's purse and keys, Rusty caught a glimpse of the old man's face: he was disgusted but had quit putting up a fight. The boy was reminded of a rabbit gone limp in the toothed jaws of a trap and felt a kind of pity for Felix, who was already falling under the authority of women again, like a little child.

Out of habit, Mathilde started to open the passenger door.

"Maybe you ought to drive, Mrs. Petitjean," Rusty suggested. "Mr. Petitjean, he only got the one hand. He'll have a hard time with the shift."

The boy saw the woman's dawning recognition of how everything in her life was about to change. Her eyes fluttered for a moment with something like fear, but then she took a deep breath and agreed. "Yeah, you right, Rusty. I don't know what I was thinking."

"It's a lot to deal with, ma'am." He didn't want to frighten her any worse than she already was, and so he added, "To deal with all of a sudden, I mean, without any warning."

"Yeah, it's all just dropping out of the blue, isn't it?"

"Yes ma'am, but ain't that always the way?"

Therese hurried back with her mother's things. "You want I should come along, Mama?"

Felix bellowed a deep, serrated "No." Everyone turned. He shook his head vigorously.

"Maybe it's better we go see the doctor by ourselves, baby. No telling how long we gonna have to be there," Mathilde agreed, calming her husband.

After they had gotten Felix into the truck and closed his door, she added in a whisper to her daughter, "I think he's embarrassed about all this, your daddy. Probably don't want a bunch of company."

Therese gave her a kiss. "Don't worry about me. You just go do whatever needs doing for Daddy. I'll take care of things around here. You just deal with him."

Mathilde hugged the girl. "I don't know what we'd do without you," she told Therese. Then she surprised Rusty with an embrace. "I don't know how we'd make it without the two of you."

"You don't have to thank me, ma'am," Rusty responded, suddenly shy. "I'm just glad to be of help."

As her mother started the truck, Therese leaned through the other window and gave her father a kiss on his grizzled cheek. She noticed a strand of drool trailing from the corner of his mouth and wiped it with her handkerchief.

Felix loudly puffed, two or three times, "Buh, buh."

Therese understood him. "Boat? That what you trying to say, Daddy? Boat?"

The old man, breathless, nodded.

"Yeah, Mama, Daddy's right. We might do a little more fishing while you run up to Magnolia."

"Take your time, baby. We gonna be a while, I'm sure."

Therese stepped down from the running board and watched her mother follow the gravel road until the truck disappeared in the trees.

"So what now?" Rusty had been standing at a distance while the family said good-bye.

"We got a hold full of ice," Therese reminded him, "and a tank full of gas."

"Fine by me," Rusty agreed. "Let's take her back out."

The two of them closed up the house, shutting the windows and checking to be sure Mathilde had left nothing heating on the stove or in the oven.

"You know where we going?" Rusty wondered out loud as they headed back to the boat.

"Not exactly," Therese admitted.

29.

When Rusty and Therese walked in the door that night after tying up the boat, Mathilde was sitting at the table, nursing a cup of tea. They sat down beside her.

"So what did the doctor say?" Therese asked.

"Strokes. A string of them."

"Any since we left?"

"No, but maybe more on the way. They can't tell, the doctors, so they keeping your daddy overnight for observation at the clinic."

"They got medicine for it?" Rusty wondered.

Mathilde slowly shook her head. "They ain't got nothing for it."

"But he'll get better on his own, won't he, Mama? I mean, not right away but eventually?"

"Don't know that, either. Everything's maybe this or maybe that with them. They don't know the first thing about it. Maybe he'll wake up talking one morning, maybe he won't."

"So there's nothing for them to do?" Rusty asked.

Mathilde shrugged. "Told him to take it easy. That's their medicine. Take it easy."

"Well, at least you'll have him home tomorrow," the boy offered, but Mathilde was not comforted.

"I'm going back to spend the night with him at the clinic. Keep an eye on things, tell them what he needs. He can't speak or write. Somebody has to be there for him."

"Then why'd you come all the way home, Mama? We could have managed by ourselves here."

"I needed my things. Your daddy, too. Toothbrush and things." She looked at her daughter. "And it wouldn't be proper, Rusty spending the night alone in the house with you. I come back to give him a ride to his house in the truck."

"Mama, you know nothing would've happened."

"Ain't a matter of what would happen, just what might happen."

Rusty nodded. "Your mother's right. You got your reputation to think of."

"You two are a pair, I'll tell you," Therese sighed.

"Well, before we do anything else," Mathilde said, taking a final sip of tea, "let me get together some dinner for us."

"You sit, Mama. I'll take care of it."

"No, you been out on that boat all day."

Mathilde started to get up, but Rusty stopped her. "I'll give Terry a hand, Mrs. Petitjean. I been cooking at home ever since my mama died. I know how to fix a thing or two."

Both women smiled. Every man they knew had his specialty—brown-sugar fudge, oyster roux in pastry shells, flounder stuffed with shrimp—but that was all he knew how to prepare. And since it usually took two or three women to clean up after the man when he was done, most families kept men out of the kitchen except on holidays, when there were plenty of aunts and female cousins around to deal with the mess the fathers and uncles left behind.

Rusty knew what women thought of men in the kitchen. "I ain't kidding. I really can cook. You just watch."

"Let's give him a try, Mama," Therese decided, still smiling. "You go lie down. We'll call you when we ready."

"But what about the boat?"

"I'll go hose it down after we get the dinner started. You go rest, Mrs. Petitjean. Me and Terry, we'll take care of it all."

"Maybe I will lie down for a little while. Y'all call me, you need any help, OK?"

"You just go on, Mama. I'll make sure Rusty don't burn down the house with his cooking."

"I tell y'all I can cook," the boy protested.

"We'll see," Therese responded skeptically.

But the girl was surprised at how skillfully Rusty handled himself in a kitchen. His knuckles guiding the big blade of a chef's knife, he made fast work of an onion Therese needed chopped for the shrimp stew she was preparing. As she whisked a roux of oil and flour to the color of cinnamon over a low flame, he diced celery and green peppers for her, then sautéed the vegetables with a bay leaf. The air filled with the nut and sugar smells of roux and sauté. They worked quietly, as on the *Mathilde*, each pausing to let the other one pass. Rusty tossed in garlic and herbs, salt and cayenne. After the onions turned soft, he stirred everything he had prepared into Therese's kettle. When the vegetables were coated with the roux, he added water to the pot and dropped in a cheesecloth sack of shrimp heads and shells along with the last of the season's tomatoes, each peeled and then quartered. The iron kettle trembled almost to a boil while rough-cut Irish potatoes he had added bobbed in the fragrant water. Therese dumped in the shrimp Rusty had peeled for her and covered the simmering pot.

"Let's go see to the boat while this cooks," the girl suggested.

When they returned, Rusty got down three bowls from the cabinet beside the sink and a ladle and three soupspoons from the drawer. Therese checked the dinner.

"We ready to go?"

"Yeah," she judged, turning off the fire. "You put it on the table, and I'll go get Mama."

Therese was surprised that her mother had not fallen asleep on the bed.

"Too much on my mind, I guess," she said, standing.

"So how'd Rusty do?" Mathilde wanted to know as her daughter walked her to the kitchen.

"Didn't cut off any fingers, at least," Therese assured her.

But when Mathilde tried the stew, she turned to the boy with respect. "You wasn't lying. You really can cook."

"Terry done most of it. I just cut things up for her."

"He done more than he lets on," Therese confided to her mother. "I tell you, we could open up a restaurant, the two of us."

"Wouldn't recommend that." Mathilde laughed. "Cooking's too hard to do for money."

"Only for love, huh, Mama?"

"That's right, baby. Do the easy things for money; save the hard things for love."

"Well, I don't know, Mrs. Petitjean. If raking oysters is one of those easy things you talking about, then what you do for love must really break your back."

Therese burst into laughter. "Rusty Bruneau, you asking a woman if what she does for love breaks her back? I never thought I'd hear such a filthy thing coming out of your mouth."

"Filthy?" the boy repeated. But then he got the joke he had inadvertently made. His cheeks turned red as cayenne pepper.

"Terry, leave the boy be. You know that's not what he meant. Just ignore her, Rusty. I know what you were getting at." Mathilde turned pensive. "And you right. Love does break our backs. All of us."

The three of them ate without speaking for a little while. Then her mother asked Therese how they had made out on their own with the boat that afternoon.

"Not so good," the girl admitted. "Those beds ain't easy to find in open water."

"Mr. Petitjean, I guess he don't believe in marking all his leases. We kept looking for our numbers, but there weren't any lease signs like everyone else got sticking up from their beds."

"I don't know." Mathilde shrugged. "He never talks to me about that sort of thing."

"Rusty, he noticed the signs were missing right away," Therese said with a hint of admiration.

"Some of his tracts he got marked, but most, not. I should've asked

Mr. Petitjean before. Just didn't think it was any of my business how he ran his leases."

"We had these beds so long," Mathilde explained. "The hurricanes, after all these years they must've knocked everything of ours flat, and nobody ever bothers to put things right out there. Figure another storm will be along soon enough, I guess, so what's the point?"

"It's true," Rusty agreed. "They got camps over near ours on Bayou Dulac had their windows blown out by Flossie—what was that, 1948 or so? They ain't never repaired the glass, even all these years later. Got squares of cardboard to keep out the rain."

Therese smirked. "Yeah, those fishing camps, that's where y'all go to get away from the women. Had just one of us out there, though, I guarantee you somebody would fix those windows in a hurry."

"Don't doubt it," Rusty said under his breath.

"Anyway, Mama, we had ourselves a real hard time finding our reefs."

"You couldn't figure it out?"

"Ain't a lot to go by out there, ma'am," Rusty explained.

"Daddy's the only one who knows where they are."

Mathilde sighed. "And he can't speak and can't write."

"Maybe he'll be better in the morning," Rusty hoped.

"Maybe, but I wouldn't count on it."

Rusty sighed. "So what we gonna do tomorrow? You want I should come by in the morning?"

"No use wasting money on fuel and ice, we don't know where we going," Therese pointed out. "On the other hand, these doctors, they ain't free—even if not a one of them has a single goddamn idea what to do about Daddy."

"You don't need to swear, Therese," her mother objected, "but you right. We got bills to pay."

Dejection settled upon the table.

"Well, it's been a long day already, and we ain't done yet," Mathilde decided. "We'll have to sort all this out tomorrow."

"Yeah, Mama, if you gonna drop Rusty off and get back to the clinic before it gets too late, you better be on your way."

"So, Terry, you want me in the morning, or no?" Rusty asked.

"Let's hold off on going out tomorrow until we figure what we gonna do about everything. Wouldn't hurt to sleep late for once, neither. Not after the last couple days."

Mathilde agreed. "Yeah, that's a good idea. You two take a holiday tomorrow."

Therese stood up. "OK, I don't want to rush you, Mama, but you better get going."

"Let me just grab my things, I'll be ready to go."

When she had left the room, Rusty helped clear the table. "We'll talk tomorrow, huh?"

"I ain't worried—except for Daddy."

"We can go through the state, get the surveys. But that's gonna take time."

"We ain't got time. Thanks to you and your brothers, we don't have months to sit around waiting for the mailman. Those notes are coming due."

"I'll talk to Darryl."

Therese sighed. "I may have to talk to Darryl."

Rusty was about to say something else when Mathilde walked in, an overnight bag in her hand. "We better be going," she said.

On the way to his house, Rusty drove the truck. "You doing OK, Mrs. Petitjean?"

"Hard not to think it's God's hand in all this."

"God's hand?"

"Like the Bible preacher says on the radio. Smiting us for what we done."

He took a quick breath. "What we done?"

"Not you, Rusty, me. What I done."

"You think bad things happen, it's a punishment from God?"

"When they happen one after another, what else can you think?"

"Bad luck."

"Maybe that's the same thing."

Rusty shook his head. "You think God was punishing Alton for something he done?"

"Alton? He was a lamb sacrificed up for what other people done. It's not the one gets struck down but the one left standing God's trying to punish."

"That's true sometimes. What's Mr. Petitjean ever done to deserve what he's going through?"

"He's a good man, my husband. Better than I ever deserved."

"Oh, no ma'am. I'm sure he could talk, he'd be the one saying he didn't deserve you."

"You a sweet boy, Rusty. Just like your mama."

For the rest of the drive, they talked about his mother, anecdotes he had never heard before and details of her life he would never have guessed: the butterfly irises Horse would bring home to her from the marsh to plant around the house, the chocolate she'd heat to dip her strawberries in, the orange hat out of a catalogue she wore to church one Sunday.

Starved for any tidbits about his mother, Rusty slowed the truck so as not to get home before Mathilde had finished her reminiscences. The woman Mrs. Petitjean described was much more spirited and vibrant than the mother he remembered. But the woman that her friend recalled with nearly painful tenderness had been defeated by the time he was a baby, leaving him to be raised by a mother always melancholy and tentative, slow to laugh and quick to wince.

As the red taillights of the Petitjean truck faded after Mathilde had left him on his porch, Rusty looked at the steps and realized he could not remember a time when flowers—butterfly irises—bordered the house. Now, only the brown stubs of weeds doused with gasoline or bleach sprouted in front of the porch.

"So old man Petitjean had a heart attack, I hear."

The voice surprised him. It was Darryl. "Stroke," Rusty corrected. "Not heart attack."

Darryl swung open the screen door and sat down on one of the rocking chairs on the porch. "People say he can't talk."

"Not properly, at least. How you hear that already?"

"Down at the launch after you and the girl off-loaded this evening. Everybody knows about it."

"Yeah, he can't talk right."

"And that ain't all he can't do, I understand."

"Mrs. Petitjean just dropped me off on the way to the clinic up in Magnolia. They keeping him tonight for observation."

"Sounds like he's in a bad way."

"Could be worse."

"Oh, yeah, it can always be worse." Darryl laughed. "And it's gonna be, time we get done with them."

"They gonna manage. Those beds of theirs, it's money in the bank."

"Not exactly. It's money at the bottom of fifteen feet of water, and the man who knows what water, he's not talking."

"They gonna send for the surveys. The state's got records on all their leases."

"Surveys? Shit, Rusty, you sound like you don't know the first god-damn thing about dredging the little bastards. You talking about a lease that's three, maybe four hundred acres of open water, and the only one can tell you where the beds are is the old man planted them there. Even with the surveys, knowing where on the fuckin' lease the oysters are, that's the real trick."

"But we been out with him."

"Oh, yeah, you been out what, a month or five weeks? You couldn't find oyster number one on those leases by yourself. Shit, you don't remember what it was like when Daddy picked up those tracts from the Turanovich widow? One empty dredge after another. If we hadn't found Tito's old crewman, we never would have figured out where those oysters were."

Rusty had been leaning against the porch railing; now he came and sat down beside his brother. "You said we could maybe work something out with them. Give them a little more time or something."

"No, we long past that. It's like I told you last time: ain't no kindness in postponing the inevitable. An animal got a broken leg, you kill it. That's the kind thing to do. And the Petitjeans, well, their leg is broke."

"No, it ain't. Just give them a day or two, see how the old man does. We gonna get together tomorrow sometime and figure out what to do next. They got a whole lot coming down on their heads all at once."

"Whose fault is that? Look, babe, we done what the sheriff suggested, sent you over there to lend a hand."

"It was Sheriff Christovich's idea, me going there?"

"He brought it up, but I'm the one decided to send you. Me and Ross, we the ones carrying the extra load with you gone. But those days are over." Darryl softened a bit. "You done a good job. Thanks to you we got a start on finding them oysters once we get our hands on the Petitjean beds. Like you say, you been out with the old man. At least you got a sense of where they are."

"That's why the hell you sent me to help?"

"Yeah, that and keeping an eye on things for us." Rusty's brother laughed. "Shit, I told Ross we could use you to sabotage them, they start making too much money and they look like they might pay off the notes. But we ain't got to worry about that now, do we? They done sabotaged themselves."

"You son of a bitch—"

"Take it easy, babe. It was the sheriff's idea. A good one, too, make people think we didn't have nothing to gain from Alton falling into that bayou. And if there was side benefits to our good deed, well, God helps them that helps themselves."

"You used me."

Darryl ignored him. "And with two boats, Ross can work our own beds with one of the boys—maybe Bascomb or Jules or even one of the niggers, if we have to—while you and me, we use the other boat to find all those Petitjean oysters. What did you call them? Money in the bank."

"What about the Petitjeans? What they gonna do?"

"You think they concerned themselves about what we were gonna do when they murdered Daddy?"

"We don't know they done that, Darryl. You the one decided it was Alton stabbed your father. And you the one deciding to ruin that family."

"You just better remember what family you part of, boy. You ain't no Petitjean. Like it or not, you one of us."

"You think I don't know that? You think there's anything I can ever do make me forget that for one goddamn minute?"

Darryl's voice edged toward anger. "You ain't got no reason to ever want to forget where you come from."

Rusty could feel the muscles in his arms tense. He took a deep breath. "Look, Little Horse, all I'm saying is we pull the rug out from under them, the Petitjeans ain't got nowhere to go but down."

"They should've worried about that before their boy went and got himself killed and the old man wore out. We done all we can for those people. They on their own from now on."

"We can't leave them like that."

"You go over there tomorrow. Take the Caddy. Tell them I don't know we can spare you as much as we did. We got our own beds to tend. Need you in a skiff with your tongs the next few weeks."

"It ain't right."

Darryl got up and stretched. "You too tenderhearted, little brother. It make you feel better, though, maybe I will give them one more chance. You go tell them the bad news in the morning. I'll go offer them a way out tomorrow night."

30.

The next day, Rusty made himself sleep until nearly noon. After he had fixed some eggs, he put off the trip to the Petitjean house, washing his clothes and hanging them out to dry. But by two o'clock his guilt overcame him, and he took the Cadillac to tell Therese his brothers needed him back on the *Squall* to help with their own oyster beds.

When he knocked on the front door, no one answered. But then he saw Therese sitting on the dock, her legs dangling above the bayou.

He stood next to her, and she squinted for a moment, looking up into the sun over his shoulder. The girl grabbed his pants leg and pulled him down beside her.

"So what's the story with your daddy? How come they ain't home yet?"

"Mama called awhile ago."

"They on their way?"

"The doctors say Daddy had another 'setback' last night."

"What they mean by that?"

"Something to do with his leg, I don't know. They want to keep him there at the clinic, but he threw such a fit, they letting him go this afternoon. Ain't of no use anyway, them doctors. They like somebody tells you to look out it might rain when the water's already up to your knees."

"So what we gonna do?"

"I wish I knew." The girl sighed. "You talk to your brother last night? He gonna give us a break?"

"Little Horse says they need me back to rake the shallow beds. He don't think you should count on me."

"The son of a bitch," Therese hissed through tight lips. "He knows he's got us now, don't he?"

Rusty nodded, ashamed to talk.

"And what you gonna do about it, boy? You gonna let Little Horse and that other asshole of a brother you got tell you to sail away and leave us to drown?"

"If we knew where the oysters were, it'd be one thing. But even with the surveys of the leases—if we had them—we could spend the next month looking for the beds and not find enough to pay for the fuel it took to do it. And your daddy can't tell us."

"What if we let him steer us out there? He just take us out and let us do the work."

"That's what we been doing. But you seen him. He ain't fit to spend the day on the water. You'll kill him, you do that. And who knows how many more setbacks he's gonna have? Your daddy, he ain't the solution to your problems."

"And I guess you ain't the solution, either, huh?" the girl taunted him.

"You tell me where your oysters are, I'll go get them for you."

Therese leaned back her head and stared into the sun with her eyes closed. "I need to talk to your brother."

Rusty watched two mallards, a drake and a hen, glide over the bayou and splash as they landed near the reeds on the far shore. "Little Horse'll be here tonight. He wants to talk to y'all."

"I bet he does," Therese murmured, her eyes still closed.

"He promised me he's gonna give you a way out. One last chance, he said."

"Yeah, I know what that chance is gonna be, too."

"What?"

"What you think, brother-in-law?"

"He ain't never said nothing about that to me."

"You just as well run along home, boy."

But when Mathilde and Felix pulled up a few minutes later, Rusty was still sitting on the dock with Therese, though neither was speaking.

The old man had trouble getting out of the truck. He had to lift his left leg with his right hand. When Rusty had helped him down onto the gravel, Felix reached back into the truck and extracted a cane from the floorboard. Leaning heavily on its curved handle, the old man hobbled into the house.

"I told you he wasn't fit no more for skippering a boat," Rusty whispered to Therese, shaking his head.

The girl ignored him and followed her father into the house. They all took seats around the kitchen table.

"The doctors give you the cane, Daddy?"

Mathilde was already in the habit of answering for him. "They said your father was lucky it wasn't no worse. Lucky not to wind up in a wheelchair, they said."

"I guess you awful glad to be home, huh, Daddy?"

He nodded his head as if it were very heavy.

"Maybe we'll brew you up some coffee. What you say to that?"

Again Mathilde answered. "He's having a hard time with liquids. 'Cause of his mouth. They gave us some paper straws to use."

"Well, we'll fix you something else then."

"Maybe you can get your daddy some water, baby. I think he's thirsty."

As Therese got up to fill a glass with water, Felix shook his head, but no one noticed.

When the girl placed the drink in front of him, Mathilde pulled a straw from her purse, positioned it in the glass for her husband, and held it to his lips. He started to shake his head again, then sighed and took a sip. His wife smiled at him, as at a child who had pleased his parent, and put down the glass on the table.

"Rusty says Little Horse is coming by tonight. Wants to give us one last chance."

"Yeah, we need to talk to him. There's no way we pay off those notes on time now. Between the funeral for your brother, these doctor bills coming, and everything else, we ain't gonna have near enough to pay what we owe."

"But, Mama, we been doing real good out on the reefs. There must be money from all them oysters we been taking."

"Yeah, you been bringing in money, but the expenses, they eat it up in a hurry."

"The fuel and the ice, they ain't that much."

Mathilde seemed embarrassed. "That ain't the only expenses we got these days."

"What other expenses?"

"I think Mrs. Petitjean's talking about me," Rusty said softly.

Therese looked to her mother, who nodded in agreement.

"Your father insisted on paying the boy."

Felix banged his cane on the floor to get the others' attention. Gravely, he nodded his head.

"I ain't saying you wrong to do it, honey. It's only fair." Mathilde turned back to Therese. "But we was just making it with Alton doing the job for nothing. You add Rusty's share, that's just about all the profit we take in. Why you think we needed these loans in the first place?"

"I don't know what we'd do either," Rusty admitted, "we had to pay a crewman. There just ain't enough oysters out there anymore."

"I guess Horse was right about that, after all," Therese sighed. "We can't neither make a go of it on our own, the Bruneaus nor the Petit-jeans."

Rusty agreed. "Daddy, if he hadn't been doing all those things on the side, I doubt we would've made it all these years."

Therese offered him a look of scorn.

"Not that he was right to do it, those things—I ain't defending all those underhanded shenanigans with them politicians—but he was just looking after his family, keeping us fed."

"Darryl always done what he had to do," Mathilde explained.

Now Rusty seemed embarrassed as he turned to Felix. "Mr. Petitjean, I got half of everything you paid me hidden in my room at home. I want you to have it. If I still had it all, I'd give you every penny back, but my brother, Little Horse, he took the rest for their share. Still, I want you to have what I got to give."

Mathilde was touched by the boy's offer. "That's real sweet of you, Rusty, but we can't take your money. You worked too hard for it. We couldn't take it even as a loan."

"I didn't crew your boat for the money, ma'am. I owed it to you."

"Owed it?" Mathilde smiled. "You were just a good neighbor, an angel sent from God, that's what you been."

Rusty turned again to Felix. "I really do have to insist, Mr. Petitjean, you take my money. I can't explain, but I'd be robbing you, you didn't take it back from me."

Therese had been watching the boy with a gaze that hardened as he spoke. "Yeah, we'll have your money," she decided for her family, not taking her eyes off him.

When her mother tried to object, she cut the woman off. "Don't be impolite, Mama. Anybody could see he's made up his mind. Least you can do is be gracious about it."

"You sure, Rusty?"

"Yes ma'am."

The woman put her hand over the boy's. "Your mama, she'd be real proud of the man you grew up to be."

"That ain't enough to make the difference, though, is it?" Therese asked skeptically.

"It'll help, but no, it still ain't enough," Mathilde admitted. "You two figure anything out about finding our beds?"

Therese shook her head.

"It just all looks the same out there, Mrs. Petitjean," Rusty explained. "You don't already know where you going, you ain't got no landmarks to fix the position, you looking for needles in a haystack."

Felix interrupted the boy with a string of powerful barks: "Buh . . . buh . . . buh . . ."

"Yeah, Daddy, we talking about the boat," Therese agreed. "We don't know where the beds are."

The old man shook his head vigorously.

"Mama, he's upset." Therese patted his shoulder, trying to calm him.

"Buh . . . kuh."

"What are you saying, Daddy?" The girl repeated the sounds. "Buck?"
Felix nodded. "Oooh . . . kuh."

Therese sounded it out. " 'Book.' Is that it, Daddy, 'book'?"

The effort had exhausted him. He sunk back in relief.

"Book." Suddenly, Therese realized what he was talking about and
stood up.

"What is it, baby?" her mother asked, but she was already hurrying
down the hall toward Alton's room.

A moment later, the girl returned, waving her brother's black notebook. "I got it," she announced triumphantly. "I got it."

"Got what?" Her mother still didn't understand.

"Alton, Mama, he wrote down everything Daddy taught him—the
landmarks, the currents, the beds, everything. We got the magnet for
those needles in the haystack." She kissed her father. "You saved us,
Daddy." Then she added, "You and Alton."

Rusty was paging through the book. "Yeah, this is good. But it ain't
enough. Which bed is which here?"

Therese turned back to her father. "Daddy, you know what Rusty is
saying?"

The old man nodded. He reached over to the page the boy was studying and tapped a crescent oyster bed Alton had drawn. He nodded again.

"Rusty, run go get Daddy's charts off the boat."

The boy looked up and smiled. "Yeah, that'll work." He hurried to the
dock.

"We know where the oysters are, Mama. We ain't done for yet."

By the time Rusty drove home in the Cadillac two hours later to get
what was left of his pay for the Petitjeans, he had plotted the locations of
their oyster beds on Felix's charts and copied Alton's notes onto the backs
of the old maps of the whole Barataria system. When Therese suggested
that they could just take Alton's notebook with them on the *Mathilde*,
Rusty refused. "You don't take nothing on the water you not willing to

lose. And we can't afford to lose this," he said, tapping the black book. "From now on, it's our bible." In fact, before he left, the boy had copied the coordinates from the charts into Alton's notebook. "Everything we need to know," he assured Mathilde as he handed over her son's book, "it's all right here. You take care of this, you hear?"

When Rusty got home, though, he found not a single dollar in the cigar box of childhood mementos in which he had hidden the money earned from his work for the Petitjeans. He searched everywhere in the room he shared with his brother—under the mattress, behind the armoire, in all of Ross's things. But he found nothing.

Holding the empty box in his hand, Rusty confronted Darryl about the missing money.

"Don't ask me. I don't sleep in that room. That's between you and Ross, what happened to the money."

"The son of a bitch stole it."

"I don't know that's what happened. And like I already told you, by rights it ain't your money anyway. Me and Ross, we the ones making the sacrifice, pulling your load while you off eating Mrs. Petitjean's pie and pancakes."

"Don't give me that crap. You got your half just like we agreed. The rest of it, that's my money."

"What you want it for, anyway?"

"None of your fuckin' business."

"Hey, little brother, don't you forget who you talking to. So what you gonna do with all that money you got?" Little Horse laughed. "Give it back?"

Rusty blushed.

"Oh, don't tell me that's what you planning to do with it. How can you be such an asshole?"

"It's my money. I'll do whatever I want with it."

"Well, if you had any money left, I guess you might be right. If you had any money left."

"Where's Ross off to?"

"Just like me." Darryl smiled smugly. "Got a date tonight."

"You may think it's a date you got, but the Petitjeans, they all waiting for you over at their house."

"And I bet you already promised them, too, the Petitjeans, didn't you? Play the big hero, save the day, huh? I tell you, they gonna be some disappointed they find out you all talk and no money."

"Y'all not gonna get away with this, I'm warning you."

"You warning me? You just lucky I'm all dressed up to go see those poor folks. Otherwise, I'd teach you not to be so careless with our money. I'd teach you real good."

"I didn't lose my money. Ross stole it."

"I ain't talking about a hundred dollars in a goddamn cigar box. I mean our money—a boat, a house, and a shitload of oyster beds." Darryl turned his back on him and started out the door.

"We know where the oysters are."

Darryl stopped. "What did you say?"

"They got charts with everything marked—reefs, currents, landmarks. I plotted them myself," Rusty boasted. Then he added with contempt, "You know that broke leg they got you was talking about last night? Well, it healed."

"Think that changes anything?" Darryl scoffed. "Just makes it easier for us in the long run, them charts. We home free, babe. I told Ross we could count on you to do the right thing."

Rusty saw that he had made a mistake in revealing what he and the Petitjeans had worked out that afternoon at their house.

Darryl gave the boy a scornful smile. "You done real good, little brother. You couldn't have done no better if you tried."

31.

As Rusty had promised, the Petitjeans were waiting when Darryl arrived in his pale blue Cadillac. Mathilde showed him in with a deferential courtesy he took for submission. They knew he had them, Darryl thought with undisguised satisfaction as he accepted the woman's offer of coffee. On the table were freshly baked molasses crisps.

"We were sorry to hear about you getting sick, Mr. Petitjean."

Felix's face showed its contempt.

"I'm sure he appreciates your sympathy, Darryl," Mathilde answered from the stove where she was lighting a burner under a kettle of water. "He can't speak so good since yesterday."

"So I hear. And from what I understand, that's not all."

"No, the doctors call them some kind of strokes, what he's got."

"Well, we real sorry to hear it. I know it must be hard on y'all, especially on top of losing Alton."

Mathilde was measuring coffee into a white enameled pot. "Tell you the truth, Darryl, we don't know what we gonna do. If it wasn't for your brother Rusty, I don't know how we'd have made it this far."

"Well, that's the thing, Mrs. Petitjean. I wanted to come tell y'all, Rusty, we ain't gonna be able to keep sending him over here no more."

"But Darryl, without him—"

"I feel terrible about it, ma'am, but our own beds, they chockablock full of oysters. Me and Ross, we out there night and day on the *Squall*. We just can't manage by ourselves."

"You can't manage with two, how we gonna manage with none?"

"Well," Darryl smiled, "you do have Therese. My brother says she puts a man to shame the way she handles a boat."

Therese had been listening silently until now. "You know damn well, Darryl Bruneau, I can't rake no oysters by myself."

"I wish there was something I could do, but we need Rusty and his tongs out in a skiff over our shallow beds. We haven't touched them since the last time he come with us."

"Neither of you can handle a pair of tongs?" Therese sneered.

"That's right, Miss Petitjean. We got bigger fish to fry. The tongs, that's Rusty's job."

"And you gonna tell me this ain't connected to the notes coming due we owe you?" the girl went on.

"Did I have something to do with Mr. Petitjean's illness? You want to blame somebody, you blame God. Me, I just got oysters need harvesting, and I can't do it without my little brother."

"Yeah, maybe you didn't get Daddy sick, but whether you had something to do with what happened to Alton, that's a whole other question."

"I don't know where you get this idea we had anything to do with that. Another act of God, that's the way you gotta look at it."

"So all these acts of God you didn't have nothing to do with, I don't guess they change the due dates on the loans we owe you, do they?"

"We got bills, too, you know. Wouldn't be fair to those we owe to put off you paying and then we can't pay them." Darryl took a deep breath and smiled. "Look, Miss Petitjean, if we could come up with some solution here tonight, I'd be tickled pink. All the trouble you folks have had the last few weeks, nothing'd please me more than to help you find some way out of this predicament. Y'all got any ideas?"

The kettle hummed into a piercing whistle. Mathilde turned off the fire and slowly poured the boiling water over the ground coffee. Without looking up from the pot, she offered, "Your brother, he's bringing us his earnings—half of them, at least. That ought to cover this month's payment."

Darryl clucked. "I'm sorry to disappoint you, Mrs. Petitjean, but Rusty talks a better game than he plays. He ain't got no money. Half of it went to pay for food and such at the house, that's true. But the half he kept, well, he don't have a penny left of it. You ask him, he don't know where it went, neither, the money. Just gone. So if you counting on my little brother to bail you out, that dog won't hunt."

"All right," Therese sighed. "You tell us what you got in mind, Little Horse."

"I been thinking about it, yeah. Have the sheriff come over here and throw y'all out of your own house, that's just awful, the very idea of it. Particularly with Mr. Petitjean in the condition he's in now. I mean, to think of the Petitjeans reduced to that, it's just terrible, isn't it?"

Mathilde poured a cup of coffee for Darryl. "You want some milk or sugar?"

"No ma'am, I take my coffee black."

"How about something to eat?"

"I just might. I remember your molasses cookies from when I was a little child."

"That was your mama who made them, not me. She was the one taught me how."

"You don't say. I never knew that."

"She loved her sweets, your mama. Always had something sweet in her pocket, Arlene."

Therese interrupted. "So what's your idea gonna keep the sheriff from throwing us out?"

"We postpone the due dates on your two loans in return for considerations received."

" 'Considerations received'?" Therese mocked. "Where'd you learn to talk like that? From some lawyer?"

Darryl was offended. "Matter of fact, that's exactly where I learned the expression. Wouldn't hurt you none to familiarize yourself with the law, Miss Petitjean, particularly when you on the wrong side of it."

Therese eyed the man, trying to divine whether he was talking about only the loans. "So what's these considerations you looking for?"

"You gonna want to keep the house, leastways as long as you can. And the boat, well, that don't do me no good unless I got more beds to dredge. That's how I come up with the idea. You all sign over some of your leases to us, we count that as value received for extending your loans. Sort of like interest, you might say."

"Value received? You spending a lot of time with them lawyers, ain't you?"

"All I'm trying to do, Miss Petitjean, is make it easy on you. Y'all can't rake your leases, not with your daddy sick and nobody but you to run your boat. You sign some of them beds over to me, way I see it, everybody comes out ahead."

Therese's eyes narrowed. "But hold on, Little Horse. You said interest. These beds we give you, they don't count against the principal of the loan, do they? We still owe just as much as we do now."

Darryl smiled. "Sounds like you been socializing with some lawyers, too, little girl."

"Don't take no lawyer to know when you getting robbed," she retorted.

"You got a better idea, I'm all ears. But I don't see no other way."

"And so we choose some oyster beds to give you, Darryl, and in return you let us have more time to pay off the loans," Mathilde summarized. "Is that how it works, what you got in mind?"

"Yes ma'am, that's it exactly—'cept I choose which leases my brothers and I get."

"How would you know which leases are worth having?" Therese challenged him.

Darryl gave her the same look she had seen on the face of Suzanne Peljesich just before her friend declared, "Checkmate," the one time in her life Therese had played chess. Suzanne's face had betrayed a mixture of pride in surprising Therese and pity that the opponent across the board had allowed herself to be surprised. The look on Darryl's face slowly curled into a smile. "Rusty," he answered.

Therese frantically searched the board for a move to save the game. "So either we turn over our best beds to you right now, or you take our house and boat when the notes come due. But if you get our boat, then we can't work our leases anyway, so you pick them up at auction for next to nothing. Sounds like either way, you wind up with everything."

"I didn't say it was a perfect solution, what I was suggesting," Darryl admitted.

"Oh, it's perfect, all right. It's just what your daddy had in mind when he wrote those loans in the first place."

"With all due respect, it was your mother came begging for the money."

A pounding of wood against wood startled the group.

Felix had sat silently at the table listening to the exchange. Now, agitated, the old man pounded his cane on the wooden planks of the floor, growling a nearly unintelligible curse.

Therese was angry, too. "My mother never begged for nothing in her life. Your father lent us money, it was 'cause he saw a chance to beat us out of everything we had."

"I ain't looking for a fight with none of y'all. I didn't have to come here tonight. Could've let the time run out on you and gotten everything anyway, just like you said. I just thought there might be an easier way for everybody concerned."

"So your easier way is throw us out later rather than throw us out now, is that it?"

"Like I say, I didn't need to come over here tonight in the first place. You not interested in a helping hand, that's your business."

"What good those leases gonna do you anyway?" Therese countered, considering why Darryl had bothered to make his offer. "You don't know where the hell the beds are. And you'll never find them. They needles in a haystack, that's what they are."

The man moved the same piece with which he had checked her earlier. "Rusty, he knows where those beds are. And thanks to all that work you folks done this afternoon, we got everything we need."

Therese was taken aback. "You know about the charts?"

"How'd Rusty put it to me—reefs, currents, landmarks, he plotted everything, didn't he?"

"That's what he's been doing here, spying on us?"

Darryl shrugged. "He's smarter than he looks, that boy."

"So now he got everything he needs from us, we ain't gonna see him again. That how it works?"

"Wish I could spare him, I really do."

"You don't need to do this, Darryl."

"I'm waiting for you to give me a reason not to, little girl. Why you think I came here tonight?"

Therese took a breath, defeated. "Maybe you and me, we should take a drive together. Last time you was here, you said we ought to see what we got in common. Maybe you right."

Darryl finished his coffee and turned to Mathilde. "Thank you, ma'am, that was real good." Then he looked at Therese. "Tell you what, Miss Petitjean, I'll even let you drive my Cadillac. What do you think of that?"

"I ain't never driven one before."

"You be surprised how quick you get used to it. The finer things, I mean."

Darryl and Therese stood up.

Suddenly, Felix brought his cane crashing down across the table, shattering the coffee cup and its saucer. A deep, bellowing "No" issued from the old man.

Mathilde was standing, too, now. She looked at her husband's face, contorted with fury and frustration. Then she turned to her daughter. "You sure you ought to go out tonight, baby? They say that hurricane is in the Gulf now."

"It's a long ways off, Mama. Days away, if it comes at all." She avoided her father's eyes. "I won't be late. And this might be my one chance to drive a Caddy."

Outside, only a scar of moonlight chipped the dark sky, thickening with clouds. Tomorrow night would have a new moon, Therese noted. She had grown observant of the weather and the tides since beginning to sail with her father. And the ground now seemed to push back against her feet with more force than it had before she started spending her days on the yielding deck of a rocking boat. She liked the way you could ride the waves standing up once you learned their slow dance of lift and dip, but a person could never master the rhythm of dry land. You pushed; it pushed back. The sea, though, that was all give-and-take.

Walking behind the Cadillac with Little Horse, the girl noticed a sticker on the rear bumper of the car: EAT OYSTERS, LOVE LONGER. She shook her head at what morons men could be.

"Here, you drive," Darryl said, flipping her the keys.

It was big inside. The long, broad bench of the front seat seemed as wide as her bed. The baby blue leather upholstery was chafed from years under a Louisiana sun, but she liked its feel against the back of her thighs where her dress had hiked up. She liked the smell of it, too. You could tell it had been alive once, she thought, the leather.

The engine hummed until it caught. Then, with the shift still in neutral, she gave it some gas and the engine climbed an octave like a man breaking into song.

"Some car, huh?" Darryl boasted.

"Yeah," Therese agreed, "it's something, all right."

"Go ahead," the man encouraged her, "shift it into gear."

The car crushed the gravel beneath its tires without a hint of effort. "Rides smooth," the girl conceded.

They headed toward the highway, but after a few hundred yards, Darryl told Therese to stop the car and turn off the engine. She could not see the lights of her house in the rearview mirror.

"I thought we were going for a ride," she complained.

"We got some talking to do first."

"About what?" Her voice was still laced with defiance.

"Don't start. You start again, and you can just walk on back to your mama and daddy and tell them to get busy packing."

Therese held up her hands. "I ain't starting."

"All right, then," Darryl began, "you can see I'm holding all the cards. Y'all got nothing in the hole—no money from my brother and nobody to work your leases."

The girl nodded.

"So, here's the deal. Same deal my daddy offered you. We put our beds together, you and me."

"That some kind of proposal?" she asked sarcastically.

"You want romance, it don't come with no house and boat you get to keep."

"So I marry you, we keep our house and boat?"

"Your parents, I take care of them. Don't make no difference to me which house I live in. You choose. My brothers and me, we work all our leases, Petitjean and Bruneau beds alike, with the *Squall* and the *Mathilde*."

"What about me? I like going out on a boat."

Little Horse laughed. "No wife of mine'll ever have to work a lugger. You can stay at home, have babies, do whatever it is y'all do."

"Why you asking? You don't need me no more. You won. You got it all, whether I marry you or no."

"A man's got to say it?"

"You sure you don't just want what your daddy never got?"

"Let's just say I been watching you. Even before my daddy came calling, I was thinking about you."

"Well, Little Horse, you can strip us naked and throw us out of our own house, but it don't change nothing. I can't marry you."

Darryl seemed shocked. "Why not?"

"I got to say it? All right, I will. You the son of a bitch murdered my brother."

"You know you ain't got no proof of that."

"I was standing there in that cemetery when you told my mama what you was gonna do."

"Did I say anything about killing that boy? Did I?"

"Don't make no matter what you did or didn't say. You were plain enough."

"Listen, girl, I ain't sure your brother's even the one killed my daddy. I been thinking might be somebody else. Maybe you ought to consider the one looks like he done it ain't always the one with bloody hands."

That brought Therese up short.

"You say Alton didn't kill Daddy. Fine," Darryl went on. " 'Course, ain't nobody else in this whole damn town thinks he didn't do it but you. Let's say, though, everybody is wrong and you right. Let's say Alton had nothing to do with it. Then the son of a bitch looks the guiltiest to everybody, your brother, he's completely innocent. Right?"

She saw his point.

"Now take me. You sure I killed your brother, sure as everybody else is he killed my daddy. If they all wrong about Alton, how come you can't be wrong about me?"

"Then who else done it if you didn't?"

Darryl hesitated. "I hate to say it, but I wouldn't put it past Ross. Tell you the truth, I don't know where he was the night your brother died."

Therese hadn't considered the possibility Ross might have done it by himself.

"I mean, look what he nearly done to you the other night on our sofa." Darryl shook his head. "Never be able to prove it, of course. And you can't expect a brother to testify against a brother. Wouldn't never expect you to testify against Alton, he was the one killed somebody."

"No, I wouldn't."

"Who could blame you? That's just a matter of blood."

"And blood trumps all the rest," the girl sighed.

"Don't get me wrong. I ain't sure Ross done what happened to your brother. All I do know for sure is I got questions about who killed my daddy. I'm starting to think maybe I have an idea who the murderer is. But you ask for proof, I got none to show. So me, I got to put aside my suspicions. Maybe this person killed Daddy, maybe not. And if this person was to have suspicions of me about Alton dying, well, that person ought to realize it ain't so obvious as it seems what happens sometimes."

The two of them sat silently in the dark car for a few moments.

"What you say makes sense," Therese acknowledged, "about the oyster beds, I mean."

"Your mama and daddy keep their house, I get the prettiest wife in these parts, and you wind up the richest woman Egret Pass ever seen."

"I gotta think about it."

"What's there to think about? This is a gift falling out of heaven at your feet. All you got to do is stoop to pick it up."

"You must be used to dealing with a lot of foolish women, Darryl."

"I tell you," he sighed, shaking his head, "sometimes I think you more man than woman."

"Just depends on what's needed at the moment, I guess," she explained.

"Well," he said softly, "what's needed at this moment is a woman. Think you can manage that long enough for me to give you a kiss?"

"Suppose so."

The man leaned over and took her in his arms. His muscles felt like smooth stones wrapped in silk. When she looked into his eyes this time, she didn't let herself think of her brother. Instead, she let the man lean her back against the seat.

With one hand, he slid her whole body closer to his. It had been a while since she had been with a man, and she felt herself lifting up toward him, clinging. She wanted to make a decision before things went too far. Buttons seemed to be flicking open all over her clothes, like silent little explosions. After a few moments, she could barely distinguish cloth from flesh, the cotton skirt on her thighs from his hand. He was moving her, limb by limb. From the ankle of a leg slung over the seat back, she was aware of her panties dangling. Then she felt the cracked leather against one side of her face as a hand pressed her down.

"You got a rubber on?" she groaned.

"I don't need no rubber. You my fiancée."

That woke the girl from the dream into which she was slipping. "The hell I am." She tried to twist her body free of the muscular man, but the more she fought, the harder he leaned on her. Suddenly, she felt a shudder run through his body.

"If you wasn't before, you is now," he whispered, breathless.

A few minutes later, her dress crumpled, her hair disheveled, Therese slammed the car door and walked the few hundred yards through the black trees home, following a dark path of small stones and crushed shells that shifted beneath her feet with each step.

32.

The knocking on the front door woke everyone in the Petitjean house well before dawn.

Mathilde looked out the window to see who was there. "It's Rusty," she called out to her husband, still in bed, and her daughter, who waited on the stairs in a pink chenille robe. Opening the door, she greeted the boy more coldly than had been her habit.

Rusty stood beside the sofa, awkwardly shifting from foot to foot. "Little Horse, he told me to take the Cadillac and come on over here to help you with the boat today," he announced. "Said Therese would understand."

"He sent you over here in his Cadillac?" the girl asked almost angrily.

"Yeah, and he don't never allow us to drive it when we working."

"Darryl didn't say nothing last night about Rusty coming, did he?" Mathilde appealed to her daughter.

"No, Mama, he didn't. But I understand." The girl nodded to Rusty. "I know what you doing here."

"Wish I did," Rusty sighed. "First, Little Horse says he needs me on the *Squall*. Next thing I know, he's waking me up to come over here." The boy turned to Mathilde. "Ma'am, about that money I promised you yesterday—"

The woman shook her head. "You don't need to say nothing. Your brother explained you don't have it."

"He told you about that?"

"We had a real direct conversation with Darryl last night. I think we all know where we stand now. Ain't that so, baby?" she asked Therese.

"Yeah," the girl agreed, glaring at Rusty, "we know where we stand all right, every one of us."

"Look," the boy apologized, "there wasn't nothing I could do about it. Ross took every dollar I had while I was over here working."

"Ross?"

"Yeah, Ross stole it all. Why? What did Darryl tell you?"

Mathilde softened a bit toward the boy. "I'll tell you what he didn't say. He didn't say nothing about Ross taking your money."

"If it had been where I hid it, I would've come right back here with the money last night. I was just ashamed not to have anything for you after making a promise."

"Nothing to be ashamed of. Not your fault," Mathilde told him, as if making up her mind about something. "You two gonna need some breakfast, you heading out today. I'll get it started. Therese, you go get dressed."

"Terry," Rusty called up the stairs after Mathilde had gone into the kitchen, "you want I should go get the charts from the boat? Figure out where we going?"

"You leave those charts be," she shouted back. "Don't you lay a hand on them."

Puzzled, Rusty took a seat and waited quietly for breakfast.

The charts proved invaluable. Rusty and Therese triangulated their position on a lease among the islands of Bay Ronquille using two dead trees and a navigational buoy Alton had noted in his black book. In copying the information onto the charts, Rusty had even included the names Therese's brother had given the landmarks. One of the trees had been dubbed "Gator's Head," apparently because of the jagged cleft of its branchless trunk. The other one was enigmatically named "Miss Sally"; neither Therese nor Rusty could unravel the connection between the weathered cypress rising above a stand of low palmettos and the name it had been christened.

Following the outline of the oyster bed copied onto the chart of the bay, Therese maneuvered the *Mathilde* over the field as Rusty brought up dredge baskets sagging under the weight of their hauls. It was clumsy at first, the two of them figuring out the new routine of working the beds without Felix, but by afternoon, they had fallen into a rhythm. Therese handled the wheel while Rusty raised one dredge and dropped another; then Rusty steered for a few minutes while Therese cracked the clusters of oysters apart with a hammer and sorted the selects into sacks.

At the wheel, circling above a bed, Rusty considered why he was so much happier on a boat than on solid ground.

Everything is simple on the water, he thought. It's not like the woods, where things are tangled and twisted. The water runs off as far as you can see all the way to the horizon; then the sky races back overhead, same color, same surface. Like two hands praying, they seemed to him, sea and sky. And everything that happens goes on between those two hands. There's nowhere to hide on the water. But three steps into the woods, and you don't know where you are. Being lost on the water, that's not like losing your way in a forest's labyrinth of trees. It was closer to a desert, he realized, the ocean.

The image seemed to him so strange—a desert made of nothing but water—he lost the idea he had been pursuing.

Therese, moody all day, was preoccupied with her own thoughts. Rusty tried to keep his distance, but on a boat, that was difficult to do. Tense disagreements flared like summer rainstorms. The girl, as far as he could tell, seemed to be mulling something over.

Toward the end of the afternoon, as they were making the final run of the day, Rusty took a break after he got the dredge in the water. He sidled up to Therese in the wheelhouse and tried to tease her out of her testiness, but she would have none of it.

"You gonna joke with me after what you done?"

"Done? What did I do?"

"Don't play the innocent with me. Darryl told us last night what you been up to, spying on us."

"Spying on you? That's what he was after me to do, keep tabs on y'all. Let him know when there was trouble. Maybe even make a little trouble for you, things got going too good. But no, I never told him nothing, not a word."

"You a lying son of a bitch, Rusty Bruneau. Your brother, he knew all about what we copied onto the charts when he come over last night. You didn't tell him, where he found out about that?"

"I did tell him, yeah, but not like you think. I was trying to stop him from taking away your beds. Let him know y'all still had a chance now we know where the oysters are."

Therese relented a little. "And that's all you told him?"

"All I can remember. I get angry with Darryl, sometimes things slip out."

"So you wasn't no spy?"

"How can you even ask that? Where'd you be right now without me?"

"I should've known not to believe him, Little Horse. He's slick, though. Always got his eye on something over your shoulder."

"That's my brother, all right."

"Well, I guess it don't make no difference, anyway."

"How's that?"

"Looks like we gonna be related, you and me."

"You gonna marry Little Horse?"

"Ain't got no choice. I don't, we lose everything."

"But with these charts, we gonna make us some money. And you can forget about paying me a salary. After the fuel for the boat and the ice for the shrimp, it'll all be profit."

"Why you think Darryl sent you over here today? You think I tell him no, he gonna let you come anymore? Then where's that leave us? I don't do like he says, he'll fix it we lose everything. I gotta think of my parents. Particularly now with Daddy sick as he is."

"I bet Little Horse didn't let you forget that, the shape your Daddy's in."

"Darryl made it crystal clear where we'd stand, we don't take his help."

"Why the hell I need his permission to come work your boat, anyway?" Rusty fumed. "I'll give you a hand whenever I damn well please. He can go jump in the lake, my brother."

"You sweet, but you ain't really the problem. Mama and me, we talked last night after I got home from seeing Darryl."

"I thought he come by your house?"

"Yeah, but then we took a drive, just him and me. When I got back, Mama told me the truth about how much money we got. It ain't near enough for what we owe. You and me, we could be hauling up dollar bills in our nets, wouldn't make the difference."

Rusty was angry. "I don't know how you can even think about marrying him—after what he done."

Therese slowed the throttle. "What he done?"

The boy didn't regret that it had slipped out, but now he insisted, "I can't say nothing. He's my brother."

The girl shifted the engine into neutral, and the boat drifted on its momentum. "What you meant yesterday when you said you owed us? What you owe us for?"

Rusty took a breath. "I can't talk about it. I can't never talk about it, what happened."

Try as she might the rest of the trip, Therese was able to get nothing else out of Rusty.

When they got back to the house, Mathilde was cooking. "Your daddy, I'm fixing him a proper meal. It's gonna be a while, but you welcome to stay, Rusty."

"Yeah, Mama, he'll stay," Therese declared firmly.

"Little Horse, he said I had to come home tonight. He wants me to rake a shallow reef tomorrow with him and Ross."

"We'll get you home, don't you worry about that," Therese promised. "Now let's go see to the boat."

Hosing down the deck and the compartments they had filled with oysters during the day, the girl reminisced to Rusty about her brother. She told the boy about the time Alton had tried to keep a baby crab his father had caught with a net full of shrimp, the lengths he had gone to feed the creature that night in a bowl of water beside his bed, the worry he divulged to his little sister the next morning that his pet might be lonely for its mama, and how he had set the tiny crab free in the bayou before breakfast.

"You know anybody actually keep one of those little crabs alive long enough to even get it home in one piece, let alone set it free later on?" she asked Rusty as she scrubbed mud from the teeth of one of the dredges.

Therese could see the toll her anecdotes were taking on the boy, and she continued right through dinner with tales of her brother's gentleness and pity. She reminded Rusty, especially, of Alton's courage in standing up to somebody in the wrong. "Seems like I remember you telling me about my brother sticking up for you against Ross one day. Why don't you tell Mama and Daddy that story? It's got Alton written all over it, what he done for you." She filled his glass again from the bottle of wine she had opened to celebrate, she explained, the end of all their problems.

After dinner, Therese let her mother clean the dishes, and she took Rusty out to the dock. In her hand, she carried a second bottle of wine she had uncorked. The boy was already unsteady on his feet.

The only light outside was cast from the house. The sky was dark with a new moon and clouds already driving inland from the hurricane spinning hundreds of miles out in the Gulf.

"So it looks like I'm gonna be your sister-in-law," Therese began, sitting on the edge of the dock and swinging her bare feet over the water.

Rusty lumbered down beside her. She passed him the bottle.

"Therese Bruneau," she went on. "Ain't as pretty as Therese Petit-jean, is it?"

"You really gonna marry that son of a bitch?"

"Unless you give me a reason not to," she teased flirtatiously.

The boy took another swig of the red wine. "Oh, I could give you a reason, all right."

"What reason?"

He turned grumpy. "Nothing. You go ahead and marry Little Horse, you want to. Why should I care?"

Therese took back the bottle and sipped. "You know, it's so dark out here tonight, nobody could see nothing from the house."

"See what?"

"You want to go for a swim in the bayou? It's still warm, the water."

"Ain't got no bathing suit."

The girl put down the bottle between them and whispered in his ear, "Don't need no bathing suit."

Rusty was too drunk to stop her, so he tried to avert his eyes. He could hear her clothes rustle as she undressed on the dock next to him. When she leapt into the water, his pants legs got soaked from the splash.

"Come on in," she called. "It's warm as a bath."

"Don't think so," the boy said, trying not to look.

Suddenly, he felt her hugging his legs, as if she were about to tug him into the bayou. When he reached down to disentangle her arms from him, even in the darkness he saw her, half out of the water as she clasped him, her hair over one shoulder like a swirl of wet cloth, a breast cupped in the crook of an arm, and her face smiling up into his. It took his breath away.

He helped her back up onto the splintery dock and wrapped his arm around the shivering, naked girl.

"You gotta tell me," she whispered, pressing herself against his body for warmth. "You gotta tell me what Darryl done to my brother."

They stayed out there a while, talking and drinking.

After her hair had dried enough to tie up in the bandanna she kept on the boat, they went back into the house, and Rusty, drunk from all the wine, fell asleep on the sofa.

"How'd your hair get wet?" Mathilde wondered.

"We were playing" was all the explanation Therese offered.

"Well, let's get this boy a blanket," her mother decided. "He ain't going nowhere tonight in his condition."

"Mama, you better call the Bruneaus, let them know Rusty's spending the night."

"Yeah, you right, Terry. Us, we'd be worried sick, somebody didn't come home one night."

Therese saw the woman, realizing what she had just said, wince ever so slightly. "Yeah, Mama, I guess we would."

Mathilde shook her head. "It won't never go away, will it, baby?"

"Missing Alton? You really want that to go away?"

"Just the surprise of it. You forget, just for a flash, he's gone, and then, out of the blue, you remember. It's like you hearing about it for the first time, every time it comes back to you."

"Well, I ain't forgot for one single moment about Alton," the girl fiercely maintained. "And I ain't never gonna forget."

Mathilde put her arm around her daughter. "No, baby, don't you ever forget your brother. Nobody else will ever love you the way he did."

The girl started to cry. "You better call Little Horse," she whispered, her throat rough.

"Yeah, let me go telephone."

The girl wiped her eyes while her mother dialed the Bruneaus.

"Darryl, this is Mrs. Petitjean. How you?"

Therese kept one ear on her mother's conversation.

"Thing is, your little brother's had too much to drink. Not much of a drinker, that boy, is he? He ain't fit to drive your daddy's car home tonight." She paused while Darryl said something on the other end of the line. "No, he's already asleep on our sofa. We'll send him over to y'all in the morning. We going to bed now ourselves."

Therese smiled. She knew Darryl didn't stand a chance of changing her mother's mind.

"No, that's all right. Y'all just stay home and get yourselves a good night's sleep. Rusty has your Cadillac. He can run himself over to your boat in the morning." There was another pause. "So good night, Darryl. And Darryl, we appreciate you coming by last evening, yeah. You sleep tight now, you hear?"

33.

Therese waited until past midnight before she slipped down the stairs from her bedroom, carrying her shoes in her hand. Tiptoeing across the dark living room to the sofa where Rusty gently snored under a blanket Mémère had crocheted, she eased the keys to the Cadillac out of the boy's pocket. He didn't even stir.

Ain't used to liquor, I guess, Therese told herself.

Like most nights, the front door wasn't locked. The girl took her time turning the knob and pulling the door shut behind her to avoid any noise. Slipping on her shoes, she hurried to the boat to get some things she would need.

Therese worried about the sound of the tires on the gravel, so she drove as slowly as she could manage until the yard light disappeared in her rearview mirror, obscured by the trees lining the turns of the road. Only then did she flick on the car's headlights and speed up a little. The highway was deserted in both directions when she slowed at the end of the gravel road, and once on the asphalt, she accelerated.

A few minutes later, she approached the taillights of a truck a hundred yards or so up ahead and slowed the Cadillac to keep her distance. After a minute or two, the truck pulled off the highway at the junction with the old road to the river and kept going.

The launch, down the embankment from the highway, was dark as she approached. She slowed, looking for any trucks parked beside the boats, but nobody was there. It was hard to see on such a moonless night; only a streetlight rigged at the far end of the boat slips provided any illumination. So she drove past to be sure she would have no company, then turned around in the lot of the closed bait and grocery shop just down the highway.

Returning to the launch and parking the Cadillac behind a stand of cypresses that screened the car from the highway, Therese quickly found the *Squall*. The Bruneau boat rocked under her foot as she boarded it.

She pulled open the deck panel nearest the engine. With the flashlight she had taken from the wheelhouse of her own boat, she found the fuel pump. It was filthy, and bilge sloshed beneath it. The pump, the line, the carburetor—she recognized everything immediately from the lesson Rusty had given her only a few days ago on the *Mathilde*. She had a screwdriver to loosen the clamp on the fuel line, but she was dismayed to discover a length of garden hose jammed onto the nipple of the fuel pump. There was no fitting, only some kind of wire wrapped round and round the hose, tightening it against the nipple of the pump.

Therese tried to loosen the wire, but it had rusted solid, corroded from the salt water in the bilge. She knew she could not waste time playing with it, so she put the screwdriver down on the towel in which she had wrapped all the tools she'd brought from her boat. Picking up something else she'd taken from the *Mathilde*, she drew Alton's knife from its sheath.

She played with the hose until she felt it bend, an inch or two past the nipple it concealed. Reaching underneath it with the edge of the blade, she sliced a slash along the bottom of the hose, as if she were cutting a very small throat. She wiped the knife on the towel and shined the light on her work. Nothing was visible from the top. But when she ran her finger along the notch she had cut, she could feel gasoline beading. She held her finger up to her nose to be sure. Her face recoiled from the sweet, metallic smell.

It took only another minute to replace the deck panel and cut the towel into squares to stop up the hooded vents on the deck and the transom. She checked with her flashlight to be sure no trace of her work was visible and counted to make sure she was not leaving any of her tools behind.

Just as Therese was about to hop from the boat to the dock, she saw headlights approaching on the highway. Jumping down, she crouched behind a stack of baskets in the stern.

Though she couldn't see from where she hid, it sounded to her as if the vehicle, whatever it was, had slowed and then resumed its speed as it passed the boats. Frightened, she took her things, jumped onto the dock, and hurried to the Cadillac. She was relieved that she could barely see it, concealed behind the trees.

Therese drove too fast on the way home, but there were no other cars out on the highway. Still trembling from adrenaline, she took the turn onto her own road too fast and felt the rear of the car slide sideways on the gravel. The heavy car seemed to catch itself, and the girl slowed, and then slowed again when the yard light began to flicker between the trees.

Even more quietly than she had left, Therese entered the house, again with her shoes in one hand and the keys to the Cadillac in the other. She climbed the stairs to her room one step at a time. When she flipped on the light next to her bed, she checked to be sure she had wiped all the grease from her hands with the towel back on the Bruneau boat.

She had done a good job, she congratulated herself. She hadn't forgotten anything.

Changing into a thin nightgown and her robe, Therese descended the stairs barefoot and slipped the keys back into Rusty's pocket without waking him. Then, loosening the belt of her robe, she knelt beside the sleeping boy and tickled his ear until he opened his eyes.

"Hey, sleepyhead," she whispered in the dark room.

"What time is it?" Rusty wondered, confused and still a little drunk.

"Nearly two. I couldn't sleep."

"Well, I wasn't having any trouble." He yawned loudly.

"Hush, you'll wake my parents." She looked toward the door of their bedroom, but the light stayed off. "Come on. We can talk upstairs where we won't bother them."

Rusty sat up and rubbed his eyes. "Talk about what?" he whispered.

She took his hand. "Just come on upstairs before Mama and Daddy hear us."

The boy had never been in her room before. Nestled beneath the slope of the roof, it was a cozy place, fluffy with stuffed animals and rag dolls and embroidered pillows. Everything was too small for her, the chair beneath the short desk, the narrow bed, the little pink bookcase. This side of Therese, the girl only a few years out of childhood, rarely revealed itself. But showing herself to him in this way, quietly, without all the bluster he was used to, touched him.

With the steep roof descending along one wall, Rusty had to watch his head. Not sure where to stand, he sat on her bed beside her.

"You ain't gonna marry him are you, now you know?"

"Marry the son of a bitch murdered my brother? What do you think?"

"I shouldn't have said nothing, I guess, but the idea of you married to Little Horse, it just didn't sit right. Not after what him and Ross done your brother."

"Go against blood, I know that ain't easy. But what kind of man lets a girl marry the murderer of her brother? You tell me that." She put her hand on his. "Not a man like you, at least."

Embarrassed, Rusty withdrew his hand from hers. "Like I said, I'll tell you, but I won't tell nobody else. I ain't testifying against my brothers in court or anything like that. So this stays between us, you and me. It don't go no further."

"I won't ask nothing else of you. I just had to know for myself what happened, that's all."

Rusty lowered his head. "Little Horse, he says I'm just as guilty as him and Ross. But I don't see it that way." The boy turned his face toward Therese. "Maybe I should've known what they were up to, figured it out sitting in that truck waiting for Alton to come home. Truth is, though, I never thought in my wildest dreams that's what they had in mind, what they done him."

The girl nodded. "If anybody has the right to call you guilty, it's me. But you ain't. What you said before, out by the bayou, sounds like you were just as surprised as my brother what happened."

"I didn't have the slightest idea what was coming."

"Don't know how many times Alton sat right here where you sitting, just like this. And I promise you, the dead could talk, he'd tell you the same thing. It ain't your fault what happened. His murder, that's on the heads of Darryl and Ross alone."

"I ain't slept good in a long time," Rusty sighed.

"Well," Therese promised, "you gonna sleep good tonight. Just like a little baby you gonna sleep."

Rusty leaned forward as if to get up. "I ought to get on home. Darryl wants me in a skiff tomorrow morning out on some shoals with my tongs."

Therese pulled him back by the shoulder. "You still too drunk to drive. You take a little nap, then you go."

"I guess I got time."

"Sure you do. You got hours. Take off your boots and lie down. I'll see you ain't late."

Rusty sagged under the exhaustion of the last weeks and the lingering effects of the wine Therese had poured him all night. "Maybe just a nap," he conceded, slipping off his boots.

"You lie back and leave it all to me," she soothed him. "Here, take off your shirt and loosen that belt, too. You'll never fall asleep like that." She helped lift the shirt over his shoulders. "There, ain't that better? Now you just lie back and close your eyes." She flicked off the lamp. The room disappeared into an obliterating darkness.

Rusty had been asleep only a moment, it seemed, when he felt her next to him in the small bed. He tried to make room for her by slipping his arm under her head and shifting onto his side. As he did, his other arm fell across her hip. He let his hand slide along the curve of her thigh. She wasn't wearing anything, he realized.

Before he could speak, her hand slipped down his pants, drawing a slow sigh from his lips. That first, long breath seemed not to whisper into silence until all the clothes had fallen from his body and he poised, trembling, above the smaller body shifting beneath him in the dark.

"Don't we need . . . ?" The boy, embarrassed, tried to remember a polite phrase for it. "Don't we need some kind of protection?"

The girl smiled to herself. "You so sweet I could eat you up." She pulled him down on top of her. "Don't you worry about nothing. You just leave it all to me, you hear?"

Rusty had to stop himself from answering, "Yes ma'am."

He had spent so many nights imagining what it would be like with a woman, he was shocked at how different it really was. The smells, of course, he could not have guessed, the intimate fragrances of the woman teased out by desire, and her taste. The feel, too, of flesh against flesh, of a woman's flesh clinging to a man's—that had not occurred to him. The tangle of limbs, the uncertainty of whose finger, exactly, lolled on a lip, he could not have expected. But if these unanticipated pleasures had surprised him, he was totally unprepared for the thrill of her voice, the song of her rising breaths in rhythm with the plunging of his body, breaching and falling back like a dolphin breaking the waves.

Afterward, dazed and tingling, Rusty felt Therese's hand upon his thigh, tracing the furrow of his scar.

"Who done this to you?" she asked, her voice foggy and full of sleep.

The boy told her the story of the snapped cable on his father's boat.

"They should've taken better care of you," she insisted, angry yet again with the Bruneaus.

"I lived," he answered simply.

She nuzzled her face against his shoulder. "Lucky for me," she whispered.

They lay in the dark, quiet for a little while.

"Can we do it again?" Rusty asked shyly but eagerly.

"You ain't had enough already, boy?" Therese laughed.

"No ma'am."

This time when Rusty rolled off the girl, he was asleep before he could think to kiss her. Therese worked loose the bedspread and top sheet on which they lay and covered the sleeping boy. She snuggled beside him and was soon asleep, too.

Dawn was staining the curtains in the dormer window when Rusty shook the girl awake. "What time is it?" he asked her, panicked.

"It's the middle of the night. Go back to sleep, baby."

"No, it ain't. Look out the window. It's morning coming. I'm supposed to be on the boat with Darryl and Ross. They probably waiting for me right now down at the slip."

Therese rolled over and looked at the window. "That ain't the sun. It's just moonlight on the curtains."

"There wasn't no moon last night."

"Well, you can't go," she told him crossly. "Don't make no difference what time it is."

"Why not?"

The girl smiled. " 'Cause I ain't done with you."

Rusty already had his pants on and was bending under the slope of the roof. Therese grabbed him by the belt and tugged him back toward the bed.

"But I gotta go rake oysters with my brothers."

"Oysters don't care you catch them today or tomorrow. They ain't going nowhere. They stuck for life on that reef."

"Little Horse, he ain't gonna like this one little bit, me not doing what he says."

"Maybe it's time you start raking your own oysters."

"I ain't got none."

"You take that rake out your pants, I bet you find yourself an oyster right here in this bed. Sweet, too, and salty."

"You something, girl," he said with a sigh and let his pants fall around his ankles.

34.

Just as on the morning before, Mathilde was awakened by a fist pounding on the front door. Today, though, the knocking seemed frantic.

The sun was already well up. Mathilde swung the door open to find Sheriff Christovich, his hat in his hand, standing on the porch.

"Matthew, what's wrong?"

"Mathilde, is Rusty Bruneau here?"

"I don't think so, Matthew. He slept here, on the sofa, but you can see he's not there now. He was supposed to go out with his brothers on their boat this morning. I talked to Darryl about it myself last night. Rusty was gonna meet them at their slip."

"How was he supposed to get there?"

"Their Cadillac. Darryl had him drive it over here yesterday. Why you ask?"

" 'Cause Horse's Cadillac is sitting outside next to my squad car right now."

"Well, I don't know," Mathilde replied, "maybe he's asleep in Alton's bed. That's where he usually spends the night."

"Could you check?"

They walked down the hall together. Alton's bed hadn't been slept in.

"What's this all about, Matthew?"

"I got bad news, I'm afraid."

"I don't know we can take any more bad news."

"An hour or two ago, way out in the channel, the *Squall* exploded."

"The Bruneau boat?"

"Yeah, I'm afraid so. We know Little Horse and Ross were on board, but nobody seen Rusty down at the launch when they were fueling up. I'm hoping he didn't make the trip."

"And Darryl and Ross?"

The sheriff shook his head. "They dead."

Mathilde sat down. "Arlene's poor little babies."

"It was quite an explosion, they saying."

"The poor things."

"You think Terry might know where Rusty went? If he's OK, I don't want him hearing what happened from somebody else."

"Let me go ask."

Mathilde climbed the staircase to Therese's room and knocked on the door. There was no answer. She was about to knock again when the girl opened the door just wide enough to see who was there. "What you want, Mama? I'm sleeping."

"Baby, it's Sheriff Christovich downstairs. He's looking for Rusty. There's been an accident."

"What kind of accident?" Therese asked.

"It's his brothers," her mother answered grimly.

Suddenly, the door swung open wider. Rusty was standing behind the girl, wearing nothing but his pants. "What about my brothers?"

Mathilde was taken by surprise to find the boy in her daughter's bedroom. Sheriff Christovich, looking up at them from downstairs, answered for her. "Your boat, son, it blew up in the channel a little while ago. Your brothers, they gone."

"What?" Rusty pushed past the women out onto the landing and leaned on the balustrade, staring down at the sheriff and at Felix, who had hobbled with his cane into the living room in his pajamas.

Mathilde, now behind the boy, put her hand on his shoulder. "Ross and Darryl, they dead, baby."

Rusty's chin slumped against his chest. "They dead, both of them? On the boat?"

"You go get dressed," Mathilde said softly. The boy retreated into the bedroom. Then the woman turned to her daughter. "And you put some clothes on, too, and get downstairs right now. We'll talk later about all this." She waved vaguely in the direction of the girl's bed.

"Yes ma'am," Therese answered meekly and closed the door.

Felix, his face red with anger and embarrassment to have his daughter's shame paraded before the sheriff, spit two or three unintelligible words at his wife while shaking his cane at the upstairs bedroom.

"What you want me to do about it?" Mathilde sighed. "We'll deal with her later. Right now, it's Rusty we better be worrying over."

Christovich chose his words carefully. "Mathilde's right. That boy's lost his whole family. This ain't the moment to straighten out anything else. There'll be plenty of time for that later."

Upstairs, Therese stroked the boy's hair as he pulled on his boots.

"I should've been out there with my brothers," he kept repeating.

"The only difference that would've made, you'd be dead now, too. We just lucky we done what we done last night."

Rusty turned his head toward the girl. "I guess you saved my life this morning."

"Maybe I saved both our lives this morning."

"How you mean?"

"I don't know what I would've done, something happened to you."

The boy studied her face. "I love you," he said.

Therese nodded. "They waiting downstairs for us."

"Yeah," Rusty agreed, "we better get down there."

The sheriff was sitting in the kitchen with Felix when the boy walked in. Mathilde was at the stove.

"We real sorry, all of us, Rusty, about your brothers," Christovich told him.

"Thank you, Sheriff."

The man took a sip of the coffee that Mathilde had just brewed. "We gonna need you down at the launch, I'm afraid. Another lugger, they bringing the bodies in."

The boy pulled out a chair and sank down on it.

"You have some coffee before you go anywhere," Mathilde insisted.

"Yes ma'am, whatever you say."

"Yeah," the sheriff agreed, "you take your time, Rusty. We ain't in no rush."

The boy turned to Felix. "I'm sorry, Mr. Petitjean, about me and Terry. It was all my doing. I shouldn't have drunk so much last night."

Rusty could see the old man was trying to restrain his anger.

"I'm ashamed what I done. But I'll do right by your daughter, don't you worry."

"We'll sort all that out later, Rusty," Mathilde explained softly, bringing the boy's coffee to the table. "You got other things to see to this morning."

They sat, no one quite sure what to say, until Therese walked in.

"There's coffee on the stove," her mother announced without so much as glancing at the girl.

"Thanks," she said, getting a cup down from the cabinet. She looked around the table for a place to sit.

"Here, Terry, you take my chair," Rusty said. "I'm just going."

Sheriff Christovich stood up. "Me, too. We better be on our way."

Mathilde and Therese walked Rusty and Christovich to the porch.

"Like I told Mr. Petitjean," Rusty apologized again, "I'm real sorry, ma'am—"

Mathilde cut him off. "We'll talk about all that later." Then she kissed him on the cheek. "We here for you, you need us."

"Yes ma'am, thank you. Thank you for everything."

Terry caught his eye. "I'll talk to you later on, huh?"

The boy nodded.

He slipped his hand in his pants pocket for the keys to his car. "That's funny," he said, sinking his hand in deeper. Then he tried the other pocket. "How'd my keys get on this side?" he wondered, fishing them out with his left hand.

Therese tried to laugh it off. "You was so drunk last night, you lucky you didn't wind up with your keys in your mouth and your pants on your head."

Mathilde, still upset about finding the boy in her daughter's bedroom, added, with some sarcasm, "I'd say he just about did wind up like that, didn't he?"

The boy, deeply embarrassed, excused himself and drove off to the boat slips in his pale blue Cadillac.

"Terry, why don't you walk me out to my car?" Christovich, still standing on the porch saying good-bye to Mathilde, suggested.

The girl waited for the sheriff to say something as she walked beside him.

"You remember that talk we had? Rusty ever tell you anything, one way or another, about what happened to your brother?"

Therese looked up at the man. "No, Sheriff, not a word. He hasn't so much as let drop a hint about what went on that night."

"How about Darryl? Your mama tells me he come around once or twice to see you."

"See me?" She smiled, as if flattered. "No sir, he come by to talk money with my daddy. Don't get me wrong, he was pleasant enough. Even took me for a ride in his Cadillac one night. But we like oil and water, the two of us. Just didn't mix, you know."

"Maybe them two brothers, Rusty and Darryl, they the ones didn't mix. Particularly with you in the middle."

Now Therese sounded like a much older woman. "What you seen this morning, Sheriff, that just begun last night. Me and Rusty, we started drinking last evening at dinner . . ."

The sheriff finished the sentence for her. "And you didn't stop till way too late."

"That about sums it up," she confessed.

They came to the squad car, and the sheriff opened the door. "You know my hands are tied, Terry, I don't have no evidence."

"Maybe you don't have no evidence 'cause there ain't no evidence to have. Tell you the truth, I don't know the Bruneaus had anything to do with it, my brother's murder."

"Well, who you think killed him, then?"

"I don't know about you, Sheriff, but I'm finding out you got to learn to live with mysteries."

Christovich got into his car and smiled at the girl. "See, you'd never make a lawman with an attitude like that. A mystery, hell, it drives me goddamn crazy."

Therese smiled back. "Hope you find a cure for that."

The sheriff started his engine. "Only one cure I know."

"What's that?"

"Put the bastard in jail."

It was late afternoon before Rusty returned to the Petitjean house. Therese was sitting on the porch, cleaning shrimp for dinner. Her hands glistened with their slime.

The boy walked slowly toward her. She could see he was exhausted.

"They found the bodies," he told her.

"Yeah, the sheriff told us this morning."

"That's right," Rusty recalled. "Everything today, it's just sort of jumbled up."

"Here, you sit down for a minute, baby. Let me go wash my hands and put this in the icebox."

Rusty rocked in Felix's chair. He watched a mockingbird attack a cat slinking across the yard. The cat, nipped on its hindquarters, leapt up, turning in midair to claw the screeching bird, which veered away and perched on the branch of a pine tree.

"I'm sorry for them, your brothers. Despite everything." It was Therese; he hadn't noticed her come back onto the porch.

"They were all the family I had left, Ross and Little Horse."

"Ain't so," she disagreed, leaning against the porch railing. "You got me."

"Yeah, we ought to talk."

"It can wait. You got a lot on your mind."

Rusty tried to think of something else to say. "Your mama and daddy gone? I didn't see the truck."

"Yeah, the doctors want to see Daddy every few days for a while since he won't stay in the clinic like they told him to."

The boy couldn't keep away from talking about the accident. "It was bad, the explosion."

"They got any idea what happened?"

"Sheriff says they scooped up some pieces of the boat when they found the bodies. Ain't a whole lot, though. The explosion just about splintered the *Squall*."

"Any chance more of the boat'll turn up?" the girl wondered.

"They dragging the channel right now looking for more debris, but the tide's running. They won't find much out there."

"So nobody knows?"

"Had to be the engine or the fuel tank or something, to blow that way. They were always so goddamn sloppy about everything, especially Ross. I begged them to fix it up, the boat. But they wouldn't listen."

"You and Daddy told me how dangerous it can be, that gasoline. Just like dynamite, you said."

"Yeah, that's true, but it still don't add up, what happened."

"How you figure that? You say they were sloppy, your brothers. Maybe it was something like us, a gas leak they didn't tend to."

"It just don't feel right."

"Sure, they leaking gas in the bilge, the fumes build up—just like you told me—and somebody lights a cigarette. Up she goes. It could happen to anybody."

"Ross maybe. But it just don't sound like Darryl, something like that happening to him."

"Hell, the way y'all had that boat rigged, garden hoses wrapped round with baling wire—"

Rusty stopped rocking. "What you just say?"

Therese paled. "Nothing. I was just supposing."

"How you know about garden hoses and baling wire? You never been on the *Squall*."

"I say that? I don't know, you must've told me."

"I don't think so. Far as I remember, I ain't never talked to you or nobody else about how Daddy fixed that leaking hose we had."

"I was just making examples, is all. Horse actually use a garden hose in place of something else, that what you mean?"

Rusty was deadly serious now. "Yeah, that's exactly what I mean."

"Coincidence. I say something as a for instance, turns out you got it. Ain't nothing but coincidence."

"So how come my keys was in the wrong pocket this morning? Another coincidence."

"You don't know how drunk you was last night. You could've put your keys in your ear, wouldn't have noticed."

"I always put my keys in the right-hand pocket. Drunk or sober, that wouldn't be no different."

"What you saying, boy? I got something to do with what happened? After what you done me last night, and you come round today talking like this? Shit, I can't believe you."

Rusty didn't blink. "I don't know can I believe you. That's the real question."

The girl sighed. "Last night, you tell me you and your brothers ambush Alton like a pack of cowards and dump his body in the bayou. And what do I do? I forgive you and take you into my bed." She turned her back on him and looked out across the bayou and the marsh beyond it. Suddenly, her voice changed. "You want to know about Darryl and Ross? Yeah, I cut that garden hose all right and sent your brothers to hell. But you remember what I done this morning to keep you from going down with them?"

"Yeah, I remember," he whispered behind her.

"I'll tell you something else, too. Alton never killed your daddy. Alton never hurt nobody in his whole life. You boys ambushed the wrong Petitjean that night. You want to kill your daddy's murderer, you take a knife to me. I'm the one done it—and I'd do it again."

She could hear the shock in the boy's voice. "You?"

"Yeah, me. Horse thought he could buy me for his wife. Well, I ain't for sale."

"Jesus, girl," Rusty exclaimed.

Therese turned back around and faced him. "Now you know the whole story. I know what you done, and you know what I done. We even, the way I figure it. You didn't do no different from me, and I didn't do no different from you."

"So you get away scot-free?"

"Free?" she said angrily. "You forgetting Alton's dead. I already paid my price. You the one walking away from all this free and clear. You ask me, it's just like you told Mama—you the one owes us." She took a breath and added softly, "Especially after last night."

He looked up past the girl and saw clouds racing west, scudding before the hurricane still somewhere far out in the Gulf.

"So what you gonna do, boy?" she asked with a sigh. "Now you know, what you gonna do?"

Five

35.

Though the sky sagged with low gray clouds and the cypresses and pines had rusted with winter, the day was warm for this time of year. Still, Sheriff Christovich was surprised to see Mathilde standing on the dock as he eased to a stop beside the Petitjean house. The breeze off the bayou was raw, and the woman wore only a shawl over her dress.

Stepping on the thin thatch of brown pine needles beneath the scattered trees leading down to the water, Christovich treaded lightly so as not to startle Mathilde, who seemed lost in thought.

When he was a few yards away, he called her name.

She turned, and he was struck, once again, by how handsome a woman she was.

As if she had raised the two corners of a veil to reveal her face, the melancholy he had glimpsed as she looked over her shoulder lifted, and speaking his name forced her lips into a smile. "Matthew."

"So how your daughter like the married life?" Christovich asked as he stepped onto the dock.

"Guess I'll be a grandma before long." The woman laughed.

"I heard Terry was expecting. When's the baby due?"

Mathilde smiled and shook her head. "A little early. But I guess after that morning we found Rusty upstairs in her room, shouldn't come as no surprise, should it?"

Christovich nodded. "Won't be the first baby show up a little too soon after the wedding, huh?"

"Terry tells me that's the night she think it happened, too. That night the Bruneau boys died." Mathilde sighed. "Doctor says with her due date, it had to be somewhere around there she got herself pregnant."

"Does seem you never have a funeral without a baptism on its heels. And vice versa."

"Maybe we ought to go buy ourselves a charm from Mary Two-Dogs, protect us when this baby gets christened," Mathilde joked.

Christovich smiled. "You must be freezing, standing out here in the middle of winter with nothing but that flimsy little thing over your shoulders."

"Ain't so cold today." She sighed. "I was just tired of being inside all the time. Thought I'd take a little walk, but I didn't get no farther than this."

The two of them looked out over the dull leaden surface of the bayou, like an old mirror whose silver had flaked away. Something squawked in the reeds on the far side.

"Sounds like mallard," the man observed.

"Calling for his mate," the woman agreed.

Christovich saw the melancholy slipping down over Mathilde's face again. "You know why they call it a bayou?" he asked.

Mathilde smiled. Matthew had once confessed to her, long after they both had married, that when he was a teenager he had memorized jokes so he'd have a way to make girls laugh. He still remembered a few of them. "No, why do they call it a bayou?"

"Because a bayou's the water run by you house."

"That's an old joke, Matthew."

"Well," he conceded, "it's an old man telling the joke. What you expect?"

"You ain't so old."

"No? My old girlfriend, she's nearly a grandma. So what's that make me, huh?"

She sighed again. "A good old friend, Matthew, that's what it makes you. Come over here to cheer me up."

"How you managing with Felix gone?"

"It was a shock at first, even sick as he was. Everyone says, though, it was for the best. Maybe they right. At the end, it seemed like he was getting hacked to death, bit by bit—couldn't speak, his face all twisted up, one leg useless, the other twitching so bad he banged it black-and-blue against the bed rail in the clinic one night."

"At least he saw his daughter married."

"Yeah, that was a blessing, all right. And to see we wasn't gonna lose everything after all, the house and the beds. That was a comfort to him, I know. The doctors say no, but I think the worry, that's what brought them on, the strokes. When those first ones hit, the dead arm and the talking funny, him and me was sure we already lost it all. Didn't tell Terry—no point. But we thought it was a done deal, Little Horse taking everything."

"Funny the way it works out, huh? You walk away with a son-in-law and all the Bruneau holdings."

"You could just as well say," Mathilde objected, "Rusty walks away with a bride and all the Petitjean holdings."

"Either way, a happy ending all around."

"Except for my Alton buried in that cemetery," the woman lamented bitterly.

"And don't forget poor old Horse and those boys of his."

"May they rest in peace." Mathilde looked away. "I wouldn't call that a happy ending, Sheriff. Me, I'd call it a tragedy, what happened."

"Yeah, you right."

The woman wrapped the shawl more tightly around her.

"You are cold," Christovich admonished her.

"That icy gust just now, chilled me right to the bone."

"Come on inside. Let me buy you a cup of coffee to warm you up."

She smiled at his joke, and they started back to the house. "So why you come all the way out here, Matthew? I don't think I seen you since Felix's funeral."

"Yeah, I'm sorry about that. I've had my hands full with Candy."

The woman nodded.

"Tell you the truth, I'm looking for your daughter. She wouldn't be inside, would she?"

"Just like every other day, she out with Rusty in the boat. Terry said they was gonna make a run to Lake Grande Écaille today."

"She ain't slowing down, that girl, even with a baby on the way."

"No, Matthew, she loves the water. The two of them, they doing real good, too. Between Rusty's leases and ours, they got the pick of the beds to choose from."

"What she gonna do when the baby comes?"

"Terry'll be back at the wheel of the boat first chance she gets. My guess, I'll wind up raising the child."

Christovich smiled as they stepped onto the porch. "People start calling you Maw-Maw, you don't watch out."

"You laugh, but who you think sleeps in the upstairs room now?"

"Oh, Grandma, just like you and Felix done his mother."

The sheriff held the door for Mathilde as they went in.

"You were right, Matthew, it does feel better in here," the woman said, though she kept on her shawl.

"Terry and Rusty, they take your old room?"

"Yeah, with Felix gone, I couldn't sleep in there anymore. And they gonna make Alton's room the nursery, so they want to be near the baby."

"What y'all gonna do with the Bruneau house?"

"Don't know. Sell it, probably. You ought to go see. Terry, she fixed it all up before the wedding when they thought they'd be living there. All painted, new curtains, a garden dug and planted—I tell you, you wouldn't recognize it."

"Hard to imagine," the sheriff agreed, "considering the way the Bruneaus lived after the mother died." He gave Mathilde's house an admiring glance. "Like most run-down places, I guess. Not half so bad as you thought, once you put a woman in it."

Mathilde smirked. "I don't know how men can live the way they do."

"Ain't all men," Christovich protested.

"No, not all," the woman agreed, "just the ones I ever met."

"We ain't so dependent," the sheriff teased, "on creature comforts as y'all."

"Creature comforts?" Mathilde sniffed. "You mean like soap and water?"

"Where's that cup of coffee I was gonna buy you?"

"Let me go ask the waitress in the kitchen. Come on, boy, you come, too."

They were enjoying themselves, the two old friends.

"So why you need Terry?" Mathilde wondered as she began to make the coffee.

The sheriff took a seat at the table. "Arcie Ardois, he's got himself the lease just off the channel where the *Squall* blew up."

"Yeah, I know. Rusty said he was the one brought the bodies in on his lugger the morning it happened."

"Well, Arcie pulled up something yesterday in one of his dredge baskets. Didn't know what it was, at first. The thing was so deep in the mire down there, it come up looking like a monster oyster or something covered in clay. But when he dips it over the side and washes it down, turns out it's most of a fuel pump from an engine."

"What use is that, after it's been in the water?"

"None. But considering where he finds it, Arcie figures it might be from the *Squall*, so he drops it off at the jail last night when he gets in."

Mathilde sat down while she waited for the water to boil. "Can you tell if it's theirs?"

"Still got a few inches of the fuel line attached. Garden hose wrapped with wire for a clamp at the nipple. A typical Horse Bruneau one-tack job. Instead of using a decent piece of rubber hosing, he jury-rigs a damn fuel line out of what he finds on the dock."

Mathilde nodded. "Yeah, Darryl was famous for that kind of thing." She smiled, remembering the man. "But it always worked."

"This time, too. Even an explosion couldn't rip it off the fuel pump."

"So what this got to do with Terry?"

"Thing is, the hose broke right in front of the nipple where the fuel line attaches to the pump."

"Isn't that where they tend to crack? Like on cars?"

"Oh, yeah, if it's gonna crack, that's the spot, all right. But it's real ragged when it happens. This one, it's a clean cut, at least on the bottom. Tell you the truth, looks to me like somebody took a knife to it."

Mathilde laughed. "You don't think Terry did that, do you? Why would she?"

"Alton. She says different, but I think she blamed the Bruneau boys for what happened to her brother. Probably right, too."

"She married one of them."

"After all the rest were dead."

Mathilde shook her head. "Anyway, that girl don't know any more about motors than I do. She wouldn't have the slightest idea what to cut, even if she wanted to."

"Probably. Of course, Terry, she'd been going out on the boat regular after Alton died. You pick things up, you go to work every day doing something."

"Matthew," the woman said, still smiling, "she'd only been out there a few weeks when all that happened."

"There's something else, too."

The kettle was shrieking and trembling. Mathilde rose to turn off the heat.

The sheriff continued. "Somebody thinks they saw a Cadillac down at the boat launch the night before those boys died. Couldn't do nothing with it at the time, that report. And the man, he wasn't a hundred percent certain what he saw. But now there's this other thing—"

"Rusty was here all night—and you know where. When you come by the next morning, he was still here. We all sat down with you right at this very table."

"I ain't talking about Rusty."

"Then who you . . . you don't mean Terry?"

"You didn't make nothing of those car keys of his being in the wrong pocket? A man's right-handed, he keeps his keys in his right-hand pocket. Simple as that."

"Sheriff, that boy was so drunk—"

"Drunk or no the night before, he was stone-cold sober when he walk out of here the next morning. You think he gonna make a big show—in front of the sheriff, no less—about his car keys being in the wrong pocket if he was the one drove down to the launch in the middle of the night to cut the fuel line on his brothers' boat? Somebody else put those keys in the wrong pocket."

"Who says that fuel line was cut, anyway? All you got is a piece of garden hose don't look right to you after sitting buried in the mud for three or four months. You call that proof of anything?"

The sheriff smiled. "Proof? No, can't say what I got would convince a jury."

Mathilde set the coffeepot on the table and put out two cups and saucers. "Sounds like you got a whole lot of nothing, then."

"Maybe. And to be fair, on the other side of the ledger, Harley Boudreaux, he was down at the icehouse that morning, looking for work. He tells Ross he smells gas when the *Squall* ties up."

"See, there you go, Sheriff. What did Ross say to that?"

"You know Ross. Said it wasn't gas, just spilled liquor old Boudreaux was smelling on his own shirt. And Darryl was in a big hurry. They were getting a late start."

"From waiting for Rusty, probably."

"I warned those boys, too, they had gasoline in their bilge, one day I was down at their slip. Just like their daddy, though. Too smart not to be stupid. Never done nothing about it, I guess."

"It's a shame, but sounds like they done it to themselves."

"That's what most people think."

The woman looked at him. "But not you?"

"Alton kills Horse. Darryl and Ross kill Alton. That's all simple enough. Now who's got a reason to kill the two Bruneau boys? Rusty, he ain't got no real motive, except he's stuck with two assholes for brothers—excuse my language. And like I said, he didn't do it, anyway. Felix, the night they die, he can't walk, he can't lift his arm. That leaves you and Therese. And I ain't got to prove you didn't do it, 'cause you know you didn't."

"You still can't prove that boat blowing up, it wasn't no accident."

"Mathilde, the truth's the truth—whether I can prove it or not. And it all works out real sweet for your daughter. Saves her parents their house, their boat, their leases, and walks away with a husband owns the second-best oyster beds in the parish."

"Matthew, you loved me once. I'm asking you, let it go."

The sheriff sighed. "What do I know, anyway? I haven't got any proof. Just the truth, that's all I got."

"The truth?" Mathilde laughed. "When's the truth ever had anything to do with us, you and me?"

"Anyway, like you say, I can't prove nothing, can I?"

The woman shook her head tenderly.

"You tell Terry something for me, though?"

" 'Course."

"You tell her we neither one of us have to live with mysteries anymore."

"She'll know what you talking about?"

"She'll know."

The woman poured his coffee.

"What they gonna call their baby, anyway?" he asked. "They decide yet?"

"Oh, yeah, they made up their mind. Arlene, if it's a girl, after Rusty's mother. It'll be nice to have another Arlene around here."

"Yeah, it will. And what about they have a boy?

"Felix."

"Would've pleased your husband, I bet, having a grandson named after him."

"He would've liked that, carrying on his name. Even if there won't be no Petitjean named after him." Mathilde spooned some sugar into her coffee. "And how's Candy? She doing any better?"

"I had to take her back to the Touro Infirmary two days ago. The doctors say it's just a matter of time now."

"I'm sorry to hear." Mathilde smiled sadly. "That's what Darryl always used to say, wasn't it, it's all just a matter of time?"

"Maybe so," the sheriff said, trying his coffee. "Maybe old Horse, he'll prove right in the end."

ecco

Also by John Biguenet:

*If the stories in this first collection
engage the world in sometimes
shocking ways, they are virtuoso
engagements, eloquent in their prose,
sly in their plotting, acute in their
form. Biguenet, by turns, reminds one
of Richard Ford and Tobias Wolff.
Constantly shifting among voices
and narrative strategies, he imposes
upon the conflicts he depicts neither
a single style nor a repeated structure.*

ISBN 0-06-000745-1 (paperback)

"These fourteen erudite, deeply religious,
deeply moral stories are stunningly impressive. . . .
A superb collection from a fascinating writer."
—*Esquire*

"*The Torturer's Apprentice* is full of bold risks, taken with
intelligence and humor and pitch-perfect narrative voices."
—Robert Olen Butler

"*The Torturer's Apprentice* deserves the highest praise. . . .
A showcase for an astonishing, occasionally daunting imagination."
—*Minneapolis Star Tribune*

**Want to receive notice of events and new books by John Biguenet?
Sign up for John Biguenet's AuthorTracker at www.AuthorTracker.com**

Available wherever books are sold, or call 1-800-331-3761 to order.